THE TEMPLAR KNIGHT

About the Author

Jan Guillou was born in Sweden in January 1944. He made his name as a journalist and rose to fame when he exposed a secret intelligence organization, was convicted of espionage and spent 10 months in prison, 5 of which were spent in solitary confinement. He is now a bestselling novelist and writes regularly for Sweden's leading tabloid, commenting on current affairs.

JAN GUILLOU

The Crusades Trilogy

The Templar Knight

Translated by Steven T. Murray

HARPER

Harper
An imprint of HarperCollins*Publishers*
77–85 Fulham Palace Road,
Hammersmith, London W6 8JB

www.harpercollins.co.uk

A Paperback Original 2009
4

A catalogue record for this book
is available from the British Library

ISBN: 978 000 7285860

Set in Sabon by Palimpsest Book Production Limited,
Grangemouth, Stirlingshire

Translation copyright © Steven T Murray 2009

Printed and bound in Great Britain by
Clays Ltd, St Ives plc

'The road to hell is paved with good intentions'

Jacula Prudentum, 1651, no. 170

PRINCIPAL CHARACTERS

KNIGHTS TEMPLAR
Al Ghouti - Arn de Gothia
Arman de Gascogne, his sergeant
Arnoldo de Torroja, Master of Jerusalem
Odo de Saint Armand, Grand Master
Siegfried de Turenne
Harald Øysteinsson
Grand Master Roger des Moulins

CHRISTIANS
Count Raymond III de Tripoli
Reynald de Châtillon
Gérard de Ridefort
King Baldwin IV
Baldwin d'Ibelin, later Baldwin V
Guy de Lusignan, later King Guy
Agnes de Courtenay
Father Louis
Heraclius

MUSLIMS
Yussuf ibn Ayyub Salah al-Din - Saladin
Fahkr - his brother
al Afdal, Saladin's son
Ibrahim ibn Anaza

INHABITANTS OF GUDHEM MONASTERY
Abbess Rikissa
Cecilia Algotsdotter (Rosa), betrothed of Arn
Cecilia Ulvsdotter (Blanca), betrothed of Knut Eriksson
Sister Leonore
Ulvhilde Emundsdotter
Fru Helena Stensdotter

FOLKUNG CLAN
Birger Brosa, Arn's uncle
Magnus; Arn and Cecilia's son
Eskil Magnusson, Arn's brother

King Knut Eriksson
Philippe Auguste, King of France
Richard the Lionheart, King of England
Babarossa, Emperor of Germany

THE TEMPLAR KNIGHT

In the name of God, most benevolent, ever-merciful.

'God is great in His glory, Who took His votary in the night
to a wide and open land from the Sacred Mosque
to the most distant Mosque whose precincts We have blessed,
in order to show him Our sign;
Verily He is all-hearing and all-seeing.'

The Holy Koran, Sura 17, Verse 1

ONE

During Muharram, the holy month of mourning, which occurred when the summer was at its hottest in the year 575 after Hijra, called Anno Domini 1177 by the infidels, God sent His most remarkable deliverance to those of His faithful He loved best.

Yussuf and his brother Fahkr were riding for their lives and right behind, shielding them from the enemies' arrows, came the Emir, Moussa. Their pursuers, who were six in number, were steadily gaining on them, and Yussuf cursed his arrogance, which had made him believe that something like this would never happen since he and his companions possessed the swiftest of horses. But the landscape here in the valley of death and drought due west of the Dead Sea was just as inhospitably arid as it was rocky. This made it dangerous to ride too fast, although their pursuers seemed completely unhampered by this. But if one of them happened to take a spill, it would be no less fateful than if any of the men being chased should fall.

Yussuf suddenly decided to cut across to the west and head up toward the mountains, where he hoped to find cover. Before long the three pursued horsemen were following a *wadi*, a dry riverbed, up a steep slope. But the *wadi* began to narrow and deepen so that they were soon riding in a long ravine, as if God had caught them in flight and was now steering them in a specific direction. Now there was only one road, and it led upward, growing steeper and steeper, making it harder and harder to keep up their speed. And their pursuers were coming steadily closer; they would soon be within shooting range. The men being chased had already fastened their round iron-clad shields to their backs.

Yussuf was not in the habit of praying for his life. But now, as he was forced to decrease his speed more and more among all the treacherous boulders at the bottom of the *wadi*, a verse came to him from God's Word, which he breathlessly rattled off with parched lips:

He who has created life and death in order to test you and allow you to prove who among you, by his actions, is the best. He is the Almighty. The One who always forgives.

And God did indeed test His beloved Yussuf and showed him, first as a mirage against the light of the setting sun, and then with terrible clarity the most horrific sight that any of the faithful in such a hunted and difficult situation could see.

From the opposite direction in the *wadi* came a Templar knight with lowered lance, and behind him rode his sergeant. Both of these foes were riding at such speed that their cloaks billowed behind them like great dragon wings; they came like *jinni* out of the desert.

Yussuf abruptly reined in his horse and fumbled with his shield, which he now had to pull around to the front to face the infidel's lance. He felt no fear, only a cold excitement at the nearness of death, and he steered his horse over to the steep wall of the *wadi* to present a narrower target and increase the angle of the enemy's lance.

But then the Templar knight, who was only a few breaths away, raised his lance and waved his shield, as a signal to

Yussuf and his brother to move aside and get out of their way. They complied at once, and the next moment the two Templar knights thundered past as they let their cloaks fall, which fluttered to the dust behind them.

Yussuf quickly issued an order to his companions. With difficulty, their horses' hooves slipping, they clambered up the steep slope of the *wadi* until they reached a spot from which they had a good view. There Yussuf turned his horse around and stopped, for he wished to understand what God meant by all of this.

The two others wanted to take advantage of the opportunity and escape while the Templar knights and bandits settled matters as they saw fit. But Yussuf rejected all such arguments with a curt gesture of annoyance because he truly wanted to see what would happen next. He had never in all his life been this close to a Templar knight, those demons of evil, and he felt strongly, as if God's voice were advising him, that he had to see what was going to happen; mere common sense would not stop him. Common sense dictated that they should continue their ride toward Al Arish for as long as the light permitted. But what he now saw he would never forget.

The six bandits had few choices once they discovered that instead of chasing three wealthy men they were now facing two Templar knights, lance to lance. The *wadi* was much too narrow for them to be able to stop, turn around, and affect a retreat before the Franks were upon them. After a brief hesitation they did the only thing they could do: They grouped themselves so they were riding two by two and spurred their horses so as not to be killed by standing still.

The white-clad Templar knight who rode in front of his sergeant first feigned an attack to the right of the first two bandits, and when they held up their shields to counter the dreaded blow of his lance – Yussuf wondered whether the bandits understood what now awaited them – the Templar

5

knight spun his horse around with a swift movement that shouldn't have been possible in such tight quarters. This gave him a whole new vantage point, and he thrust his lance right between the shield and body of the bandit on the left. At the same time, he released his lance so as not to be wrenched out of his saddle. Just at that moment the sergeant came in contact with the astonished bandit on the right, who was huddled behind his shield, waiting for the blow that never came, and who now looked up only to see the other foe's lance coming towards his face from the wrong direction.

The white-clad man with the loathsome red cross now faced the next two enemies in a passageway so narrow that there was barely room for three horses abreast. He had drawn his sword, and at first it looked as if he intended to attack head-on, which would have been unwise with a weapon on only one side. But suddenly he turned his handsome steed sideways, a roan at the height of its powers, and lashed out behind him, striking one of the bandits and toppling him out of the saddle.

The second bandit then saw a good opportunity since the enemy was approaching him sideways, almost backwards, with his sword in the wrong hand and out of reach. What he did not notice was that the Templar knight had dropped his shield and switched his sword to his left hand. When the bandit leaned forward in the saddle to strike with his sabre, he exposed his whole neck and head to the blow, which now came from the opposite direction.

'If the head can retain a thought at the moment of death, if only for a brief breath, then that was a very surprised head that fell to the ground,' said Fahkr in amazement. He too was now captivated by the drama and wanted to see more.

The last two bandits had exploited the moment of decreased speed that had befallen the white-clad Templar knight as he dispatched the other bandit. They had turned their horses around and were now fleeing down the *wadi*.

At that moment the black-clad sergeant reached the godless dog who had been knocked to the ground by the Templar knight's horse. The sergeant dismounted, calmly grabbed the reins of the bandit's horse with one hand and with the other used his sword to stab the dazed, reeling, and no doubt bruised bandit in the throat at the spot where his steel-plated leather coat of mail ended. But then the sergeant no longer made any attempt to follow his master, who had now put on speed to chase down the last two fleeing bandits. Instead, the sergeant hobbled the horse he had just caught with the reins and then cautiously began rounding up the other loose horses, seeming to talk to them reassuringly. He did not appear at all worried about his master, whom he had been following so closely to offer protection. Instead, he seemed to think it more important to gather up the enemies' horses. It was truly a strange sight.

'That man,' said Emir Moussa, pointing toward the white-clad Templar knight who was far down the *wadi* and about to disappear from the sight of the three faithful, 'that man there, sire, is Al Ghouti.'

'Al Ghouti?' said Yussuf, puzzled. 'You say his name as if I should know him. But I do not. Who is Al Ghouti?'

'Al Ghouti is a man you should know, sire,' replied Emir Moussa resolutely. 'He is the man God sent to us for our sins, he is the one among the devils of the red cross who sometimes ride with the Turcopoles and sometimes with their heavy horsemen. Now, as you can see, he is riding an Arabian stallion as a Turcopole does, but carrying a lance and sword as if he were seated on one of the slow and heavy Frankish horses. He is also the emir of the Knights Templar in Gaza.'

'Al Ghouti, Al Ghouti,' muttered Yussuf thoughtfully. 'I would like to meet him. We will wait here!'

The two others looked at him in horror but realized at once that he had made up his mind, so it would do no good to offer any objections, no matter how wise.

7

While the three Saracen horsemen waited at the top of the *wadi*'s slope, they watched the Templar knight's sergeant. Seemingly unperturbed and as though carrying out the most ordinary daily task, he had rounded up the horses of the four dead men. He then tied them together and started lugging and dragging the corpses of the bandits. With great effort, although he appeared to be a very powerful man, he hoisted them up and bound them hand and foot, each dead man slung over his own horse.

The Templar knight and the two remaining bandits, who had been the pursuers but were now the pursued, could no longer be seen.

'Very clever,' muttered Fahkr as if to himself. 'That is clever. He ties the right man to the right horse to keep the animals calm in spite of the blood. He is obviously thinking of taking the horses along with them.'

'Yes, they are truly fine horses,' agreed Yussuf. 'What I do not understand is how such criminals could have horses that are fit for a king. Their horses kept pace with our own.'

'Worse than that. They were closing on us at the end,' objected Emir Moussa, who never hesitated to speak his mind to his lord. 'But haven't we seen enough? Wouldn't it be wise to ride off now into the darkness before Al Ghouti comes back?'

'Are you certain that he will come back?' asked Yussuf, amused.

'Yes, sire, he will come back,' replied Emir Moussa morosely. 'I am just as certain of that as the sergeant is down there; he hasn't even troubled to follow his master when there are only two enemies to fight. Didn't you notice that Al Ghouti had thrust his sword into its sheath and had pulled out his bow and stretched it taut just as he came around the bend down there?'

'He pulled out a bow? A Templar knight?' asked Yussuf in surprise, raising his slender eyebrows.

'Yes he did, sire,' replied Emir Moussa. 'He is a Turcopole, as I said; sometimes he travels light and shoots from the saddle like a Turk, except his bow is bigger. Far too many of the faithful have died from his arrows. I would still dare to suggest, sire, that –'

'No!' Yussuf cut him off. 'We will wait here. I want to meet him. We have a truce with the Knights Templar right now, and I want to thank him. I owe him my gratitude, and I refuse even to consider being indebted to a Templar knight!'

The two others could see it would do no good to argue any further. But they were uneasy, and all conversation ceased.

They sat there in silence for a while, leaning forward with one hand resting on the pommel of their saddles as they watched the sergeant, who was now done with the bodies and horses. He had started gathering the weapons and the cloaks that both he and his master had flung off right before the attack. After a while he picked up the severed head in one hand, and for a moment it looked as if he were wondering how to pack it up. At last he pulled the headdress off one of the bandits, wrapped it around the head, and made a parcel which he tied onto the pommel of the saddle over which the body with the missing head was slung.

Finally the sergeant was finished with all his tasks. He made sure all of the packs were fastened securely and then mounted his horse and began slowly leading his caravan of linked horses past the three Saracens.

Yussuf then greeted the sergeant politely in Frankish, with a wave of his arm. The sergeant gave him an uncertain smile in return, but they could not hear what he said.

Dusk began to fall, the sun had dropped behind the high mountains to the west, and the salt water of the sea far below no longer gleamed blue. The horses seemed to sense their masters' impatience; they tossed their heads and snorted now and then, as if they too wanted to get moving before it grew too late.

9

But then they saw the white-clad Templar knight returning along the *wadi*. In tow behind him came two horses with two dead men draped over the saddles. He was in no hurry and rode with his head lowered, making him look as if he were lost in prayer even though he was probably just keeping an eye on the rocky, uneven ground. He did not appear to have seen the three waiting horsemen, although from his vantage point they must have been visible, silhouetted against the light part of the evening sky.

But when he reached them, he looked up and reined in his horse without saying a word.

Yussuf felt at a loss, as if he had been struck dumb because what he now saw did not coincide with what he had witnessed only a short time ago. This spawn of the Devil, who was openly called Al Ghouti, radiated peace. He had hung his helmet by a chain over his shoulder. His short fair hair and his thick, unkempt beard of the same colour framed a demon's face with eyes that were as blue as you might expect. But here was a man who had just killed three or four other men; in the excitement Yussuf had not been able to keep track of how many, even though he usually could recall everything he saw in battle. Yussuf had seen many men after a victory, just after they had killed and won, but he had never seen anyone who looked as if he had come from a day's work, as if he had been harvesting grain in the fields or sugarcane in the marshes, with the clear conscience that only good work can provide. His blue eyes were not the eyes of a demon.

'We were waiting for you . . . we wish to thank you . . .' said Yussuf in a semblance of Frankish that he hoped the other man would understand.

The man who was called Al Ghouti in the language of the faithful gazed at Yussuf steadily as his face slowly lit up with a smile, as if he were searching his memory and had found what he sought. This made Emir Moussa and Fahkr, but not

Yussuf, cautiously, almost unconsciously, drop their hands to their weapons beside their saddles. The Templar knight quite clearly saw their hands, which now seemed to be moving of their own accord toward their sabres. Then he raised his glance to the three on the slope, looked Yussuf straight in the eyes, and replied in God's own language:

'In the name of God the Merciful, we are not enemies at this time, and I seek no strife with you. Consider these words from your own scripture, the words which the Prophet himself, may peace be with him, spoke: *"Take not another man's life – God has declared it holy – except in a righteous cause."* You and I have no righteous cause, for there is now a truce between us.'

The Templar knight smiled even wider, as if he wanted to entice them to laugh; he was fully aware of the impression he must have made on the three foes when he addressed them in the language of the Holy Koran. But Yussuf, who now realized that he had to be quick-witted and swift to take command of the situation, answered the Templar knight after only a slight hesitation.

'The ways of God the Almighty are truly unfathomable,' and to that the Templar knight nodded, as if these words were particularly familiar to him. 'And only He can know why He sent an enemy to save us. But I owe you my thanks, knight of the red cross, and I will give you some of the riches that these infidels wanted. In this place where I now sit, I will leave a hundred dinars in gold, and they belong by rights to you for saving our lives.'

Yussuf now thought that he had spoken like a king, and a very generous king, as kings should be. But to his surprise and that of his brother and Emir Moussa, the Templar knight replied at first with a laugh that was completely genuine and without scorn.

'In the name of God the Merciful, you speak to me out of

both goodness and ignorance,' said the Templar knight. 'From you I can accept nothing. What I did here I had to do, whether you were present or not. And I own no worldly possessions and cannot accept any; that is one reason. Another reason is that the way around my vow is for you to donate the hundred dinars to the Knights Templar. But if you will permit me to say so, my unknown foe and friend, I think you would have difficulty explaining that gift to your Prophet!'

With these words, the Templar knight gathered up his reins, cast a glance back at the two horses and the two bodies he had in tow, and urged his Arabian horse on, as he raised his right hand with clenched fist toward the men in the salute of the Templar knights. He looked as if he found the situation quite amusing.

'Wait!' said Yussuf, so quickly that his words came faster than his thoughts. 'Then I invite you and your sergeant instead to share our evening meal!'

The Templar knight reined in his horse and looked at Yussuf with a thoughtful expression.

'I accept your invitation, my unknown foe and friend,' the Templar knight replied, 'but only on the condition that I have your word none of you intends to draw a weapon against me or my sergeant as long as we are in one another's company.'

'You have my word on the name of the true God and His Prophet,' replied Yussuf quickly. 'Do I have yours?'

'Yes, you have my word on the name of the true God, His Son, and the Holy Virgin,' replied the Templar knight just as quickly. 'If you ride two fingers south of the spot where the sun went down behind the mountains, you will reach a stream. Follow it to the northwest and you will find several low trees near some water. Stay there for the night. We will be farther west, up on the slope near the same water that flows toward you. But we will not sully the water. It will soon be night and you have your hour for prayers, as do we. But afterwards, when we come in the darkness to you, we will make enough noise so you hear us, and not come quietly, like someone with evil intentions.'

The Templar knight spurred his horse, again saluted in farewell, got his little caravan moving, and rode off into the twilight without looking back.

The three faithful watched him for a long time without moving or saying a word. Their horses snorted impatiently, but Yussuf was lost in thought.

'You are my brother, and nothing you do or say should surprise me anymore after all these years,' said Fahkr. 'But what you just did really surprised me. A Templar knight! And the one they call Al Ghouti at that!'

'Fahkr, my beloved brother,' replied Yussuf as he turned his horse with an easy movement to head in the direction described by his foe. 'You must know your enemy; we have talked a great deal about that, haven't we? And among your enemies, isn't it best to learn from the one who is most monstrous of all? God has given us this golden opportunity; let us not refuse His gift.'

'But can we trust the word of such a man?' objected Fahkr after they had been riding for a time in silence.

'Yes, we can, as a matter of fact,' muttered Emir Moussa. 'The enemy has many faces, known and unknown. But that man's word we can trust, just as he can trust your brother's.'

They followed their foe's instructions and soon found the little stream with fresh cold water, where they stopped to let their horses drink. Then they continued along the stream and, exactly as the Templar knight had said, came to a level area. There the stream spread out to a small pond where low trees and bushes grew, with a sparse pasture area for the horses. They unsaddled the animals and took off the packs, hobbling the horses' forelegs so that they would stay close to the water and not go in search of grazing land farther away, where none existed. Then the men washed themselves, as prescribed by law, before prayers.

At the first appearance of the bright crescent moon in the blue summer night sky, they said their prayers of mourning for the dead and of gratitude to God for sending them, in His unfathomable mercy, the worst of their foes to rescue them.

They talked a bit about this very subject after prayers. Yussuf then said that he thought God, in an almost humourous way, had shown His omnipotence: revealing that nothing was impossible for Him, not even sending Templar knights to rescue the very ones who in the end would conquer all Templar knights.

Yussuf tried to convince himself and everyone else of this. Year after year new warlords arrived from the Frankish lands; if they won, they soon returned home with their heavy loads.

But some Franks never went back home, and they were both the best and the worst of the lot. Best because they did not pillage for pleasure and because it was possible to reason with them, making trade contracts and peace agreements. But they were also the worst because some of them were fierce adversaries in war. The worst of them all were the two cursed devout orders of competing monks, the Templars and the Hospitallers of St John. Whoever wanted to cleanse the land of the enemy, whoever wanted to take back Al Aksa and the Temple of the Rock in God's Holy City, would have to conquer both the Knights Templar and the Hospitallers. Nothing else was possible.

Yet they seemed impossible to conquer. They fought without fear, convinced that they would enter paradise if they died in battle. They never surrendered since their laws forbade the rescue of captured brothers from imprisonment. A captured Hospitaller knight or Templar knight was a worthless prisoner that they might just as soon release or kill. Thus they always died.

It was a rule of thumb that if fifteen of the faithful met

five Templar knights out on a plain, it meant that either all or none of them would live. If the fifteen faithful attacked the five infidels, none of the faithful would escape with his life. To ensure victory of such an attack, they had to be four times as many and still be prepared to pay a very high price in casualties. With ordinary Franks this was not the case; ordinary Franks could be defeated even if there were fewer men on the side of the faithful.

While Fahkr and Emir Moussa gathered wood to make a fire, Yussuf lay on his back with his hands behind his head, staring up at the sky where more and more stars were appearing. He was pondering these men who were his worst enemies. He thought about what he had seen right before sundown. The man called Al Ghouti had a horse worthy of a king, a horse that seemed to think the same thoughts as his master, that obeyed instinctively.

It was not sorcery; Yussuf was a man who ultimately rejected such explanations. The simple truth was that the man and the horse had fought and trained together for many years, in the most serious fashion, not just as a pastime to be taken up when there was nothing else to do. Among the Egyptian Mamelukes there were similar men and horses, and the Mamelukes, of course, did nothing but train until they were successful enough to obtain commissions and land, their freedom and gold granted in gratitude for many good years of service in war. This was no miracle or magic; it was man alone and not God who created these kinds of men. The only question was: What was the most crucial characteristic for attaining that goal?

Yussuf's answer to this question was always that it was pure faith, that the one who wholeheartedly and absolutely followed the words of the Prophet, may peace be with Him, regarding the *Jihad*, the holy war, would become an unconquerable warrior. But the problem was that among the

Mamelukes in Egypt it was impossible to find the most faithful of Muslims; usually they were Turks and more or less superstitious, believing in spirits and holy stones and giving only lip service to the pure and true faith.

In this case it was worse that even the infidels could create men like Al Ghouti. Could it be that God was demonstrating that man uses his own free will to determine his purpose in life, in this life on earth, and that only when the holy fire separates the wheat from the chaff will it be apparent who are the faithful and who are the infidels?

It was a disheartening thought. For if it was God's intention that the faithful, if they could unite in a *Jihad* against the infidels, should be rewarded with victory, why then had He created enemies who were impossible to defeat, man to man? Perhaps to show that the faithful truly had to unite against the enemy? The faithful had to stop fighting among themselves because those who joined forces would be ten to a hundred times more numerous than the Franks, who would then be doomed, even if they were all Templar knights.

Yussuf again recalled the image of Al Ghouti: his stallion; his black, well-oiled, and undamaged harness; his equipment, none of which was merely for the pleasure of the eye but for the joy of the hand. Something could be learned from this. Many men had died on the battlefield because they couldn't resist wearing their stiff, new, glittery-gold brocade over their armour, which hindered their movements at the crucial moment, and thus they died more from vanity than anything else. Everything they had seen should be remembered and learned from, otherwise how were they going to conquer the devilish enemy that now occupied God's Holy City?

The fire had already begun to crackle. Fahkr and Emir Moussa had spread out the muslin coverlet and were starting to set out provisions and drinking vessels of water. Emir Moussa squatted down and ground up his mocha beans to prepare his black Bedouin drink. With the descending darkness a cool breeze came racing down the mountainside from Al Kahlil, the city of Abraham. But the cool air after a hot day would soon give way to cold.

The westerly direction of the wind brought Yussuf the scent of the two Franks at the same time as he heard them out in the darkness. It was the smell of slaves and battlefields; no doubt they would come unwashed to the evening meal, like the barbarians they were.

When the Templar knight stepped into the light of the fire, the faithful saw that he was carrying his white shield with the red cross before him, as no guest ever should. Emir Moussa took several hesitant steps toward his saddle where he had stacked up their weapons with the harnesses. But Yussuf quickly caught his nervous eye and quietly shook his head.

The Templar knight bowed before each of his hosts in turn, and his sergeant followed his master's lead. Then he surprised the three faithful by lifting up his white shield with the loathsome cross and setting it as high up as he could in one of the low trees. When he then stepped forward to unfasten his sword and sit down, as Yussuf invited him to do with a gesture of his hand, the Templar knight explained that as far as he knew, there were no malicious men in the area, but you could never be certain. For that reason the shield of a Templar knight would probably have a chilling effect on their fighting spirit. He generously offered to let his shield hang there overnight and come back to get it at dawn when it would be time for all of them to move on.

When the Templar knight and his sergeant sat down near the muslin coverlet and began setting out their own bundles – dates, mutton, bread, and something unclean were visible – Yussuf could no longer hold back the laughter he had tried so hard to suppress. All the others looked up at him in surprise, since none of them had noticed anything amusing.

The two Templar knights frowned, suspecting that they might be the objects of Yussuf's merriment.

He had to explain, saying that if there was one thing in the world he had never expected to have as night-time protection, it was in truth a shield with the worst emblem of the enemy. Although on the other hand this confirmed what he had always believed, that God in His omnipotence truly was not averse to joking with His children. And at this he thought they could all laugh.

Just then the Templar knight discovered a piece of smoked meat among the items his sergeant was setting out, and he said something harsh in Frankish and pointed with his long, sharp dagger. Red-faced, the sergeant removed the meat while the Templar knight apologized, shrugging his shoulders and saying that what was impure meat for one person in this world was good meat for another.

The three faithful now understood that a piece of pork had been lying in the middle of the food, and thus the entire meal was unclean. But Yussuf quickly whispered a reminder about God's word in those cases when a man finds himself in need, when laws are not laws in the same way as when a man is in his own house, and they all had to be content with that.

Yussuf blessed the food in the name of God the Merciful and Gracious, and the Templar knight blessed the food in the name of the Lord Jesus Christ and the Mother of God, and none of the five men showed any disdain for the beliefs of the others.

They began offering each other food, and finally, at Yussuf's invitation, the Templar knight accepted a piece of lamb baked in bread, slicing it in two with his grey, unadorned, extremely sharp dagger. He then handed half of it on the tip of his knife to his sergeant, who stuffed it into his mouth, hiding his distaste.

They ate in silence for a while. The faithful had placed the lamb baked in bread along with chopped green pistachios baked in spun sugar and honey on their side of the muslin coverlet. On their own side, the infidels had dried mutton, dates, and dry white bread.

'There is something I would like to ask you, Templar knight,' said Yussuf after a while. He spoke in a low, intent voice, the way his closest friends knew he always talked when he had been thinking for a long time and wanted to understand something important.

'You are our host, we have accepted your invitation, and we will gladly answer your questions, but remember that our faith is the true faith, not yours,' replied the Templar knight with an expression as if he were daring to joke about his own faith.

'Doubtless you know what I think about that matter, Templar knight, but here is my question. You rescued us, we who are your foes. I have already acknowledged that this is true, and I have thanked you. But now I want to know why you did it.'

'We did not rescue our foes,' said the Templar knight thoughtfully. 'We have been after those six bandits for a long time. We've been following them at a distance for a week, waiting for the right moment. Our mission was to kill them, not to rescue you. But at the same time God happened to hold a protective hand over you, and neither you nor I can explain why.'

'But you are the real Al Ghouti himself?' Yussuf persisted.

'Yes, that is so,' said the Templar knight. 'I am the one the nonbelievers in their own language now call Al Ghouti, but my name is *Arn de Gothia*, and my mission was to free the world of those six unworthy men, and I completed my mission. That is the whole of it.'

'But why should someone like you do such a thing? Aren't you also the emir of the Knights Templar in your fortress in Gaza? A man of rank? Why should such a man take on such a lowly mission, and a dangerous one at that, setting out for these inhospitable regions just to kill bandits?'

'Because that was how our order came into being long before I was even born,' replied the Templar knight. 'From the beginning, when our troops had liberated God's Sepulchre, our people had no protection when they went on a pilgrimage down to the River Jordan and the site where Yahia, as you call him, once baptized the Lord Jesus Christ. And back then pilgrims carried all their possessions with them, instead of leaving them in safekeeping with us, as they do now. They were easy prey for bandits. Our order was created to protect them. Even today it is considered a mission of honour to offer protection to pilgrims and kill bandits. So it is not as you think, that this is a lowly mission we give to just anyone; on the contrary, it is the heart and soul of our order, a mission of honour, as I said. And God granted our prayers.'

'You are right,' Yussuf concluded with a sigh. 'We should always protect pilgrims. How much easier life would be here in Palestine if we all did so. By the way, in which Frankish country is this Gothia located?'

'Not exactly in any *Frankish* country,' replied the Templar knight with an amused glint in his eye, as if all his solemnity had suddenly vanished. 'Gothia lies far north of the land of the Franks, at the ends of the earth. But what country do you come from? You don't speak Arabic as if you came from Mecca.'

'I was born in Baalbek, but all three of us are Kurds,' replied Yussuf in surprise. 'This is my brother Fahkr, and this is my . . . friend Moussa. Where did you learn to speak the language of the faithful? Men like you do not usually end up in long captivity, do they?'

'No, that is true,' replied the Templar knight. 'Men like me don't end up in prison at all, and I'm sure that you know why. But I have lived in Palestine for ten years; I am not here to steal goods and then go home after half a year. Most of the men who work for the Knights Templar speak Arabic. My sergeant's name, by the way, is Armand de Gascogne;

20

he's quite new here and doesn't understand much of what we're saying. That's why he is so silent, not like your men, who don't dare speak until you give them permission.'

'Your eyes are sharp,' murmured Yussuf, red-faced. 'I am the eldest, you can already see grey hairs in my beard; I am the one who administers the family's money. We are merchants on our way to an important meeting in Cairo, and . . . I don't know what my brother and my friend would want to ask one of the enemy's knights. We are all peaceful men.'

The Templar knight gave Yussuf a searching glance but said nothing for a while. He took his time eating some of the honey-drenched almonds. He paused and held up a piece of the delicacy to the firelight to examine it, concluding that these baked goods must have come from Aleppo. Then he pulled out his wine-skin and took a drink without asking permission or offering an apology, and handed the skin to his sergeant. Afterwards he leaned back comfortably and drew his big, thick white cloak around him with its terrifying red cross, looking at Yussuf as if he were assessing his opponent in a game of backgammon, not as a foe but as someone who must be evaluated.

'My unknown friend and foe, what use do any of us have for falsehoods when we eat together in peace and both have given our word not to harm each other?' he said at last. He spoke very easily, with no rancour in his voice. 'You are a warrior, as I am. If God wills, we shall meet next time on the battlefield. Your clothes betray you; your horses betray you, just as your harnesses do, and your swords, which are leaning against the saddles over there. They are swords made in Damascus; none of them costs less than five hundred dinars in gold. Your peace and mine will soon be over; the truce is about to be ended, and if you don't know this now, you will know it soon. Let us therefore enjoy this strange hour.

It's not often that a man gets to know his enemy. But let us not lie to each other.'

Yussuf was struck by an almost irresistible urge to tell the Templar knight honestly who he was. But it was true that the truce would soon be ended, although it had not yet been felt on any battlefield. And their mutual oath not to harm each other, the reason they could sit and eat together at all, was valid only for this evening.

'You're right, Templar knight,' he said at last. '*Insh'Allah*, if God wills, we will someday meet on the battlefield. But I also think, as you do, that a man should get to know his enemies, and you seem to know many more of the faithful than we know of the infidels. I now give my men permission to speak to you.'

Yussuf leaned back, also drawing his cloak closer around him, and signalled to his brother and emir that they were allowed to speak. But they both hesitated, accustomed as they were to sitting an entire evening and just listening. Since none of them made any attempt to speak, the Templar knight leaned toward his sergeant and carried on a brief whispered conversation in Frankish.

'My sergeant wonders about one thing,' he then explained. 'Your weapons, your horses, and your clothes alone are worth more than those unfortunate bandits could ever have dreamed of. How did it happen that you chose this perilous road west of the Dead Sea without sufficient escort?'

'Because it is the quickest route, because an escort arouses a great deal of attention . . .' replied Yussuf slowly. He did not want to embarrass himself by again saying something that wasn't true, so he had to weigh his words. Any escort of his would certainly have attracted attention because it would have consisted of at least three thousand horsemen if it was to be considered safe.

'And because we trusted our horses. We didn't think a few

worthless bandits or Franks would be able to catch us,' he added swiftly.

'Wise but not wise enough,' the Templar knight nodded. 'But those six bandits have been plundering these regions for almost half a year. They knew the area like the backs of their hands, they could ride faster on these stretches than any of us could. That was what made them rich. Until God punished them.'

'I would like to know one thing,' said Fahkr, who now spoke for the first time and had to clear his throat because he was stumbling over his own words. 'It is said that you Templar knights who reside in Al Aksa had a *minbar* there, a place of prayer for the faithful. And people have also told me that you Templar knights once struck a Frank who tried to prevent one of the faithful from praying. Is this really true?'

All three of the faithful now gave their full attention to the enemy. But the Templar knight smiled and first translated the question into Frankish for the sergeant, who at once nodded and burst out laughing.

'Yes, there is more truth to that than you know,' said the Templar knight after thinking for a moment, or pretending to think in order to spur his listeners' interest. 'We do have a *minbar* in *Templum Salomonis*, as we call *Al Aksa*, *"the most remote of prayer sites."* But that is not so unusual. In our fortress in Gaza we have a *majlis* every Thursday, the only day possible, and the witnesses then swear on God's Holy Scriptures, on the Torah, or on the Koran, and in some cases on something else entirely that they regard as holy. If the three of you were Egyptian merchants as you claimed, you would also know that our order conducts a great deal of business with the Egyptians, and none of them share our beliefs. *Al Aksa*, if you wish to use that name, is where we Templar knights have our headquarters, and where many people come as our guests. The problem is that every September new vessels arrive from Pisa or Genoa or the southern lands of the Franks with new men filled with the spirit and the zeal, perhaps not to enter paradise at once, but to kill unbelievers or at least lay hands on them. These newcomers create great difficulties for the rest of us, and each year, shortly after September, we always have disturbances in our own quarters because the newcomers turn against people of your faith, and then of course we have to deal with them harshly.'

'You would kill your own kind for the sake of our people?' gasped Fahkr.

'Of course not!' replied the Templar knight with sudden vehemence. 'For us it is a grave sin, just as it is in your faith, to kill any man who is a true believer. That can never come into question.'

He went on after a brief pause, his good humour restored, 'But nothing prevents us from giving rogues like that a good thrashing if they refuse to be persuaded. I myself have had the pleasure on several occasions . . .'

Quickly he leaned toward his sergeant and translated. When the sergeant began nodding and laughing in agreement, a great sense of relief seemed to come over everyone, and they all joined in with hearty laughter – perhaps a bit too hearty.

A gust of air, like the last sigh of the evening wind from the mountains near Al Khalil, suddenly carried the stench of the Templar knights toward the three faithful, and they shrank back, unable to hide their feelings.

The Templar knight noticed their embarrassment and rose to his feet immediately, suggesting that they change sides and wind direction around the muslin coverlet, where Emir Moussa was now setting out small cups of mocha. The three hosts complied with his suggestion at once, without saying anything offensive.

'We have our rules,' explained the Templar knight apologetically as he settled into his new place. 'You have rules about washing yourselves at all times of the day, and we have rules that forbid doing so. It is no worse than the fact that you have rules permitting hunting while we have ones forbidding it, except for lions; or that we drink wine and you do not.'

'Wine is a different matter,' objected Yussuf. 'The prohibition against wine is a strict one, and it is God's word to the Prophet, may peace be with Him. But we are not like our enemies; just consider God's words in the seventh *Sura*: *"Who has forbidden the beautiful things that God has granted His servants and all the good He has given them for their sustenance?"'*

'Well yes,' said the Templar knight. 'Your scriptures say many things. But if, for the sake of vanity, you want me to expose my modesty and make myself fair-smelling like worldly men, I might just as well ask you to stop calling me your enemy. For just listen to the words of your own scriptures, from the sixty-first *Sura*, words of your own Prophet, may peace be with Him: *"Faithful! Be God's disciples. Just as Jesus, the son of Mary, said to the white-clad: 'Who will be my disciple for the sake of God?' And they answered: 'We will be God's disciples!' Among the children of Israel, some came to believe in Jesus while others rejected him. But we supported those who believed in him against their enemies, and the faithful departed with victory."* I particularly like the part about the white-clad . . .'

At these words Emir Moussa sprang to his feet as if he were about to reach for his sword, but halfway there he restrained himself and stopped. His face was red with anger when he stretched out his arm and pointed an accusatory finger at the Templar knight.

'Infidel!' he cried. 'You speak the language of the Koran; that is one thing. But twisting God's words with blasphemy and ridicule is another matter that you would not be allowed to survive if it weren't for His Majes . . . because my friend Yussuf has given you his word!'

'Sit down and behave yourself, Moussa!' shouted Yussuf harshly, regaining his composure as Moussa obeyed his command. 'What you heard were indeed the words of God, and they were from the sixty-first *Sura*, and they are words you ought to consider. And don't think, by the way, that the phrase "the white-robed" refers to what our guest spoke of in jest.'

'No, of course it does not,' the Templar knight hurried to smooth things over. 'It refers to those who wore white robes long before my order existed; my clothing has nothing to do with it.'

'How do you happen to be so familiar with the Koran?' asked Yussuf in his customary and quite calm tone of voice, as if no disruption had occurred, and his high rank had not been almost revealed.

'It is a wise thing to study your enemy; if you like, I can help you to understand the Bible,' replied the Templar knight, as if trying to joke his way out of the topic, seeming to regret his clumsy invasion of the faithfuls' territory.

Yussuf was about to utter a stern reply to his lighthearted talk of entering into blasphemous studies, when he was interrupted by a long drawn-out, horrifying scream. The scream turned into something that sounded like scornful laughter, rolling down toward them and echoing off the mountainsides above. All five men froze and listened; Emir Moussa immediately began rattling off the words the faithful use to conjure up the *jinni* of the desert. Then the scream came again, but now it sounded as if it came from several spirits of the abyss, as if they were talking to each other, as if they had discovered the little fire below and the only people in the area.

The Templar knight leaned forward and whispered a few

26

words in Frankish to his sergeant, who nodded at once, stood up, and buckled on his sword. He drew his black cloak tighter, bowed to his unbeliever hosts, and then, without saying a word, turned on his heel and disappeared into the darkness.

'You must excuse this rudeness,' said the Templar knight. 'But the fact is that we have the scent of blood and fresh meat up in our camp, and horses that must be tended to.'

He didn't seem to think he needed to offer any further explanation, and with a bow he stretched out his mocha cup for Emir Moussa to refill it. The emir's hand shook slightly as he poured.

'You send your sergeant into the darkness and he obeys without blinking?' said Fahkr in a voice that sounded slightly hoarse.

'Yes,' said the Templar knight. 'A man must obey even if he feels fear. But I don't think that Armand does. The darkness is more of a friend for the man who wears a black cloak than the one who wears white, and Armand's sword is sharp and his hand steady. Wild dogs, those spotted beasts with their horrid barking, are also known for their cowardice, are they not?'

'But are you certain it was only wild dogs we heard?' asked Fahkr doubtfully.

'No,' replied the Templar knight. 'There is much we do not know between heaven and hell; no one can ever be certain. But the Lord is our shepherd, and we shall not want, even though we wander through the valley of the shadow of death. That is doubtless what Armand is praying as he walks along in the dark right now. That is what I would pray, at any rate. If God has measured out our time and wishes to call us home, there is nothing we can do, of course. But until then we cleave the skulls of wild dogs as we do those of our enemies, and in that respect I know that you who believe in

27

the Prophet, may peace be with Him, and deny the Son of God, think exactly as we do. Am I not right, Yussuf?'

'You are right, Templar knight,' Yussuf confirmed. 'But then where is the borderline between reason and belief, between fear of and trust in God? If a man must obey, as your sergeant must obey, does that make his fear any less?'

'When I was young . . . well, I am not yet a particularly old man,' said the Templar knight, seeming to think deeply, 'I was still preoccupied with that sort of question. It is good for your mind; your thoughts grow nimble from exercising your mind. But nowadays I am afraid I grow sluggish. You obey. You conquer evil. Afterwards you thank God – that is all.'

'And if you do not conquer your enemy?' asked Yussuf in a gentle voice, which those who knew him did not recognize as his normal voice.

'Then you die, at least in the case of Armand and myself,' replied the Templar knight. 'And on Judgment Day you and I will be measured and weighed, and where you will then end up, I cannot say, even though I know what you yourself believe. But if I die here in Palestine, my place will be in paradise.'

'You truly believe that?' asked Yussuf in his strange, gentle voice.

'Yes, I believe that,' replied the Templar knight.

'Then tell me one thing: Is that promise actually in your Bible?'

'No, not exactly; it does not say that exactly.'

'But you are still quite certain?'

'Yes, the Holy Father in Rome has promised . . .'

'But he is only a man! What man can promise you a place in paradise, Templar knight?'

'But Muhammed too was merely a man! And *you* believe in his promise, forgive me, may peace be to his name.'

'Muhammed, may peace be with him, was God's messenger, and God said: *"But the messenger and those who follow him in faith and strive for the sake of God, offering up their property and lives, shall be rewarded with goodness in this life and in the next, and everything they touch will prosper."* Those words are very clear, are they not? And it goes on . . .'

'Yes! In the next verse of the ninth *Sura,*' the Templar knight interjected brusquely. '*"God has prepared for them gardens of pleasure, watered by streams, where they shall remain for all eternity. This is the great and glorious victory!"* So, we understand each other, I presume? None of this is foreign to you, Yussuf. And by the way, the difference between us is that I have no possessions, I have put myself in God's hands, and when He decides, I will die for His sake. Your own beliefs do not contradict what I say.'

'Your knowledge of God's word is truly great, Templar knight,' said Yussuf, but at the same time he was pleased that he had caught his enemy in a trap, and his companions could see this.

'Yes, as I said, you should know your enemy,' said the Templar knight, for the first time a little uncertain, as if he too realized that Yussuf had backed him into a corner.

'But if you speak in this way, you are not my enemy,' said Yussuf. 'You quote from the Holy Koran, which is God's Word. What you say does apply to me, but not to you for the time being. For the faithful, all of this is as clear as water, but what is it for you? In truth, I know as much about Jesus as you know about the Prophet, may peace be with him. But what did Jesus say about the Holy War? Did Jesus speak a single word about you entering paradise if you killed me?'

'Let us not quarrel about this,' said the Templar knight with a confident wave of his hand, as if everything had suddenly become petty, although they could all see his uncertainty. 'Our beliefs are not the same, even though they have many similarities. But we have to live in the same land, fighting each other in the worse case, making treaties and conducting business in the best case. Now let us speak of other matters. It is my wish, as your guest.'

They were all aware how Yussuf had driven his opponent into a corner where he had no more defences. Jesus had clearly never said anything about it being pleasing to God to kill Saracens. But when pressed harder, the Templar knight had still managed to wriggle out of the difficult situation by referring to the faithfuls' own unwritten laws of hospitality. And so his wish had to be granted; he was the guest, after all.

'In truth, you do know a great deal about your enemy, Templar knight,' said Yussuf. Both his voice and expression showed that he was very pleased at having won the discussion.

'As we agreed, it is necessary to know your enemy,' replied the Templar knight in a low voice, his eyes downcast.

They sat in silence for a while, gazing into their mocha cups, since it seemed difficult to start up the conversation in a natural way after Yussuf's victory. But then the silence was again shattered by the sound of beasts. This time they all knew it was animals and not some devilish creature, and it sounded as if they were attacking someone or something, and then as if they were fleeing, with howls of pain and death.

'Armand's sword is sharp, as I said,' murmured the Templar knight.

'Why in the name of peace did you take your corpses with you?' asked Fahkr, who was thinking the same thing as his brothers of the faith.

'Of course it would have been better to take them alive. Then they would not have smelled so foul on the way home, and they could have travelled with ease. But tomorrow it will be a hot day; we must start our journey early to get

30

them to Jerusalem before they begin to stink too much,' replied the Templar knight.

'But if you had taken them prisoner, if you had taken them alive to Al Quds, what would have happened to them then?' persisted Fahkr.

'We would have turned them over to our emir in Jerusalem, who is one of the highest ranking in our order. He would have turned them over to the worldly powers, and they would have been disrobed, except for that which covers their modesty, and hung up on the wall by the rock,' replied the Templar knight, as if it were quite obvious.

'But you have already killed them. Why not disrobe them here and leave them to the fate they deserve? Why do you defend their bodies against the wild animals?' asked Fahkr, as if he did not want to give up or did not understand.

'We will still hang them there,' replied the Templar knight. 'Everyone must see that whoever robs pilgrims will end up hanging there. That is a holy promise from our order, and it must always be kept, as long as God helps us.'

'But what will you do with their weapons and clothes?' wondered Emir Moussa, speaking as if he wanted to bring the conversation down to a more practical level. 'Surely they must have had quite a few valuables on them.'

'Yes, but they are all stolen goods,' replied the Templar knight, some of his old self-assurance back. 'Except for their weapons and armour, for which we have no use. But their thieves' cache is in a grotto up where Armand and I have our camp. We will take heavily laden horses home with us tomorrow; keep in mind that those beasts have been plundering here for more than half a year.'

'But you are not allowed to own anything,' objected Yussuf mildly, raising his right eyebrow, as if he thought that he had once again won the argument.

'No, I am not allowed to own anything!' exclaimed the

Templar knight in surprise. 'If you think we would take the thieves' treasures for our own, you are greatly mistaken. We will place all the stolen goods outside the Church of the Holy Sepulchre next Sunday, and if those who have been robbed can find their possessions, they can have them back.'

'But surely most of those who were robbed are now dead,' said Yussuf quietly.

'They may have heirs who are alive, but whatever is not claimed will be donated to our order,' replied the Templar knight.

'That is a most interesting explanation for what I have heard, that you consider yourselves too good to plunder a battlefield,' said Yussuf with a smile, seeming to think he had won another exchange of words.

'No, we do not take plunder from battlefields,' replied the Templar knight coldly. 'But that should not present a problem, since there are so many others who do. If we have taken part in a victory, we turn at once toward God. If you would like to hear what your own Koran has to say about plundering a battlefield . . .'

'Thank you, no!' Yussuf interrupted him, holding up a hand in warning. 'We would prefer not to return to a topic of conversation since it would seem that you, an infidel, know more than we do about the Word of the Prophet, may peace be with him. Let me instead ask you a very candid question.'

'Yes. Ask me a candid question, and it shall be given the answer it deserves,' replied the Templar knight, holding up his hands, palm out, to show, in the manner of the faithful, that he agreed to change the topic of conversation.

'You said that the truce between us would soon be over. Is it Brins Arnat you are referring to?'

'You know a great deal, Yussuf. Brins Arnat, whom we call Reynald de Châtillon, has begun plundering again.

And by the way he is no "prince" but an evil man who is unfortunately allied with the Knights Templar. This I know, and I regret it. I would rather not be his ally, but I obey orders. But no, he is not the major problem.'

'Then it must be something about that new *prince*, who came from the land of the Franks with a great army. What is it he is called: *Filus* something or other?'

'No,' said the Templar knight with a smile. 'He is indeed *Filus*, meaning the son of someone. His name is Philip of Flanders, he is a duke, and yes, he came with a great army. But now I must warn you before we continue this conversation.'

'Why is that?' asked Yussuf, feigning nonchalance. 'I have your word. Have you ever broken a vow you have sworn?'

'I once made a vow that I have not yet been able to fulfil; it will take ten years before I can do so, if it is God's will. But I have never broken a promise and, may God help me, I never will.'

'Well then. Why should our truce be broken because of the arrival of someone named *Filus* from some Flamsen? Surely such things happen all the time.'

The Templar knight gave Yussuf a long, searching look, but Yussuf did not avert his eyes. This went on for some time; both refused to give in.

'You wish to keep secret your identity,' said the Templar knight at last, without taking his eyes off Yussuf. 'But few men could know so much about what goes on in the world of war; certainly not someone who claims to be a merchant on his way to Cairo. If you insist on speaking more about this, I can no longer pretend that I do not know who you are; a man who has spies, a man who knows. There are not many such men.'

'You have my word also; remember that, Templar knight.'

'Of all the unbelievers, your word is no doubt the one most of us would trust most.'

'You honour me with your words. So, why will our truce be broken?'

'Ask your men to leave us if you will continue this conversation, Yussuf.'

Yussuf pondered this for a moment as he pensively tugged on his beard. If the Templar knight truly understood who he was talking to, would it then be easier for him to kill and at the same time break his word? No, that was unlikely. Considering how this man had behaved when he killed earlier in the evening, he had no need to make it easier to betray his vow; he would have drawn his sword long ago.

Yet it was difficult to understand his demand, which seemed unreasonable. At the same time, no one would particularly benefit if it were met. In the end Yussuf's curiosity won out over his caution.

'Leave us,' he commanded curtly. 'Go to sleep close by; you can clean up here in the morning. Remember that we are in the field, under camp rules.'

Fahkr and Emir Moussa hesitated. They started to get to their feet as they looked at Yussuf, but his stern glance made them obey. They bowed to the Templar knight and withdrew. Yussuf waited in silence until his brother and his closest bodyguard had moved far enough away and could be heard arranging their bedding.

'I don't think my brother and Moussa will have an easy time falling asleep.'

'No,' said the Templar knight. 'But neither will they be able to hear what we say.'

'Why is it so important for them not to hear what we say?'

'It is not important,' said the Templar knight, smiling. 'What *is* important is that you know they won't hear what *you* say. Then our conversation will be more candid.'

'For a man who lives in a monastery, you know a great deal about human nature.'

'In the monastery we learn much about human nature; more than you imagine. Now to what is more important. I will speak only of things that I am positive you already know, since anything else would be treason. But let us examine the situation. As you know, a new Frankish prince is coming. He will remain here for some time; he has everyone's blessing back home for his holy mandate in God's service, and so on. He has brought a great army along with him. So what will he do?'

'Acquire riches as fast as possible since he has had great expenses.'

'Precisely, Yussuf, precisely. But will he go against Saladin himself, and Damascus?'

'No. Then he would risk losing everything.'

'Precisely, Yussuf. We understand each other completely, and we can speak freely, now that your subordinates are out of earshot. So where will the new plunderer and his army go?'

'Towards a city that is sufficiently strong and sufficiently wealthy, but I do not know which one.'

'Precisely. Nor do I know which one. Homs? Hama? Perhaps. Aleppo? No, too far away and too strong a city. Let us say Homs or Hama, as the most obvious. What will our worldly Christian king in Jerusalem and the royal army do then?'

'They do not have much choice. They will join in with the plundering even though they would rather use the new forces to attack Saladin.'

'Precisely, Yussuf. You know everything, you understand everything. So now we both know what the situation is. What do we do about it?'

'To begin with, you and I will both keep our word.'

'Of course, that goes without saying. But what else do we do?'

35

'We use this time of peace between us to understand each other better. I may never have the chance to talk to a Templar knight again. You may never have the chance to talk to . . . an enemy such as myself.'

'No, you and I will probably meet only on this one occasion in our lives.'

'The singular whim of God . . . But then let me ask you, Templar knight, what is needed more than God if we, the faithful, are to vanquish you?'

'Two things. What Saladin is now doing: uniting all Saracens against us. That is already taking place. But the other thing is treason among those of us on the side of Jesus Christ, betrayal or grave sins, for which God will punish us.'

'But if not betrayal or these grave sins?'

'Then neither of us will ever win, Yussuf. The difference between us is that you Saracens can lose one battle after another. You mourn your dead and you soon have a new army on the march. We Christians can lose only a great battle, and we are not that foolish. If we have the advantage, we attack. If we are at a disadvantage, we seek refuge in our fortresses. It can go on in this fashion forever.'

'So our war will last forever?'

'Perhaps, perhaps not. Some of us . . . Do you know who Count Raymond de Tripoli is?'

'Yes, I know . . . know of him. And?'

'If Christians like him should win power in the kingdom of Jerusalem, and you have on your side a leader like Saladin, then there can be peace, a just peace, in any case something better than eternal war. Many of us Templar knights think as Count Raymond does. But to return to our previous topic concerning what is going to happen right now. The Hospitallers followed the royal army and the "prince" up to Syria. We Templar knights did not.'

'I already know that.'

'Yes, doubtless you know this; because your name is Yussuf ibn Ayyub Salah al-Din, the one we call Saladin in our language.'

'May God be merciful to us, now that you know this.'

'God is merciful to us by granting us this strange conversation during the last hours of peace between us.'

'And we will both keep our word.'

'You surprise me with your uneasiness about that point. You are the only one of our enemies who is known for always keeping his word. I am a Templar knight. We always keep our word. Enough said about that matter.'

'Yes, enough about that matter. But now, my dear enemy, at this late hour before a dawn when we both have urgent errands, you with your foul-smelling corpses and I with something else that I will not discuss but which you certainly can imagine, what do we do now?'

'We take advantage of this only opportunity that God may give us in life to speak sensibly with the worst of all enemies. There is one thing that you and I can agree on . . . forgive me if I address you so plainly now that I know you are the Sultan of both Cairo and Damascus.'

'No one but God hears us, as you so wisely arranged. I wish for you to use the informal means of address on this one night.'

'We agreed on one thing, I think. We are risking eternal war because neither side can win.'

'True. But I will win, I have sworn to win.'

'As have I. Eternal war then?'

'That does not sound promising for the future.'

'Then we will continue, even though I am merely a simple emir among the Knights Templar, and you are the only one of our foes in a long time that we have had reason to fear. Where should we begin now?'

They began with the question of the pilgrims' safety. That

was the most obvious. That was the reason they had met in the first place, if they sought a human explanation for it and did not look solely to God's will in all things. But even though they both firmly believed, at least when they spoke aloud, that God's will guided everything, neither of them was a stranger to the idea that man, with his free will, could also bring about great calamities as well as great happiness. This was a cornerstone in both of their faiths.

They talked for a long time that night. At dawn, when Fahkr found his older brother – the glorious prince, the light of religion, the commander of the faithful in the Holy War, the water in the desert, the Sultan of Egypt and Syria, the hope of the faithful, the man whom the infidels for all time would call by the simple name Saladin – he was sitting with his chin resting on his knees, huddled under his cloak which was wrapped around him, and staring into the dying embers.

The white shield with the evil red cross was gone, as was the Templar knight. Saladin wearily looked up at his brother, almost as if he had awakened from a dream.

'If all our foes were like Al Ghouti, we would never win,' he said thoughtfully. 'On the other hand, if all our foes were like him, victory would no longer be necessary.'

Fahkr did not understand what his brother and prince meant but supposed it was mostly meaningless weary mutterings, as had happened so many times before when Yussuf stayed up too long and brooded.

'We must head out; we have a hard ride to Al Arish,' said Saladin, getting stiffly to his feet. 'War awaits, we will soon be victorious.'

It was true that war awaited; that was as written. But it was also written that Saladin and Arn Magnusson de Gothia would soon meet again on the battlefield, and that only one of them would come away victorious.

TWO

Jerusalem was located in the middle of a world from which even Rome seemed a distant place. Farther away was the kingdom of the Franks, and almost at the ends of the earth, in the cold, dark North, lay the land of Western Götaland which was known to very few. It was said among learned men that beyond was nothing but dark forest stretching to the edge of the earth, inhabited by monsters with two heads.

Nevertheless the true faith had reached up here to the cold and the dark, mostly thanks to Saint Bernard, who in his mercy and love of humankind had found that even the barbarians up in the dark North had a right to salvation of the soul. It was he who sent the first monks to the wild, unknown lands of the Goths. Soon the light and truth had spread from more than ten cloisters among the Northmen, who were now no longer lost.

A convent located in the southern part of Western Götaland had the loveliest of all cloister names. It was called Gudhem, God's Home, and it was dedicated to the Virgin Mary. The convent stood atop a hill, and from there could be seen the distant blue mountain Billingen, and if a person strained his eyes a bit, he might see the two towers of the cathedral in

Skara. North of Gudhem glittered Hornborga Lake, where the cranes appeared in the spring before the pike began to play. Surrounding the cloister were farms and fields and small groves of oaks. It was a very peaceful and beautiful landscape and did not at all lead the mind to thoughts of darkness and barbarity. For the older woman who had made a substantial donation and travelled here to conclude her life in peace, the name of Gudhem sounded like a caress, and the region was the loveliest that an aging eye could see.

But for Cecilia Algotsdotter, who had been locked up at Gudhem at the age of seventeen because of her sins, the convent for a long time seemed a home without God, a place that was considered more of a hell on earth.

Cecilia was familiar with cloister life, and that was not what frightened her. She also knew Gudhem, because at various intervals in her life she had spent more than two years inside among the novices, young women who were sent to the convent by wealthy families to be disciplined and taught good manners before they were married off. She already knew how to read; she knew the Book of Psalms by heart and the words tumbled from her lips like running water, because she had sung every psalm more than a hundred times. So in this there was nothing new and nothing frightening.

But this time she had been consigned to convent life, and the sentence was harsh – twenty years. She had been sentenced together with her betrothed Arn Magnusson of the Folkung clan, because they had committed a grave sin when they united in carnal love before being married before God. It was Cecilia's sister Katarina who had reported them, and the proof of their sin was such that no argument would avail. The day that the convent gate closed behind Cecilia, she was already in her third month. Her betrothed Arn had also been sentenced to twenty years, but he was to serve his time as a monk in God's holy army in the far reaches of the Holy Land.

Over the portal of Gudhem convent there were two sandstone sculptures depicting Adam and Eve driven out of Paradise after the Fall, hiding their shame with fig leaves. The image was meant to be a warning, and it spoke directly to Cecilia as if it had been cut and chiselled and polished out of stone expressly for her sake.

She had been separated from her beloved Arn only a stone's throw from this portal. He had fallen to his knees and sworn with the passion that only a seventeen-year-old youth can swear, and even upon his sword that was blessed by God. He vowed to endure all fire and war and promised to come back and fetch her when their penance was paid.

That was a long time ago now. And from Arn in the Holy Land she had heard not a word.

But what frightened Cecilia from the very start, when Abbess Rikissa dragged her in through the gate with a hard and undignified grip round her wrist, as if leading a thrall to her punishment, was that Gudhem had now become an utterly different place. It was not the same as when she had previously spent time here with the novices.

That is, on the surface Gudhem was still the place she knew, and only a few new outbuildings had been added. But inside much was changed, and she truly had good reason to feel fear.

The land for Gudhem had been donated from the royal holdings by King Karl Sverkersson. Consequently, the Abbess Rikissa belonged to the Sverker clan, as did most of the consecrated sisters and almost all the novices.

But when the pretender to the throne, Knut Eriksson, the son of Saint Erik Jedvardsson, returned from his exile in Norway to reclaim his father's crown and avenge his murder, he himself had murdered King Karl Sverkersson out on the island of Visingö. And among the men who abetted him in this deed was his friend and Cecilia's lover Arn Magnusson.

So in the world outside the cloister walls war now raged anew. On one side were the Folkung clan and the Erik clan with their Norwegian allies; on the other were the Sverker clan and their Danish allies.

Cecilia thus felt like a butterfly dragged into a hornets' nest, and she had good reason to feel this way. Since most of the sisters belonged to the Sverker faction, they hated her and they showed it. All the novices hated her as well and did nothing to hide their animosity. No one spoke to Cecilia, even when talking was permitted. They all turned their backs on her.

In the early days it was possible that Mother Rikissa had actually tried to drive her to her death. Cecilia had come to Gudhem in the months when the turnips had to be thinned. It was hard, hot work out in the fields, and none of the elegant sisters or the novices took part.

Mother Rikissa had put Cecilia on bread and water from the very first day. At mealtimes in the *refectorium* Cecilia was seated alone at an empty table at the far end of the hall, where she had to sit silently. As if this were not punishment enough, Mother Rikissa had decreed that Cecilia had to work with the lay sisters out in the turnip fields, crawling along bit by bit with the baby kicking in her belly.

As if that wasn't bad enough, or perhaps because Mother Rikissa was cross that Cecilia hadn't lost her child from the hard labour, the young woman was sent for bloodletting once a week during her first and hardest time at the convent. It was said that bloodletting was good for one's health, and that it also had a salutary effect that suppressed carnal desires. And since Cecilia had obviously fallen prey to such desires, she should have her blood let often.

As Cecilia crawled along in the turnip fields, growing ever paler, she constantly murmured prayers to Our Lady to protect her, forgive her for her sin, and yet hold Her gracious hand over the child she bore inside her.

Cecilia almost gave birth to her son out in the cold November mud in the turnip fields. It was near the end of the harvest time when she suddenly sank to the ground with a sharp cry. The lay sisters and the two supervisors who stood nearby to monitor virtue and silence during the work understood at once what was about to happen. At first they acted as if they thought nothing needed to be done. But the lay sisters would not stand for this; without uttering a word, even to ask permission, they hurried to carry Cecilia to the *hospitium*, the guest house outside the walls. There they laid her in bed and sent a messenger to fetch Fru Helena, who was a wise woman and one of Gudhem's pensioners who had given a large donation to the convent.

Fru Helena came quickly, taking pity on Cecilia, although she herself was of the Sverker clan. She ordered two of the lay sisters to stay in the *hospitium* and assist her; let Rikissa – she didn't say *Mother* Rikissa – think or say what she would. Women had a hard enough time in this world without heaping stones on one another's burdens, she told the two astonished lay sisters who stayed with her. At her command they heated water, fetched linens, and washed the mud and dirt from the suffering Cecilia, now almost out of her mind with pain.

Fru Helena had come to her rescue, and she must have been sent by the Holy Virgin herself. She had given birth to nine children, seven of whom had survived. Many times she had assisted other women in this difficult hour, when women are alone and only other women can help. She scoffed at the thought that this young woman was supposed to be her enemy. She told the two lay sisters that the position of friend or foe could change overnight, or even as the result of a sorry little war between the menfolk.

Cecilia did not remember much of the hours that night when she gave birth to her son Magnus, as they had decided

43

he should be named. She remembered the moment when it was all over and, drenched in sweat and hot as if with fever, she was given the infant by Fru Helena, who pressed him to her aching breasts. And she recalled Fru Helena's words that he was a fair boy in good health with all his limbs in the proper place. But after that a haze shrouded her mind.

Later she learned that Fru Helena had sent word to Arnäs, and a large escort came to fetch the babe and take him to safety. Birger Brosa, the mightiest of the Folkungs and the uncle of her beloved Arn, had sworn that the lad – he had never spoken of the anticipated child as other than 'the lad' – would be taken into the clan and proclaimed at the *ting* as a true Folkung, whether he was born in whoredom or not.

Of all the trials in young Cecilia's life, the hardest of all was that she would not see her son again until he was a man.

Mother Rikissa had a heart of stone where Cecilia was concerned. Shortly after giving birth Cecilia was once again set to hard labour, although she still had a fever. She was often bathed in sweat, she was very pale, and she had trouble with her breasts.

As Christmas approached in her first year at the cloister, Bishop Bengt came from Skara on visitation, and when he noticed Cecilia shuffling past out in the arcade, seemingly oblivious to everything, he blanched. Then he had a brief conversation with Mother Rikissa in private. That same day Cecilia was placed in the *infirmatorium*, and she was given daily pittances, extra helpings of food that those outside were allowed to donate to the residents of the cloister: eggs, fish, white bread, butter, and even some lamb. Gossip spread at Gudhem about these pittances that Cecilia received. Some believed that they came from Bishop Bengt, others that they came from Fru Helena or perhaps from Birger Brosa himself.

She was also excused from bloodletting, and soon the colour returned to her face, and she started to regain her health. But all hope seemed to have left her. She went about mostly muttering to herself.

When winter swept into Western Götaland with cold and ice, all outside work ceased for both the lay sisters and Cecilia. This was a relief, yet at the same time the nights became an even greater torment.

Since it was against the rules to have heating in the *dormitorium*, it was important where in the room one's bed stood. The farther away from the two windows the better. Naturally Cecilia was assigned the bed right next to the stone wall, beneath a window where the cold came flowing down like ice water; the other novices slept on the other side of the room, against the internal wall. Cecilia and her worldly sisters were separated by the eight lay sisters who never dared to speak to her.

The regulations permitted a straw mattress, a pillow, and two woollen blankets. Even if they all went to bed fully dressed, the nights could sometimes get so cold that it was impossible to sleep, at least for someone who always shook with cold.

It was at this most difficult time at Gudhem for Cecilia, that it seemed as though Our Lady sent her some consolation; a few words that would not have meant very much to anyone else, but here warmed her to the heart.

One of the other maidens close to the door had been found unworthy of the best bed location when someone revealed one of her secrets. On Mother Rikissa's express order she was forced to move to the bed next to Cecilia's. One evening she came with her bedclothes in her arms and stood with bowed head, waiting until the lay sister in the bed next to

Cecilia grasped that she was supposed to toddle off to the warmer side of the room. When the lay sister had taken her bedclothes and gone, the new maiden slowly and carefully made her bed, glancing over at the sister who stood in the dark by the door to the stairs and kept a watchful eye on the proceedings. When she was done the maiden crept into bed, turned on her side, and sought out Cecilia's gaze. Then without blinking she broke the rule of silence.

'You're not alone, Cecilia,' she whispered, so quietly that no one else could hear.

'Thank you, Our Lady be praised,' Cecilia signalled back in the sign language they used at Gudhem when no words could be spoken. But she no longer felt cold, and her thoughts were directed to different matters, something other than the loneliness and unhappy longing in which she'd been circling for so long that sometimes she feared for her sanity. Now she lay for a while looking with curiosity into the eyes of her unknown companion who had spoken so kindly to her, even when it was forbidden to speak. They smiled at each other until the darkness came, and that night Cecilia did not shiver from the cold and she quickly fell asleep.

When they were awakened to go down to *matins*, she was sleeping deeply, and the unknown maiden next to her had to give her a gentle shake. Later, down in the church, Cecilia sang along in the hymns for the first time in full voice, her clear tones rising higher than all the others'. Singing had after all been her one great joy in past years at Gudhem, back when she knew that she would be released after only a few months.

And she fell asleep easily after *matins*, so when it was time for *lauds*, the morning praise song, the stranger had to wake her again. It seemed she had a need to catch up on lost sleep.

After the first mass of the day, when it was time to gather in the chapter hall, Cecilia found that her new neighbour had to sit close to the door, just as she did, and again she contemplated the words that she was no longer alone, that now they were two.

After Mother Rikissa read the day's Bible text, she recited a list of names of deceased brothers and sisters in the Cistercian order for whose souls they must pray. Cecilia froze briefly, for sometimes the list included a foreign name or the name of a fallen Templar knight, who was counted as equal to brothers or sisters. But today there was no such name.

The punishments were saved till last during the morning convocation. The most common infraction punished by Mother Rikissa was breach of the code of silence. Six or seven times Cecilia had been punished for this, despite the fact that no one ever spoke to Cecilia, nor did she speak to anyone else.

It so happened, explained Mother Rikissa with something that looked more like a smile than an expression of sternness, that it was now time to punish Cecilia again. The sisters then lowered their heads with a sigh, while the worldly maidens raised theirs and stared with inquisitive malice at Cecilia.

However, it was not the usual Cecilia who was to be punished; not Cecilia Algotsdotter but Cecilia Ulvsdotter. And now that there were two Cecilias who apparently displayed the same breach of conduct, the red-haired Cecilia Algotsdotter would hereafter be called Cecilia Rosa, and the blonde one would be called Cecilia Blanca.

The punishment was usually a day or two on bread and water, a common penalty meted out during the period when Mother Rikissa had seemed intent on tormenting Cecilia to death after her childbirth. But now Mother Rikissa ordered, more with scorn than with the grace of God, that Cecilia Blanca be led to the *lapis culparum*, the punishment stone at the far end of the room. The prioress and one of the sisters promptly went over to Cecilia Blanca and took her by both arms to lead her to the punishment stone; there they removed her woollen mantle so that she stood there in only her linen shift. They stretched her hands above her head and fastened them with two handcuffs of iron.

Then Mother Rikissa fetched a scourge and took up position next to the bound Cecilia Blanca and looked at her congregation, again showing more triumph than divine benevolence. She paused for a moment, testing the scourge by slapping it against her hand.

Then she signalled for them to say three *Pater Nosters*, and they all bowed their heads obediently and began reciting.

When the prayers were concluded, she summoned one of the worldly maidens, Helena Sverkersdotter, handed her the scourge, and asked her in the name of the Father, the Son, and the Holy Virgin to administer three lashes.

Helena Sverkersdotter was a clumsy, bumbling girl who seldom got the chance to stand out from the crowd. Now she looked at the other sisters with delight, and they all nodded at her in encouragement; someone signalled for her to give Cecilia Blanca a good thrashing. And so she did. She did not do it in the usual way, which was intended to mark the memory and alter the mind rather than to cause injury to the body. She struck as hard as she could, and with the last blow two lines of blood seeped through Cecilia Blanca's white shift.

Cecilia Blanca moaned between clenched teeth during the beating, but she did not scream nor cry.

Now she turned around, difficult as it was in her bound position, so that she could look the flushed and exhilarated Helena Sverkersdotter in the eye. And then, snarling between clenched teeth and with her eyes black with hate, she said something so appalling that a gasp of horror passed through the hall.

'One day, Helena Sverkersdotter, you shall regret those lashes more than anything else in your life, I swear it by the Holy Virgin Mary!'

These words were unconscionable. Not just because they expressed threats and anger *intra muros*, nor because she had involved Our Lady in her sin, but primarily because these words showed that Cecilia Blanca had not accepted the justice of her punishment and thus had not obeyed Mother Rikissa.

What everyone now anticipated was three times three new lashes with the scourge, as an immediate result of the blasphemous words. But Mother Rikissa went over to take the scourge away from Helena Sverkersdotter, who had already raised her hand to begin anew.

Cecilia Rosa over by the door thought she saw Mother Rikissa's eyes glowing red like a dragon's or some other evil creature, and all the others bowed their heads as if in prayer, although what they really felt was horror.

'Three days in the *carcer*,' said Mother Rikissa at last, drawing out her words. 'Three days in the *carcer* on bread and water, with solitude and silence and prayer, and with only one blanket – that's where you shall seek forgiveness!'

No one had been sentenced to the *carcer* as long as Cecilia Rosa had been at Gudhem; that was a punishment mentioned only as a scary story. The *carcer* was a dark little hole beneath the *cellarium*, the seed storage areas. Sitting there among the rats in the wintertime was a torment that would be terrible to endure.

Over the next few days Cecilia Rosa did not feel cold, because she was occupied with praying for her new friend Cecilia Blanca. She prayed with a burning soul and tears running from her eyes, and she did all her tasks without thinking; she wove and sang and ate without thinking. She put her whole soul and all her thoughts into her prayers.

On the evening of the third day, Cecilia Blanca returned, her legs stiff and unsteady, completely white in the face. She was escorted by two sisters up to the *dormitorium* after the period of silence. They led her to her bed, shoved her in, and heedlessly tossed the covers over her.

Cecilia Rosa, as even she now called herself, sought out her friend's eyes in the dark. But Cecilia Blanca's gaze was rigid and empty. Considering how she looked, she had to be chilled to the bone.

Cecilia Rosa waited a while until it was quiet in the *dormitorium* before she did the unthinkable. She took her two blankets and climbed into her friend's bed as quietly as she could, pulling the covers over both of them and lying close to her. It was like lying next to ice. But soon, as though Our Lady were holding her hand over them even in this difficult hour, the warmth slowly crept into their bodies.

After *matins* Cecilia Rosa did not dare repeat her sin, which was an act of charity. But she loaned one of her blankets to her friend and no longer felt cold herself, even though it was one of the last hard winter nights, with the stars sparkling with utter clarity in the black sky.

Their crime was never discovered. Or perhaps the lay sisters who slept nearby and had the best opportunity of discovering the sinful deed of sleeping together found no reason to tell tales. For those who did not have hearts of stone or, unlike the other worldly maidens among the novices, did not hate the two Cecilias, it was not hard to imagine the suffering that three nights in the *carcer* had caused during the coldest part of winter.

Winter at Gudhem was the time for spinning and weaving. For the lay sisters this was monotonous work, since the important thing was that they produce as much cloth as possible for Gudhem to donate or sell.

But for the worldly maidens it was more a matter of learning a task that would keep their hands occupied. *Ora et labora*, pray and work, was the most important rule next to obedience at Gudhem, as in other cloisters. For this reason the maidens had to look as though they were working even during the time when the cold kept them all indoors.

If one of the younger novices was totally ignorant of this type of work, she would first have to sit next to someone more skilled, at least until she was able to manage her own loom or distaff.

Cecilia Blanca had proved completely unfamiliar with this work, while Cecilia Rosa could perform the tasks almost as well as a lay sister. This presented a problem that could be solved in only one way, since none of the six young women who belonged to the Sverker clan, or wanted to belong, would sit with the one they disdained and hated most at Gudhem, the fiancée of the regicide Knut Eriksson. That was the secret they had discovered. So the only solution was to put the two Cecilias together at the same loom.

Cecilia Rosa soon discovered that her friend Blanca had actually mastered all the arts of the loom; she furtively demonstrated as much, using a secret sign between them. Her feigned ignorance was merely a ruse so that the two friends could be near each other. Now no imposed silence could prevent them from speaking together, since during the work they constantly had to use sign language. No supervising sister was sharp-eyed enough to see what they were talking about at every moment. And when the supervisor turned her back, they could exchange a surreptitious whisper.

Soon Cecilia Blanca had told her what she knew about the hatred of the others for the two of them, and about her hopes for the future.

Outside in the world of men, things were no longer as simple as before; it took more than chopping off a king's head to become king oneself. Her betrothed Knut Eriksson would manage it in time, and with the help of God and his dead father, Erik the Holy. But it would not be accomplished in the blink of an eye.

So immediately after the betrothal ale, Knut had seen to it that his betrothed Cecilia Blanca was sent to the convent, where she could find sanctuary while the men fought it out. Even in an enemy cloister her life and limb would not be endangered, although it would not be an enjoyable time. One stumbling block was that the few convents in the country were all associated with the Sverker clan; that was something that would have to be changed in the future. But that was how things now stood, with great uncertainty about what was to come. It would be bleak indeed for them both if the Sverkers were victorious; maybe they would never get out, never have children and servants to manage, never be able to stride freely across their own fields, ride horses, or sing worldly songs.

Yet the joy would be all the greater if their side won, if her beloved Knut were proclaimed king and then peace descended upon the realm. Then all the dark times would be transformed to blinding white. Then Cecilia Blanca would become the true consort of her beloved Knut and become queen. This was the threat that Mother Rikissa, the sisters, and the stupid geese among the novices, worst of all that Helena Sverkersdotter, tried to ignore.

Cecilia Blanca thought that the two of them, friends only to each other, had to pray for this every day: pray that the Folkungs and the Eriks would prevail. Their lives and their happiness depended more on this victory than on anything else.

Although they could never be sure. When peace was made, many peculiar things could happen, and the men often found that it was easier to keep peace through marriage than to win it by the sword. So if the Sverkers won, they might very well arrange a suitable bridal ale with any one of the enemy's women. If that were to happen, the two Cecilias might be collected one miserable day and married off to some old men in Linköping – an unkind fate, but still not as unpleasant as doing the cleaning and suffering under Mother Rikissa's scourge.

Cecilia Rosa, who was some years younger than her new and only friend, sometimes had a hard time following Blanca's stern train of thought. She protested more than once that for her part, she hoped for nothing more than that her beloved would come back just as he had sworn to do. Blanca, on the other hand, had no time for such sentimental talk. Love might be pleasant to dream about, but they couldn't dream themselves out of their imprisonment at Gudhem. They might be taken from there to a bridal ale, and then they would see if their husband was to be a drooling old codger from Linköping or a handsome young man. But nothing in this earthly life could be worse than being forced to show obedience each day to Mother Rikissa.

Cecilia Rosa said that nothing could be worse than betraying her vows of love, but Cecilia Blanca had no idea what she meant.

The two young women were altogether different. Cecilia, the red-haired Rosa, was quiet in both speech and thought, as if she dreamed a good deal. Cecilia, the blonde Blanca, was choleric in her speech and had many hard thoughts of revenge for the day when she would become King Knut's queen. She often repeated what she had sworn, to make the stupid goose Helena regret the lashes she had delivered more than anything else in her life. Perhaps the two Cecilias would not have grown so close to each other if they had met out in the free world, say if they had been the mistresses of neighbouring farms. But since life had now brought them to

53

Gudhem among all these malicious, cowardly, and hostile women, their bond of friendship had been forged as if in a glowing furnace, linking them forever.

They both wanted to rebel, but neither of them wanted to go to the *carcer*, the cold hole in the ground with the rats. They wanted to break as many rules as they could, but it was vexing to be discovered and punished, since what stung most about the punishment was the malicious pleasure of the other young women.

With more than a little cunning they found more ways to cause trouble as time passed. Cecilia Rosa sang perfectly on-key and more beautifully than anyone else at Gudhem, and she demonstrated her ability as often as she could. Cecilia Blanca was no slouch of a singer either, but she tried to spoil the song as often as she could, especially during the sleepy *lauds* and *prime* services, by singing loudly and a bit off-key, singing too fast or too slow. It was hard to sing falsely in that manner, but Cecilia Blanca became increasingly skilled at doing so, and it was something for which she could never be punished. In this way they took turns; Cecilia Rosa sometimes sang so that the others stopped their own singing, put to shame by the beauty of her voice. At other times, when Cecilia Rosa felt out of form or too tired, Cecilia Blanca would sing and ruin everything. She would be chided and then promise with her head bowed that she would improve and learn to sing as well as all the rest.

Over time the two friends grew quite skilled at their art of creating annoyance during the seven or eight song sessions each day.

Cecilia Rosa played the part of the weak and submissive one, and always replied in a low voice with her head bowed when spoken to by Mother Rikissa or the prioress. Cecilia Blanca did the opposite, answering in a loud voice with head held high, even though her speech was such that the words themselves were unimpeachable.

Each day, *prandium* was eaten at exactly twelve minutes past four in the afternoon, a repast of bread and soup. They all had to eat in silence, while the lector read texts aloud that were considered especially appropriate for young women. Cecilia Blanca would often make a point of loudly slurping up a piece of bread dipped in the soup just as the reading reached a crucial point. This would cause some of the Sverker maidens to giggle aloud, sometimes to draw Mother Rikissa's attention to the naughtiness of Cecilia Blanca's behaviour. But Mother Rikissa would be more strict in her reproaches to those who giggled than to the one who slurped.

After *prandium* all the women had to walk in a procession from the *refectorium* to the church for prayers of thanksgiving, singing along the way. The intent was that they were to walk with great dignity. But Cecilia Blanca often had occasion to clear her throat loudly, to clump along and act like a lout, or pretend to stumble and disturb the order of the procession. Next to her walked Cecilia Rosa, because the two of them always had to bring up the rear. She was singing with her gaze fixed on the distance and a dreamy expression that seemed almost heavenly.

It was like a game the two played, constantly talking about their little tricks and trying to think up new ones. But since they talked to each other even when it was forbidden, Mother Rikissa would often punish them, but not as hard as one might expect. And she no longer allowed any of the worldly maidens to wield the scourge. She did the whipping herself, first Cecilia Blanca, then Cecilia Rosa. The strange thing was that the longer their rebellion went on, the less Mother Rikissa countered it with sternness, which at first they couldn't understand.

To both of them Mother Rikissa was an evil person who

had no belief in the fear of God which she was always trying to drum into others. She was as ugly as a witch, with big protruding teeth and rough hands, and they were sure she would have had to hold a very powerful position in the Sverker clan to be married off with those looks. She could hardly have gained power through the marriage bed; it was much easier to do so by becoming an abbess.

And since both Cecilias were women at their loveliest age, with slender waists and eyes full of life, they believed that this was precisely what put Mother Rikissa's back up.

When the summer came and the masses of Ascension Day were past, Mother Rikissa changed again. Now she found constant reason to punish the two hated Cecilias. Since bread and water didn't seem to have much effect on what she called their roguishness, she employed the scourge almost daily. And now she forced the Sverker maidens, but never again Helena Sverkersdotter, to carry out the whipping. Of course none of the girls struck as hard as Helena had done when Cecilia Blanca issued her curse, but the repeated punishment still resulted in more pain in their backs.

It was Cecilia Blanca who at last figured out how they could escape this misery. She figured that Mother Rikissa would not be honest enough to follow the rule of inviolable secrecy in the confessional, and that she would worm information out of any father confessor who came to Gudhem.

The confessor who came most often was a young *vicarius* from the cathedral in Skara. Even the worldly maidens had to make confession to him. But they were never allowed to see him, because he sat inside the church, and the one who was confessing sat out in the arcade next to a window with a wooden grating and a cloth between them.

One mild morning in early summer Cecilia Blanca found herself at confession, overcome by a feeling of nervousness, for she knew quite well that what she intended to do was a serious sin; it was a mockery of the holy confession. On the other hand, she consoled herself, if this stratagem succeeded then it would show that it was actually Mother Rikissa and the *vicarius* who were mocking the confessional.

'Father, forgive me, for I have sinned,' she whispered so rapidly that the words stumbled over each other. Then she drew a deep breath in anticipation of what she had to do.

'My child, my dear daughter,' replied the *vicarius* with a sigh on the other side of the grating, 'Gudhem is not a place that induces one to grave sins, but let us hear your confession.'

'I've been thinking evil thoughts about my fellow sisters,' Cecilia Blanca continued with a will, now that she had taken the leap into sin. 'I have vindictive thoughts and I can't forgive them.'

'What and whom can't you forgive?' the *vicarius* asked cautiously.

'The Sverker girls and their lot. They run around telling tales, and they wield the scourge when my friend and I are repeatedly punished because of their gossip. And forgive me, father, but I must speak the truth. I think that if I become queen, then I will never be able to forgive either them or Mother Rikissa. I think that I will have to take a lengthy and harsh revenge; I think that their kinsmen's farms will burn and that Gudhem will be emptied of all folk, and not one stone will be left standing at this place.'

'Who is your friend?' asked the *vicarius* with a slight quaver in his voice.

'Cecilia Algotsdotter, father.'

'The one who was betrothed in the Folkung clan to a man named Arn Magnusson?'

'Yes, exactly, father, the one Birger Brosa holds so dear. She is my friend, and she is tormented by everyone here the same as I am, and this is why I'm filled with these unworthy and sinful thoughts of revenge.'

'As long as you are at Gudhem, my daughter, you must follow the holy rules that apply here,' replied the *vicarius*, trying to sound stern. But there was a clear note of uncertainty and fear in his voice that did not escape Cecilia Blanca's attention.

'I know, father, I know that this is my sin, and I seek God's forgiveness,' said Cecilia Blanca in a low, demure voice, but with a broad smile on her face; the *vicarius* could no more see her than she could see him.

It took a moment before the *vicarius* answered, and Cecilia Blanca considered it a good sign that her ploy was having an effect.

'You have to seek peace in your soul, my daughter,' he said at last in a strained voice. 'You have to reconcile yourself with your lot in life, like all the rest here at Gudhem. I tell you now that you must meditate on your sinful thoughts, you must say twenty *Pater Nosters* and forty *Ave Marias* and you must refrain from speaking a word to anyone for twenty-four hours while you repent your sin. Do you understand?'

'Yes, father, I understand,' whispered Cecilia Blanca, biting her lip to keep from breaking into laughter.

'I forgive you in the name of the Father, the Son, and the Holy Virgin Mary,' whispered the *vicarius*, obviously shaken.

Cecilia Blanca hurried off along the arcade in jubilation, but with her head demurely bowed. At the other side of the cloister she found her friend Cecilia Rosa hiding by the fountain in the *lavatorium*. Cecilia Blanca was red in the face with excitement.

'That ploy did some good, by God I think it helped,' she whispered as she came in, looked around, and then embraced her friend as if they were free women in the other world, an embrace that would have cost them dearly if anyone had seen.

'How so, how can you know that?' asked Cecilia Rosa as she anxiously pushed her friend away and looked around.

'Twenty Our Fathers and forty Hail Marys for confessing such hatred – that's nothing at all! And only one day of silence. Don't you see? He was scared, and now he'll run and spill it all to that witch Rikissa. Now you have to do the same thing!'

'I don't know, I don't know if I dare . . .' said Cecilia Rosa. 'I have nothing to use as a threat. You can threaten them with the prospect of becoming a vengeful queen, but I . . . with my twenty-year sentence, what can I threaten them with?'

'With the Folkungs and with Birger Brosa!' whispered Cecilia Blanca excitedly. 'I think something has happened outside or is about to happen. Threaten them with the Folkungs!'

Cecilia Rosa envied her friend's courage. It was a bold venture they had undertaken, and Cecilia Rosa could never have done it by herself. But now the first move had been made. Cecilia Blanca had taken the risks for them both, and now Cecilia Rosa had to do the same.

'Trust me, I will do it too,' she whispered, crossing herself and pulling her hood over her head. She walked off rubbing her hands together as if she had just washed them in the fountain. She walked along the arcade to the confessional without hesitation, and she did as friendship now demanded she do; she overcame her fear of committing the unprecedented act of mocking the confessional.

She was not quite sure what part of their plan had actually worked, but the fact that it did work was certain.

Silence still surrounded the two Cecilias at Gudhem; no one spoke to them, but neither did anyone look at them with the same hatred as before. It was as though everyone's eyes had become frightened and furtive. And none of the other maidens gossiped about them any longer or reported that they had spoken during the periods of enforced silence, which they now began to do quite openly. Without shame they could walk and converse like free people outside, although they were walking in the arcade inside Gudhem.

It was a brief period of unexpected happiness that also brought a tantalizing feeling of uncertainty. The others obviously knew so much more and did what they could to keep their two enemies in ignorance. But something big was happening outside the walls; otherwise the scourge would have been taken out long ago.

The two Cecilias now found greater joy in their shared tasks, for no one prevented them from working together at the looms, although it was now obvious that Cecilia Blanca was certainly no beginner who needed help. They had started working with linen thread now that winter was long past. They received help from Sister Leonore, who came from southern climes and was the one responsible for the convent's vegetable garden outside the walls as well as for the garden inside the walls and all the rosebushes that grew along the arcade. Sister Leonore taught them how to mix various colours and dye the linen, and they began to experiment with different weaving patterns. What they made could not be used inside Gudhem, of course, but it could be sold on the outside.

They turned to Sister Leonore all the more, because she had no friends in the lands of the Goths and thus had nothing to do with the feuds that were going on outside the walls. From her they learned how to take care of a garden in the summertime, how each plant had to be nurtured like a child, and how too much water was sometimes just as harmful as too little.

Mother Rikissa left them alone with Sister Leonore, and in this way a sort of equilibrium was restored at Gudhem;

the enemies had been separated although they all lived under the same roof, recited the same prayers, and sang the same hymns.

But the two Cecilias were not allowed to go outside except to the garden just beyond the south wall. Mother Rikissa was hard as stone on that point. And when two sisters and all the novices were going to the midsummer market in Skara, Cecilia Rosa and Cecilia Blanca were forced to stay behind at Gudhem.

They clenched their teeth when told and once again felt a fierce hatred for Mother Rikissa. At the same time they knew that there was something going on that they didn't understand, something the others seemed to know about but refused to discuss.

Later that summer something happened that was as frightening as it was surprising. Bishop Bengt in Skara had come rushing over to Gudhem and locked himself in with Mother Rikissa in the abbess's own rooms. Whether it was merely a lucky coincidence or whether one thing had to do with the other, the Cecilias never found out.

But some hours after Bishop Bengt arrived at Gudhem, a group of armed riders approached. The alarm was sounded on the bell, and the gates were closed. Since the riders came from the east, the two Cecilias hurried up to the *dormitorium* to look out the windows up there. They were filled with hope, almost jubilant. But when they spied the colours of the riders' mantles and shields, they felt as if death itself had seized hold of their hearts. Some of the riders were bloody, others gravely wounded and leaning forward over their saddles, and some were physically unhurt but with wildly staring eyes. All of them belonged to the enemy.

Up by the barred cloister gate the riders came to a halt, but their leader began to yell something about turning over the Folkung whores. Cecilia Rosa and Cecilia Blanca, who were now hanging halfway out the *dormitorium* windows so they could hear everything, didn't know whether to start praying or stay there to hear more. Cecilia Rosa wanted to pray for her life. Cecilia Blanca absolutely wanted to hear everything that was said. She thought they had to learn why wounded enemies would attempt an act as serious as abducting women from a convent. So they both stayed in the window and pricked up their ears.

After a while Bishop Bengt came out and the gate was locked behind him. He spoke in a low voice and with dignity to the enemy riders. The two Cecilias in the window could hear very little of what was said, but the gist of the exchange was that it was an unforgivable sin to direct violence against the peace of the cloister. And that he, the bishop, would rather be struck down by the sword than allow any such thing. Then the men spoke so low that nothing could be heard from the window. It ended with the entire group slowly and reluctantly turning their horses and riding off to the south.

The two Cecilias held each other tight as they sank to the floor beneath the window. They didn't know whether to pray to the Holy Virgin Mary and give thanks for their rescue or to laugh out loud with joy. Cecilia Rosa began to pray; Cecilia Blanca let her do so while she herself used the time to think hard about what they had witnessed. Finally she leaned over, embraced Cecilia Rosa once again, even tighter, and kissed her on both cheeks, as if she had already left this stern world.

'Cecilia, my beloved friend,' she whispered excitedly, 'my only friend in this evil place they so unfairly call Gudhem, the home of God. I think we just saw our salvation arrive.'

'But those were the enemy's retainers,' Cecilia Rosa whispered uncertainly. 'They came to abduct us, and we were fortunate that the bishop was here. What was so good about that? Imagine if they come back when the bishop isn't here.'

'They won't come back. Didn't you see that they were defeated?'

'Yes, many of them were wounded . . .'

'That's right. And what does that mean? Who do you think defeated them?'

'Our men?'

Just as she uttered the simple answer to that simple question, Cecilia Rosa felt a pain and sorrow that she couldn't understand, since she should have been happy. If the Folkungs and the Eriks had now won, she ought to be happy, but that also meant that she would be separated from Cecilia Blanca. And she herself had many years left to serve.

That day a dark mood of fear descended over Gudhem. Not a single woman dared look them in the eye except for Sister Leonore, who was probably the one who knew least, along with the two Cecilias.

Mother Rikissa had retreated to her own rooms and did not emerge until the following day. Bishop Bengt had left in a great hurry, and then they all carelessly tended to the work, the songs, and to holding mass. At evensong the two Cecilias sang together as they had never done before, and now there were absolutely no false notes from the one called Blanca. And the one called Rosa sang louder, more boldly, almost with a worldly boldness, sometimes putting entirely new variations into her voice. No one corrected her, and there was no Mother Rikissa to frown at this song of joy.

The next morning riders came galloping from Skara to Gudhem to bring a message to Mother Rikissa. She received the messengers out in the *hospitium* and then shut herself in the abbess's quarters without meeting anyone until *prime*, which would be followed by the first mass of the day.

The Host had been blessed out in the sacristy by an unknown *vicarius* or someone else from the cathedral in

Skara, and it was distributed in the usual order, first the sisters, then the lay sisters, and the worldly maidens last.

The sacred wine was brought in, the bell rang to proclaim the miracle, and the chalice was passed from one to the next by the prioress, with her other hand giving each her own *fistula*, a straw to use for the wine.

When it was Cecilia Rosa's turn to drink of God's blood, she did it demurely and with a genuine feeling of thanksgiving inside, for what was now happening confirmed her greatest hopes. But when it was Cecilia Blanca's turn to drink there was a loud slurping, perhaps because she was the last to drink and there was little wine left. Or perhaps because she again wanted to show her contempt, not for God but for Gudhem. The two Cecilias never talked about it, or discussed which was the truth.

After that everyone was so tense when they headed out to the chapter hall that they moved as stiffly as puppets. Out there Mother Rikissa was waiting, looking exhausted with dark circles under her eyes and almost a bit shrunken in her chair, where she usually sat like an evil queen.

The prayer session was short. As was the reading of the Scripture, which this time dealt with grace and mercy, which made Cecilia Blanca give her friend an encouraging wink to signify that everything seemed to be going as they might hope. Mercy and grace were certainly not Mother Rikissa's favourite topics during the Scripture reading.

Then there was silence and the mood was tense. Mother Rikissa began in a quiet voice, not at all like her normal one, to read aloud the names of brothers and sisters who were now wandering the fields of Paradise. Cecilia Rosa briefly listened for any name of Templar knights to be added to the list, but there was none.

Then there was silence again. Mother Rikissa wrung her hands and looked almost on the verge of tears, something that neither of the Cecilias would have believed possible from the evil witch. After sitting a while in silence and trying to collect herself, Mother Rikissa plucked up her courage and unrolled a parchment. Her hands trembled a bit as she recited in a monotone, 'In the name of the Father, Son, and the Holy Virgin, we must pray for all those, friends or not, who have fallen on the fields of blood, as these sites are always called, outside of Bjälbo.'

Here she paused to collect herself once more, and when the two Cecilias heard the word Bjälbo, their hearts contracted in fear. Bjälbo was the mightiest fortress of the Folkungs; it was Birger Brosa's estate and home. So the war had reached that far.

'Among those who fell, and they were many . . .' Mother Rikissa went on, but she had to force herself to continue. 'Among the many who fell were the jarls of God's grace Boleslav and Kol, and so many of their kinsmen that I cannot count them all. We will now pray for the souls of the dead. We will be in mourning for a week and take nothing but bread and water; we will now . . . suffer a great sadness.'

There Mother Rikissa fell silent and sat with the text held loosely in her hand, as if she no longer felt like reading. Sniffling was already heard in the hall.

Then Cecilia Blanca stood up and took her friend boldly by the hand; they were sitting together at the back of the hall closest to the door. And without hesitation in her voice, but also without showing contempt or malice, she now broke her vow of silence.

'Mother Rikissa, I beg your forgiveness,' she said. 'But Cecilia Algotsdotter and I will be leaving you now to the sorrow in which the two of us cannot participate. We're going out to the arcade to reflect in our own way on what has happened.'

It was an unheard-of way of speaking, but Mother Rikissa

merely waved her hand weakly in acknowledgment. Cecilia Blanca then took a step closer to her friend and bowed with courtly dignity, as if she were the queen herself, before she left the hall, still holding her friend's hand.

When they reached the arcade they quickly ran as far away as they could so as not to be heard by the mourners. Then they stopped, embraced, kissed each other in the most immodest way, and spun round and round with their arms around each other's waists, moving along the arcade as if they were dancing. Nothing needed to be said; now they knew all that they needed to know.

If Boleslav and Kol were dead, then the battle was over. If the Sverkers had attacked Bjälbo itself, then the Folkungs, even though they had hesitated before, must have emerged with all their forces, either to conquer or die. There would have been no other choice if the battle was at Bjälbo.

And if both the pretenders to the throne on the other side had fallen, it meant that not many of their men had escaped the battle alive, since the noble lords were the last to fall in war. Birger Brosa and Knut Eriksson must have won a great and decisive victory. So that's why the fleeing Sverkers had come to Gudhem in the belief that they would be able to purchase safe conduct for themselves by kidnapping Knut Eriksson's betrothed.

The war was over, and their side had won. In the first moment of joy when they danced down the arcade with their arms around each other, this was the thought that filled their minds.

Only later did they realize that what had happened on the bloody fields outside Bjälbo also meant that now they would be separated from each other. Cecilia Blanca's hour of release would soon arrive.

THREE

Armand de Gascogne, sergeant of the Order of the Knights Templar, was a man who knew neither fear nor dread. Not only was it against the Rule – a Templar knight was forbidden to feel fear – it was also against his image of himself and against his most fervent wish in life, to be taken into the Order as a full-fledged brother in arms.

But when he spied the walls of Jerusalem in the setting sun, the centre of the world, looming up before them, it seemed that he did feel dread, and as if a chill went through him and the hairs on his forearms stood on end. But instantly the heat was back in his face.

Their ride had been very hard; his master Arn had allowed them only a brief rest at midday, and they had ridden in silence without any stops except to dismount now and then for a moment and rearrange the cumbersome loads on the horses. The six corpses had grown rigid in awkward positions, and as the sun climbed in the sky and the heat increased, they had gathered greater and greater clouds of flies around them. But the corpses were not the most difficult things to handle; they could be bent to fit better among the packs. On the other hand, the robbers' loot in the little grotto had been sizable and hard to load. There was everything from Turkish weapons to Christian communion goblets of silver, silks and brocades, jewellery and Frankish arms ornaments, spurs of silver and gold, blue stones of the Egyptian sort, and gemstones that Armand had never seen before coloured violet and blue-green, small golden crucifixes affixed to leather cords or chains of hammered gold. These items alone told them that more than a score of the faithful souls, peace be upon them, must now be in Paradise after meeting a martyr's death on their way to or from the place where John the Baptist had immersed the Lord Jesus Christ in the waters of the Jordan.

Armand's tongue had swollen up so that it felt like a piece of thick leather in his mouth, and it was as dry as desert sand. This wasn't because their water had run out, for with each step the horse took, Armand could hear water sloshing in the leather sack by his right thigh. But it was the Rule. A Templar knight controlled himself. A Templar knight must be able to withstand situations that other people could not endure. And above all, a sergeant could not drink without the permission of his lord, just as he could not speak without being spoken to or halt without orders.

Armand sensed that his lord Arn was tormenting him, but not without purpose, since he was also tormenting himself. It had something to do with that morning. That morning he had responded truthfully, as the Rule demanded. The question he was asked was whether he wished to be admitted as a knight and bear the white mantle. His lord Arn had merely nodded pensively at his reply without showing any emotion, and since then they had not spoken a word. They had ridden for eleven hours with only one brief stop to rest; they had halted occasionally whenever they found water to give the horses, but not themselves, and all this during one of the hottest days of the year. For the past hour Armand had seen how the horses' quarter muscles had quivered with each step as they moved forward; for the horses too it had been a very hard day. But the Rule also seemed to apply to the horses of the Knights Templar. One never gave up. One obeyed orders. One endured what others could not.

When they finally neared the port in the city wall that was called the Lion's Gate, a fog clouded Armand's eyes briefly and he had to grab the pommel of the saddle so as not to fall off his horse. But then he rallied, if for no other reason than out of curiosity to see the tumult that arose at the city gate as he and his lord and their unusual cargo approached. Or perhaps it was because he thought that he would soon get something to drink, in which case he was mistaken.

By the city gate stood guards who were the king's soldiers, but also a Templar knight and his sergeant. One of the royal soldiers came over to Arn de Gothia's horse to take it by the bridle as he questioned the rider about his intentions and right to enter the city. The white-clad Templar knight behind him instantly drew his sword and held it in his path, ordering his sergeant to keep the curious away. And then Armand and his lord rode into the centre of the city without needing to utter a word, because they belonged to God's holy army, and they obeyed no person on earth except the Holy Father in Rome.

The sergeant from the city gate escorted them down narrow cobblestone streets towards the temple square, shooing off street urchins and other bystanders who, if they were Christian, wanted to flock around their cargo and spit on the corpses; or if they were unbelievers, wanted to see whether they recognized any of the dead. A myriad of foreign languages buzzed around Armand's head; he heard Aramaic, Annenian, and Greek, but many others he failed to recognize.

When they neared the temple square they rode down towards the stables located beneath the Temple of Solomon. Down there was a high vault furnished with huge wooden gates, and more guards stood there who were all sergeants in the Order of the Knights Templar.

Now Armand's lord slowly dismounted, handed the reins to one of the sergeants waiting politely, and whispered something before he turned to Armand and in a rough voice issued the order to dismount and keep a tight rein on the horses. A white-clad Templar knight came hurrying up and bowed to Arn de Gothia, who bowed in return, and then they were allowed to enter the long colonnade of huge stables. They halted inside at a table where green-clad sub-chaplains did the bookkeeping. Sir Arn and his brother knights in white had a brief conversation which Armand couldn't hear, and then the sergeants began to unload the horses and prepare to show object after object to the scribes, while Arn beckoned to Armand to follow him.

They passed through the endless stables. The stables were very beautiful and clean; not a horse-dropping in the corridors, not even a wisp of straw, nothing but clean cobblestones. Row after row of horses stood either lost in their own dreams or being curried, shoed, watered, and fed by an army of brown-clad grooms. Here and there a black-clad sergeant was working with his horse, or a white-clad brother knight with his. Each time they passed by a sergeant, Armand bowed. Each time they passed a Templar knight, Arn did the same. What Armand saw was a power and a force he never could have imagined. He had been to Jerusalem only once before, to visit the Church of the Holy Sepulchre with a group of recruits; every recruit was required to have visited the church at least once. But he had never been inside the Templars' own quarters in Jerusalem. Despite all the rumours he had heard, it was larger and mightier than he could have ever imagined. The value in gold of these beautiful and well-cared-for horses of Arabian or Frankish or Andalusian blood would be enough to defray the cost of a small army.

When they came to the end of the stables they saw narrow spiral staircases leading upward. Armand's lord seemed to know his way like the back of his hand. He had no need to ask directions of anyone, and he chose the third or fourth staircase without hesitation. They walked up the stairs in the dark in silence. When they suddenly emerged in a large courtyard, Armand's eyes were blinded by the light as the setting sun flashed off a great *cupola* of gold and a smaller one of silver. His lord stopped and pointed, without saying a word. Armand crossed himself before the holy sight and then was amazed, now that he stood so close, to discover that the golden dome he had previously seen from a distance was covered with rectangular plates of something that could only be solid gold. He had always imagined that it was made of tiles with a gold-coloured glaze. That the entire roof of a church could be made of pure gold was beyond comprehension.

His lord still said nothing, signalling after a while that they should move on. Armand now followed him into a separate world of gardens and fountains nestled inside a network of buildings constructed in every colour and style. Some of them looked like Saracen dwellings, others like Frankish ones; some had plain whitewashed facades, others were covered in blue, green, and white-glazed Saracen tiles in patterns that were obviously not Christian. Several houses of the type with small, round but simply whitewashed domes were attached in a row, and this was where they now entered, Armand two paces behind his lord.

They stopped outside wooden doors that all looked the same – three or four white doors with the red cross of the Knights Templar on the surface, but no larger than the palm of a hand. Arn turned and gave his sergeant a searching and slightly amused glance for a moment before he said anything. Armand's head felt utterly empty and he hadn't the slightest idea what was going to happen; he knew only that he would be given an order which he had to obey. And he was almost dying of thirst.

'Now, my good sergeant, you shall do as I say, and nothing more,' said Arn at last. 'You will go in through this door. There you will find a room that is empty except for a wooden bench. There you shall . . .'

Arn paused and cleared his throat. His mouth was too dry to be able to speak without difficulty.

'There you shall remove all your clothes. *All* your clothes: your surcoat, chain mail, hose, shoes, and . . . and even the outer lambskin girdle covering the impure parts of a man's body, and even more, also the inner part of the lambskin girdle which you never take off. And then you will remove the shirt that you wear under the chain mail and the belt around it so that you stand there completely naked. Have you understood what I'm telling you?'

'Yes, lord, I understand,' whispered Armand, blushing as he bowed his head. Then he had to make an effort to get his dry mouth to squeeze out more words. 'But you tell me, lord, that I must take off all my clothes. The Rule says that –'

Arn cut him off. 'You are in Jerusalem; you are in the holiest of cities in the holiest of our quarters in the entire world, and here other rules apply! So, when you have done as I command, you will walk through the next door into the next room. There you will find water in which you can immerse your whole body, and oils which you shall use, and you will find things for washing yourself. You will wash, you will immerse your body completely in water, also your hair, and you will clean yourself thoroughly. Have you understood all I say?'

'Yes, lord, I understand. But the Rule . . . ?'

'In the inner room you must wash yourself,' Arn went on without concern, as if he no longer was having difficulty forcing the words out through his dry mouth, 'and you shall do so until you see darkness fall; yes, there are windows in there. And when darkness falls and you hear the *muezzin*, the one who calls the unbelievers to prayer, claiming that "Allah is the greatest," and whatever else they may shout, then you must return to the outer room. There you'll find new clothes, although of the same type as those you now wear. You will dress in those clothes. I shall be waiting outside in the corridor here. Have you understood all this?'

'Yes, lord.'

'Good. Then I have only one more thing to say to you. You will wash yourself in water, you will immerse your whole body in water, you will have water all around you and over you and a great deal more. But you may not drink a drop. Obey!'

Armand was unable to reply, he was so shocked. His lord had already turned on his heel and with one long stride he reached the next door and was on his way in. But just as he was about to disappear from Armand's sight, he seemed to remember something, stopped, turned around and smiled.

'Don't worry, Armand. Those who bring your new clothes will never see you naked, and they have no idea who you are. They simply obey commands.'

And so the Templar knight vanished from Armand's sight behind a door which he firmly closed.

At first Armand stood utterly still. He could feel his heart pounding in his breast at the peculiar instructions he'd been given. But then he collected himself and went into the first room without hesitation. Just as his lord had said, there was nothing but a wooden bench and another door. The floor was a gleaming white, the walls were covered with sky-blue tiles with no pattern, the ceiling was of white plaster and formed a small dome with star-shaped skylights.

He first took off his stinking battle mantle which he had carried over his left arm as his lord did. He unbuckled his sword and then removed his soiled and bloody surcoat without hesitation. Nor was it so strange to remove his chain mail and the mail-clad hose, and with them the steel-covered shoes that went with the hose.

Then, as he stood in his wet inner shirt reeking with sweat, he hesitated. But orders were orders, so he pulled off his inner shirt and its belt, hesitating once more at his double lambskin girdles; he shut his eyes and stripped them both off. Then he paused for a moment before he dared open his eyes, utterly naked. He felt like he was in a dream, and he didn't know whether it was a good or bad one, only that he had to proceed, and he had to obey. With manly resolve he pulled open the door to the next room, stepped inside, hastily shutting it behind him as he closed his eyes again.

When he forced himself to open his eyes he felt as if assaulted by beauty. The room had three rounded arched windows with wooden blinds, so that the light came in but did not escape. He could see some of Jerusalem's towers and spires and also hear all the sounds coming from the city. Doves flapped past out in the summer evening, but no one could see into the darkness behind these wooden slats set high on the wall.

The walls of the room were decorated in blue, green, black, and white Saracen patterns that reminded him of the wall of the church with the golden dome. Thin columns of white marble supported the vault of the ceiling, and they were shaped as though they had been twisted up from floor to ceiling. The floor was made of black-glazed tile and solid gold, laid in a chessboard pattern, each plate a double hand's-breadth square. To the left in the room was a large alcove filled with water and steps leading down into something that looked like a pond big enough for two horses, and to the right the same thing. Two tables stood between the two ponds, with inlays of mother-of-pearl forming Arabic script, and on the tables were arranged

74

silver bowls containing oils of various bright colours, and two small oil-lamps, also of silver, were burning. On a bench of almond wood inlaid with African ebony and red rosewood there were big white lengths of cloth.

Armand hesitated. He repeated to himself in a murmur the instructions he'd been given and must obey. He went uncertainly over to one of the ponds and proceeded down the steps until the water reached up to his knees, but he regretted it at once. The water was much too hot; now he noticed the vapour rising off the surface. Then he went over to the other pond, leaving wet footprints behind him on the warm gold of the floor and tried again. The water was cool like a stream, and he stepped in up to his thighs and then stood for a moment, unsure what he should do next. He cautiously looked at his body. His hands were brown to an inch or two above his wrists, but everything else he could see was as white as the feathers of seagulls back home by the river in Gascony. Along his arms he saw stripes of salt and dirt that were crusted in layers inside small wrinkles and recesses. It occurred to him that the Rule prohibited any form of pleasure, but at the same time he knew that he must obey. So he proceeded down all the steps and immersed his whole body in the cool water as he glided out into the pond and floated as he now remembered one could do. He imagined that he was swimming in the river below the fortress at home in Gascony, back when he was a child and there were no clouds in the sky, and life was perfect. He submerged his head, got water up his nose, and stood up snorting in the middle of the pond. He took a tentative swimming stroke but came immediately to the edge decorated in blue tile. He dove under and kicked his legs across the water, but foolishly closed his eyes and hit his head hard on the tile on the other side. He yelled, swearing since it was not against the Rule, stood up, and rubbed the sore spot on his scalp. All of a sudden he felt happy in a way he couldn't explain. He dipped his cupped hand down to the water and splashed a handful into his mouth. But he stopped himself at once and spat out the forbidden liquid in terror, trying to wipe off the last of it from his tongue with his finger; he had been prohibited from drinking, after all.

He inspected the various oils on the table between the two pools, rubbing himself carefully with them over the parts of his body that he could touch without sin, trying out the various colours in the bowls until he found the one he thought he should use for his hair. At last his entire body was smeared with oil. Then he stepped back into the cool water of the pool and washed himself, immersing himself completely. He even washed his hair and beard. He lay still for a moment, floating in the water and staring up at the Saracen patterns decorating the vault of the ceiling. It was like an atrium of Paradise, he thought.

After a while he began to feel cold, so he went over to the hot pool, which had now cooled to such a comfortable temperature that at first it felt like climbing into nothingness. He shuddered and shook his body like a dog or a cat. Then he lay still in the warm nothingness and managed to wash even the impure parts of his body that one must not touch. Without being able to stop himself he sinned. He knew that the first thing he had to do when he returned to the castle in Gaza was to confess this sin, which for so long he had been able to refrain from committing.

He lay dreaming for a long time, totally motionless in the water, as if floating in his dreams. He was here in the ante-room of Paradise but at the same time far away, back home as a child by the river in Gascony, back when the world was good.

The shrill, ungodly sound from the unbelievers screeching out their prayer over the crepuscular city woke him up as if

76

by alarm. Horror-stricken and filled with guilt he climbed hastily out of the water and reached for the two soft white cloths to dry himself.

When he returned to the little outer room, all his old clothes were gone, even the felt layers he wore against his skin beneath his chain mail. There lay a new black mantle of precisely the same type he had worn into Jerusalem, and other new clothing that all fitted perfectly.

Soon he was ready to leave the two strange rooms and go out to the corridor with his mantle over his arm. His lord Arn was waiting, also attired in new clothes. His mantle with the black border showing his rank was fastened around his neck and his beard was combed. Both of them had hair cropped so short that they only needed to run their hands through it.

'Well, my good sergeant,' said Arn without expression. 'How did you like that?'

'I obeyed orders; I did everything as you said, lord,' replied Armand uncertainly with his head bowed. He was suddenly apprehensive because of the blank look Arn gave him, as if he had been tested and failed.

'Fasten your mantle and follow me, my good sergeant,' said Arn with an amused little laugh, slapping Armand lightly on the back, then hurrying down the hall. Armand hastened after him as he struggled to don his mantle, not understanding whether he had broken some rule or whether he had missed a joke.

Arn seemed able to find his way without hesitation through these endless corridors, stairways, small courtyards with fountains and shuttered houses that seemed like private residences. He led his sergeant over to the Temple of Solomon. They descended through some sort of back entrance and suddenly stood in the huge long hall covered with Saracen rugs. There a multitude of writing-desks and tables stood in long rows. The hall was filled with men in green, the guardians of the faith, and men in brown who were apparently workers, but also knights in white who were reading or writing or had meetings with all sorts of foreigners in worldly garb. Arn led his sergeant past all this activity to the far end, where white gates separated the hall from a large rotunda with a high *cupola*. This was the sanctuary itself, the holy of holies of the Order of the Knights Templar.

As they entered and approached the large high altar with the cross beneath the *cupola*, water was still dripping from their beards onto the cold marble set in black-and-white star patterns. At the high altar they fell to their knees; Armand copied everything his lord did and was given a quick whispered instruction to say ten *Pater Nosters* and a personal thanks to the Mother of God for their fortunate homecoming from their mission.

When Armand knelt like that, reciting the prescribed number of prayers, he was struck anew by a burning thirst. It seemed so powerful that he briefly thought he might go crazy, and almost lost count of the number of prayers he had said.

No one took any particular notice of them; there were people praying everywhere inside the round sanctuary. Armand was a bit concerned about why they were kneeling before the large altar when nobody else had dared approach it, but he soon pushed away such thoughts. He acknowledged that he did not yet comprehend all these new rituals, and he continued to keep a precise count of his prayers.

'Come, my good sergeant,' said Arn when they were finished. They got up and crossed themselves one last time before God's cross. And then they resumed their labyrinthine wanderings down long corridors, across new courtyards with fountains and flowers in sumptuous profusion, and again into dark corridors that were illuminated only by occasional torches. Suddenly they were in a huge whitewashed hall decorated solely with banners of the Order and knightly shields lining the walls. Here there were no Saracen decorations or other colours to break the whiteness and the strict lines of the setting. High vaults soared overhead and an arcade supported by pillars ran down one side of the hall as in a cloister. That was all Armand managed to notice before he caught sight of the Master of Jerusalem.

Jerusalem's Master, Arnoldo de Torroja stood erect and stern in the middle of the hall with the white mantle bearing the two small black lines indicating his rank fastened at his neck and his sword at his side.

'Now do as I do,' Arn whispered to his sergeant.

They approached the Master of Jerusalem, stopped at a respectful six paces away as the rules prescribed, and instantly dropped to their knees and bowed their heads.

'Arn de Gothia and his sergeant Armand de Gascogne have returned from their mission, Jerusalem's Master,' said Arn in a loud voice but with his gaze fixed on the floor.

'Then I ask you, master of the Gaza fortress, Arn de Gothia, was the task successful?' said the mighty one in a loud voice.

'Yes, brother knight and Jerusalem's Master,' replied Arn in the same formal manner. 'We sought out six ungodly robbers and the spoils they had taken from believers and infidels. We found what we sought. The six are already hanging from our walls. All their goods can be set out before the rock tomorrow.'

Jerusalem's Master at first did not reply, as though he wanted to draw out the silence. Armand did as his lord did, staring at the floor before him without moving, hardly daring even to breathe loudly.

'Have you both washed as our Jerusalem rules prescribe? Have you thanked the Lord and the Lord God's Mother, the special protectress of our Order, in the Temple of Solomon?' asked the Master of Jerusalem after his long pause.

'Yes, Jerusalem's Master. I therefore beg respectfully for a bowl of water after a long day's work, the only wages we deserve,' replied Arn quickly, keeping his tone neutral.

'Castle master Arn de Gothia and sergeant Armand de . . . de Gascogne, right? Yes! That's what it was, de Gascogne. Rise, both of you, and embrace me!'

Armand did as his lord did, standing up quickly, and when Jerusalem's Master embraced Arn he also embraced the sergeant Armand, though without kissing him.

'I knew you could do it, Arn, I knew it!' Jerusalem's Master then exclaimed in a completely different tone of voice. Gone were the dull, thundering words; now he sounded like a man inviting two good friends to dinner. At the same moment two Templar knights hurried up, each carrying a silver bowl with ice-cold water, which they handed to Arn with a bow. He in turn handed one to Armand.

And Armand again followed Arn de Gothia's example, swallowing the entire contents of the bowl in one gulp so that the water ran down his surcoat. Panting, he removed the empty bowl from his lips, surprised to find one of the white-clad knight-brothers ready to take it from him with a bow. He hesitated; he had never imagined being waited on by a knight. But the man in white facing him saw his embarrassment and understood it. He gave a nod of encouragement to Armand, who handed over his bowl with a deep bow.

Jerusalem's Master had thrown one arm around Arn's shoulders, and they were carrying on a lively conversation, almost like worldly men, as they walked toward the far end of the hall where cook's servants in green were setting the table for dinner. Armand followed after receiving another encouraging nod from the knight-brother assigned to serve him.

They took the seats that Jerusalem's Master proffered, with Arn and the Master at one end of the table, then the two knight-brothers, and at the far end sergeant Armand. On the table were placed fresh bacon, smoked lamb, white bread, and olive oil, wine and vegetables and great steaming silver bowls of water. Arn said grace over the food in the language of the church as they all bowed their heads, but then they pitched in with good appetite and drank wine without hesitation. At first only Jerusalem's Master and Arn spoke; they seemed immersed in memories of the old days and old friends, matters that the others at the table could not share. Armand stole a glance now and then at the two high brothers who seemed to know each other very well, behaving like close friends, which was not always the same thing within the Order of the Knights Templar. Armand was careful not to eat more or faster than his lord; he kept checking that he wasn't ahead of him in either wine or bread or meat. He had to show moderation even though it was a banquet, and not gobble his food like worldly men.

And as Armand had suspected, the meal itself was brief. Suddenly Jerusalem's Master wiped off his dagger and stuck it back in his belt, and so all the others did the same and stopped eating. The cook's servants in green came over to the table at once and began clearing it off, but they left the bowls of water, the Syrian glass goblets, and the ceramic wine carafes.

Arn thanked the Lord for the gifts of the table while all bowed their heads.

'So! That was surely a well-deserved wage for your efforts, brothers,' said Jerusalem's Master, wiping his mouth carefully with the back of his hand. 'But now I want to hear how you acquitted yourself, young sergeant. My brother and friend Arn has given you a favourable accounting, but now I want to hear it from you.'

He regarded Armand with a look that seemed quite friendly, but Armand noticed something sly in his gaze, as if he were now going to be subjected to another of the endless tests. He thought that the most important thing was not to boast.

'There isn't much to say, Master of Jerusalem,' he began uncertainly. 'I followed my lord Arn, I obeyed his orders, and the Mother of God showed mercy on us, so we were victorious,' he muttered with his head bowed.

'And you feel no pride for the part you played? You simply proceed humbly along the path that your lord Arn assigns you and accept gratefully the grace that the Mother of God shows you and so on and so forth?' the Master of Jerusalem went on, his tone barely disguising the irony of his words. But Armand did not dare understand the meaning of this irony.

'Yes, Jerusalem's Master, that is so,' he replied modestly with his eyes focused on the table. At first he didn't dare look up, but then he thought he heard some merriment from the other end of the table. He glanced up at Arn and saw him laughing broadly and almost shamelessly. For the life of him Armand couldn't understand what was wrong with his answer, or what could be so funny when they were speaking of serious matters.

'Oh, I see!' said Jerusalem's Master. 'I see that you have an ingrained concept of the way a sergeant should speak to high brothers in the Order. Then let me put it this way. Is it true, as my dear brother Arn here has told me, that you want to be accepted as a knight in our circle?'

'Yes, Jerusalem's Master!' answered Armand with sudden enthusiasm that he could not hide. 'I would give my life to . . .'

'No, no, not like that,' Jerusalem's Master laughed, raising his hand. 'As a dead man we have not much use for you. But one thing you must now learn. If you want to become one of us, one of the brothers, then you have to learn never to lie to a brother. Think about that, now. Don't you think that my beloved brother Arn and I were once young like you? Don't you realize that we were sergeants like you?

82

Don't you think that we can see through your dreams, because they were our dreams too? Don't you imagine that we understand what pride you feel for what you have accomplished, which as far as I can see was fully worthy of a knight-brother? But a brother must never lie to another brother, and you must never forget that. And if you're ashamed of unworthy thoughts, if you're ashamed because you're proud of what you did, then it's all right that you feel such shame. But it's always worse to lie to a brother than to feel pride, or what you may think is pride. You can always confess your pride. But faithfulness to the truth before brothers is what you must never forsake. It's that simple.'

Armand sat with his head bowed, staring at the tabletop, and could feel his cheeks aflame. He had been reprimanded, even though the words of Jerusalem's Master were friendly and his tone brotherly.

'Now we'll start again,' said the older man with a weary little sigh that didn't sound quite genuine. 'What happened and what did you accomplish in the battle, my good young sergeant?'

'Jerusalem's Master,' Armand began, feeling his head turn to air and all his thoughts flee like birds, 'we had been tracking the robbers for a week, we had studied their tactics, and we realized that it would be hard to catch them in the act. We had to find a position where we could meet them face to face.'

'Yes? And then . . . did a good situation present itself?'

'Yes, Jerusalem's Master, at last it did,' Armand went on with renewed courage, having convinced himself that he only had to present a normal account of battle. 'We discovered them as they were pursuing three Saracens unknown to us up into a *wadi* which formed a trap like a sack. It was just what we were hoping for when we saw them begin pursuit from a distance, because they had used

83

that tactic before. We took up position and attacked when the time was ripe; my lord Arn first, of course, and I on his flank behind him as the rules prescribe. The rest was easy. My lord Arn signalled to me with his lance how he would first launch a feint against the robber on the left in front, and that opened a good gap for me to aim and strike with my lance.'

'Did you feel fear at that moment?' asked Jerusalem's Master in a suspiciously gentle voice.

'Jerusalem's Master!' replied Armand loudly yet hesitantly. 'I must admit that I did feel fear.'

He looked up to see how the others around the table reacted to this. But neither Jerusalem's Master nor Arn, or the other two high knight-brothers, betrayed by their expressions what they thought about a sergeant who showed fear in battle.

'I felt fear, but also resolve. This was the opportunity we had waited for so long, and now we could not fail! That was what I felt,' he added so rapidly that his words stumbled over each other.

Now Arn carefully pounded his Syrian wine glass on the table and then Jerusalem's Master did the same, followed by the two knight-brothers, and then they all burst out in laughter that was hearty but not malicious.

'So you see, my good young sergeant,' said Jerusalem's Master, shaking his head and chuckling to himself, 'what one must endure as a brother in our Order. You confess to fear, eh? But let me tell you this. Any one of us who does not feel some fear at the crucial moment is a fool. And we have no need for fools among our brothers. So, when can he be initiated as a brother in our Order?'

'Soon,' said Arn. 'Very soon indeed. I shall go through the first conversations prescribed by the Rule as soon as we return to Gaza.'

'Excellent! Then I will make a visitation in person for the initiation, and I will be the one to give you the second welcome kiss after Arn.'

The Master raised his wine glass to Armand, and the other Templar knights followed suit. With heart pounding Armand tried to keep his hand from shaking as he raised his glass and bowed in turn to his four superiors before he drank. He felt suffused by a great joy.

'But right now the situation is critical, and it may be difficult to find the three days required for the initiation ceremony, at least in the near future,' said Arn, just as the talk should have taken a less sombre turn. There was no comment, but they all shifted their attention to Arn to hear what he had to say.

'Among the three Saracens whom we rescued from a tight situation was no less than Yussuf ibn Ayyub Salah al-Din,' Arn began abruptly. 'In the evening we broke bread and conversed, and from that talk I understood that we shall soon have war upon us.'

'You broke bread and sat with Saladin?' Jerusalem's Master said harshly. 'You ate with the greatest enemy of all Christendom and you let him escape alive?'

'Yes, it is true,' replied Arn. 'And about this there is much to say, but the easiest is that he was allowed to get away alive. First of all, we have a truce, and second, I gave him my word.'

'You gave Saladin your word?' asked the Master in astonishment, his eyes narrowing.

'Yes, I gave him my word before I realized who he was. But now we have more important things to discuss,' Arn went on in the tone he used on the battlefield.

Jerusalem's Master sat in silence for a moment, rubbing his fist on his chin. Then he pointed suddenly at Armand, who was now sitting with his gaze fixed on his lord Arn with wide, frightened eyes, as if only now did he understand what had happened, and with whom he too had broken bread.

'My good sergeant, now you must leave us,' commanded Jerusalem's Master. 'Brother Richard Longsword here will show you around our quarters and our part of the city. Then he will escort you to the sergeants' night quarters. May God be with you. May I soon have the pleasure of giving you a welcome kiss.'

One of the Templar knights then stood up and indicated to Armand the direction they would be going. Armand stood up, bowed hesitantly to the now grim-visaged knights at the table, and left.

When the iron-clad wooden door closed after Armand and his high escort, a heavy silence settled over the room.

'Now I'll begin,' said Jerusalem's Master after a moment. 'You know Brother Guy, who has just been made weapons master here in Jerusalem. You two hold the same rank, and the three of us have serious problems that concern us all. Shall we start with the matter of breaking bread with our enemy?'

'By all means,' said Arn lightly. 'What would you have done? We have a truce, which is hanging by a thin thread, as we all know, and Saladin knew it as well. The robbers were the ones who had to be punished, not peaceful travellers of one faith or another. I gave him the word of a Templar knight. And he gave me his word. A moment later I understood to whom I had granted safe passage. So, what would you have done?'

'If I had given my word I could have done no differently than you,' agreed Jerusalem's Master. 'You worked here under Odo de Saint Armand, didn't you?'

'Yes, that's true, and it was when Philip de Milly was the Grand Master.'

'Hmm. You and Odo became good friends, I heard?'

'True. And we still are.'

'But now he is Grand Master, and that's good. That solves the problem of supping with the greatest enemy of Christendom. Some brothers may be upset by it, as you know.'

'I do. And what do you think about this matter?'

'I'm on your side. You kept your word as a Templar knight. And if I understood correctly you gained some information?'

'Yes. War will be upon us in two weeks at the earliest, and no later than two months from now. That is what I believe I learned.'

'Tell us. What more do we know? And what can we believe?'

'Saladin knew a great deal: that Philip of Flanders and a vast host of the worldly armies and the Hospitallers are on their way up into Syria, presumably heading for Hama or Homs, not for Damascus and Saladin himself. But having learned of this, Saladin is travelling with great haste and without an escort south toward El Arish, I believe, though he told me he was on his way to Cairo. He is not making this journey because he wants to flee the Christian army in the north. So his intention is to attack us from the south now that he knows that more than half our forces are located far to the north. That is my conclusion.'

Jerusalem's Master exchanged a glance with his brother and weapons master Guy, who gave him a curt nod of agreement to his unspoken question.

War was on its way. Saladin trusted that his forces in the north were sufficiently prepared to be able to hold the enemy in place. If at the same time he could drive an Egyptian army up through Outremer, then he could penetrate deep without meeting stiff resistance, perhaps all the way to Jerusalem. It was a terrifying thought, but they could not close their eyes to the possibility.

In that case the first battle would take place near Gaza, where Arn was in command as master of the fortress. The castle in Gaza was by no means one of the stronger ones, and it was defended by only 40 knights and 280 sergeants. It was inconceivable that Saladin would stop there and beat himself bloody against the walls. With a large enough army and good siege engines he could take Gaza. Few castles were as impregnable as Krak des Chevaliers or Beaufort. But the effort would cost him much more than it would benefit him. No one took a castle of the Knights Templar without great losses. And if they won, there would be no captives of any value to make up for all the costs; such a long and bloody siege would also mean a great loss of time.

So Saladin's army would probably bypass Gaza, possibly leaving a small siege force outside the walls. But what would be their next objective? Ashkelon. Taking back Ashkelon after twenty-five years would not be a stupid idea. It could be a victory of significance and provide a Saracen stronghold along the coast north of Gaza. It would cut off the Knights Templar in Gaza from Jerusalem. Ashkelon was a plausible objective.

But if Saladin did not meet particularly great resistance, and it didn't look as though he would, what would prevent him from heading straight for Jerusalem itself?

Not a thing.

The unpleasant conclusion was impossible to avoid. Saladin had first united Syria and Egypt under one commander and one sultan, just as he had said he would do. But he had also sworn to retake the holy city, which the infidels called Al Quds.

Decisions had to be made. The Grand Master, Odo de Saint Armand, who was now in Acre, had to be warned. Brothers of the Order had to be called in to reinforce both Jerusalem and Gaza. The king, that unfortunate leprous boy, and his court riddled with intrigue had to be warned.

Messengers would have to ride off that very night at full speed in many directions.

Because momentous decisions are often easier to make than small, unimportant ones, the whole matter was soon settled. Weapons master Guy left the other two alone to take care of all the tasks that had to be accomplished before dawn.

Arnoldo de Torroja, Jerusalem's Master, had remained seated at the table the whole time he was leading the discussion and issuing orders. But after the iron-clad door had closed behind the swiftly departing weapons master, he stood up with an effort and gestured to Arn to follow him. The two men then crossed the big, empty space of the Order Hall, heading for a side entrance that led out to an arcade with a view. They stood there a while with their hands propped on the stone railing, looking out over the darkened city and taking in the smells carried on the mild summer breeze: meat frying and spices, garbage and decay, perfumes, incense, and camel and horse droppings, all combined in the same sort of mixture that God had created of life itself: high and low, ugly and beautiful, delightful and loathsome.

'What would you have done, Arn? I mean if you were Saladin, if you'll pardon the impudent comparison,' asked Arnoldo de Torroja at last.

'There's nothing to apologize for; Saladin is a magnificent foe and we all know it, even you, Arnoldo,' replied Arn. 'But I know what you're thinking; both you and I would have done something altogether different in his place. We would have tried to draw the enemy into our area, extending the test of strength, harassing the enemy with constant small attacks by Turkish knights, disturbing his sleep, poisoning the fountains in his path – all the things that Saracens usually do. If we had the chance to defeat a large Christian army, then we would have seen a huge advantage before spring, when we would have moved on Jerusalem.'

'But Saladin, who knows how much we know of him and the way he usually thinks, will instead do something completely unexpected,' said Arnoldo. 'He will purposely risk Homs or Hama because he has set his sights on a larger prize.'

'You have to admit that it's both a bold and a logical plan,' Arn continued the thought.

'Yes, I have to admit that it is. But thanks to your . . . unusual measures, or whatever we should call them, may God have mercy on you, at least now we are prepared. It could mean the difference between keeping Jerusalem in our hands and losing it.'

'In that case I believe God does have mercy on me,' Arn muttered in annoyance. 'Any chaplain could set about praising the Lord and say that the Lord had sent the enemy into my arms in order to save Jerusalem for us!'

Arnoldo de Torroja, who was not used to being reprimanded by subordinates, turned in surprise and gave his young friend a searching look. But the dim light in the arcade made it hard to interpret the other's gaze.

'You're my friend, Arn, but don't abuse that friendship, for it could cost you someday,' he said peevishly. 'Odo is the Grand Master now, but you may not have that protection forever.'

'If Odo falls you will probably be the next Grand Master, and you too are my friend,' said Arn as if commenting on the weather.

This made Arnoldo completely lose all intention of showing stern leadership and instead he burst out laughing. If anyone had seen them, such behaviour would have seemed extremely out of place at this difficult hour, both for the Knights Templar and for Jerusalem.

'You have been with us a long time, Arn, since you were very young, and you are like one of us in everything but your speech. Sometimes, my friend, one might think you were speaking with audacious candour. Is everyone of your Nordic race like this, or is it merely that we haven't whipped the rascal out of your body yet?'

'My body has been well whipped, don't worry about that, Arnoldo,' said Arn in the same unconcerned tone of voice. 'It's true that up there in the North, in what was once my home, we might speak with less fuss and fawning than do some Franks. But a Templar knight's words must always be compared with his actions.'

'Still the same impudence, the same lack of respect for your superiors. And yet you're my friend, Arn. But watch your tongue.'

'Right now it's more my head that is at stake. Down there in Gaza we'll be taking the first blow when Saladin arrives. How many knights can you spare me?'

'Forty. I'll put forty new knights under your command.'

'Then we'll be eighty knights and fewer than three hundred sergeants against an army that I suspect will be no less than 5,000 Egyptian cavalry. I hope you'll leave it to my judgment as to how to confront such an army. I wouldn't care to receive an order to meet them out on the open field lance to lance.'

'Are you afraid to die for a holy cause?' Arnoldo de Torroja wondered, with clear irritation in his voice.

'Don't be childish, Arnoldo,' Arn replied. 'I find it almost blasphemous to fall in battle for nothing. We've seen far too much of that here in Outremer; new recruits who want to go straight to Paradise, causing the rest of us unnecessary losses and benefiting the enemy. In my opinion such stupidity should not be rewarded with the forgiveness of any sins, because such behaviour is itself a sin.'

'So you think that the Templar knight who knocks on the gates of Paradise, out of breath after having rushed into death, might have an unpleasant surprise awaiting him?'

'Yes, but I wouldn't say that to any brothers except my closest friends.'

'I would agree with that wholeheartedly. Nevertheless, attend to your command in accordance with whatever situations arise and your own best judgment. That is my only order to you.'

'Thank you, Arnoldo, my friend. I swear I will do my best.'

'I don't doubt that, Arn, I certainly don't. And I'm glad that you were the one to be given the new command in Gaza now that the first battle of the war will take place there. We actually had not intended to put you there in such a high position; many men can handle a high position, but you are much too valuable in the field to sit and manage a fortress all day long.'

'But?'

'But that is how things have turned out. Odo de Saint Armand is holding a protective hand over you; I think he wants you to move up in the ranks. I'm holding my hand over you too, for what it's worth. But God was apparently standing by us. Against all rhyme and reason it was you, our Turcopole, who won the position, even though it meant a poor allocation of fighting forces.'

'And now it turns out that the enemy is coming to Gaza, of all places.'

'Precisely. God has a plan for everything. May He now stand by you and all your men when the storm comes. When are you leaving?'

'At dawn. We have much to build in Gaza, and very little time.'

The city of Gaza and its fortress represented the southern-most outpost of the Knights Templar in Outremer. Since the fortress was built, the city had never been besieged, and the armies that had passed by had always been their own, coming from the north on their way to war in Egypt. But now the roles would be reversed; the enemy was not going to be attacked, but would instead attack them. It could be regarded as a sign of the times, a warning that from now on the Christians would have to pay more attention to defence than to offence. They now had an enemy whom they had greater reason to fear than all the men who had come before – men like Zenki and Nur al-Din. But none of these Saracen leaders could measure up to the man who had now assumed leadership: Saladin.

For the new young master of Gaza it was an unusual assignment to be preparing himself for defence. For ten years Arn de Gothia had taken part in hundreds of battles out in the field, but almost always as part of the forces that attacked the enemy first. As a Turcopole he had commanded the mercenary Turkish cavalry who with light arms and light, fast horses rode against the enemy to spread turmoil and confusion. In the best case, the cavalry's aim was to force the foe to close ranks so that the Frankish forces could attack. At the very least the cavalry would cause the enemy to suffer losses.

Arn had also ridden with the heavily armoured knights, and then the aim was to attack at the right moment and wreak havoc on the order in the enemy's cavalry by smashing straight through it. Sometimes he'd had to wait with reserve forces out of the fray of battle and not join the action until it was time to decide the situation and win. Or, even worse, a situation arose when a desperate counter-attack from the best troops would gain time for the Frankish army to retreat in an orderly fashion instead turning it into a rout.

Arn had also been involved in a number of sieges at the two previous fortresses where he had been stationed, first as a sergeant in the Templar fortress in Tortosa in the duchy of

Tripoli and later as a full brother-knight at Acre. These sieges would sometimes last for months, but they had always ended with the besiegers giving up and pulling back their troops.

But here in Gaza something entirely different awaited them. The important thing now was to make plans and prepare in a new way, as if no previous experience could tell them very much. The city of Gaza included about fifteen villages with Palestinian peasants and two Bedouin tribes. The master of Gaza was thus the lord of all these peasants and Bedouins; he ruled over both their lives and their property.

Consequently the primary concern was to set the right level of taxation for the villages and the Bedouins; he had to raise the tax in years of good harvests and lower it in the meagre years. This year there had been an unusually good harvest, particularly in the lands surrounding Gaza, but much worse in other places in Outremer. This led to a thorny problem, since the master of the castle in Gaza had decreed that the villages be emptied of all their harvest and almost all livestock. The intent, of course, was to save everything from being plundered by the approaching Egyptian army. But it was hard to explain to the peasants when stern-looking Templar knights arrived with columns of empty carts. It looked as if the plundering had already begun, and from the point of view of the Palestinian peasants, it didn't matter whether they were plundered by Christians or by the faithful.

So Arn spent a lot of time on his horse, riding from village to village to try to explain what was happening. He gave his word that it was not a matter of taxes or confiscation, and that everything would be returned when the plundering army had gone. He tried to explain that the less there was to nourish their enemies in the region, the sooner they would go away. But he found to his surprise that in many villages the people doubted his word.

Then he had a new regulation introduced, proclaiming

94

that every load of grain, every cow and every camel, as well as their calves, should be entered into the books with a receipt. That delayed the whole process, and if Saladin had attacked earlier than planned, all this book-keeping would have cost both the Knights Templar and the peasants dearly. Slowly but surely the villages around Gaza were emptied of livestock and grain. Inside the city walls a great confusion reigned as grain storehouses were filled to overflowing and congestion grew from the constant transports of foodstuffs and livestock.

But this was the most crucial part of the preparations for war. War was more about economics and supplies for an advancing army than it was about bravery on the field. That was the view of the new master of the fortress, even though he avoided communicating such profane ideas to his subordinate knights. Reinforcements began arriving from other fortresses in the country until the forty new knights promised by Jerusalem's Master were in place inside the walls of Gaza.

The next most important preparation was to widen the moats around Gaza and reinforce the city walls. The first line of defence would be out there, but if it collapsed the people and their animals would take refuge inside the fortress itself. The 280 sergeants and all the hired civilians, even the scribes and customs men, laboured around the clock, using torchlight at night, on this construction work, and the master of the fortress himself made constant inspections of their progress.

Saladin was delaying his attack, but no one understood why. According to the Bedouin spies that Arn sent down to the Sinai, Saladin's army had assembled in Al Arish, a good day's march from Gaza. Possibly the delay had to do with the way the war was going up in Syria. The Saracens did have an uncanny way of sending messages from one part of the country to the other, and no one really knew how they did it. The Bedouins in Gaza thought that the Saracen troops were using birds as messengers, but that was hard to believe. The Christians used smoke signals from one fortress to the next, but Gaza lay too far south and was thus prevented from using this system.

The Bedouins who reported back to Arn estimated Saladin's army at 10,000 men, and the vanguard consisted of Mameluke knights. This was terrible news; such an army would be impossible to defeat on the field. On the other hand, Arn suspected that his spies might be exaggerating, since they were given new assignments and more pay if they brought bad news rather than good.

When almost a month had passed without an attack by Saladin, a certain calm fell over Gaza. They had largely managed to complete their task. They had even begun to distribute grain and livestock to the peasants, who now stood in long, loud queues outside the grain storehouses in the city, the ones that were to be emptied before the storehouses within the fortress walls.

The young master of the fortress was constantly attending to these queues, listening to complaints and trying to resolve misunderstandings and dissension. It was obvious to all that he truly believed that this was not a matter of confiscation of goods but merely an attempt to save the grain from plunder and fire. His intention had been to see to it that each family in every village had enough to live on for a week at a time before they would have to go to Gaza and get more supplies. This way they could also bring along everything edible if they had to flee, leaving only empty villages to the enemy.

Arn's quartermaster Brother Bertrand thought that the process of writing everything down and explaining things to the peasants took up an unreasonable amount of time. But his superior refused to yield an inch; a promise from a Templar knight could not be broken.

In the calmer work atmosphere that came about after the

first month of nervous, rushed preparations, Arn finally took time for his sergeant. Armand de Gascogne may have thought he'd been transformed into a masonry worker rather than a sergeant in preparation, which he had become the moment that Jerusalem's Master had expressed his blessing. But now he was summoned from working on the walls by the weapons master himself and ordered to report, washed and in new clothes, to the master of the castle after the midday meal. Armand's hope flared up anew. He had not been forgotten, and his chances of being accepted as a full brother had not died with the approaching war.

The master's *parlatorium* was in the western part of the castle, high up with two large, vaulted windows looking out on the sea. When Armand arrived at the appointed time he found his lord tired and red-eyed, but still in a calm frame of mind. The beautiful room, with the afternoon sun streaming in, was simply furnished; no decorations on the walls, a large table in the centre covered with maps and documents, and a row of chairs along one wall. Between the two windows facing the sea there was a doorway leading to a balcony. The master's white mantle lay flung over one of the chairs, but when Armand entered the room and stood at attention, Arn went to fetch his mantle and tied it under his neck with practiced hands. Then he greeted Armand with a slight bow.

'You have dug and dug, and I should think you probably feel more like a mole than a sergeant in preparation,' said Arn in a jocular tone, which instantly put Armand on his guard. The high brothers had a habit of laying traps in their words, even those that sounded most friendly.

'Yes, we did a lot of digging. But it had to be done,' replied Armand cautiously.

Arn gave him a long, searching look without revealing what he thought of that answer. Then he became serious and pointed to one of the chairs as if issuing an order. Armand sat down in the appointed place as his lord went over to the cluttered table and swept aside some documents. Arn sat down on the table with one leg dangling, leaning on his right hand.

'Let us first do what has to be done,' he said curtly. 'I have summoned you so that we can go over some matters that you must answer truthfully. If this goes well for you, there are no more hindrances to your acceptance into our Order. If it goes badly, you will probably never become one of us. Have you prepared yourself for this moment with the prayers as prescribed by the Rule?'

'Yes, lord,' replied Armand with a nervous swallow.

'Are you married or are you engaged to any woman, and is there any woman who can make a claim on you?'

'No, lord, I was the third son and –'

'I understand. Please answer only yes or no. Now, the next question. Were you born legitimately of parents who were united before God?'

'Yes, lord.'

'Is your father or his brother or your father's father a knight?'

'My father is the baron of Gascogne.'

'Excellent. Are you in financial debt to anyone of worldly position or to any brother or any sergeant in our Order?'

'No, lord. How could one be in debt to a brother?'

'Thank you!' Arn interrupted him, holding up a warning hand. 'Just answer my questions, do not argue and do not question!'

'Forgive me, lord.'

'Are you healthy in your body, hale and hearty? Yes, I know the answer, but I must ask the question in accordance with the Rule.'

'Yes, lord.'

'Have you paid any gold or silver to enter into our Order, and is there anyone who has promised against compensation to make you one of us? This is a serious question; it deals with the crime of simony, and if anything is later discovered, your white mantle will be taken from you. The Rule says that it is better that we know now than later. Well?'

'No, lord.'

'Are you prepared to live in chastity, poverty, and obedience?'

'Yes, lord.'

'Are you prepared to swear before God and Our Holy Virgin Mary that you will do your utmost in every situation to live up to the traditions and customs of the Knights Templar?'

'Yes, lord.'

'Are you prepared before God and Our Holy Virgin Mary to swear that you will never leave our Order, in its moments of weakness or its moments of strength, that you will never betray us and never leave us other than with special permission from our Grand Master?'

'Yes, lord.'

Arn did not seem to have any more questions; he sat silent and meditative for a while, as if he had already moved far away to other concerns. Then his face brightened suddenly. He jumped down from his half-sitting position on the table, and went over to Armand to embrace him and kiss him on both cheeks.

'This is what our Rule prescribes from paragraph 669 on. Now you know this section that has been revealed to you, and you have my permission to go and read it again with the chaplain. Come now, we'll go out on the balcony.'

In a daze, Armand of course did as he was told, following his lord out to the balcony and, after some hesitation, standing just as he did with both hands resting on the stone railing, gazing down at the harbour.

'That was the preparation,' Arn explained, a bit wearily. 'You will be asked the same questions once again at the initiation itself, but then it's more of a formality, since we already know your answers. It was this moment that counted, and I can now tell you for certain that you will be accepted as a knight as soon as we have time for it. Until then you will wear a white band around your upper right arm.'

For a moment Armand felt a dizzy happiness inside, and he was incapable of replying to this good news.

'Naturally, we have a war to win first,' Arn added thoughtfully. 'And it doesn't look easy, as you know. But if we die then the matter is no longer of this world. If we survive then you will soon be one of us. Arnoldo de Torroja and I myself will conduct the initiation ceremony. So be it. Do you feel happy about this?'

'Yes, lord.'

'I wasn't very happy when I was in your position. It had to do with the first question.'

Arn had revealed this remarkable admission as if in passing, and Armand didn't know how to reply, or whether he should say anything at all. They stood for a while looking down at the harbour, where hard work was in progress unloading two lighters that had moored that same day.

'I have decided to make you our *confanonier* for the time being,' Arn said as if he'd returned from his reverie about the first question. 'I don't need to explain what a special honour it is to bear the banner of the Temple and the fortress in war; you know that already.'

'But mustn't a knight . . . can a sergeant be given that assignment?' Armand stammered, overwhelmed by the news.

'Under normal circumstances it would be a knight, but you would have been a knight by now if the war hadn't intervened. And I'm the one who decides, no one else. Our *confanonier* has not recovered from serious wounds; I visited him in the infirmary and have already spoken with him of this. Now let me hear what you think about the war we're about to re-enter.'

They went in and sat down next to one of the big windows, and Armand tried to tell him what he thought. He presumed it would be a long siege that would be hard to endure but quite possible to win. He did not think they should ride out, 80 knights and 280 sergeants, to meet an army of Mameluke knights on the field. Scarcely 400 men against perhaps 7000 to 8000 knights – that would be very brave but also very stupid.

Arn pensively nodded his agreement, but added, almost as if thinking out loud, that if that army bypassed Gaza and headed for Jerusalem itself there would no longer be any question of what was wise, stupid, or brave. Then there would be only one choice. So they would have to hope for a long and bloody siege. Because no matter how such a long battle would end, they would have saved Jerusalem. And there was no greater task for the Knights Templar.

But if Saladin headed straight for Jerusalem, there would be only two choices for them all. Death, or salvation through a miracle of the Lord.

So in spite of all its terrors, they would have to pray for a long siege.

Two days later Armand de Gascogne rode for the first time as the *confanonier* in a squadron of knights led by the master himself. They rode south along the seacoast in the direction of Al Arish, fifteen knights and a sergeant in tight formation. According to the Bedouin spies, Saladin's army was on the move but had split in two, with one regiment heading north along the coast and the other inland in a circular movement across the Sinai. It was not easy to grasp what the intention of such a manoeuvre might be, but the information would have to be verified.

At first they rode close to the seacoast on the west, giving them full view of the beach to the southwest. But since there was a risk that they might end up behind enemy lines without realizing it, Arn soon ordered a change of course. Then they headed east, up toward the more mountainous part of the coast where the caravans passed during the seasons when storms made the coast itself impassable.

Up by the caravan road they altered course again, so that they stayed in the heights above it and had a clear view of the road for a great distance. When they passed a curve where the view along the road was obscured by a protruding cliff, they suddenly made contact with the enemy.

Both parties discovered each other at the same time, and both were equally surprised. Along the road below came an army of knights riding four abreast, stretching as far as the eye could see.

Arn raised his right hand and signalled to regroup in attack position, so that all sixteen knights spread out in a row facing the enemy. He was obeyed at once, but his men also gave him some questioning, nervous looks. Below were at least two thousand Egyptian knights carrying yellow banners, and their yellow uniforms shone like gold in the sun. So they were Mamelukes, an entire army of Mamelukes, the absolutely best knights and soldiers the Saracens had.

When the Templar knights high above them regrouped to attack, the valley soon echoed with commands and the clatter of horses' hooves as the Egyptians hastily prepared to meet the assault. Their mounted archers were sent to the front rank.

Arn sat silently in his saddle watching the mighty foe. He had no intention of ordering an attack, since it would result in the loss of fifteen knights and a sergeant without much gain from such a sacrifice. But neither did he want to flee.

And the Mamelukes seemed reluctant as well. All they could see from their low vantage point was an enemy force of sixteen, which they could easily defeat. But since the enemy sat there calmly watching their opponents, there had to be more than sixteen of them, and it could be seen from far off that they were the infidels' most terrifying knights of the red cross. The Mamelukes, who also must have seen Armand holding the commander's banner, undoubtedly surmised that this was a trap. The sixteen may have been the only ones in sight, but the commander's banner signified a much larger formation, perhaps 500 to 600 similar knights who were now readying themselves in case the bait of the sixteen knights was taken.

Finding themselves on low ground before an attacking Frankish army of knights was the worst imaginable situation for the Saracens, whether they were Turks or Mamelukes. Soon new orders echoed off the cliffs from the commanders down below, and the Egyptian army began to retreat. At the same time a party of lightly armed scouts fanned out onto the surrounding slopes to locate the enemy's main force.

Then Arn gave the order for an about face, a new tight formation, and retreat at a walk. Slowly the sixteen knights disappeared out of the field of vision of their apprehensive foes.

As soon as the squadron was safely out of sight, Arn ordered a brisk trot in the direction of Gaza, taking the fastest route.

When they approached the city they saw that all roads were filled with refugees seeking protection and fleeing the plundering marauders. In the distance to the east could be seen several black columns of smoke. Gaza would soon be full of refugees.

War was finally upon them.

FOUR

The war had finally ended, but Cecilia Rosa and Cecilia Blanca were now about to learn that an end to fighting was not at all the same thing as good order and peace; the effects of a war did not cease overnight. Even though a war ended when the last men fell on the battlefield, that did not mean instant happiness and serenity, even for the side that had won.

One night during the second month after the battle on the fields of blood outside Bjälbo, when the first autumn storms were lashing at the windows and shingled roof of Gudhem, a group of riders arrived. With great haste the men removed five of the maidens from the Sverker clan who were among the novices. It was whispered that they would be fleeing to relatives in Denmark. A few days later three new maidens belonging to families defeated in the war arrived to seek the serenity of the Gudhem cloister, which was beyond the reach of the victorious Folkungs and Eriks.

With them they brought tidings about what was happening in the outside world. When the last Sverker maiden arrived, everyone at Gudhem found out that King Knut Eriksson, as he was now called, had ridden into Linköping itself with his

104

jarl Birger Brosa to accept the surrender of the town and confirm the peace that now prevailed, in accordance with his terms.

For the two Cecilias this was cause for great joy. Cecilia Blanca's betrothed was now actually the king. And the uncle of Cecilia Rosa's beloved Arn was now jarl. All power in the kingdom was now in their hands, at least all worldly power. However, there was still one big black cloud in this bright sky, because they'd had no word whether King Knut had any intention of bringing his betrothed, Cecilia Ulvsdotter, home from Gudhem.

In the world of the men, nothing was ever certain. A betrothal could be broken because a man had lost in war, just as it could be broken if he was victorious. In the men's struggle for power, anything was possible. The winning clans might now want to bind themselves tighter together through marriage, but it was also possible that they would have the notion of marrying into the losing side so as to seal the peace. This uncertainty consumed Cecilia Blanca, but the situation also meant that she did not assume victory in advance. She directed no harsh words to the unfortunate sisters who belonged to the losing side, and Cecilia Rosa followed her lead.

The behaviour of the two Cecilias had a good and healing effect on the emotions prevailing inside Gudhem; Mother Rikissa, who was sometimes wiser than the two Cecilias suspected, viewed this as an opportunity to quell blood that was much too hot. She decided to relax the rules for conversing by the stone benches at the northern end of the arcade. Previously the silence rule had only been relaxed at the reading hours and when reciting the few writings at Gudhem, or during edifying discourses on sin and punishment when the worldly maidens were to be schooled there. But now Mother Rikissa invited Fru Helena Stenkilsdotter several times during the late summer to these discussions in order to learn what she knew about the struggle for power – and she knew a good deal. She knew even more about how women should react to such matters.

Fru Helena was not merely wealthy and of royal lineage. She had lived her life under five or six kings, three husbands, and many wars. What she didn't know about a woman's lot was not worth knowing.

Chiefly she impressed on them how important it was for women to learn to stick together to the very last. A woman who chose her adversaries and friends based on the shifting fortunes of men at war would end up alone in life with nothing but enemies. As delightful as it was to belong to the side that was victorious in war, it was equally miserable to be on the losing side. But if a woman lived long enough, as Fru Helena herself had done – and she hoped to God this would also be granted to the maidens now listening to her – then she would experience both sweet victory and the black feeling of defeat many times in her life.

And if women had only had the wit to stick together more steadfastly in this world, how many unnecessary wars could then have been prevented? And if women hated one another without having any sensible reasons for doing so, how much unnecessary death would that not promote?

'For let us play freely with the idea that anything at all might happen, which is often the case,' she said. 'We shall imagine that you, Cecilia Blanca Ulvsdotter, will become King Knut's queen. And we shall imagine that you, Helena Sverkersdotter, in the near future will drink the bridal ale with one of blessed King Sverker's kinsmen in Denmark. So, which of you two now wants war? Which of you wants peace? What would it mean if you had hated each other ever since the brief years of your youth at Gudhem? What would it mean if instead you were friends ever since that time?

I shall tell you: it means the difference between life and death for many of your kinsfolk, and it can mean the difference between war and peace.'

She paused, breathing heavily as she shifted position on her chair and fixed her little red eyes on her young listeners, who were sitting bolt upright, not showing any sign of comprehending. They neither agreed with nor opposed her words. Not even Cecilia Blanca revealed what she was thinking, even though she knew the least that Helena Sverkersdotter would suffer would be three times the number of blows with the scourge that she had dealt out.

'You look like geese, all of you,' Fru Helena went on after a moment. 'You think that I'm only preaching the Gospel to you. One must act peaceably; anger and hatred are deadly sins. You must forgive your enemies, as they in turn must forgive you; you must turn the other cheek, and all the other admonitions we try to pound into your small, empty heads here at Gudhem. But it's not that simple, my young friends and sisters. For you don't believe that you have any power of your own – you think that all power resides in the hilt of a sword and the point of a lance, but in this you have made a fundamental mistake. That's why you run across the court-yard like a flock of geese, first in one direction, then the other; first one maiden is your enemy, then someone else. No man in his right wits – and may the Virgin Mary hold her protective hand over you so that you all may wed such men – can refrain from listening to his wife, the mother of his children and the mistress of his home. Girls of your young age might simply believe that this applies only to trivial matters, but it is true in large matters as well as small. You must not go out into the world as silly little geese; you must go out in possession of your own free, strong will, precisely as the Scriptures prescribe, and do something good instead of something evil with that free will. Just as men do, you decide over life and death, peace and war, and it would be a great sin if you shirked that responsibility out there in life.'

Fru Helena signalled that she was tired, and because she looked very ill with her constantly running eyes, two sisters stepped forward to lead her back to her house outside the walls. But a flock of maidens with their thoughts aflame stayed behind, not saying a word and without looking at each other.

A mood of conciliation descended over Gudhem, not least thanks to Fru Helena's many wise words to the young girls, and as the calm follows the abating storm, Mother Rikissa acted promptly and wisely.

Four maidens from Linköping had come to Gudhem, and only one of them had any previous experience of convent life. They were all mourning fallen kinsmen, and they were all terrified, crying themselves to sleep every night.

But one could make something good come from their pain, as one can make a virtue out of necessity, Mother Rikissa thought. And so she decided two things. First, that for an unspecified period the vow of silence at Gudhem would be lifted, since none of the new girls knew sign language. Second, since the sisters themselves had other more important things to do, Cecilia Blanca and Cecilia Rosa would be given special responsibility for the new girls. They would teach them to speak with signs, to obey the rules, to sing and to weave.

Cecilia Blanca and Cecilia Rosa were astonished when they were summoned to Mother Rikissa in the chapter hall and given these instructions. And they were filled with ambivalence. For one thing, it permitted them a freedom they could never have imagined inside Gudhem, to determine their own workday and also be able to talk freely without risk. And yet they would be forced to be together with four daughters of the Sverker clan. Cecilia Blanca wanted as little to do with such girls as possible; even though she suspected that her hatred had more to do with their fathers and mothers, it still didn't feel right, she claimed. Cecilia Rosa begged her to consider how she would have felt if the battle on the field of blood outside Bjälbo had turned out differently. They had to obey; they had no choice.

All six were embarrassed when they met the first time out in the arcade after the midday rest. Singing would be the easiest, since they had no idea what to say, Cecilia Rosa thought. And because she knew exactly where they were in the continual progression through the Psalter, she knew which songs were coming up in three hours, when it was time for *None*, the mid-afternoon prayers. And so the lessons began, with Cecilia Rosa singing lead. They repeated each song so many times that their pupils seemed to have them memorized, at least temporarily. And when *None* was then to be sung inside the church, it was evident that the new girls really could join in with the singing.

When they came out to the arcade after the songs, the weather was blustery with the chill of autumn. Cecilia Blanca then went to the abbess's residence, returning at once, clearly pleased, and told them that they'd been given permission to use the chapter hall.

They sat there for an hour or so, practicing the simplest signs in Gudhem's silent language, and the inexperienced teachers soon noticed that this was an art that they had to teach in small portions, and that it was no use continuing for too long at a time. After half the work shift before *Sext*, the midday prayers, they went straight across the arcade to the weaving rooms, where surly lay-sisters reluctantly moved aside. There both Cecilias began chattering away as they explained about the weaving and began to giggle. Then they joked that they were both trying to talk at once so that all six of them for the first time had something to giggle about together.

It turned out that one of the new girls, the youngest and smallest, a maiden with coal-black hair named Ulvhilde Emundsdotter, was already very adept at the art of weaving. She had said nothing to anyone before, or perhaps no one had bothered to listen to her since she had arrived at Gudhem. Now she began with growing fervour to tell them that there was a way to blend linen and wool that would produce a cloth that was both warm and supple. This fabric was ideal for mantles for both men and women. And they all belonged to families in which there was great need of mantles for both religious and worldly occasions.

Then the conversation abruptly stopped short because they still felt embarrassed in one another's company: two from the clans of the blue mantles and four from the clans of the red and black mantles. But a seed had been sown.

A short time later Cecilia Rosa discovered that little Ulvhilde seemed to be tagging after her, not in a hostile way as if she wanted to spy on her, but shyly, as if she had something she wanted to say. The Cecilias had now divided up their time as teachers, with Rosa taking care of the singing and Blanca the weaving, and then they were all together during the lessons in sign language. Cecilia Rosa soon found an occasion to conclude the singing a bit earlier than usual. She frankly asked Ulvhilde to sit down for a moment and tell her what it was that she so obviously wanted to discuss. The other girls stole out cautiously and closed the door to the chapter hall so quietly behind them that Cecilia Rosa had the feeling they already knew what was on Ulvhilde's mind.

'So, now that we're alone,' she began, sounding almost as authoritative as an abbess, but was instantly embarrassed and caught herself. 'I mean . . . I've sensed that there's something you want to talk about in private. Am I right about this?'

110

'Yes, dear Cecilia Rosa, you are completely right,' replied Ulvhilde, looking all at once as if she were making a brave attempt to hold back the tears.

'My dear little friend, what is it?' Cecilia Rosa asked uncertainly.

But the answer was not forthcoming. They sat together for a while, neither of them daring to be first to break the silence, although by now Cecilia Rosa had begun to have her suspicions.

'The thing is, Emund Ulvbane was my father, blessed be his soul,' whispered Ulvhilde at last, her gaze fixed on the limestone floor.

'I don't know any Emund Ulvbane,' said Cecilia Rosa timidly, at once regretting it.

'Yes, you do, Cecilia Rosa; your betrothed Arn Magnusson knew him, and everyone in both Western and Eastern Götaland knows the story. My father lost his hand in that duel.'

'Yes, of course I know about the duel at Axevalla *ting*,' Cecilia Rosa admitted in shame. 'Everyone does, just as you say. But I wasn't there and had nothing to do with that affair. Arn was not yet betrothed to me. And you weren't there either. So what do you mean by this? Do you intend for this matter to stand like a fortress wall between us?'

'It's much worse than that,' Ulvhilde went on, no longer able to hold back the tears. 'Knut Eriksson killed my father at Forsvik, even though he had promised that father would be allowed to come for me, my mother, and my brothers. And on the fields of blood . . .'

Then Ulvhilde could go no farther, but bent forward sobbing as if the pain had cloven her across her tender waist. Cecilia Rosa at first felt altogether at a loss, but she put her arms around little Ulvhilde, knelt down next to her, and awkwardly stroked her cheeks.

'There, there,' she consoled her. 'What you started to tell me must come out, and you may as well do it now. So tell me what happened on the fields of blood, because I know nothing about it.'

Ulvhilde struggled for a moment, trying to catch her breath between sobs before she was able to utter the words that had to come out.

'On the fields of blood . . . both my brothers died . . . killed by the Folkungs . . . and then they came to our farm where mother . . . where mother was still in hiding. And they burned her alive with the livestock and servants!'

It was as if Ulvhilde's wild grief spread like a coldness between their limbs so that it was now inside Cecilia Rosa as well. They clung to each other without being able to speak. Cecilia Rosa began rocking back and forth as if she were lulling the younger girl to sleep, although now there would be no sleep. And yet something more had to be said.

'Ulvhilde, my little friend,' Cecilia Rosa whispered hoarsely. 'Keep in mind that it could have been you in this position and that neither of us is at all to blame. If I can console you then I will try. If you want me to be your friend and support, I will try that too. It's not easy to live at Gudhem, and you should know that here we need friends more than anything else.'

The death throes of Fru Helena Stensdotter took a long time. For ten days she lay dying, and during most of that time her mind was utterly clear. It made the matter that much more delicate for Mother Rikissa, who now had to send various messages far and wide.

It would not do simply to bury Fru Helena as any of Gudhem's pensioners, because she was of royal lineage, and she had married into both the Sverker and the Erik clans. At a time when the wounds of war had been better healed, a huge retinue should have come to see her to her final rest. But as things now stood, with the fields of blood outside Bjälbo fresh in everyone's memory, only a small but very resolute group showed up. Almost all the guests arrived several days before her death; they had to spend the time waiting in both the *hospitium* and other buildings outside the cloister – Folkungs and Eriks in one group, and Sverkers in another.

Cecilia Blanca and Cecilia Rosa were the only novices who were allowed to go outside the walls to sing at the graveside in the churchyard. This was not because of their clan lineage, but because their singing voices were among the loveliest at Gudhem.

Bishop Bengt had come from Skara to pray over the grave. Standing slightly removed from everyone else he wore his light-blue, gold-embroidered bishop's vestments, and he seemed able to remain upright only by clutching his staff. On one side stood men from the Sverker and Stenkil clans in red, black, and green mantles. On the other side stood the Eriks in gold and sky-blue, and Folkungs in the same blue but with silver. In two long rows outside the churchyard were all the shields fastened to lances stuck into the ground: the Folkung lion, the three Erik crowns, the black Sverker griffin, and the Stenkil wolf's head. Some of the shields still bore clear marks of sword-edges and lance-points, while some of the guests' mantles bore traces of both battle and blood. Peace had reigned for too short a time for the marks of war to have been washed away in the rain.

The two Cecilias did their utmost during the singing of the hymns, and they had not the slightest thought of attempting any mischief that might cause discord among the clans. Slight as their acquaintance with Fru Helena was before she died, it was more than sufficient for them to like her and feel great respect for her.

When the singing was over and Fru Helena had been consigned to the black earth, there was naturally no question but that the Cecilias, and any of the other sisters, would quickly disappear behind the convent walls. A grave-ale would be drunk in the *hospitium*, but that was something only for Bishop Bengt, Mother Rikissa, and the worldly guests. They would now have to associate more closely with one another than they had done in the churchyard, where none had shown any desire for fellowship.

When Bishop Bengt and his cathedral dean started off, as if intending to lead the procession toward the *hospitium* and the waiting grave-ale, the hostility among the various group was obvious to the worldly guests. The Eriks made the first move to start walking, so they were in the front of the procession. But when the Sverkers discovered that, they hastened to ensure that they would come before the Folkungs. In stifled silence the colourful retinue headed off toward the northern end of Gudhem where the guest quarters stood.

The two Cecilias had hung back to observe the fine clothing and the ritual. When Mother Rikissa noticed them she strode over and gave them a good dressing-down, fuming about things that were unsuitable for the eyes of Christian maidens, and she ordered them to hurry off behind the walls, and to be quick about it.

But Cecilia Blanca then answered her so gently that she surprised even herself, saying that she had seen something that might further the cause of peace and also serve Gudhem. Many of the mantles worn by the guests needed to have the traces of war removed, and that was something which would be easy to arrange inside Gudhem. Just as Mother Rikissa opened her mouth to speak more harsh words, an idea seemed to dawn on her. Instead she turned around and looked at the morose procession of guests shuffling off.

'You know, I think that maybe even a blind hen can find

114

the grain,' she said pensively, but not at all unkindly. And then she shooed off the two Cecilias as if they were geese.

Mother Rikissa had two worries that she kept from everyone else at Gudhem. One involved a great event that would soon take place, inevitable as a new season, and for Cecilia Blanca at least it would mean a tremendous change. The second had to do with Gudhem's business affairs and was somewhat more difficult to comprehend.

Gudhem was a rich cloister even now in its early days, although less than a lifetime had passed since the church was consecrated as a cloister church and the first sisters moved in. But riches alone could not feed mouths, since the wealth was based on the ownership of land, and this ownership had to be transformed into food and drink, clothing and the construction of buildings. And what the earth produced came to Gudhem from near and far in the form of casks of seed, bales of wool, salted fish, dried fish, flour, oil, and fruit. A portion of all these goods had to be stored for use at Gudhem; a greater portion had to be shipped to various marketplaces, mostly the one in Skara, to be sold and transformed into silver. This silver would then be spent primarily to pay all those from foreign lands who worked on the various buildings of the cloister. All too often the sale of goods took some time, so that the convent's cache of silver ebbed away. This was a constant source of worry for Mother Rikissa. No matter how she tried to involve herself in the various details of administration, the *yconomus*, a canon from Skara whom Bishop Bengt viewed as useless in church work but who had a good head for business, always had a rejoinder for her suspicious questions. If the harvests had been good, then it would be difficult to sell very much grain at one time. If the harvests had been poor, then they had to wait to sell until the prices rose a bit. And it was never good to sell everything at once, but rather to spread the sale over the entire year.

So in the late autumn when most of the rent payments from tenants came flowing in, all their storehouses were filled to bursting, and toward the end of each summer all these storage places stood empty. The *yconomus* claimed that this was the natural order of things.

Mother Rikissa had tried to discuss these problems with Father Henri, who was the abbot of Varnhem and in that capacity her superior. But Father Henri had been unable to give her any particularly good advice. There was a big difference between a cloister populated only by men and a convent with only women, as he explained with a concerned expression. At Varnhem they took in direct payments in silver for the many different sorts of work they did. They had twenty different quarries where they manufactured millstones; they had smithies that fabricated everything from farming tools to swords for noblemen; and they did all their construction work with their own labour force without spending any silver. What Gudhem needed was its own business that could bring in silver directly, Father Henri had told her. But that was easier said than done.

When Mother Rikissa heard Cecilia Blanca talking about the guests' stained and tattered mantles it had given her an idea, and she would always remember it as being of her own devising. At Gudhem wool was spun and woven; linen was harvested, retted, dried, braked, scutched, combed, spun, and woven – the entire process from the flax plant to finished fabric. And Sister Leonore, who took care of Gudhem's gardens, knew how to dye fabrics in many different ways. Except for black, this knowledge was never put to use because there was no need for garish worldly colours inside Gudhem.

Thought precedes action just as the dawn precedes the day, and Mother Rikissa now set the new plan in motion. When she returned from the grave-ale in the *hospitium*, which was as brief as it could be among the victors and the vanquished, she took with her two threadbare and sloppily mended mantles, one red and one blue. She had been careful to acquire a mantle from each side.

All the new work that would now have to be done brought a change for the better to Gudhem, just as Mother Rikissa had hoped. Apart from her worries about obtaining silver, she was in a race against time with another concern that she had not confided in anyone. She had to make the girls cease their hostility toward one another.

The maidens would be given the greatest responsibility for the new work, and this suited Mother Rikissa's new hidden agenda all the better. Now, in early autumn, the lay sisters needed to devote all their attention to the harvesting work. Besides, the lay sisters all came from families that never dressed in clan colours to go to church or to market or to bridal ales. Lay sisters – lay-sisters, whom Mother Rikissa regarded with a contempt she could scarcely conceal – were women from poor families who could not afford to marry off their daughters. So the young women were sent to the convent to work for their own food instead of staying at home with poor peasant fathers and costing more than they could contribute. Lay-sisters had never in their lives been in a noble household so had never seen a Folkung mantle or a Sverker one either. So this new work had to be done entirely by the consecrated sisters and the more or less temporary guests among the novices: the two Cecilias and the Sverker daughters.

It soon turned out, however, that Gudhem had taken on no easy task. Everything had to be tested, and many trials were failures before something good finally emerged. And yet all these early difficulties merely intensified the maidens determination to succeed; they hurried to take up each job in a way that seemed almost indecorous. And when Mother Rikissa went past the weaving workshop, she heard eager words spoken in a tone that hardly seemed proper in a house dedicated to the Mother of God. But Mother Rikissa decided to bide her time, and for now the giggling was permitted. There would be time enough to restore decorum. Until the great event took place it would be unwise of her to treat the girls in a heavy-handed fashion.

Ulvhilde Emundsdotter had persuaded the others to try and weave the fabric she had spoken about, in which wool and linen were mixed. A mantle of pure linen would be too soft, and a mantle of only wool would be too thick and unwieldy and would not drape well over the shoulders and back. So the first task was to produce the cloth. But it wasn't easy, because if the woollen threads were woven too loosely, too many strands would pull out from the cloth; if the linen thread was woven too tightly, it would bunch up the cloth too much. Through trial and error they would have to find the proper techniques.

Then there were difficulties with Sister Leonore's various dye samples. Red proved to be the simplest to produce, though the maidens had to be careful to ensure that it was exactly the right shade of red. The red of beet juice was too vividly purple and too bright; the red that came from St John's wort was too light and too brown, although it could be mixed with alder to darken it. The correct red colour was soon developed using dyes from Sister Leonore's many clay pots. It proved harder to produce the right blue.

And a dyed piece of cloth had to be marked and dried, since the colours when wet did not look at all the same when dry. Many pieces of cloth, which were useless for any other purpose afterwards, were given over to all this testing.

It took a lot of work to produce a single finished mantle. And as if that weren't enough, there was the matter of how to line the mantles and where the pelts would come from. Winter squirrels, marten, and foxes didn't grow on trees, after all. So instead of bringing in silver, the new work ended up adding to the cloister's expenses. The *yconomus* was finally ordered by a reluctant Mother Rikissa to go to Skara and buy skins, travelling all the way to Linköping if need be. He whined and complained about the expense. He thought it was risky to lay out silver for something one wasn't certain could be sold, and in any case it would be a long time before the costs could be recouped as income. Mother Rikissa replied that silver did not multiply on its own at the bottom of a chest; something had to be done with it. But the *yconomus* argued that doing so could bring losses as soon as gains. At a calmer period for Gudhem Mother Rikissa might have paid more attention to the *yconomus* and his grumbling. But in view of its current situation it was important that the girls had no reason to complain or that the cloister still had silver in its coffers.

The harbinger of the great event at Gudhem was a convoy of ox-carts from Skara. It arrived on a calm, clear autumn day and was taken in hand as something that had been expected, although the cargo consisted of tents and wood, casks of ale and mead, and even some barrels of wine that had been brought up from Varnhem. There were also animal carcasses that had to be hung in cold storage, and a great number of roast-turners and labourers. They began to raise a tent city outside the walls of Gudhem, and their hammer-blows, laughter, and coarse words rang throughout the cloister.

Inside the walls rumours were buzzing like a beehive. Some simply believed that war was coming again, that an army would arrive and claim Gudhem as the enemy's fortress. Others thought that it was merely the bishops who were holding a meeting and had selected a neutral spot where no one had to bear the entire expense. Mother Rikissa and the nuns, who knew or at least ought to know what it was all about, gave not the slightest hint of anything.

In the *vestiarium*, which was the new, more formal term for the weaving chamber where the Cecilias and the Sverker daughters now spent most of their time, the idea soon arose that one of them was to be fetched and married off – a thought that inspired both hope and trepidation. It even seemed most probable, since preparations were being made for a feast. They let their imaginations run wild, as if they were no longer enemies at all, picturing which of them would end up with a drooling old man from Skara. That was how the Cecilias taunted the Sverker daughters, who then retaliated with the prospect of a drooling old man from Linköping who had done the king a favour or promised loyalty in return for once again being allowed to creep into the bed-straw with an innocent maiden. The more they spoke of this possibility, the more excited they became, because it would be splendid to have a different life outside the walls, yet terrible was the thought of a drooling old man, whether from Linköping or Skara. What was perceived as both liberation and punishment could just as well befall someone on the red Sverker side as on the blue side. Half in jest each tied a piece of yarn around their right arm, a red one for the Sverker daughters and a blue one for the two Cecilias.

When talk turned to this matter it felt as though a hard hand were squeezing Cecilia Rosa's heart. She found it hard to breathe and broke out in a cold sweat. She had to leave the room for a few moments, breathing in the chill air in the arcade and panting as if with a cramp. If they decided to marry her off, what could she do about it? She had sworn to remain faithful to her beloved Arn, as he had sworn to her. But what did such promises mean to men who were settling scores after war? Of what significance was her will or her love?

She consoled herself with the fact that she had been sentenced to many years of penance, and that it was the judgment of the Holy Roman Church. No Folkungs or Eriks or other men who had either won or lost in war could change that fact. She calmed down at once, but also found it odd that her lengthy punishment might become a consolation. At least she wouldn't be married off.

'I will love you forever, Arn. May God's Holy Mother always hold her protective hand over you wherever you are in the Holy Land and whatever godless enemies you may encounter,' she whispered.

Then she prayed three *Ave Marias*, and in her own prayers she turned to the Mother of God and begged forgiveness for having let herself be overwhelmed by her worldly love, promising that her love for the Mother of God was greatest of all. Having regained a sense of calm, she then went back inside to the others, and seemed just as usual.

After *prandium* and the prayers of thanksgiving the next day, when it was time for rest, a great commotion arose at Gudhem. Messengers came and knocked loudly at the gate, sisters ran back and forth, Mother Rikissa came from the church, wringing her hands in distress, and all the women were summoned to a procession. Soon they were walking slowly, in the order prescribed by the cloister rules, out of the great port underneath Adam and Eve. Singing, they then circled the walls three times before they stopped before the southeast side of Gudhem and lined up with Mother Rikissa in front, behind her the consecrated nuns, and behind them the lay-sisters. But it was strange that the maidens had to stand near the consecrated nuns in a little group by themselves.

In the tent city that had now been raised, men in ordinary brown work clothes made ready by cleaning up all that was untidy. They finished in a great hurry and then fetched poles with furled pennants. All the worldly men lined up, and soon only whispers were heard from them.

All the men and women now stood tensely, staring off to

121

the south-east. It was a lovely day, at that time of autumn when all the colours were still bright and had not yet faded in advance of winter. There was a light breeze and only a few clouds in the sky.

The first thing that could be seen to the south was the flashing glint of lance-points in the sunshine. Soon a great host of horsemen came into view, and the colours became apparent, mostly blue. Everyone knew that the Folkungs or Eriks were approaching.

'It's our men, our colours,' Cecilia Blanca whispered excitedly to Cecilia Rosa standing beside her. Mother Rikissa turned at once and shot her a stern look, raising her finger to her lips to shush her.

The mighty host came ever closer, and now they could see the shields. Those in the vanguard all bore three crowns on a blue field, or Folkung lions against the same background, and all their mantles were blue.

When the retinue came closer they could see that there were red mantles farther back, as well as green and black with gold and other colours that did not belong to any of the more powerful clans.

Now they could see that one of the horsemen in front wore flashing gold around his brow instead of a helmet. No, two of them in front were wearing crowns.

When the column was less than an arrow-shot away it was easy to make out the three riding in front. First came Archbishop Stéphan on a plodding chestnut mare with a large belly. Behind the archbishop to his right rode Knut Eriksson himself on a lively black stallion. His crown was that of a king. And next to him rode Birger Brosa, the jarl, wearing a smaller crown.

Mother Rikissa stood with her back straight, almost defiant. Now the procession was so close that those waiting outside the cloister could speak with the horsemen. Then Mother Rikissa sank to her knees, as she was compelled to do before both the secular and ecclesiastical power. Behind her knelt all the sisters, all the lay-sisters, and finally all the worldly maidens. When all the women were in this position with their eyes on the ground before them, all the men knelt down too. King Knut Eriksson had come to Gudhem on his royal tour of the realm.

The three riders in front stopped only a few paces from Mother Rikissa, who had not yet raised her glance from the ground. Archbishop Stéphan managed to dismount from his horse, muttering in a foreign language about the difficulty of doing so. He straightened his clothing, and stepped up to Mother Rikissa to offer her his right hand. She took it and kissed it humbly, and he gave her leave to rise. Then all were allowed to rise and stood silent.

King Knut now dismounted, though with the ease of a victorious young warrior, raised his right hand, and waited without looking around as a rider from the rear ranks quickly galloped up and handed him a blue mantle with three Erik crowns of gold and a lining of ermine. It was the mantle of a king or queen, like the one he wore himself.

He took the mantle over his left arm and walked slowly, as all the others at Gudhem stood motionless, over to the worldly maidens. He stood behind Cecilia Blanca without a word, raising the mantle high so that all could see it. Then he hung his queen's mantle over her shoulders and took her by the hand to lead her to the royal tent, where four banners with the three Erik crowns waved. Cecilia Rosa realized that she hadn't even noticed when these banners were raised.

The two Cecilias were still holding hands, which they had been doing ever since they recognized Knut Eriksson. But as the king began to lead his Cecilia away, their fingers released their grip. Cecilia Blanca, soon to be the new queen of the Swedes and Goths, quickly turned and gave her friend for life a kiss on both cheeks.

The king frowned at this, but his face instantly brightened as he led his betrothed Cecilia to the royal tent. All the others stood still or remained on their horses until the king and his betrothed had entered the tent.

Then a great rattling and din arose as the whole company dismounted and all began leading their horses toward the oat pastures and haycocks the workers had arranged. The archbishop turned to Mother Rikissa, blessed her, and gave her a dismissive sign as if shooing away a fly before he headed for the royal tent.

Mother Rikissa clapped her hands as a sign for all the women under her supervision to return inside the walls without delay. Inside the cloister there was now much talking and commotion, which not even the strictest rules in this world could have prevented. The holy sisters of the Virgin Mary were jabbering away at each other almost as loudly as the worldly maidens.

It was time for singing, and Mother Rikissa sternly tried to restore order and get them all into the church, forcing upon them the dignity and silence required for the singing hour and the prayers. During the hymns she noticed that Cecilia Rosa sang with a rare power. Tears flowed down the cheeks of this young and now dangerous woman. Everything had gone as badly as Mother Rikissa had feared.

Everything had gone as well as Cecilia Rosa had hoped, but also feared. Her dear friend would become queen, that was as clear as water. And for that reason she felt great joy. But now she would be alone, without her dear friend for many hard years to come. And for that reason she felt sorrow. She couldn't tell which feeling was stronger.

Inside the walls of the cloister the rest of the day passed like any other day, even though it could not be the same. It was a novelty for all the maidens and lay-sisters at Gudhem that the king would come here on his tour of the country and take his rest near the cloister. Mother Rikissa had found it best not to say anything about what she had known for several weeks. She hadn't even mentioned it to Cecilia Blanca, even though she'd been given a royal greeting to deliver, but it would have made Cecilia Blanca impossible to control and also would have unsettled all the other girls.

The king had made a detour from the anticipated route. After passing Jönköping he and his retinue had headed for Eriksberg, which was the king's birthplace. It was also the place where his father, who was now more often called Holy Saint Erik, had been born and where the Erik clan had built their church with the most beautiful frescoes in Western Götaland. The king now entered the most pleasant part of the journey for him, the heartland of the Erik clan.

Many travellers came and went, and there was a constant clatter of horses' hooves. In the *vestiarium* not much orderly work was done by Gudhem's maidens, since they were fantasizing about what the smells and sounds from outside might tell them regarding about was happening. But amid the eager chatter, a distance arose between Cecilia Rosa and the others. Now she was the only one inside Gudhem with a piece of blue yarn around her right arm, alone among the Sverker daughters. It was as if some of the old hostility had come creeping back, mixed with fear or caution since she, even though alone, was the dearest friend of the future queen.

After vespers Mother Rikissa was to attend the banquet outside the walls, so she refrained from following all the others to the *refectorium* for a supper of lentil soup and rye bread. But the prioress had scarcely managed to say grace over the meal in the *refectorium* before Mother Rikissa returned and spread anxiety all around her. She was livid with barely contained anger. Pressing her lips tight, she ordered Cecilia Rosa to come with her at once. It seemed as though Cecilia Rosa might now be taken for punishment, in the worst case to the *carcer*.

She got up at once and followed Mother Rikissa with her head bowed, for rather than fear a bright hope had ignited inside her. And just as she hoped, she was not being led to the *carcer* but to the gate and then to the *hospitium*. There merry voices were heard from the banquet in progress. In the tents outside the smithy and stables, many men were drinking ale.

The *hospitium*, however, was large enough to hold only the most highly honoured guests. At the oak table inside the hall sat the king himself and his jarl Birger Brosa, the archbishop and Bishop Bengt from Skara, four other men whom Cecilia Rosa did not recognize, and far down at the short end of the table sat Cecilia Blanca wearing her blue mantle with the three crowns and ermine trim.

When they entered the room Mother Rikissa roughly shoved Cecilia Rosa before her, seizing her by the scruff of the neck to make her curtsey to the dignitaries, as if she wouldn't have thought to do so herself. Knut Eriksson frowned and gave Mother Rikissa a stern look that she pretended not to notice. Then he raised his right hand so that all talking and whispering ceased in the room at once.

'We welcome you to our banquet here at Gudhem, Cecilia Algotsdotter,' he said with a kind glance at Cecilia Rosa. Then he continued, with a less kind look at Mother Rikissa.

'We welcome you most gladly since your presence here is the wish of our betrothed. Just as we may invite Mother Rikissa if we so choose, our betrothed may invite you.'

With that he gestured toward the place where Cecilia Blanca was sitting, where there was still some room. Mother Rikissa then led Cecilia Rosa with a firm grip to the far end of the table. When she sat down Mother Rikissa angrily tore from her arm the blue piece of yarn, turned away, and went to her place at the other end of the table.

Mother Rikissa's contemptuous handling of the blue colour did not escape the attention of anyone in the hall, so at first there was an embarrassed silence. The two Cecilias held each other's hand under the table. Everyone could see that the king was incensed by the unwise action of the mother superior.

'If you, Mother Rikissa, feel an aversion to blue yarn, then perhaps you would not feel comfortable sitting here with us this evening,' he said, his tone suspiciously gentle as he pointed to the door leading out.

'We have rules at Gudhem that not even kings can alter, and at Gudhem no maiden may wear clan colours,' replied Mother Rikissa brusquely and without fear. But then jarl Birger Brosa slammed his fist on the table so hard that the ale tankards jumped, and there was a silence like that between a lightning strike and the thunder. Everyone cringed involuntarily when he stood up and pointed at Mother Rikissa.

'Then you should know, Rikissa,' he began in a much quieter voice than anyone in the room expected, 'that we Folkungs also have our rules. Cecilia Algotsdotter is a dear friend, and she is betrothed to an even dearer friend of both myself and the king. It is true that she was sentenced to harsh punishment for a sin that many of us have escaped with no punishment at all, but you shall know that in my eyes she is one of us!'

He had raised his voice toward the end of his speech and now he strode with slow, decisive steps down the table and stood directly behind the two Cecilias, giving Mother Rikissa a hard stare as he swept off his mantle and carefully, almost tenderly, draped it around Cecilia Rosa's shoulders. He gave the king a glance, and the king nodded his approval in return. Then Birger Brosa returned to his place, hoisted his ale tankard and drank several mighty drafts, before he held out the tankard toward the two Cecilias, and then sat down with a loud grumble.

For a long while the conversation flagged. Roast-turners brought in both venison and pork, along with ale and sweet vegetables and white bread, but the guests touched only enough food as was considered polite.

The two Cecilias had no opportunity to talk, although they were bursting with impatience to discuss events. That which was called women's prattle would not have been appropriate at the table when the mood was so solemn. They bowed their heads demurely, picking cautiously at the food which after such a long time on a cloister diet, they otherwise would have gobbled right up.

For Archbishop Stéphan, the roast-turners had brought in special food, including lamb cooked in cabbage, and unlike all the others at the table he drank wine instead of ale. He had not allowed the dispute between Mother Rikissa and the king's jarl to interrupt his earthly enjoyments. Now he held up his wine glass and scrutinized the colour of the wine before once again putting it to his lips and rolling his eyes.

'It's like being home in Burgundy again,' he sighed as he set down his glass. '*Mon Dieu!* This wine certainly suffered no harm from its long journey. But speaking of journeys . . . how are the affairs in Lübeck going, Your Majesty?'

Just as Archbishop Stéphan had intended, Knut Eriksson brightened at this question and at once launched into an animated response.

At that very moment Eskil Magnusson, who was Arn's brother and the nephew of Birger Brosa, was in Lübeck to draw up a trading contract, signed and sealed, with no less than Henrik the Lion of Saxony. As large a portion of the trade from the Gothic lands as could be imagined would now be rerouted to the Eastern Sea and pass between Eastern Götaland and Lübeck. If their own lighters were not sufficient, the Lübeckers would generously make their vessels available. The great new wares that the Lübeckers wanted included dried fish from Norway, which Eskil Magnusson had begun to buy in copious quantities, shipping it from the Norwegian Sea up into Lake Vänern and on via river and lake to Lake Vättern, then out from ports in Eastern Götaland. Iron from Svealand, pelts and salt herring, salmon and butter would soon be shipped the same way, and the goods that the Lübeckers had to offer in return were just as favourable, but best was all the silver that changed hands.

Soon all the men, worldly as well as clerical, were involved in a lively, cheerful conversation about what the new trade route with Lübeck might entail. Their hopes were high, and they were all agreed that trade belonged to new and better times. They also seemed convinced that the wealth that would come from greater trade would also lead to increased concord and peace.

The discussion grew louder, and more ale was brought in with ever-growing haste so that the feast at long last got under way.

The two Cecilias could now begin to talk to each other, since nobody could hear what they were saying at the far end of the table. Cecilia Blanca first reported how long ago Knut Eriksson had sent a message that he would be coming to Gudhem on this day, and that he would be bringing with him a queen's mantle. So Mother Rikissa had known about it for quite a while, but malicious as she was she had decided to say nothing. That woman's only true joy was not to love God but to torment her neighbour.

Cecilia Rosa quietly replied, saying that happiness must seem all the greater now that it was here. For it would have been so hard to go on counting the days for over a month in constant worry that something might have changed.

They had no chance to say more because the men's dreams

129

of all the gold and silver to be made from trading with Lübeck began dominating the room, and Bishop Bengt was careful to turn the conversation to himself. He told them what fear he had felt for his life, but how he had prayed that God might make him brave, and then he resolutely dared to intervene and rescue the two Cecilias from being abducted, and from a convent at that – the worst sort of abduction. His story droned on, nor did he omit a single insignificant detail.

Since the Cecilias couldn't very well interrupt when a bishop was speaking, especially when he was talking about them – although mostly about himself – they chastely bowed their heads and continued to communicate in sign language under the table.

True that he chased away the boors, but where was the courage in that? Cecilia Rosa signed.

His courage would have been greater if the Sverkers had won on the fields of blood, Cecilia Blanca replied. Neither of them could hold back a giggle.

But King Knut, who was a sharp-eyed man and not yet very drunk, saw this female merriment from the corner of his eye. He turned suddenly to the Cecilias and asked in a loud voice whether this incident did not occur exactly the way Bishop Bengt had related it.

'Yes, absolutely true, it happened just as the bishop tells it,' replied Cecilia Blanca without the slightest hesitation. 'Foreign warriors came and demanded with words so coarse that I can't repeat them here that Cecilia Algotsdotter and I be delivered from the walls of Gudhem at once. Then Bishop Bengt stepped up and admonished them in stern terms and they retreated without doing harm.'

During a brief silence the king and the other men pondered these angelic words from the king's own betrothed, and the king then promised that this matter would not go unrewarded. Bishop Bengt was quick to point out that he sought no reward for acting in accordance with his conscience and as his duty to the Lord commanded, but if something good might fall to the church then joy would arise among God's servants, just as in Heaven. Soon the conversation took another turn.

Cecilia Rosa now asked in sign language why the lying bishop was let off the hook so easily. Cecilia Blanca answered that it would have been unwise for a future queen to disgrace one of the kingdom's bishops before other men. But that did not mean that anything was forgotten, and the king would soon be told the truth, although at a more suitable time. By now they were signing even more excitedly above the table, and they suddenly realized that Mother Rikissa was staring at them with an expression that was anything but loving.

Birger Brosa had also seen something, although he was not one to talk much at a feast; he preferred to watch and listen. He was sitting in his usual way, leaning back slightly with that amused smile that had given him the nickname Brosa – meaning Cheerful – and with his ale tankard lazily propped on one knee. Now he quickly leaned forward and slammed down the tankard with a bang, so that the conversation stopped and all eyes turned to him. They knew that when the jarl did this he had something to say, and when the jarl had something to say everyone listened, even the king.

'It seems fitting to me,' he began with a thoughtful look on his face, 'that we might talk a bit about what we could do for Gudhem, now that we are finally gathered here and have heard about Bishop Bengt's heroic action. Does Rikissa have any suggestion, perhaps?'

All eyes turned to Mother Rikissa, for the jarl was not one to ask a rhetorical question. Mother Rikissa thought carefully before replying.

'Land is always being donated to cloisters,' she said. 'Gudhem too has acquired more property as the years go by.

131

But right now what we need at Gudhem are squirrel furs and good wintertime white fox and marten pelts.'

She looked a bit sly when she fell silent, as if she understood quite well what astonishment her answer would arouse.

'Squirrel and marten pelts? It sounds as though you and your sisters have been struck by worldly temptations, but surely things can't possibly be as bad as that, can they, Rikissa?' asked Birger Brosa in a kindly tone and with a bigger smile than usual.

'Not at all,' Mother Rikissa snorted. 'But just as you gentlemen deal in trade, a subject which you have all been boasting of so freely, the servants of the Lord must do so as well. Look at all these soiled and torn mantles that your men are wearing. Here at Gudhem we have begun to make new mantles, better and more beautiful than the ones you had before. And for these mantles we are counting on receiving an honest price. Since we are women, you can't demand that we cut millstones like the monks at Varnhem.'

Her reply provoked both surprise and amusement. So involved in business matters as all the men had just been feeling, and as men always felt, they could do no less than nod in agreement and attempt to look wise.

'And what sort of colours are possible for these mantles that you and your sisters are sewing?' asked Birger Brosa in a kindly tone that scarcely concealed the cunning of his thoughts.

'My good jarl!' replied Mother Rikissa, feigning equal surprise at the question that Birger Brosa had just posed so innocently. 'The mantles that we sew are of course red with a black griffin head . . . as well as blue with three crowns, or blue with the lion that you yourself, although not at this moment, usually wear on your back . . .'

After a brief hesitation Birger Brosa began to laugh, and Knut Eriksson joined in, so that in no time all the men around the table were laughing.

'Mother Rikissa! You have a sharp tongue, but we also find you have an amusing way with words,' said Knut Eriksson, taking a swig of ale and wiping his mouth before he went on. 'The pelts you asked for shall soon be at Gudhem, we give you our word on that. Was there anything else, while we're still in a good mood and willing to make new business deals?'

'Yes, perhaps so, my king,' replied Mother Rikissa hesitantly. 'If those Lübeckers have gold and silver thread, we could make the coats of arms much lovelier. Surely both Cecilia Ulvsdotter and Cecilia Algotsdotter can attest to that, since they have both been very industrious in this new venture at Gudhem.'

All eyes now turned to the two Cecilias, who modestly had to agree with what Mother Rikissa had said. With such fine foreign thread they could embroider beautiful coats of arms on the back of the mantles.

So the king immediately promised to see to it that not only the desired furs but also Lübeck thread would arrive at Gudhem as soon as possible. He added that it was not only a better deal than bestowing land, it could also mean a more beautiful assembly at the coronation ceremony if the guests were well appointed by the women of Gudhem.

Mother Rikissa got up at once and excused herself, saying that duty called, and she thanked the king most gratefully for both the meal and the promises. The king and the jarl both nodded good night, and she was free to go. But she remained standing there, giving Cecilia Rosa a stern look, as if she were waiting for her.

When Knut Eriksson noticed Mother Rikissa's silent demand, he looked at his betrothed and she shook her head. He made up his mind.

'We wish you good night, Rikissa,' he said. 'And as far as Cecilia Algotsdotter is concerned, we would like her to spend the night with our betrothed so that no one can say

133

that Knut spent the night under the same roof and in the same bed as his intended.'

Mother Rikissa stood utterly still, as if she could not believe her ears. She had a hard time deciding whether she should agree and simply leave, or whether she should argue the point.

'For we all know,' interposed Birger Brosa quietly, 'what misery it could mean for the Cecilias if the betrothed are not kept scrupulously apart until the bridal ale. And no matter how much it might please you, Rikissa, to be allowed to hold *both* the Cecilias in the nurture and admonition of the Lord for twenty years, our king would probably be less glad of it.'

Birger Brosa smiled as always, but there was poison in his words. Mother Rikissa was a contentious woman and now her eyes were flashing fire. The king intervened quickly before more damage wrought by harsh words could be done.

'We believe that you can sleep peacefully with regard to this matter, Rikissa,' he said. 'For your archbishop has given his blessing for what we have now decreed and arranged. *N'est-ce pas, mon cher Stéphan?*'

'*Comment?* Oh . . . *naturellement . . . uh, ma chère Mère Rikissa* . . . it is just as His Majesty has said, a small matter, a mere trifle . . .'

The archbishop dug into his roast lamb once again, the third serving that had been brought in to him, and then he raised his wine glass and seemed to be inspecting it as if everything was settled. Mother Rikissa turned without a word and strode off, her heels clacking on the oaken floor as she headed toward the door.

With that the king and his men were rid of the person who by her presence most hampered their speech – a desire for candour that soon began to make itself felt just as implacably as the need to relieve themselves outside in the pine boughs. It was a hindrance to have the abbess at their feast, no two ways about it.

But it was not much better with two maidens whose young ears would probably be badly singed by the long talks that the night still promised.

The king explained that they had arranged beds for the Cecilias in a chamber on the upper floor, and that a guard would be placed outside their door all night so that no malicious tongues could do harm. For the Cecilias this leavetaking was just as important as it was for the men, because they had only one last night together to say everything that they might otherwise long regret not having said. They withdrew in a courtly manner, although Birger Brosa cleared his throat and stopped them on their way, pointing at his mantle. Cecilia Rosa flushed and took off the mantle. When Birger Brosa turned his back in amusement, she placed the jarl's mantle adorned with the Folkung lion over the shoulders where it belonged.

Soon the two Cecilias climbed into bed upstairs among the linens and thick pelts so that they were able to sleep in only their shifts and still find the night unusually warm and pleasant. Affixed to one of the log walls were tallow candles that would burn much longer than ordinary wax ones.

They lay for a while side by side, staring at the ceiling and holding hands. On a bench next to the bed lay the queen's mantle, a majestic blue with three glinting crowns of gold reminding of all the wondrous things that had happened on this day. For a while they were so absorbed in this thought that neither of them spoke.

But the night was still young, and from downstairs came noise and laughter from the now female-free company. The men could concentrate on enjoying a good feast with liveliness and vigour, an honour demanded when dining with the king.

'I wonder if the archbishop is started on his fourth helping of roast lamb by now,' Cecilia Blanca giggled. 'And I wonder if he's as simple-minded as he seems. Did you see the way he brushed aside Mother Rikissa as if a fly had got into his wine glass?'

'That's exactly why he's not the simpleton he makes himself out to be,' replied Cecilia Rosa. 'He couldn't feign obedience to the king's slightest whim. Nor could he feign that he thought it was important to decide for the king and against Mother Rikissa, so he pretended there was a fly in his wine glass, and that was that. Besides, Arn always spoke well of Archbishop Stéphan, even though he sentenced both of us to such a harsh punishment.'

'You're far too good and you think too well of people, my dearest of friends,' Cecilia Blanca said with a sigh.

'What do you mean, dearest Blanca?'

'You have to think more like a man, Rosa, you have to learn to think as they do – the way all men think whether they bear the crown of a jarl or carry a bishop's staff. It was not at all a fair sentence that you and Arn were given. As Birger Brosa said so clearly, many have committed the same sin without being punished at all. You were both judged too harshly, that's clear as water, don't you realize that?'

'No, I don't understand. Why would they do that?'

'Rikissa. There you have the malevolent soul behind the entire matter. I was at Gudhem when your sister Katarina, who is probably no longer so dear to you, urged Rikissa to begin spinning her web. Arn, your beloved as you say, was Knut Eriksson's friend and a Folkung. That was the relationship that Rikissa was intent on destroying; she wanted to harm the king's friend and sow dissension. And Arn was a swordsman who could vanquish all others; many stories were told about him. That was a skill that the archbishop was intent on using.'

'But what would the archbishop and Father Henri want with another swordsman?'

'My dear beloved friend!' Cecilia Blanca burst out impatiently. 'Don't make yourself the stupid goose that Fru Helena talked about. Bishops and other prelates are constantly talking about how we must send men to the war in the Holy Land, as if we didn't have enough to do with our own wars, and how anyone who takes up the Cross will enter Paradise. Yet they have had scant success with such speech. Do you know anyone who took the Cross and went there voluntarily? No, me neither. But they could send Arn, and they surely said many prayers of thanksgiving afterward. The truth is sometimes hard and cold. If Arn Magnusson hadn't gained a saga-like reputation after the duel at Axevalla, had he been a man like all the others with sword and lance, you would have received a sentence of two years, not twenty.'

'You're starting to think like a queen. Is this the talent you wish to practice?' asked Cecilia Rosa after a moment. She seemed deeply affected by her friend's claim that the sword was the reason for the harsh judgments levied against Arn and herself.

'Yes, I am trying to learn to think like a queen. Of the two of us, I'm probably the one most suited to it. You are much too good, my dear Rosa.'

'Is that how you talked them into bringing me over here to this feast, because you were thinking like a queen? By the way, Mother Rikissa looked like she was about to burst with hatred when she came to get me.'

'She probably could have, that hag; she has to learn that she is certainly not the will of God. No, I tried first with normal cunning and caresses. But Knut did not seem to be very taken by my arts. He went and asked his jarl, so there I was disappointed. I have a long way to go to be treated as a queen.'

'So it was Birger Brosa then who decided that I should be invited?'

137

'He and no other. In him you have a supporter whom you must tend well. When he went over and draped the Folkung mantle around you, it was not meant merely to protect you from the cold.'

They fell silent because the salvos of laughter were now thundering up through the floor planks, and because they felt somewhat embarrassed that their conversation had taken such a sombre turn. It felt as if the queen's mantle, lying in the darkness close to them, had forced them to become something other than simply the dearest of friends. And even though the hour was not yet late, the night would end as all nights did, even nights spent in the *carcer*. And with that they would be separated for a very long time, perhaps even forever. Surely there was something else to talk about besides the struggle for power.

'Don't you think he's a handsome man? Does he look the same as you remember him?' Cecilia Rosa asked at last.

'Who? Knut Eriksson? Yes, though I no doubt remember him as younger and more handsome. It's been a few years since we've seen each other, and even then we met only seldom. He's still tall and looks quite strong, but his hair is starting to thin so that soon he'll resemble a monk, even though he's not very old. He isn't exactly an old man from Linköping, but my choice could have been better, of course. And he isn't as smart as Birger Brosa. *Summa summarum*, the betrothal could have been better, but also much worse. So I'm fairly satisfied.'

'Fairly satisfied?'

'Yes, I have to admit as much. But it's not that important. The important thing is that he's the king.'

'Then you don't love him?'

'The way I love the Virgin Mary, or the way they love in the sagas? No, it's obvious that I don't. Why should I?'

'Haven't you ever loved a man?'

138

'No. But there was once a stable boy . . . ah, I was only fifteen at the time. My father caught us together and there was an awful row. The stable boy was shown the gate after being whipped, but he swore that he would come back someday with many retainers. I cried for days, and then I got a new horse.'

'When I get out of here I'll be thirty-seven years old,' Cecilia Rosa whispered although they had been talking quite loudly to be heard over the feast downstairs.

'Then you may still have a lot of your life before you,' Cecilia Blanca replied in a much louder voice. 'You can come to me and the king. You and I are friends for life; that's the one thing that Mother Rikissa can do nothing about.'

'But I'll probably only get out of here if Arn comes back as he vowed to do. Otherwise I'll dry up and spend the rest of my life in the convent,' said Cecilia Rosa in a somewhat louder voice.

'You must pray every night for Arn until that day comes,' said Cecilia Blanca, squeezing her friend's hand harder. 'I promise you that I'll pray for the same thing, and maybe together, if we both keep trying, we can persuade God's Holy Mother.'

'Yes, maybe we can. Because it's well known that Our Lady has many times been persuaded by prayers of love if only they are persistent enough. I know a story about such a case that is very beautiful.'

'What if I ask you the same thing you asked me – do you really love Arn Magnusson? Or is he just your footbridge that will carry you across this chasm called Gudhem? Do you love him the way you love Our Lady, or the way they love in the sagas?'

'Yes, I do,' said Cecilia Rosa. 'I love him so much that I'm afraid of the sin of loving a man more than God. I will love him forever, and when these cursed twenty years have passed, I will still love him.'

'You may not be able to understand this, but I envy you,' said Cecilia Blanca after a while. She turned in the bed and threw her arms around her friend.

They lay like that for a while as tears came to them both. Finally they were interrupted by the necessity that can intervene at any time after a feast. Cecilia Blanca had to get up and relieve herself in the wooden bucket that had been thoughtfully placed under their bed.

'I have to ask you two things that can only be asked of one's dearest friend,' Cecilia Blanca resumed when she crept back in under the sheepskins. 'How does it feel to have a son and yet not have a son? And is it as bad as many women say it is to give birth to a child?'

'You're certainly asking a lot all at once,' said Cecilia Rosa with a wan smile. 'Having to give up a son like mine, a boy named Magnus who is growing up with Birger Brosa and with Brigida as his mother, was so hard that I force myself to think of him only in my prayers. He was so beautiful and so little! It's a misfortune greater than my captivity with Mother Rikissa, not to be with him. Yet in spite of this misfortune, I am happy that he will be raised by a man as good as Arn's uncle. Does this seem a bit crazy? Is it hard to understand?'

'Not at all, I believe it's exactly as you say. But what was it like to give birth?'

'Are you starting to worry already? Isn't it a little early for that, now that they've put a guard outside your bedchamber and taken all these precautions?'

'Don't make fun of the matter. Yes, I am worried. I'm sure that I will give birth to more than a few sons. What is it like?'

'What do I know? I've had only one. Do you want to know if it hurts? Yes, it hurts terribly. Do you want to know if you feel glad when it's over? Yes, you do. Now have you found out from an experienced woman anything that you didn't already know?'

'I wonder if it hurts less if you love the man who is father to your child,' Cecilia Blanca mused after a while, half in earnest and half in jest.

'Yes, I think that's true,' replied Cecilia Rosa.

'Then it's probably best if I start loving our king,' joked Cecilia Blanca with a sigh.

They both burst out laughing, and their laughter felt cleansing and liberating. They wriggled around in bed so that they lay entwined, almost like the night when a nearly frozen Cecilia Blanca was brought up from the *carcer*. And as they lay there they both came to think of that night.

'I believe and will always believe that you saved my life. I was frozen to the bone, and my life felt like it was the last blue flame that flickers just before the last ember dies out,' Cecilia Blanca whispered in her friend's ear.

'Your flame is no doubt stronger than that,' said Cecilia Rosa sleepily.

They fell asleep but awoke when it was time for *lauds*. Both of them stumbled groggily out of bed and started to get dressed before remembering that they were in the *hospitium*, and bellowing could still be heard downstairs.

As they crept back underneath the sheepskins they were wide awake and couldn't go back to sleep. But the candle had burned out and it was pitch dark outside the window.

They began again where they had left off, talking of eternal friendship and eternal love.

FIVE

When Saladin arrived at Gaza he was not fooled by any of
the defenders' traps. He had been a warrior much too long
for that; he had laid siege to too many cities, and defended
too many cities from besiegers, to believe what he first saw.
The city of Gaza at this moment looked easy to take, as if
they could simply ride straight in, as if the city had given up
and would surrender voluntarily. But from the tower above
the wide-open city gate and the lowered drawbridge across
the moat waved the black-and-white banner of the Knights
Templar and their standard bearing the image of the mother
of Jesus, whom they worshipped like a goddess. It was those
banners that should be kept in mind and not what the enemy
wanted the advancing troops to see. The idea that a Templar
knight would surrender without a fight was almost ridiculous; it was even more of an affront that their commander
thought they could succeed with such a simple trick.

Annoyed, Saladin waved off the emirs who came riding
up to him with one idiotic proposal for a lightning attack
after another. He held to his orders. They would do as he
had planned, and not change their tactics because of an open
gate and what looked like an unguarded approach.

Arn stood up on the city ramparts along with his weapons master Guido de Faramond and his *confanonier* Armand, tensely watching the incoming enemy army. In the city beneath and behind him the streets had been cleared of rubbish and everything flammable; all the windows were closed with wooden shutters or stretched skins soaked in vinegar. The refugees had been herded into the grain storehouses made of stone that had been emptied when they filled the storehouses inside the fortress, and the city's inhabitants were either in their homes or with the groups that were responsible for fighting fires.

The city of Gaza stood on a hill that sloped down to the sea toward the fortress and the harbour. Atop the hill was the city gate, so that any enemy would have to attack uphill. Between the city gate and the gates of the fortress on the shore, the way was clear and without obstacle, like a practice field for equestrian games. Visible up on the city walls were mostly Turkish archers and an occasional black-clad sergeant; from the outside it must have looked like a surprisingly meagre defence. That was because two hundred sergeants, mostly armed with crossbows, were sitting with their backs against the breastwork walls so that they were invisible from outside. In an instant Gaza's defence forces would more than double if Arn gave the order.

Just inside the closed but not barred gates to the fortress itself sat eighty Templar knights mounted and ready to ride to the attack.

Arn had hoped that the enemy's army would advance in groups and not in a body. He had hoped that some emir, in a lust for glory, then wouldn't be able to keep from showing his bold valour so as to reap rich praise when Saladin himself arrived. The excitement was often greatest, just as the dread was the worst, at the beginning of an attack.

If the Mamelukes had sent in their cavalry through the

open city gate, it would have been closed when the crush was sufficiently great, after about four hundred men. Then the gates would have opened down in the fortress and the knights would have emerged, hacking at the Mamelukes in the perfect situation, crowded and hard-pressed, where Saracen speed was no longer an advantage. And from the city wall the sergeants would have turned their crossbows inward and downward. The enemy would have lost a tenth of his force in the first hour. And anyone who then initiated a siege would encounter much trouble afterwards. Actually this had been more of a pious hope than a cunning plan. It was well known that as a foe, Saladin was not to be easily fooled.

'Is it time to give our knights something else to do?' asked the weapons master.

'Yes, but they must remain on high alert, because there may be another opportunity,' Arn replied without revealing either disappointment or hope in his voice.

The weapons master nodded and hurried off.

'Come on!' said Arn to Armand, leading him out on the breastwork next to the tower by the city gate so that they ended up standing immediately below the colours of the Knights Templar and in full view of the enemy. Arn himself was the only white-clad knight now visible among Gaza's defenders.

'What happens now that they weren't fooled?' asked Armand.

'Saladin will first show his strength, and when that is done there will be some swordplay that is not intended to be taken seriously,' said Arn. 'We'll have a calm first day, and only one man will die.'

'Who's going to die?' asked Armand with a puzzled frown.

'A man of your own age, a man like you,' said Arn in a tone that almost sounded a bit sad. 'A brave young man who believes he'll have a chance to win great glory and perhaps for the first time take part in a great victory. A man who believes that God is with him, although God has already marked him as the one who will die today.'

Armand couldn't bring himself to ask any more about who was going to die. His lord Arn had answered him as if he were miles away in his thoughts, as if his words might mean something completely different from what they at first seemed to mean. It was the way that the exalted knight-brothers often spoke.

Soon Armand's attention was entirely absorbed by the drama outside the walls, where Saladin, exactly as Lord Arn had predicted, now showed his strength. The Mameluke cavalry paraded forward on their beautiful, lively steeds in ranks of five by five, their uniforms gleaming with gold in the sun. They shook their lances and raised their bows as they rode past the city wall by the tower gate where Arn and Armand stood. It took almost an hour to finish the parade, and even though Arn lost count towards the end, he had a good idea that the enemy cavalry was probably more than six thousand strong. It was the largest mounted army Armand had ever seen; to him it seemed utterly invincible, especially since everyone knew that these glistening gold Mamelukes were the best soldiers of the entire Saracen enemy. But his lord Arn did not seem especially worried by what he saw. And when the parade of horsemen was over he even smiled at Armand, rubbing his hands together with satisfaction. He began to loosen up his fingers as he did before practicing with the longbow that now stood inside the tower by the gate, along with a beer barrel filled with more than a hundred arrows.

'It looks good so far, Armand, don't you think?' said Arn, clearly exhilarated.

'That is the largest enemy army I've ever seen,' replied

Armand cautiously, since he certainly did not think it looked good.

'Yes, that's true,' said Arn. 'But we're not going out there to race with them across the plain as they apparently think we will. We're going to stay here inside the walls, and they'll never be able to climb over them with their horses. But Saladin hasn't shown his real force yet; this procession was mostly to keep up the morale of his own men. He will show his strength after what is coming now.'

Arn again turned to look out over the breastwork and Armand did the same. He didn't want to admit that he had no idea what was coming next, or how Saladin's force would look once he decided to show it.

What followed, however, was an entirely different sort of display of riders. The huge army had ridden off and was now busy unsaddling their mounts and pitching camp. But about fifty riders had gathered as if to launch a direct attack on the city gate. They raised their weapons, shouted their quavering battle cries, and then came riding at full gallop towards the open city gate with their bows in their hands.

There was only one spot where they could cross the moat, and that was at the city gate. The moat on the east side of the city was filled with sharpened poles pointing outward, and anyone who rode down into it at full speed would impale both himself and his horse.

But the entire group of Saracens had halted before they reached the crossing and entered into a loud discussion. Then one of them suddenly spurred his horse, riding at full speed toward the city gate, releasing the reins as he raised his bow and drew it without pausing, as almost none but Saracen riders could do. Arn stood utterly still. Armand glanced at his lord and saw him almost smiling sadly as he sighed and shook his head.

The rider down below loosed his arrow at Arn, the intended

target, the only man in a white mantle who was now visible on the walls of Gaza. The arrow whizzed past Arn's head but he didn't move a muscle.

The rider had turned just as he loosed his shot and was now on his way back at a furious speed. When he reached his comrades he was greeted with loud cries and lances that slapped him lightly on the back. Then the next rider made ready and soon came galloping up the same way as his comrade had done. He missed his shot by much more than the first archer, but he had dared to come even closer.

As the Saracen rode for his life back to the other young emirs, Arn gave Armand the order to go and fetch his bow and a few arrows from inside the tower. Armand obeyed at once and came back out of breath, carrying the bow, just as the third rider was rushing forward.

'Cover me on the left with your shield,' Arn ordered as he grabbed his bow and nocked an arrow. Armand held the shield ready; he knew that he had to wait until the rider down there came closer and prepared to shoot.

When the young Mameluke emir thundered over the covered part of the moat, dropped his reins, and drew his bow, Armand raised the shield to cover most of his master as Arn drew his longbow, aimed, and let the arrow fly.

Arn's arrow struck the foe at the base of his throat, flinging him back and down to the ground with gouts of blood spurting from his mouth. From the twitching of his body in the dust they surmised that he must have died even before he hit the ground. His horse continued without a rider straight in through the open city gate and vanished down the main street toward the fortress.

'He was the one I meant,' said Arn in a low voice to Armand, as if he felt more sorrow than triumph at having killed an enemy. 'It was written that he was the one who would die, and that he would be the only one today.'

147

'I don't understand, lord,' said Armand. 'You told me that I should always ask when I don't understand, and this is one of those times.'

'Yes, it's right for you to ask,' said Arn, leaning his bow against the stone wall. 'You have to ask about anything unfamiliar so that you can learn. It's really much better than pretending you know more than you do just because your pride forbids you from showing your ignorance. You will soon be a brother, and a brother always receives an answer from another brother, always. So this is how it is. Those young emirs know very well who I am, and that I'm a fairly good shot with a bow. So one who rides against Al Ghouti is courageous, and one who survives it has been spared by God because of his courage. Yes, that is how they think. It is most courageous to ride the third time; that's when it is decided, according to their belief. Now no one will ride a fourth time, since it's not possible to ride any closer than the first three. Anyone who does so will only die for the sake of a game. Courage, and everything that both unbelievers and believers imagine about courage, is harder to comprehend than honour. Indecision is the same as cowardice, many believe. And look how indecisive they are out there now! They wanted to taunt us, and now they're the ones who have put themselves in a most difficult position.'

'What will they do now that their comrade is dead; how will they be able to avenge him?' asked Armand.

'If they're smart they won't do anything. If they're cowardly and choose to take cover by attacking in a group all at once to bring back his body for a proper burial, then we'll kill almost all of them when our crossbowmen step forward. Order the archers to make ready!'

Armand obeyed at once, and all the sergeants who sat concealed behind the wall with their crossbows now cocked their weapons and prepared to pop up over the breastwork at the next command and send a deadly rain of bolts down on the group of cavalry if they attacked.

But the young riders seemed too indecisive to go on the attack, or perhaps they sensed that it was a trap. As the walls of Gaza looked from their vantage point, with a sparse defence of Turkish archers, it might look suspiciously simple and innocuous – just like a trap.

When the group no longer seemed eager to attack, Arn ordered the captured Mameluke horse brought out. Then he walked down the stone steps, took the horse by its reins, and led it out through the city gate. He did not stop until he reached the man he had killed. The Mamelukes sat silently watching him, tense and ready to attack, just as Armand up on the city wall was tense and ready to order forward all the crossbowmen if the cavalry decided to attack.

Arn hoisted the body of his dead foe over the saddle and tied him on carefully with the stirrup straps around one arm and one leg so that he wouldn't slip off. Then he turned the horse toward the now utterly silent group of opponents and gave the steed a quick rap on the haunches so that it set off at a trot. Arn turned on his heel and walked slowly back to the city gate, without looking back.

Nobody attacked him and nobody shot at him.

He seemed quite pleased and in a good mood when he reached Armand up on the breastwork. His weapons master had now returned from down in the fortress; he shook Arn's hand heartily and embraced him.

The Mamelukes had taken charge of their dead comrade and were now riding slowly away to bury him as their customs prescribed. Arn and the weapons master watched the departure of the gloomy company with pleased expressions on their faces.

But Armand felt like a goose; he didn't understand what his lord had done, nor did he understand the satisfaction of the two high brothers over what he regarded as a gesture of foolish bravery. It seemed to him an irresponsible way for Arn to risk his life, especially since he was responsible for all their lives.

'Forgive me, master, but I have another question,' Armand finally said after long hesitation.

'Yes?' said Arn cheerfully. 'Is there something in my behaviour that you don't understand?'

'Yes, master.'

'You think that I risked my life in a foolish way?'

'It might appear so, my lord.'

'But I did not. If they had come riding toward me to get within range, most of them would have died before they managed to nock their arrows, for they would have ridden straight into the range of the crossbows. I'm wearing a double coat of mail on my back, so their arrows would have stuck in the felt layer but not penetrated, and I would have walked through our gate looking like a hedgehog. That would have been the best turn of events, of course. But we had to be content with second best.'

'I'm still not sure I understand all this,' Armand appealed to him, while the two knight-brothers gave him a paternal smile.

'Our enemies this time are the Mamelukes,' explained the weapons master. 'You, who will soon be a brother among us, Armand, must learn to know them especially well, both their strength and their weakness. Their strength is their riding skill and bravery, and their weakness is in their mind. They believe in spirits and the wandering of the soul from one body to the next and even to stones in the desert; they believe that a man's courage is his true soul, and many other things. They believe that he who displays the most courage will be the one who is victorious in war.'

'I see,' said Armand, abashed. But they could see that he was still brooding.

'For them the number 3 is sacred in war,' Arn went on to explain. 'In a way that makes sense: it's the third blow in a swordfight that is the most dangerous. But now their third rider has died. Now the enemy they call Al Ghouti showed greater courage than they did, so I will win the war and not Saladin, and that rumour will spread throughout their encampment tonight.'

'But what if they had come riding toward you when you were standing out there, master?'

'Then most of them would have been killed. And the few who escaped would have seen that I was struck time after time without dying, so they would have spread the legend of my invulnerability tonight. I'm not sure which would have been better. But now it's time for Saladin's next move, which we will witness before nightfall.'

Arn, who no longer thought there was any danger of an enemy attack, sent off more than half the defenders from up on the walls to rest and eat. He himself went back through the streets of Gaza and into the fortress to sing vespers and pray with the knights before it was time for the evening meal. Then half of the force would rest while the other half remained on guard. Gaza's gates still stood provocatively open, but there was no indication that Saladin was preparing to storm them.

Instead, in the late evening the enemy came forward with engineers and labourers and carts loaded with wheels, rough beams, and rope. They began to assemble their catapults that would soon begin launching huge blocks of stone at Gaza's walls.

Arn stood pondering the scene from up on the breastwork; he had come as soon as he got word of the siege machines. It looked as though things were calm over in the enemy's camp, where thousands of fires burned around the tents and the men were obviously eating and drinking.

It looked as though Saladin had left his precious siege machines and engineers with much too small a guard, almost no cavalry and only about a hundred infantry.

If that was really true, it was a golden opportunity. If Saladin had known that there were eighty Templar knights inside the fortress, he never would have dared leave his workers so unprotected. If Arn ordered his men out in a massed attack now, they could burn down and destroy the siege machines and kill the engineers. But in the dark it would also be possible to hold a large force of Mameluke cavalry in readiness without being seen from the city walls. And much could be said about the enemy's most dangerous commander, but certainly not that he was stupid.

Arn ordered the drawbridge raised and the gates to the city closed. The first day of war, which had been more a war of minds than out on the battlefield, was over. Neither had fooled the other, and only one man had fallen. Nothing was decided. Arn went inside, prepared to sleep for many hours, since he suspected that this would probably be his last chance to get a good night's sleep for a long time to come.

He went back up on the walls after *matins*. When the light of dawn slowly changed from an impenetrable black to a gray haze, he discovered the huge army waiting down in a low-lying area to the right of the siege machines, where hammers still pounded indefatigably. It was just as he had thought: there was a cavalry force of at least a thousand men. If he had sent out his knights to destroy the siege machines, succumbing to the temptation that Saladin had presented to him, they would have all died. He smiled at the thought that it must have been a hard night for the enemy riders, having to keep their horses quiet as they waited for the drawbridge to be lowered at any moment so that two columns of white-clad enemy could ride out to their deaths.

He thought that whatever he did in the future, as much future as he now had left in life, he would never underestimate Saladin.

The guard was changing. Stiff and weary archers began descending from the breastwork as the new, fresh forces climbed up, greeting their brothers and taking over their weapons.

Arn's only clear intention was to delay Saladin as long as possible in Gaza. Then Jerusalem and God's Holy Grave might be saved from the unbelievers. It was a very simple plan – very simple to describe in words, at least.

But if it succeeded then he and all the knight-brothers in Gaza would be dead within a month. He had never viewed death this way before, so close and so clear. He had been wounded in battle many times but so far had been lucky. He had ridden with lance lowered into an enemy force that was superior in numbers more times than he could remember. But he had never been in a situation where he could foresee his own death. In some way he couldn't explain, he had always known that he would survive every battle. He hadn't taken any special consolation from the promise that he would go to Paradise after death, because he never believed that he would die. He wasn't going to die, that was never the intention. He would live twenty years as a Templar knight and he would return home to the woman to whom he had promised his heart, making the vow on his honour and on his blessed sword. He couldn't break his word, after all; surely it could not be God's intention for him to break his word.

Now, as he stood up on the breastwork in the rising light of dawn, Arn saw that the trap that Saladin had laid was taking shape. What had at first seemed an illusion was slowly being transmuted to reality – from the sound of snorting horses in the darkness and an occasional clinking stirrup to gold uniforms that began to glimmer in the first rays of the sun.

And he saw for the first time his own death. Gaza could not withstand such a large siege army for more than about a month. That was utterly certain, based on the deeds of men and discounting any miracle from God. But they could not expect a miracle; God was unyielding with his believers.

He could see Cecilia before him. He saw her walking toward the gate of Gudhem; he had turned around in tears before she vanished through the gate. That life was so different from his life now, after he'd spent such a long time in the Holy Land; those days seemed as if they'd never really existed. 'God, why did You send me here, what did You want with a lone knight, and why don't You ever answer me?' he thought.

He was embarrassed at once to be thinking this way about God, who heard all thoughts. He should not be so vain as to put his own interests before the great cause – he was a Templar knight after all. It was a long time since he had been affected by such weakness, and he sincerely prayed for forgiveness, on his knees by the breastwork as the sun rose over the enemy army, spreading its radiance upon weapons and pennants.

After his prayer at dawn Arn consulted with the weapons master and the six squadron leaders among the knights.

It was clear that Saladin had tried to lure them into a trap during the night. But it was also clear that it would be a very good thing if they could launch a successful sortie and demolish or burn the siege engines. Gaza's walls would not withstand an onslaught of stone blocks and Greek fire for very long. Then all the men, women, children, and livestock would have to retreat, crowding into the fortress itself.

Saladin didn't know how many knights there were behind the walls. His riders had never seen more than a squadron of sixteen men. And since no sortie had ventured out on the first night when it would have seemed most tempting, Saladin might still believe that the force of knights was far too weak for such an attack. So they ought to strike in the middle of the day, during work or midday prayers, just when the enemy decided that such an attack would not be forthcoming. The question was only how much such an action would cost in fallen brothers, and whether it was worth the price.

The weapons master thought they had a good chance. The siege engines were close to the city walls and downhill. If the attack came unexpectedly, the damage could be done before the enemy gathered themselves for a counterattack. Yes, they did have a good chance of setting fire to the siege engines. It would probably cost the lives of twenty brothers. According to the weapons master, that price was worth paying, since those twenty lives would extend the siege by at least a month, and thus Jerusalem would be saved.

Arn agreed, and all the others nodded their approval. Arn then decided that he would lead the attack himself, the weapons master would take over command inside Gaza, and all the brothers would participate, even those who normally would have been spared because of minor injuries. If they began preparing leather sacks filled with tar and Greek fire this morning, the attack could be carried out at the very hottest hour of midday, when the unbelievers were praying. As the others made ready, Arn returned to the walls to show himself to both the defenders and the enemy. As soon as he got there he ordered the city gate to be opened and the draw-bridge lowered. When this was done, it caused a great stir in the enemy camp, but when nothing further happened they all returned to their work.

Arn took a turn along the city walls, which in both the north and south were protected by the fortress and the harbour. In the western part of the city the moats were deep and filled with sea water. That was Gaza's strong point, and no attack would take place there in the early part of the siege. The weakest parts were far to the east around the city gate, and where Saladin had chosen to construct his catapults. The great cavalry army was no danger as long as the walls held; the Mamelukes would just get more and more impatient the longer they had to wait with nothing to do. The most important part of the battle would take place around the city gate, between Gaza's archers and Saladin's infantry and sappers. The enemy would attempt to cross the moat and reach the walls in order to undermine them and crack them with fire, thus causing a breach that would allow the cavalry to get inside the walls. Arn knew very well what to expect; soon the stench of all the dead Saracens around the walls would hang like a pall of smoke from roasting meat over all of Gaza. Fortunately the wind was mostly westerly and would blow it toward the enemy. But it was still a race against time. If the besiegers wanted to knock down the walls, they would eventually succeed. No relief could be expected from Jerusalem or from Ashkelon to the north along the coast. Gaza was entirely left to God's mercy.

At midday, Arn's most beloved horse Khamsiin was led up to the city gate, saddled and covered with a coat of felt and chain mail along its sides. The attack that was imminent would be considerably more dangerous for the horses than for their riders, but he had chosen Khamsiin because mobility and speed were more crucial than a heavy frontal assault. Their paths would soon part in one way or another, and it was of minor importance which of them died first.

Inside the gate of the fortress the entire contingent of knights made ready to launch the attack. They said their last prayers because they knew that many of the brothers would die; in the worst case almost all of them would perish, if they had miscalculated, if the enemy saw through the plan, or if God so willed it.

But what Arn saw as he stood in his usual spot did not

indicate that the enemy suspected any danger. There were no large groups of cavalry anywhere near. Far in the distance a large force was conducting an exercise, and down in the camp most of the horses seemed to be penned in, grazing. There could not be any hidden forces anywhere else in the vicinity, for in daylight the view was good. This was really the right moment to attack.

He knelt down and prayed to God for support in this reckless endeavour, which might result in losing everything, but might also save God's Grave for the believers. He placed his life in God's hands and took a deep breath. Then he stood up to give the order to attack and go down to the impatiently waiting Khamsiin, who was being held with some difficulty by a stable boy. Khamsiin could feel that something major and fateful was at hand; Arn could tell by the way his steed was moving.

Then he saw a group of riders approaching the gate of Gaza in tight formation and bearing Saladin's colours. They stopped a short distance from the moat and lined up in a row, and a single rider with lowered flag rode forward as a sign that he wanted to parley. Arn quickly gave the order that the rider was not to be fired on.

He ran down the stairs from the tower by the city gate, leaped up on Khamsiin, and galloped out through the gate, stopping in front of the emir who had ridden forward, within easy range of the archers on the walls. The Egyptian rider now lowered his flag almost to the ground and bowed his head as Arn approached.

'I greet you in the name of God, most benevolent and ever-merciful, you, Al Ghouti, who speaks the language of God,' said the negotiator when Arn rode up to his side.

'I greet you also with God's peace,' replied Arn impatiently. 'What is your message and from whom?'

'My message is from . . . he asked me to say only Yussuf,

although his names and titles are many. The men you see behind me are prepared to offer themselves as hostages during the time the negotiation is under way.'

'Wait here, I will come back at once with an escort,' Arn commanded, wheeling Khamsiin around and galloping back in through the city gate.

When he was out of sight, he reined in Khamsiin and walked him slowly down the cleared street towards the gate of the fortress. Inside sat the eighty mounted knights, ready to attack. If they struck now, the surprise would be great. They would hardly have another chance to burn and destroy the siege engines.

There were Christians who said that they could not win against Saracens by using deceit, since deceit could not exist between believers and unbelievers. Such a promise, according to this school of thought, would be worth nothing. Arn had entered into negotiation, and that was the same as a promise. But disagreement was great on this matter. Hadn't he a short time ago been in complete agreement with Jerusalem's Master that the word he had given to Saladin by the rocky shore of the Dead Sea must be honoured?

Was it not pride to set the value of his own honour so high? Balanced in the other pan on the scale might be Jerusalem and God's Holy Grave. A broken word, a single brief moment of deception on his part could possibly save the holy city.

No, he thought. Such a deception would only gain time. Destroyed siege engines could be replaced. The promise of his word could never be undone.

He gave the order to open the fortress gate, rode inside, and summoned the first squadron among the waiting knight-brothers to come with him. He ordered the others to dismount and rest, for he was convinced that Saladin was not preparing a deception.

Arn rode out at a brisk trot at the head of his squadron, with his *confanonier* bearing the flag of the Knights Templar at his side, up through Gaza and out the city gate. As he neared the waiting Saracen flag-bearer he commanded the whole squadron to form a straight line, and their opponents did the same. The two groups of riders approached each other slowly until they were a few lance-lengths apart. Then a group of five riders from the other side broke off and began moving toward Arn, who in turn countered their movement and rode with only his *confanonier* at his side toward the approaching hostages until the two groups met.

Among the hostages he recognized at once Saladin's younger brother Fahkr, but the other emirs were unknown to him. He greeted Fahkr, who returned his greeting.

'So we see each other sooner than we expected, you and I, Fahkr,' said Arn.

'This is true, Al Ghouti, and we meet under circumstances that none of us would have wanted. But He who sees all and He who knows all willed it otherwise.'

Arn merely nodded in agreement, and then he declined to keep any hostages other than Fahkr. He ordered Armand at his side to see to it that this man was treated as an honoured guest in every respect, but he should not be shown too much of their defences or the number of white-clad knights.

With that Fahkr rode past Arn, who in turn rode into the group of waiting Mamelukes. The Templar knights formed an escort around Fahkr and the Mamelukes around Arn, and thus the two groups rode away from each other in opposite directions.

Saladin honoured his foe with greater gestures than was proper for a man who was master of only a single fortress. A thousand riders formed two columns alongside Arn the last stretch of the way toward Saladin's tent, and not a single scornful remark was uttered during this short ride.

Outside the commander's tent stood two rows of Saladin's security guard, forming a path with swords and lances to the very opening of the tent. Arn dismounted and one of the guards hurried to take Khamsiin by the reins and lead him away. Arn did not bow and showed no expression as he now unbuckled his sword as custom demanded, handing it over to the man he judged to be of highest rank in the guard. But he was met only by a bow and the explanation that he could put his sword back on. This surprised Arn, but he did as he was told.

Wearing his sword again at his side he entered the tent. When he came into the dim light, Saladin stood up at once and hurried to meet him, taking both his hands as if old friends and not enemies were meeting.

They then greeted each other with greater heartiness than any of the other men in the tent had expected, for when Arn's eyes got used to the gloom he saw astonished faces. Saladin showed him to a place on the floor in the centre of the tent, where a camel saddle decorated with gold and silver and precious stones stood next to another just like it. They bowed to each other and sat down, as the other men sat down on mats along the walls.

'If God had brought us together at a different moment, then you and I would have had much to discuss, Al Ghouti,' said Saladin.

'Yes, but at this meeting with you, al Malik an-Nasir, "the victorious king" as you are also called, you have brought your cavalry and siege engines to my fortress. So I'm afraid that our conversation will be quite brief.'

'Do you want to hear my terms?'

'Yes. I come to decline your terms, but respect demands that I listen to them in any case. Tell them to me now, without evasion, for neither of us believes he can fool the other with sweet and guileful words.'

160

'I give to you and your men, your Frankish men, safe passage. But not to those traitors to the true faith and the *jihad* who are working for you for silver. You may all ride out without a single arrow being loosed upon you. You are free to ride wherever you like, to Ashkelon or Jerusalem or to one of your fortresses farther up in Palestine or Syria. Those are my terms.'

'I cannot accept your terms; as I said, this will be a brief negotiation,' replied Arn.

'Then you will all die, and a warrior such as yourself should know that, Al Ghouti. You of all people should know. My high opinion of you – you alone, and for reasons that only you and I know but no one else in this room – requires me to make you this good offer which my emirs find entirely unnecessary. The rules say that he who refuses such an offer cannot expect any quarter if he is defeated.'

'I know that, Yussuf,' said Arn keenly aware that he was addressing the greatest commander of the faithful solely by his first name, 'I know that. I know the rules as well as you do. You must now take Gaza by force, and we will have to defend ourselves until we can do so no longer. And those of us who afterwards, wounded or not, become your prisoners cannot expect anything other than death. I don't think we have anything else to say to each other now, Yussuf.'

'At least tell me why you are making such a foolish decision,' said Saladin, his face almost contorted with sorrow. 'I don't want to see you die, and you know that. Therefore I have given you an opportunity that no one but you would have been given when our force is so much stronger than yours, as you have seen. Why are you doing this when you could save all your men whom you now doom to death?'

'Because there is something greater to save,' said Arn. 'I believe, as you do, that if you stay here in Gaza and lay siege to us, you can defeat us in a month and I will end up dying here, unless God wills it otherwise and sends us salvation of a miraculous nature. But so be it.'

'But why, Al Ghouti, why?' persisted Saladin, obviously distressed. 'I am giving you your life, and you refuse to accept it. I give you your men's lives, and you choose to sacrifice them. Why?'

'It's not so hard to figure out, Yussuf, and I believe that you do understand,' replied Arn, suddenly feeling a faint hope begin to glimmer inside him. 'You can take Gaza, I believe you. But it will cost you half your army and it will cost you much time. And in that case I die not for any small cause; I die for the only thing I truly must die for, and you know very well what I'm talking about. I don't want your mercy to save my life. I would rather die if my death will cause your army to shrink to a size that makes it impossible for you to proceed. Now I have told you why.'

'Then we have nothing more to say to each other,' Saladin agreed, nodding sadly. 'May you go with the peace of God and say your prayers this day. Tomorrow there will be no more peace.'

'I too leave you in God's peace,' said Arn, getting up and bowing deeply and respectfully to Saladin before he turned and left the tent.

On his way back to the city gate he met Saladin's brother Fahkr, who reined in his horse and asked how things now stood. Arn replied that he had said no to Saladin's offer, which, he had to admit, had been less harsh than he might have expected.

Fahkr shook his head and muttered that he had told his brother the exact same thing, that even the most generous proposal would be met with a flat refusal.

'I say farewell to you now, Al Ghouti, and know that I, like my brother, feel sorrow for what now must come to pass,' said Fahkr.

'I feel the same way, Fahkr,' said Arn. 'One of us will die, it seems. But only God knows which one of us it will be.'

They bowed to each other in silence since there was nothing more to say, and then they each rode slowly away in opposite directions, pondering.

As Arn neared the city gate, he harboured a bright hope that Saladin might have been so humiliated in front of his own emirs when his generosity was contemptuously refused that now he would have to eradicate the affront by truly taking Gaza. That, in turn, would prevent him from continuing on toward Jerusalem. But it was true, as Saladin had said, that such an action would lead to the eventual death of all men at arms within Gaza's walls, and of all the infidels who worked for the Christians – including Arn himself. It was a certainty imbued with sorrow, because the thought that he'd had ever more often in recent years of one day returning home now seemed impossible. He was going to die in Gaza. But his joy was greater than his sorrow, because he would die to save God's Grave and Holy Jerusalem. That much was crystal clear. He could have died in any minor battle with less important foes in the past years, and it would have made no difference at all in the Holy Land. But now God had granted him and his brothers the grace of dying for Jerusalem. In truth it was a worthy cause, a favour that was granted to few Templar knights.

He would do as Saladin suggested, spend the evening and the night in prayers of thanksgiving. All his knights would have to prepare by taking Holy Communion before the next day dawned.

The following morning Saladin's army broke camp and set off in column after column north along the coast in the direction of Ashkelon. They did not leave even a small siege force behind.

The populace of Gaza stood on the city walls and watched the enemy moving off. They thanked their gods, which were seldom the true God, and they moved in long queues past Arn, bowing to the knight who stood up by the tower at the city gate. He was filled with ambiguous feelings, but the people wanted to thank him for their salvation. A rumour had spread through the city that the master of the fortress had somehow managed to scare Saladin with magic tricks or by threatening vengeance from the evil friends of the Knights Templar, the Assassins. It was a rumour that caused Arn to snort when he heard it, but he made no effort to refute the lies.

His disappointment was greater than his relief. Saladin's army, which had gone unchallenged, was now large enough to take Ashkelon, a city far more important than Gaza. And many more Christian lives were sure to be lost. In the worst case, Saladin's army was even large enough to take Jerusalem.

So Arn felt more like a failure than a victor. Nor was there any wise choice to make when it came to Gaza's force of knights. First they needed to know what was happening to the north, perhaps wait for orders that would soon arrive by sea. With good winds it didn't take many hours to sail from Ashkelon to Gaza.

While waiting for the right time to make such momentous decisions, Arn applied himself to a multitude of smaller problems. All the refugees who had taken shelter behind Gaza's walls now had to be sent back to their villages as soon as possible. They needed to start rebuilding as much as they could before the winter rains came. They also had to be supplied with livestock and grain for bread so that they could resume the routines of their everyday lives. For a day and a half he busied himself mostly with these matters, working together with his head of ordnance and his scribes.

But on the second day a messenger came sailing into the

harbour, giving Arn a reason to summon all the high brothers to the *parlatorium* at once.

The young leprous king of Jerusalem, Baldwin IV, had ventured out with the cavalry force he had scraped together – 500 knights, no more – from Jerusalem toward Ashkelon to meet the enemy on the open field. It was not a very wise thing to do; the flat landscape around Ashkelon was all too well suited to Mameluke warriors. It would have been better to concentrate on defence at the walls of Jerusalem.

When the Christians discovered what a superior force they would have to face, they hurried to flee behind the walls of Ashkelon, and there they now sat, trapped inside. Saladin had left a siege force to keep them in place. In the flat land-scape around the city the Mameluke riders would have no difficulty destroying a heavily armoured force of knights, which was also much smaller than their own.

For his part, Arn did not need to worry over what to do. Among the men in the royal army behind the walls of Ashkelon was the Grand Master of the Knights Templar, Odo de Saint Amand, and from him now came a direct written order.

Arn was to set off toward Ashkelon with all haste, bringing his knights and at least a hundred sergeants. They would ride with heavy arms, and without infantry to protect the horses, and they would attack the siege force one hour before sundown on the following day. When Arn's attack came, the army trapped in Ashkelon would simultaneously emerge from inside, and the siege army would be caught in a pincer move-ment between two shields. That was the whole plan. But it was an order from the Grand Master, so there was nothing to discuss.

Nevertheless Arn made one decision on his own; he would take with him his mounted Bedouins as spies. He would be venturing into territory that was controlled by the superior number of enemy cavalry, and the only protection he would have was reliable information about where it would be safe to ride and where it would be foolish to go. The Bedouins could acquire such information with both their camels and their fast horses; no one who saw Bedouins from a distance could say for sure which side they were fighting for, and it was seldom worthwhile trying to catch them to find out what they knew. Arn saw to it that Gaza's Bedouins were well paid in silver before it was time to set off, but more important than silver was the knowledge he imparted to them that this time there would be much to plunder. This was true no matter how things went, because now the Templar knights were riding without caution, and without infantry that could protect their horses from sudden attack by Turkish archers. Now they were riding to victory or to death; there was no other choice. Time was too short, and they were too outnumbered to worry about caution.

The Bedouins fanned out before the advancing column of Templar knights from Gaza. The first of them came riding back in a cloud of dust at top speed even before they were halfway to Ashkelon. Out of breath, he related that in the next village he had seen four Mameluke horses tied outside some clay huts. The village looked deserted, and it was hard to say what the knights were doing inside such miserable dwellings, but the horses were there in any case. Around the village lay a number of goats and sheep that had been shot with arrows.

At first Arn didn't want to waste his time on four enemy soldiers, but then Guido de Faramond his weapons master, rode up and pointed out that they could be scouts from the Egyptian siege force, and that these scouts might not be tending to their duties as well as they should. If they took the soldiers by surprise, they would be unable to sound the alarm about the approaching danger from the south.

Arn agreed with this argument at once and thanked his weapons master for not hesitating to give his opinion. Then he divided his force into four columns, which were soon heading for the village from four directions. By the time they got close enough to see the group of clay huts, they had already passed a number of dead goats and sheep, just as the Bedouin had said. Finally, the four columns of knights merged together just outside the apparently empty village and encircled it. In silence they approached. When they got nearer they could hear what was going on, because two or three women's voices were emitting heartrending wails. Outside the hut where the atrocities were taking place, four Egyptian horses with expensive saddle tack stood shaking their heads at all the flies.

Arn pointed to a squadron of knights who dismounted, quietly drew their swords, and went inside. The noise of a brief fight was heard, and then the four Egyptians were cast out into the dust and tied up with their hands behind their backs. Their clothing was in disarray and they tried to shout something about how they were worth a ransom if they were allowed to live.

Arn got down from his horse and went over to the entrance of the hut, as his knights came out, their faces pale. He stepped inside and saw roughly what he had expected. There were three women. Their faces were bleeding, but none of them seemed to have suffered any mortal injury. They hid themselves with the clothes the Egyptians had ripped from their bodies.

'What is this village called and to whom do you belong, women?' asked Arn. At first he got no sensible answer because only one of the women seemed to speak understandable Arabic.

After a halting exchange of words he gathered that both the women and the livestock came from a village that actually belonged to Gaza, but the three women had moved their animals after they were refused entry into the fortress. They had taken their sheep and goats away from one plunderer only to run right into the arms of one that was even worse.

Since their honour and that of their families had now been offended, there was only one way to redress the wrong, reasoned Arn, once the women had calmed down a bit and understood that he had no intention of continuing what the Egyptians had started. So he would leave the four bound rapists where they were, and the violated women could do with them as they saw fit to avenge their honour. They could also keep the horses and saddles as a gift from Gaza. But he asked them not to release the Egyptians alive, because he would prefer to see them beheaded. The Palestinian women swore that none of the rapists would be allowed to live, and Arn was content with that. He went outside, mounted Khamsiin, and commanded a new tight formation to continue on towards Ashkelon. They would attack one hour before sundown, regardless of whether they had time to prepare or not, because that was the order from the Grand Master himself.

When they had ridden a way off, desperate screams were heard from the captive Egyptians. No one turned around in the saddle to look back; no one said a word.

As they neared Ashkelon their approach still seemed to have gone unnoticed. Either they'd had the improbable luck to pass through the enemy's chain of scouts at the place where those four rapists, now dead, were supposed to stand guard. Or else the Mother of God had led them by the hand.

Now several other Bedouin spies came riding up and began talking all at once about how the enemy had taken up position outside Ashkelon. Arn got down from his horse and smoothed out some sand with the tip of his iron-clad boot, pulled out his dagger, and began to draw Ashkelon and its walls in the sand. Soon he had deciphered the Bedouins' reports and knew how the Mameluke siege force was deployed.

There were two possible choices. Since the woods grew close to Ashkelon, they could get nearer to the enemy if they attacked from the east. With luck they could get within the distance of two long arrow shots before the attack would have to be launched with full force and speed. However then they would be attacking with the setting sun directly in their eyes.

The second possibility was to move in a wide arc towards the northeast and then west and south. Then they would be coming from the north and avoid having the sun in their eyes. But the risk of discovery would be greater. Arn decided that they should wait where they were and spend the remaining hour before the attack in prayer instead of moving on and risking discovery. They would just have to endure having the setting sun in their eyes during the attack. The enemy's numbers were ten times their own, so everything depended on surprise, speed, and the force of the first assault.

After their prayers they rode as quietly and slowly as they could through the thinning woods that stuck out like a tongue towards Ashkelon. Arn signalled his men to halt when he could no longer ride any farther without being seen. The weapons master walked his horse cautiously up alongside him, and they sat in silence for a while, observing the enemy encampment stretching all the way along the eastern wall of Ashkelon. Most of the horses were in large pens out on the flanks, farther away from the city wall than the rest of the siege force. That told them much. It took no time or rumination to know how the attack would proceed. Arn called over his eight squadron leaders and gave them several curt orders. When they had all returned to their places and mounted up, the men prayed together one last time to the High Protectress of the Knights Templar and unfurled Her standard, which was brought to the vanguard next to Arn and raised along with the black-and-white flag of the Knights Templar.

'*Deus vult*! God wills it!' shouted Arn as loud as he could, and his cry was repeated instantly back along the whole column.

Arn and the knights closest to him on either side slowly began to move forwards as those further back trotted up and out to both sides in orderly fashion. When the Templar knights now emerged from the woods it looked as though their centre was standing almost still while two mighty wings of white-clad and black-clad knights were unfolded on both sides. When the whole force was arrayed in a straight line, the thunder of the horses' hooves rose to a mighty rumble as they all increased their speed to a gallop over the last stretch of ground before crashing into the entire length of the enemy camp.

Few enemy soldiers had managed to mount their horses, and they were the first targets of the attacking Templar knights. At the same time the horse pens of the Mamelukes were attacked out on the flanks and the fences were trampled flat, while the enemy's horses were stuck with lances so they would panic and direct their wild flight in toward the camp. The area soon became a chaos of panic-stricken horses and Mameluke soldiers running for their weapons or trying to escape the heavy cavalry of the enemy among collapsing tents and cooking fires that spread embers and sparks in every direction as they were overrun by the horses.

The gates of Ashkelon had been opened, and from there the king's secular army now attacked from two directions toward the centre of the besiegers' camp. When Arn saw this he yelled to Armand de Gascogne to ride straight south with the flag so that all the Templar knights would follow along in that manoeuvre and make room for the royal army.

Soon the Templar knights were in tight formation and riding forward in a long phalanx right through the enemy army, slashing and jabbing and trampling everything in their path. The enemy soldiers never managed to recover from their fright and surprise, so they never understood that they were being attacked by such a small force. Because few of the Mamelukes had managed to mount their horses, they didn't have a good overview, and so it might seem that an utterly superior enemy was leading the onslaught.

The battle turned into a bloodbath that went on until long after sundown. More than two hundred captives were then led in through the gates of Ashkelon, and the battlefield was left to the darkness and the Bedouins, who now appeared out of nowhere like vast numbers of vultures. The Christians closed the city gates behind them as if they wanted to spare themselves the sight of what would now take place all night long out there in the torchlight.

In the city's largest market square Arn arrayed his troops and took roll call, squadron by squadron. Four men were missing. Considering the size of their victory that was a very low price, but the important thing for the moment was to find the fallen or wounded brothers. He quickly put together a squadron of sixteen men and sent them out with spare horses to collect the missing brothers for care or for Christian burial.

Then he went to the small quarter of the city reserved for the Knights Templar and examined his wounds, which were mostly scratches and bruises. He washed himself and asked where he could find the Grand Master. He found him waiting in the chapel dedicated to the Mother of God and together they offered prayers of thanksgiving because God and His Mother had given them a glorious victory. Afterwards they went out to talk with each other.

They went up on the breastwork and sat down a short

distance from the nearest guard post so that they would be undisturbed. Down below them in the city the victory celebration was in full swing except in the Templar quarter and in the grain store that had been put at the brothers' disposal for the night. In those two buildings it was quiet and dark except for individual candles where they were tending to each other's wounds.

'Saladin may be a great commander, but he couldn't have grasped how many of you there were down in Gaza, or he wouldn't have been content to leave barely two thousand men here to watch Ashkelon,' observed Odo de Saint Amand. That was the first thing he said to Arn, as there was not much need to discuss the day's victory.

'All the knights stayed inside the fortress when he came to Gaza. There were only two of us with white mantles up on the breastwork,' Arn explained. 'But he has more than five thousand Mameluke cavalry left. How are things in Jerusalem?'

'The king's army is here in Ashkelon, as you can see. In Jerusalem, Arnoldo has two hundred knights and four or five hundred sergeants, and that is all, I'm afraid.'

'Then we'll have to attack and disrupt Saladin's army as soon as we regain our strength. And that will be tomorrow,' said Arn tersely.

'Tomorrow we probably won't have the king's army with us, since they'll still be recovering from the after-effects of this evening. Not from the battlefield, for they didn't have to do much before we were victorious, but from tonight's celebrating,' Odo de Saint Amand said fiercely.

'We won and they're celebrating the victory. So we're dividing the labour, as usual,' muttered Arn, at the same time smiling at his high protector. 'By the way, I think it best if we do not proceed too hastily. If we're lucky, not a single one of the vanquished soldiers trying to flee will make it through the Bedouins' lines out there, so it will be a while before Saladin finds out what happened. That would be to our great advantage.'

'We'll see tomorrow,' nodded Odo, getting up. Arn also stood up to receive the Grand Master's embrace and kisses, first on the left and then on the right cheek.

'I bless you, Arn de Gothia,' said the Grand Master solemnly as he held Arn by the shoulders and looked him in the eye. 'You can't imagine how it feels to stand up there on the wall and see our men come out in an attack as if there were two thousand of us and not three hundred. I had promised the secular army and the king that you would arrive at the appointed time, and you kept your promise. It was a great victory, but we have a long way to go.'

'Yes, Grand Master,' said Arn quietly. 'This victory is already forgotten. What we have before us is a very large Mameluke army. May God protect us yet again.'

The Grand Master released Arn and took a step backwards. Arn fell to his knees at once and bowed his head as his most exalted leader disappeared into the darkness along the rampart of the fortress.

Arn rose to his feet and stood alone for a moment, looking out beyond the wall and listening to the occasional screams from the wounded. His whole body was aching, but it was a lovely warm and throbbing ache and except for a scratch along one cheek he was not bleeding. As usual, he felt the most pain in his knees, which had to absorb the impact when he rode into an enemy host on horseback or struck down a soldier by riding right over him.

In the days that followed, not much happened at Ashkelon. The Mameluke prisoners were chained and set to work digging graves for their dead comrades out on the battlefield. Now and then small groups of Bedouins would bring in new captives to sell, dragging them behind their camels.

The Bedouins also brought news of Saladin's army. Contrary to what the Templars had expected, Saladin had not moved off towards Jerusalem; instead he had loosed the reins on his army and let them plunder the entire countryside between Ashkelon and Jerusalem. Perhaps he thought that it was better to plunder now, before his glorious victory. He was obviously confident that they would encounter no enemies out in the field; he knew that the enemy forces were safely bottled up inside their fortresses and behind the city walls of Ashkelon and Jerusalem. Once the hunger to pillage had been quelled in his army, he could take Jerusalem without risk that the holy city would be desecrated after his conquest. No matter what the reason for his course of action, this was still a mistake that he would regret in ten years' time.

In the fortress at Ashkelon a war council was held. King Baldwin sat in a litter chair covered in blue muslin so that from the outside he could be seen only in silhouette. It was whispered that his hands were beginning to rot away and that he would soon go completely blind.

By the king's right side sat Grand Master Odo de Saint Amand, and behind him Arn and the two fortress masters from Toron des Chevaliers and Castel Arnald. At the king's other side sat the bishop of Bethlehem, and along the walls of the hall sat the Palestinian barons with whom the king had allied himself in his desperate attempts to wage war. Behind the bishop hung the True Cross, decorated with gold, silver, and precious stones.

The Christians had never lost a battle when they carried with them the True Cross into the field, so it was precisely this question that took up the most time and was considered the most important.

Carrying the True Cross, on which Our Saviour had suffered and died for the sins of man, into a battle that could not be won was to show irreverence, a sin comparable to blasphemy, in the opinion of the brothers Baldwin and Balian d'Ibelin, who were the most distinguished of the barons in the hall.

To that the bishop of Bethlehem replied that nothing could more plainly express the prayer for a miracle from God than to take along the True Cross when only a miracle from God could ensure their salvation.

Balian d'Ibelin said that as he understood it, one could not negotiate with God by using coercion, the way one negotiated with an inferior enemy. In the impending battle the Christians in the best case could hope to disrupt Saladin for an extended period. Then the autumn rains would transform the hills around Jerusalem to a cold, red field of clay with wet snow and strong winds, so that the siege would be halted for reasons other than the defenders' bravery and good faith.

The bishop opined that he was probably the one in the hall who fully understood how to talk to God, and he therefore refused more advice from laymen in this matter. The True Cross would be their salvation in a battle that could not be won unless God granted them a miracle. What other relic in the whole world could be more powerful than the True Cross?

Arn and his two fortress master brothers never said a word during this argument. For Arn's part, this was partly because he had to remain silent when the Grand Master himself represented the Templar order. Besides, his two brothers were higher in rank than he was. But even if he were asked his opinion, he would have been hard pressed to answer, since he was inclined to think the bishop was wrong and the knight of Ibelin was right.

In the end it was the young leprous king who decided the dispute. He took the bishop's side during the second day of discussion, at the very moment when everyone in the hall had begun to feel despair that they were all wasting their time talking instead of acting. The smoke from campfires had already spread across the horizon to the east.

Saladin's army had first headed north toward Ibelin; his soldiers took the city and laid waste to it, then swung to the east and Jerusalem. From the smoke from the fires and from occasional refugees that arrived they deduced that the Egyptian troops had dispersed throughout the areas surrounding Ramle and were now plundering and destroying everything in their path. Ramle was the property of the brothers d'Ibelin, and they demanded to go in the vanguard of the secular army because they had the most to avenge. The king granted their request at once.

It was obvious who would lead the Templar knights, since Grand Master Odo de Saint Amand was in Ashkelon. But then he summoned the three knight-brothers of fortress master rank that were in Ashkelon – besides Arn from Gaza, the two masters of Castel Arnald and Toron des Chevaliers were Siegfried de Turenne and Arnoldo de Aragon. The matter immediately became more complicated. The Grand Master said that he would accompany the True Cross, and the standard of the Knights Templar with the image of God's Mother, in the centre of the army. He would take along a guard of twenty knights for this task.

Consequently one of the three fortress masters had to take command of the combined force of Templar knights. According to the rules, in that case it should be the master of Toron des Chevaliers, Arnoldo de Aragon, since he was the eldest of the three. Next in rank stood the master of Castel Arnald, Siegfried de Turenne, and third came Arn de Gothia. Yet God's Mother had so clearly held Her protective hand over Arn when he attacked and conquered the Mameluke siege army which was many times larger, so it would be an affront to Her demonstrated favour not to give Arn de Gothia this command.

The three fortress masters accepted their Grand Master's

instructions and bowed in acknowledgment that they would obey without question. The Grand Master left them alone then to attend to their own planning.

They took seats in a small and very simply furnished *parlatorium* in the quarter of the Knights Templar in Ashkelon. There was a moment's silence before anyone spoke.

'It is said that our Grand Master is fond of you, Arn de Gothia, and it seems to me that he showed as much in his decision,' muttered Arnoldo de Aragon peevishly.

'That may be true. Perhaps it is also true that it might have been wiser to assign one of you the command, since your fortresses are located in the region you know best, and there we will meet Saladin,' replied Arn, speaking slowly, as if weighing his words carefully.

After a moment of cold silence he went on, 'But tomorrow all three of us may be riding to our death. Nothing could be worse than allowing our thoughts to dwell on petty personal matters rather than vowing to do our best.'

'Arn is right; let us now agree on what is best instead of quarrelling with each other,' said Siegfried de Turenne between clenched jaws that made his accent sound even stranger than usual.

After that none of the three took any notice of the fact that the Grand Master had made a decision that might be considered contrary to the normal rules. They were short of time and had important desisions to make.

Some things were easy to agree on. The force of Templar knights would ride heavy as usual: armour on the horses' foreheads, as much chain mail along the horses' sides as possible, as few provisions as possible. All this was assumed, because the only chance of success was to take an attack position in which the Mamelukes' mobility was restricted for one reason or another; then weight and power would decide the day. In any other situation the knights' power would be wasted against a swift Mameluke cavalry, so there was no sense in trying to save weight on the horses. The enemy's speed and mobility were factors they could never equal.

The question of whether to place the Templar knights first or last in the army, however, required some discussion. In the event of a surprise attack by the enemy, which would probably come from the front, it would be best to have the strongest part of their forces in the front, which would save the most Christian lives.

But the Christian army was not very large, only five hundred secular knights, a hundred Templar knights, and about a hundred sergeants. If the enemy launched a frontal assault, the soldiers would first see the colours of the secular army and assume that their opponent was not as strong. Consequently they might attack too soon with a smaller portion of the now divided Mameluke army. Then it could be crucial for the Templar knights, under cover of the multi-coloured secular army, to ride forward and past them and meet the Mamelukes storming forward when they were too close to change direction. That seemed the wisest course. They would ride behind the secular army. Then they could also go out to the flanks and counter any attacks from the sides.

So far the three masters were agreed on all the plans. It took more time when Arn announced that he would be taking along as many Bedouins as possible.

The other two frowned at this proposal. The fortresses at Castel Arnald and Toron des Chevaliers had no Bedouins, and the other two had no experience with such dirty, un-believing and, according to rumour, completely treacherous troops. Nothing good could come of this.

Arn agreed that his Bedouins were untrustworthy unless one was victorious, and that in the worst case tomorrow could end with all three of them being dragged behind camels to be sold to Saladin. The Bedouins no doubt knew that

Templar knights were worthless captives because they could never be ransomed like worldly barons. But the Bedouins did have horses as fast as the wind, and their camels could easily traverse any mountain or rocky wasteland. So if you had them on your side, you could always get information about the enemy. As it looked now, such information, next to God's grace, was the most important component of the coming battle.

The other two reluctantly acquiesced. They had probably seen from Arn that he had no intention of yielding in this matter. And as the Grand Master had decreed, he was the one who would make the final decision whenever there was disagreement.

To anyone who like Arn and his *confanonier* from Gaza had witnessed Saladin's enormous Mameluke army parading for more than an hour simply to show off his cavalry, the Christian army that set out from Ashkelon on this early November morning must not have looked very strong.

The weather was raw and damp, with light winds from the northwest that refused to blow away the fog that came and went at will. The limited visibility could be advantageous to one side and a detriment to the other, but if any army was favoured by the bad weather it was certainly the Christians, who knew the region well. This was especially true of the two leaders of the secular army, the brothers Baldwin and Balian d'Ibelin. But in the rear guard of the Christians were also the two fortress masters from Toron des Chevaliers and Castel Arnald, and the Christian army was headed directly inland between these two fortresses.

No one could understand how the Bedouins found their way in the fog. But they appeared and then departed, carrying various messages for Arn de Gothia from the first hours of the advance.

Around midday the Christians began to encounter small groups of heavily laden Egyptians, who preferred to give the approaching soldiers a wide berth. They wanted to keep their plunder rather than throw down the loot and pick a fight. It was clear from this that Saladin now knew that his enemy was on the way. That gave him the opportunity to decide when and where to engage them.

And as could be expected, soon a mounted army in tight formation appeared right in front of the Christian vanguard. They were now in the vicinity of the fortress Mont Gisard, not far from Ramle.

The secular army immediately went on the offensive, without first ascertaining how large the forces were before them. The army's centre was left behind with the king, the bishop of Bethlehem, the massed standards, and their guards.

Behind them came the Templar knights, but Arn gave no order to engage. Rushing out into the fog against an enemy they couldn't see did not seem very wise, either to him or to his two closest officers, the two other fortress masters. Especially not when the Mameluke cavalry immediately gave way and fled in retreat. This was a well-known Saracen tactic. Anyone who chased such a fleeing centre force would almost certainly be surrounded on both sides by advancing enemy forces. And when that flanking movement was done, horn signals would sound and suddenly the fleeing group would turn around and go on the offensive, so that those who had been pursuers were quickly surrounded on all sides.

Arn's Bedouins arrived with news which showed that this was exactly what was happening, but only from one direction, from the south.

In that case Saladin would be coming straight across the lands of the Toron des Chevaliers fortress. And the fortress master Siegfried de Turenne knew the terrain like the back of his hand.

Arn ordered the column of Templar knights to halt, and they dismounted for a brief council. Siegfried drew a map on the ground with his dagger to show them a broad ravine that narrowed toward the south. Saladin would most likely be coming that way.

Quick decisions had to be made if the Christians were not to lose the opportunity. Arn sent a sergeant to the Grand Master in the centre of the Christian army, which now had halted and taken up a circular defence. He brought word of the Templar knights's plans. Then the Grand Master ordered the knights to advance at a brisk trot in the direction his brother Siegfried was riding, leading the way.

When they reached the ravine they were high atop a long, gentle slope at the place where the ravine narrowed like the neck of a Damascene bottle. If the enemy troops came that way, they would be able to surround the Christians from two directions. But right now there was only silence and the drifting fog that came and went, limiting their visibility.

There were two possibilities. Either the Templar knights had ridden to exactly the spot God had indicated for them to save the Christians, or else they were in the wrong place and risked leaving the secular army with no protection.

Arn ordered a general dismount and prayer. As quietly as possible all two hundred knights climbed down from their horses, holding the bridles as they knelt next to the horses' forelegs. When the prayer was done, Arn ordered them all to take off their mantles, roll them up, and fasten them behind their saddles. It might be chilly to wait for a long time like this, and there was a risk they would get stiff with cold before the battle. But if the enemy came soon and caught them by surprise it would be worse to try and fight with their mantles in the way.

In silence they sat and stared down into the fog until one knight thought he heard something, though another said it was only his imagination. It was difficult to endure sitting still, because if they were waiting at the wrong place the day would end in defeat, and the blame would be on the Templar knights. If nothing happened in a while, they would have to return to the part of the Christian army where the True Cross was now held in great danger with far too few defenders. If the True Cross were lost to the unbelievers, then it would be Arn's fault more than any other man's.

He exchanged a few glances with Siegfried de Turenne and Arnoldo de Aragon. They sat with heads bowed as if praying under great duress; they were thinking the same thing.

But it was as if God's Mother then filled him with confidence, as if he had received the necessary knowledge. He ordered his two fortress master brothers to ride cautiously out to the sides and each take command of one flank. They would ride out at the edges; like Arn they had a wide black border under the red cross on their horses' side armour. In the fog they would lose track of one another if there weren't at least some clear colours or signs to follow. The Templar knights' white tunics and mantles were usually considered a disadvantage since they were always visible from far away. Yet perhaps they were also a warning that made the enemy flee if he was not of superior strength. But here in the fog the Templar knights seemed to blend into the whiteness and disappear.

As quietly as possible the knights began to form a line, as if they already knew the direction in which they should attack. But it was actually as if God's Mother were holding Her hand over them, for suddenly they spied the first gleaming gold uniforms down below. They were Mameluke lancers, those who would lead the charge. They were proceeding in long columns down the hillside across from them, hidden in the fog. There was no way of telling how many they were; anything between a thousand and four thousand was possible. It depended on how large their centre force was, which now functioned as bait to draw the secular Christian army into the trap.

Arn allowed about a hundred of the enemy to pass through the ravine's bottleneck, even though Armand de Gascogne was squirming with impatience next to him. A new wave of dense fog then cloaked the entire enemy below in invisibility. Arn gave the order to advance, but at a walk so that they could better form a straight line and hopefully come so close to the enemy before being discovered that all their own men would be ready to spur their mounts on to a full gallop.

It felt unreal and dreamlike to advance at a walk. Down in the ravine the snorts of the horses and the ringing of their hooves on stone resounded from all directions, so it would be impossible for anyone to guess that two armies were now approaching each other.

Arn soon realized that he had to launch the offensive at full speed, hurtling straight out into the unknown. He bowed his head and prayed, but the Virgin Mary answered his prayer by showing something unrelated to the battle. She showed him Cecilia's face, her red hair rippling in the air as she rode, her brown eyes smiling as always, and her childlike face covered with all those freckles. It was a brief but utterly clear image in the fog. But the next instant he saw instead a Mameluke horseman scarcely a lance-length before him. The Mameluke gaped in shock and seemed unable to do anything else when he looked around and discovered that he was surrounded by ghostlike, bearded white knights on all sides.

Arn lowered his lance and roared the battle cry *Deus vult!*, which was repeated by hundreds of voices both near him and far off in the fog. In the next instant the whole valley reverberated with the thundering stallions of the Templar knights, and almost at once came the clang of metal meeting metal and the screams of the wounded and dying.

At precisely this narrow pass in the ravine where the enemy

was forced to squeeze together in multiple ranks to proceed, the iron fist of the Christian army struck hard. In an onslaught of heavy horses and sharp steel they tossed Mameluke riders in every direction, though many fell, pierced through by a lance. The Egyptian archers were in the rear and had no chance of hitting the intended targets with their arrows; soon they were overrun by riderless horses fleeing to the rear in panic. At the same time new Egyptian soldiers were rushing forward from the rear as they hurried toward the sounds of battle.

The Templar knights held the entire width of the narrow passage, and knee to knee they fought their way forward through hard-pressed Mamelukes. At such close range it was almost an impossible task to defend themselves against the long, heavy swords of the Christians which sliced their way forward like scythes during harvest.

The Egyptians who had made it through the bottleneck in the valley before the attack was launched now tried to turn around and ride to the aid of their comrades, but Arnoldo de Aragon had already anticipated this and on his own initiative countered them by taking twenty-five knights to form a front facing the other direction.

Where the battle was raging most fiercely in the middle of the valley, no man could see much farther than the end of his lance. For the Templar knights, who knew that they were so few in comparison with even those enemy soldiers they could see, this worked to their advantage, for all they needed to do was keep hacking their way forward through the heavily massed forces of the enemy. But for the Mamelukes who felt the weight of the Christians' cavalry in this worst of all possible situations, this was a nightmare to end all nightmares.

Some of the Mameluke commanders finally brought their fear and their thoughts under control and blew the signal to retreat straight back, since it was too uncertain to try and climb up the hillsides.

Arn summoned the men nearest to him and asked them to call a council and regroup instead of pursuing the enemy into the fog. Siegfried de Turenne, out of breath, appeared at his side along with the section he had led. At first he and Arn looked at each other in shock, because they each expected to find a mortally wounded temple brother. Their white clothing was so drenched with blood that the red crosses on their chests were hardly visible.

'Are you really unhurt . . . brother?' panted Siegfried de Turenne.

'Yes, as are you . . . but the battle is going well for us so far. What do we do now? How are things in the direction they fled?' said Arn, realizing that he must look much like his fortress master brother.

'We're regrouping and we'll advance in a line at a walk until we spy them again. The valley ends in that direction, so we have them in a trap,' replied Siegfried, having regained his composure with astonishing rapidity.

No more needed to be said just now. Rather than lose their advantage it was now important to re-form the whole line of attack while advancing slowly, and spreading more widely across the widening valley. A breeze had come up and there was a risk that the fog, which had served the Christians for so long, might now vanish.

The Mameluke lancers and archers had also tried to regroup as they fled down the valley. But when they realized that they were trapped by steep cliffs, they found it difficult to turn around. Once they did, they decided to attack at speed before they were pushed together again in the narrowing part of the valley where they now found themselves. The horns blew among the Egyptians, calling for a rapid attack, and the valley was filled with the thunder of light, fast horses advancing.

But at the same time the horn signals for a swift pace were

misunderstood by the supply train bringing provisions, spare horses, and plundered goods, following the fighting troops on their way down the valley. Now they tried to flee by cutting across, which led to the two Egyptian forces clashing together as if they were enemies.

At this sound Arn ordered another attack. The Egyptians who first saw the long, attacking line of Templar knights that in the fog looked like it was composed of thousands, were seized by wild panic and tried to flee to the rear through their own ranks.

The battle lasted for several hours, until finally the merciful darkness fell. The Knights Templar had never won such a brilliant victory.

As it transpired much later, the Egyptian centre force which was to have served as bait for Saladin's envelopment was finally captured by the secular army and forced to defend themselves without aid from the large force that never arrived. The realization that they were all alone without their main force stripped them of courage, and some began to flee. That was when the Egyptian defences were completely shattered and the army was routed.

When the secular Frankish army returned to celebrate its victory, which they thought they had accomplished on their own without any Templar knights, the battle of Mont Gisard was still raging.

Saladin's army was totally broken. There were still many Mamelukes left, both alive and uninjured, enough so that Saladin could have won under entirely different circumstances on another day, in another location and in better weather. But none of the groups of soldiers in the scattered and splintered army knew where the others were.

As a result of this confusion combined with the rumour of the bloodbath at Mont Gisard, a wild and unorganized flight began to the south. This retreat would eventually claim as many lives as the battle of Mont Gisard, for it was very far from the regions of Ramle to the safety of the Sinai. And all along the way, plundering and murderous Bedouins waited. Sooner or later they would seize many prisoners and an abundance of rich spoils.

Among the many captives who were dragged behind camels to the fortress in Gaza were Saladin's brother Fahkr and his friend the emir Moussa. They had been found next to Saladin when he was almost captured by a group of Templar knights, but they had sacrificed themselves without hesitation. Not even in the darkest hour of defeat did they doubt for a moment that Saladin was the one that God had chosen to lead them to victory.

The Knights Templar lost forty-six men who were wounded and thirteen who were killed. Among the dead that were found and brought back to Gaza was the sergeant Armand de Gascogne. He was one of those who tried to take Saladin; he had been only a lance-length from changing the course of history.

SIX

The worst time of Cecilia Rosa's long penance at Gudhem was the year after King Knut Eriksson came to collect Cecilia Blanca to make her his consort and queen of the three crowns. He did honour his promises to Cecilia Blanca, but like everything else in his plans it had taken longer than he had hoped. When he and his queen were finally crowned by Archbishop Stéphan, it was not as big an event as he had envisioned. The ceremony took place not at the cathedral in Östra Aros, but at the castle church at Näs out on the island of Visingö in Lake Vättern. Although of course it was annoying not to be able to make the coronation as magnificent as he'd intended, it nevertheless was valid before God and man. He was now king by the grace of God.

And Cecilia Blanca, who had taken the surname Blanca as her royal name, was also queen by the grace of God.

But it had taken a year to arrange all this, and that year was the most lamentable in Cecilia Rosa's life.

Knut's retinue had hardly disappeared from sight before everything at Gudhem changed all at once. Mother Rikissa again decreed a vow of silence inside the cloister, and it applied especially to Cecilia Rosa. She once again had to endure being whipped with the scourge whether she had broken the vow of silence or not. Mother Rikissa summoned a cold hatred which she directed at Cecilia Rosa, and the other Sverker maidens soon adopted the same attitude – all except one.

The one who refused to hate Cecilia Rosa, the one who would not run with the flock of geese across the courtyard, and the one who never reported her for anything was Ulvhilde Emundsdotter. But none of the others took any particular notice of little Ulvhilde. Her kinsmen had been wiped out in the battle on the fields of blood outside Bjälbo, and she had inherited nothing. For that reason she would also never be invited to drink the bridal ale with any man of importance; all she had left was her clan birthright, and now, in the aftermath of so many defeats, it was worth less than water.

When the first winter storm thundered in over Gudhem, Mother Rikissa decided it was time, as she slyly explained to the malevolent Sverker daughters, to begin sentencing Cecilia Rosa to the *carcer*, since that whoring woman had still not stopped imagining that she bore the Folkung colours. Clearly she thought this entitled her to be insolent in both word and deed.

Early in the winter there was plenty of grain in the storage chambers above the *carcer*, and thus many fat black rats. Cecilia Rosa had to learn how to endure more than just the cold by offering up ardent prayers. She found that easy to do compared with being startled awake by the rats or sitting up half-sleep with exhaustion to avoid contact with them. She also learned that if she fell asleep too soundly on the second or third day, when her fatigue was stronger than the cold, then the rats might nibble at her, as if wanting to see whether she was dead and had thus become food for them.

Her only warmth during these repeated visits to the *carcer* came from her prayers. But she didn't pray so much for her own sake; she spent most of the time in entreating the Holy Virgin Mary to hold Her protective hand over her beloved Arn and her son Magnus.

There was some selfishness in her prayers for Arn. She was well aware that she lacked Cecilia Blanca's ability to think like men did, to think as one who had power. Yet she fully understood that she would only be released from this icy hell of Gudhem, and the nemesis of Mother Rikissa, if Arn Magnusson returned uninjured to Western Götaland. So she prayed for him both because she loved him more than any other human being, and also because he was her only hope of salvation.

When spring came, her lungs were still healthy; she had not begun to cough herself to death as Mother Rikissa sometimes feared and sometimes hoped. And the summer of that following year was especially warm, so the *carcer* became a place of solitude and cool refuge rather than a curse. When the grain stores were at their low point, the black rats also retreated.

But Cecilia Rosa felt weak after such a hard year, and she was afraid that another such winter would be more than she could endure unless the Holy Virgin Mary sent a miracle to rescue her.

She sent no miracle. But She did send a queen by the grace of God, and that soon proved to have the same welcome effect.

Queen Cecilia Blanca came to Gudhem at the beginning of the turnip harvest with a mighty entourage. She moved into the *hospitium* as if she owned it and was in charge of everything. She bossed everyone about and ordered great quantities of food and drink. She sent word that Rikissa, whom she now addressed as the king and the jarl did without the title of Mother, should come at once to entertain her guests. As she pointed out, at Gudhem every guest should be received as if he were Jesus Christ himself. If that applied to everyone else, then it should certainly apply to a queen.

Mother Rikissa burned inside with fury when she could no longer offer any excuses. She went down to the *hospitium* to censure that impudent woman who might be a worldly queen but who in no way had control over God's kingdom on earth. An abbess was not obligated to obey either a king or a queen, crowned or not.

That was also what she pointed out as soon as she was shown to her place at the queen's table, and it was a lowly position indeed, far from the head of the table. Queen Cecilia Blanca's desire to meet her dear friend Cecilia Rosa was not something to which Mother Rikissa would agree. For as Mother Rikissa had decided, that wanton woman was now atoning for her sins in a suitable manner and could therefore not entertain visitors, royal or otherwise. Within Gudhem a divine order prevailed, and not the order of a queen. And that, in Mother Rikissa's opinion, was something that Cecilia Blanca ought to know better than most other people.

Queen Cecilia Blanca listened to Mother Rikissa's contemptuous and self-confident interpretation of the order of God and man without showing a single hint of uncertainty and without for an instant relaxing her irritating smile.

'Are you now finished with your evil prattle about God and so on? All these fine words that *we* – who have come to know your harsh ways in this place – do not think that you believe even for a moment. So now I command you to keep your goose-beak shut and listen to your queen,' she said, the words coming in a long, gentle stream, as if she were speaking kindly although her words were biting.

But what she said had an instant effect on Mother Rikissa, who actually pressed her lips together and waited for the queen to continue. She was sure of her case because she knew far better what belonged to God's kingdom and God's servants than did a queen who had recently been a maiden in the convent. But she had grossly underestimated Cecilia Blanca, as she soon discovered.

'So, now listen here, Rikissa,' Cecilia Blanca went on in her calm, almost sleepy tone. 'You are the mistress of God's order and we are only a queen in this earthly life among men, you say. We cannot rule over Gudhem, that is what you believe. No, perhaps not. And yet perhaps we can. For now you will learn something that will cause you sorrow. Your kinsman Bengt in Skara is no longer bishop. Where the poor devil has now fled with his wife after the excommunication we do not know, nor does it particularly interest us. But excommunicated he is. So you can expect no more support in this life from him.'

Mother Rikissa received this bad news about her kinsman Bengt without changing expression, even though inside she felt both dread and sorrow. She chose not to answer but rather to wait out the queen.

'You understand, Rikissa,' Cecilia Blanca went on even more slowly, 'that our dear and so highly esteemed Archbishop Stéphan is very close to the king and queen. As anyone can see, it would be utterly wrong of us to venture to say that he is eating out of our hand, that he will obey our slightest whim in his effort to keep the kingdom and its believers together in harmony. One ought not to say such a thing, for it would be the same as insulting God's high servant on earth. But let us instead say that we understand each other well: the bishop, the king, and the queen. It would be a shame if you also, Rikissa, should need to be excommunicated. And our jarl Birger Brosa, by the way, also displays great enthusiasm in such matters as relate to the church, and he talks continually of setting up new cloisters, for which he has promised a great deal of silver. Do you understand now what I'm getting at, Rikissa?'

192

'If you say that you really want to see Cecilia Rosa,' replied Mother Rikissa tersely, 'then I answer you that there is nothing preventing such a meeting.'

'Good, Rikissa, you aren't quite as stupid as you look!' Cecilia Blanca burst out, looking both cheerful and friendly at the same time. 'But just so that you truly understand what we mean, we think you should take special care not to stir up trouble when speaking with our good friend the archbishop. So! Now you may take your leave; just see to it that my guest is brought to me without delay.'

With these last words Cecilia Blanca clapped her hands and shooed off Mother Rikissa in exactly the same way that Mother Rikissa had behaved so many times before, showing the two Cecilias hardly any more respect than geese.

But Cecilia Rosa was in such a piteous state when she came into the *hospitium* that nothing needed be said to explain what she had been forced to endure since the hour when King Knut's tour of the realm left Gudhem. The two Cecilias fell into each other's arms at once, and tears flowed from both of them.

Queen Cecilia Blanca saw fit to stay three days and three nights in Gudhem's *hospitium*, and during that time the two friends were never apart.

Afterwards Cecilia Rosa was never again sent to the *carcer* in all her remaining years in the convent. And in the days following the queen's visit she received many good morsels and was soon able to eat enough to bring back the colour to her cheeks and the roundness to her flesh.

During the next years Cecilia Rosa and Ulvhilde Emundsdotter learned the beautiful art of weaving; they sewed and dyed mantles for gentlemen and ladies, and they also embroidered the loveliest coats of arms on the backs of the mantles. It did not take long before orders were coming in to Gudhem from near and far, even from less powerful clans who had to submit a mantle as a sample, which they later received back in a much more beautiful form.

There was an aura of peace about the two young women when they were working together, and the vow of silence never applied to them, since their work now brought in more silver to Gudhem's coffers, and without any fuss or bother, than did any other activity. The *Yconomus*, the old failure of a canon, took such delight in the work done by Cecilia Rosa and Ulvhilde Emundsdotter that he seldom missed an opportunity to point this out to Mother Rikissa. She showed no expression but nodded thoughtfully in agreement. She had a sword of Damocles hanging over her head and she did not forget it, for although Mother Rikissa was not a good woman, neither was she stupid.

Queen Cecilia Blanca had occasion to visit Gudhem more than once a year, and if she could she always stayed several days in the *hospitium*. Then she would demand that both Cecilia Rosa and Ulvhilde Emundsdotter should serve as her ladies in waiting, which of course never happened because the queen brought along her own roast-turners, cup-bearers, and maids. Those were delightful days for the two 'captive women', as they referred to themselves. It was clear to everyone that the queen's friendship with Cecilia Rosa was truly of the sort that would last a lifetime. This was especially obvious to Mother Rikissa, and she bowed to the queen's demands, although with clenched teeth.

In the third year Cecilia Blanca arrived with the most pleasant news. She had stopped by Varnhem to talk with old Father Henri about how, while continuing to meet all the rules, some of Brother Lucien's knowledge about gardening and healing might be transferred to the sister who had the best understanding of such matters at Gudhem, Sister Leonore of Flanders.

But this was not the most important news that Father Henri had to relate. He had received word from Arn Magnusson. Until recently Arn had been one of many knights in a stronghold of the Knights Templar named Tortosa, situated in a part of the Holy Land called Tripoli. Arn had attended to his duties well; he wore a white mantle and would soon enter the service of a high knight-brother in Jerusalem itself.

It was summertime when Cecilia Blanca arrived with this news, early summer when the apple trees were in bloom between the *hospitium*, the smithies, and the cattle stall. Upon hearing the news, Cecilia Rosa embraced her dear friend so hard that her whole body trembled. But then she tore herself loose and went out among the blossoming trees without thinking that such behaviour would have prompted Mother Rikissa in her worst period to order at least a week in the *carcer* as punishment. It was forbidden for a young woman to walk alone at Gudhem. But right now there were no such prohibitions in Cecilia Rosa's mind, and for one happy moment Gudhem did not even exist.

He's alive, he's alive, he's alive! That thought raced like a herd of gleaming horses in her head, temporarily obliterating all else.

Then she saw Jerusalem, the holiest of cities, before her. She pictured the streets of gold, the white stone churches, the gentle, God-fearing people, and the peace that was evident on their faces; she saw her beloved Arn walking toward her wearing his white mantle with the Lord's red cross. It was a dream she would carry with her for many years.

At Gudhem time seemed to pass unnoticed. Nothing happened and everything was exactly the same as usual; the same hymns repeated from the Psalter, the same mantles that were sewn and then vanished, the seasons that changed. Nevertheless changes did occur, perhaps so slowly that they went un-noticed until they suddenly could not be ignored.

The first year when Brother Lucien began coming down from Varnhem to teach Sister Leonore all about what grew in God's splendid garden, about what was good for healing people and what was good for the palate, no great changes occurred. Soon the fact that Brother Lucien and Sister Leonore worked together in the gardens for long hours was taken for granted, as if it had always been so. And it was soon forgotten that at first they were never left alone with each other. Brother Lucien came to the cloister so often that he seemed almost a part of Gudhem.

When the two of them in unashamed conversation dis-appeared together into the gardens outside the south wall, no suspicious eye noticed in the eighth month of the second year that which any eye should have seen at once during the first month.

Cecilia Rosa and Ulvhilde began seeking out Sister Leonore to learn from her knowledge, which she in turn had obtained from Varnhem and Brother Lucien. It was as if a new world full of opportunities had opened for them, and it was wonderful to see what people with God's help could accomplish with their hands in a garden. The fruit grew large and plump and lasted longer in the wintertime; the incessant soups at supper were no longer as humdrum when new flavours were added; the rules of the cloister forbade foreign spices, but what grew at Gudhem could not be regarded as foreign.

Soon Cecilia Rosa and Ulvhilde began to move more freely in and out of the convent walls. They were allowed to go down to the gardens to tend to the fruit trees or the flower beds without anyone questioning their whereabouts. This change had also developed so gradually that it was hardly noticed. Some years earlier the slightest attempt to go beyond the walls for any reason would have been met with the scourge and the *carcer*.

As the summer approached harvest time, the apples began to take on sweetness, the moon turned red in the evening, and the black earth smelled of damp ripeness. One day Cecilia Rosa had no particular errand down in the gardens, and twilight had already begun to fall, so she wouldn't have time to do any useful work. She was simply walking by herself, looking at the moon and enjoying the strong fragrance of evening. She didn't expect to find anyone else down there, and perhaps that was why she didn't discover the terrible sin until she was quite close.

On the ground between some luxuriant berry bushes that had already been picked clean, lay Brother Lucien with Sister Leonore on top of him. She was riding him voluptuously and without the slightest shame, as if they were man and wife sharing a worldly life.

That was Cecilia Rosa's second thought. Her first had been the awareness of the terrible sin. She stood there as if petrified or bewitched; she couldn't manage to scream, or run away, or even shut her eyes.

But she quickly got over her fear and instead felt a foreign, tender feeling as if she herself were taking part in the sin. The next moment she was no longer thinking of sin but of her own longing. Instead of those two, she pictured Arn and herself, although they had never done it exactly that way, which was of course doubly sinful.

The twilight descended fast as she stood there watching. Gradually the stifled sounds of desire ceased and Sister Leonore climbed off Brother Lucien and lay down beside him. As they held and caressed each other, Cecilia Rosa saw that Sister Leonore's clothes were in such disarray that her breasts were sticking out, and she let Brother Lucien play with them and stroke them as he lay on his back, breathing hard.

Cecilia Rosa could not bring herself to condemn these two, because what she saw looked more like love than the odious sin that all the rules described. As she crept away, careful to place her feet so that she would not be heard, she wondered if she were now part of the sin because she did not condemn it. But that night she prayed for a long time to Our Lady, who as far as Cecilia Rosa knew was the one who could help lovers more than anyone else. She prayed mostly for protection for her beloved Arn, but she also prayed a bit for the forgiveness of the sin committed by Sister Leonore and Brother Lucien.

That entire autumn Cecilia Rosa kept her secret without betraying a word of it even to Ulvhilde Emundsdotter. And when winter came, all the gardening work was put aside and Brother Lucien could no longer come to Gudhem on business until spring was at hand.

During the wintertime Sister Leonore worked mostly with Cecilia Rosa and Ulvhilde in the *vestiarium*, for there was much that needed to be woven, dyed, and embroidered. Cecilia Rosa often watched Sister Leonore secretly. She imagined she saw a woman who had a light inside her that was so strong that not even the black shadow of Mother Rikissa could weaken it. Sister Leonore was almost always smiling, and she hummed hymns as she worked. It was as if her sin made her both brighter in her soul and more beautiful because her eyes were so radiant.

One day Cecilia Rosa and Sister Leonore were alone in the *vestiarium* at the beginning of Lent, when work was not obligatory as usual and only those who wished to do so worked late into the evening. They were dyeing red cloth together, a process that went quickly and surely with the two of them helping each other. Then Cecilia Rosa couldn't hold back any longer.

'Don't be afraid, sister, because of what I now tell you,'

Cecilia Rosa began without really understanding where her words came from and why she now felt the need to speak. 'But I know the secret that you and Brother Lucien share, because I saw you once in the apple orchard. And if I saw you, then someone else could see you too and draw the same conclusion. Then you would both be in deep trouble.'

Sister Leonore blanched and put aside her work, sat down and covered her face with her hands. She sat for a long while before she dared look at Cecilia Rosa, who had also sat down.

'You're not thinking of betraying us, are you?' whispered Sister Leonore at last, in a voice so weak that it was barely audible.

'No, sister, I certainly am not!' replied Cecilia Rosa, offended. 'I'm sure you know that I am here at Gudhem for punishment and penance, because out of love I committed a sin like yours. I will never betray you, but I want to warn you. Sooner or later you two will be discovered by someone who will tell Mother Rikissa, or in the worst case Mother Rikissa herself will see you. You know as well as I do what an evil woman she is.'

'I believe that the Holy Virgin Mary has forgiven us and will protect us,' said Sister Leonore after a while. But she was looking down at the floor as if she were not at all sure of her words.

'You have promised Her to remain chaste. How can you so easily believe that She will forgive your broken promise?' Cecilia Rosa wondered, more bewildered than offended by the sinful thoughts which Sister Leonore so shamelessly displayed.

'Because She has protected us. No one but you, who wishes us well, has seen us and understood. Because love is a precious gift, and more than anything else it makes life worth living!' said Sister Leonore in a louder voice as if in defiance, as if she were no longer afraid that the wrong ears might hear her.

Cecilia Rosa was dumbstruck. She felt as though she were suddenly up in a high tower, looking out over vast expanses that she had only imagined could exist, but at the same time she felt the terror of losing her footing and falling. The idea that a sister consecrated to the Holy Bridegroom would betray her vows was a thought she never could have entertained. Her own sin, doing exactly what Sister Leonore had done, but doing it with her own betrothed and not with a monk who had also taken the vows, was a small sin in comparison. But it was obviously still a sin. Love was a gift from God; there was proof of that in the Holy Scriptures. The difficult thing to understand was how love could at the same time be one of the worst of sins.

Cecilia Rosa now recalled a story which she decided to tell Sister Leonore, at first a bit hesitantly, as she searched her memory.

It was about a maiden named Gudrun who was forced to agree to a bridal ale with an old man whom she loathed. But she loved a young man named Gunnar, and these two young people who loved each other never gave up the hope that they might marry. Their prayers eventually moved Our Lady so much that She sent them a wondrous salvation, and it was reported that they were living happily together to this day.

Sister Leonore had also heard that story, because it was well known at Varnhem, and Brother Lucien dwelled on it often. The salvation offered by Our Lady had put a little monk boy from Varnhem in the way of evil men. This monk boy had inadvertently and without blame killed the old man who was to have drunk the bridal ale with the maiden Gudrun. So in the presence of God's love, and with a belief in this love that never failed, all sins could be diminished.

Even a killing could become no sin at all if Our Lady had mercy on lovers who beseeched Her for support.

It was a very lovely story as far as it went. But Cecilia Rosa now objected that it was still not that easy to understand. Because the monk boy whom Our Lady sent to the young lovers' rescue was Arn Magnusson. And not long afterwards, he had been sentenced harshly for the sake of his own love, just as Cecilia Rosa had suffered from that same harsh judgment. For almost ten years now she had been brooding over the meaning of Our Lady's response, though without being any the wiser.

Now Sister Leonore was struck mute. She had never imagined that Cecilia Rosa was the betrothed of this Arn, for Brother Lucien had not told her this sad part of the story. Naturally he had mentioned that the little monk boy in time became a mighty warrior in God's army in the Holy Land. But he had viewed it only as a great and good thing, as though Our Lady had turned even this to a benevolent outcome. He had never told her what a high price love might have had to pay, although everything had ended so well for Gudrun and her Gunnar.

This first conversation, and all the others that followed later whenever they were alone, drew Cecilia Rosa and Sister Leonore closer to each other. And with Sister Leonore's permission, after Cecilia Rosa assured her that there was no fear of betrayal, she confided everything to Ulvhilde Emundsdotter. Then there were three of them, who could sit together in the *vestiarium* on late winter nights working so industriously that even Mother Rikissa commended them.

They discussed the topic of love as if in a never-ending dance. Sister Leonore had once before, when she was the same age as Ulvhilde, been in love, but it had ended unhappily. The man she loved then had, for reasons that had mostly to do with money, been wed before God to an ugly widow whom he did not love at all. Sister Leonore's father had scolded her for all her sobbing and told her not to take it to heart. Young women, he said, had no understanding in matters to do with marriage. Also, life was not over after the first youthful infatuation.

Sister Leonore was so convinced that the opposite was true that she had sought out a convent and was eager, after her first year as a novice, to take her vows.

However, now the Holy Virgin Mary had shown her that love was an act of grace that could be granted to anyone at any time. Possibly Our Lady had also shown that Sister Leonore's stern father had been right when he spoke of the first infatuation of youth and that it did not mark the end of love.

They all giggled happily at this last remark as they imagined how astonished her old father would have been to find out that he'd been right, and in what manner he had been vindicated.

Both Cecilia Rosa and Ulvhilde seemed to be drawn into Sister Leonore's sin through these conversations. When all three of them were together, they would immediately begin talking about their favourite subject. And their cheeks would grow hot and their breathing faster. Such forbidden fruit tasted heavenly, even though all they did was talk.

For Ulvhilde, what her two friends told her during these secret talks ended up changing her life. She had never believed in love. It was enjoyable to listen to these tales by firelight on cold winter nights, but they had nothing to do with real life. Just as she had never seen a wood nymph, she had never witnessed love.

She was very young when her father Emund was killed by Knut Eriksson; she was taken away in a sleigh with her mother and her little brothers. Some years later, when she no longer had any clear memory of her father, her mother took a new husband who had been given to her by a jarl in Linköping. Ulvhilde had never seen anything between her mother and this man that made her think of love.

Ulvhilde had decided that if this was all she had lost in life on the outside, then she might as well stay in the convent forever and take her vows, since a consecrated sister still lived a better life than novice. The only thing that made her doubt the wisdom of spending the rest of her life like this, was the thought of vowing eternal obedience to Mother Rikissa. But she had hoped that a new abbess might come to the convent, or that she might move to one of the cloisters that Birger Brosa was going to build. For as things now stood, Cecilia Rosa would not remain at Gudhem for the rest of her life. They would be separated, and when that day came there would be nothing left for Ulvhilde to hold on to except her love of God.

The other two were shocked at Ulvhilde's gloomy view of life. They urged her never to take the vows; she should venerate God and God's Mother but do it as a free person. Then Ulvhilde countered that she had no life outside the walls because all her kinsmen were dead. Cecilia Rosa refuted her, saying that this was something they could change, that nothing of that sort was impossible as long as they both had a good friend in Queen Cecilia Blanca.

In her eagerness to persuade Ulvhilde to give up all thoughts of taking the vows, Cecilia Rosa now said things aloud that she had only thought silently before. She admitted that she was probably being selfish, unable to stand the idea of being left once again without a friend at Gudhem. Now that the words had been said she would have to make good her plan and speak to Cecilia Blanca the next time she came to Gudhem.

For Cecilia Rosa herself, however, there was something else to consider during these conversations. When she was first sentenced to twenty years behind the walls, she was no more than seventeen. At the time, when she then tried to imagine herself at the age of thirty-seven, she had pictured an aged and stooped old woman with none of life's juices remaining. But Sister Leonore had just turned thirty-seven, and she glowed with strength and youth ever since love had blessed her.

Cecilia Rosa thought that if she refused to doubt, if she refused to lose hope, then the Holy Virgin Mary might reward her and allow her to glow at the age of thirty-seven just as Sister Leonore did.

That spring at Gudhem was like no other, either before or since. With the spring Brother Lucien began visiting again. Now there was much to do in the gardens, and it seemed as though Sister Leonore's need for instruction was inexhaustible. Since Cecilia Rosa and Ulvhilde also were making more use of things grown in the gardens, it seemed well and proper that they were out tending the crops at the same time as the visiting monk, so that no one would believe that a man was left alone with either a sister or maiden at Gudhem.

Yet Cecilia Rosa and Ulvhilde were particularly unsuited for this intended supervision, since they were actually protecting the sinners by standing guard. In this way Sister Leonore and Brother Lucien spent more hours in blissful union than they otherwise would have dared.

One vexation, however, was that everything they had sewn during the winter had already been sold long before summer arrived. It was good for Gudhem's silver coffers, but it also forced Cecilia Rosa and Ulvhilde to spend more time in the *vestiarium*. Brother Lucien had then explained to Sister Leonore how this problem could be remedied. She in turn told her two friends, for the two maidens never spoke to Brother Lucien themselves. If the goods they fabricated vanished too quickly, that was merely because the price was too low. But if they raised the price, then the goods would stay at Gudhem longer, they could give more attention to their work, and in the long run it would produce more silver.

This plan sounded like white magic and was hard to understand. But Sister Leonore came back from Brother Lucien with written pages and text that made it clearer. At the same time she told them how he had laughed about the *yconomus* who worked at Gudhem. According to Brother Lucien it was quite clear that this stray canon from Skara had very little sense of money or bookkeeping, since he couldn't even keep proper accounts.

All this talk about bookkeeping, and altering deals with figures and ideas as much as with the work of their hands intrigued Cecilia Rosa. She harped at Sister Leonore for an explanation, and the sister in turn nagged Brother Lucien so that finally he brought the account books from Varnhem and showed them how it would work.

It was as if a whole new world of utterly different ideas had opened up to Cecilia Rosa, and soon she ventured to take up her ideas with Mother Rikissa, who scoffed at first at all thought of this new plan.

But in the late spring after the long fast, Queen Cecilia Blanca usually came to visit, and during these visits Mother Rikissa always softened in the spine, if not in her heart. Eventually both parchment and books were ordered from Varnhem, which offered a more than willing Brother Lucien the opportunity to make extra trips. He also obtained Mother Rikissa's permission to teach accounting to both the *yconomus*, the runaway canon Jöns, and Cecilia Rosa so as to help them put Gudhem's affairs into order. The condition was that there would be no direct talking between Cecilia Rosa and Brother Lucien; all communication between them had to go via *yconomus* Jöns, acting as intermediary. This led to annoying moments, since Cecilia Rosa grasped every-thing much more quickly than did the unwilling Jöns.

According to Brother Lucien, whose skill at keeping books was shared by every other brother at Varnhem, the state of Gudhem's affairs was lamentable. Actually there was no lack of income; that wasn't the problem. But there was no balance between how much of the income was in silver and how much was in outstanding invoices or in goods already received but not sold. Jöns the *yconomus* didn't even know how much silver they had. He said that he usually estimated it by the number of handfuls. If there were more than ten handfuls, he knew from experience that would last a good while without any more coming in, but if there were fewer than five hand-fuls then they would have to bring in more.

It also turned out that Gudhem was due rent payments that hadn't been made in many years because they'd simply been forgotten. In everything that Brother Lucien discussed, Cecilia Rosa was as quick to learn as *yconomus* Jöns was stubborn and obtuse. He was sure that what had been good enough in the past would be good enough in the future. To such talk Brother Lucien could only shake his head. He said that Gudhem's income might be almost doubled if they had orderly bookkeeping, and that it was a sin to administer God's kingdom on earth as badly as it was being done at Gudhem. Such remarks incited Mother Rikissa's wrath, although she still didn't know what she would do about the matter.

That spring, though, Brother Lucien and Sister Leonore had many hours to themselves, so many that it was soon visible in Sister Leonore's waistline. She understood that now it was only a matter of time before her crime was revealed, and she wept in anguish. Even Brother Lucien's visits could not console her.

Cecilia Rosa and Ulvhilde had seen what was going on; the rapid sale of everything they had sewn during the winter, however, gave the three a reason to spend extra time together in the *vestiarium*. Cecilia Rosa then tried to be smart and think like a man without resorting to whining; at least she tried to think the way her friend Cecilia Blanca would have done.

Soon everyone would know that Sister Leonore was with child. Then she would be excommunicated and cast out of Gudhem. Since a man had to be involved in the sin, Brother Lucien would not escape either.

The couple ought to flee before they were forced out and excommunicated.

They would be excommunicated anyway if they fled, Sister Leonore objected.

Well, better to flee together before that happened. The question was only how to do it. One thing was clear: a runaway nun out on the road would soon be caught, and even sooner if she was travelling with a monk, Cecilia Rosa reasoned.

They turned the problem over and over; then Sister Leonore talked to Brother Lucien about the matter, and he told her about cities in the south of the kingdom of the Franks where people could obtain asylum. People like themselves, who were believers and devoted to God in everything except what had to do with earthly love. But travelling to the south of France without money and in the clothing of a nun and monk would not be easy.

The three women could make garments that looked like worldly clothes in the *vestiarium*. Obtaining silver for the journey was another matter. Cecilia Rosa mentioned that Gudhem's accounts were in such a shambles that nobody would miss a couple of handfuls of silver.

But stealing from a cloister was a sin worse than the one Sister Leonore had already committed. She begged in despair that no one should steal for her sake; she would rather go out on the road without a single *penning*. She thought that such a theft would be a real sin, unlike her love and the fruit that it had produced, which she no longer viewed as a sin at all. If only she could get to the south of France that sin would be dissolved into nothingness. But stealing from the house of the Holy Virgin Mary could never be forgiven.

Queen Cecilia Blanca sent word to Gudhem three days in advance to announce her visit. The arrival of the messenger came as a relief for the three who were privy to Gudhem's great secret – Sister Leonore was now in her third or fourth month; but the message imposed a heavy burden on Mother Rikissa. Archbishop Stéphan had died, to be sure, but as far as she knew the new Archbishop Johan was just as much in the king's pocket. Mother Rikissa was thus still subject to the slightest whim of Queen Cecilia Blanca. And because of this the cursed Cecilia Rosa was still just as big a threat to Mother Rikissa. Vengeance was not something she worried about; she knew how she would take her revenge. But excommunication was a greater threat to her than anything else. And she could be excommunicated by the archbishop if the two Cecilias truly set their minds to it.

Cecilia Rosa understood full well that Mother Rikissa's present mental state was advantageous for certain conversations. She sought out Mother Rikissa in the abbess's own rooms and bluntly laid out her plan: she herself would take over all the activities for which *yconomus* Jöns was now responsible at Gudhem. She would put the bookkeeping in order and this would improve Gudhem's standing. The *Yconomus* would then have more time for the trips to market-places that now took up an unreasonable number of hours, since he claimed he had far too many other things to do.

Mother Rikissa feebly tried to argue that no one had ever heard of a woman being *yconomus*, and that was indeed why it used the masculine form of Latin.

Without hesitation Cecilia Rosa replied that women were

particularly well suited to taking care of such work at a convent, as it did was not manual labour. And as far as the gender of the Latin word, all they had to do was change it to '*yconoma*'.

So that was what she wanted her job at Gudhem to be called from now on, *yconoma*. When Mother Rikissa seemed about to give in, Cecilia Rosa quickly pointed out that the *yconoma* was naturally the one who would decide where the man Jöns would be sent in the future. He would travel with messages from Gudhem but not take part in any trading, since his decisions had proved to be greatly lacking.

Mother Rikissa was now very close to anger, as was clearly apparent since she was sitting motionless and hunched up, rubbing her left hand on her right – all signs that in previous years had been a bad omen at Gudhem, since it presaged shouts about the scourge and the *carcer*.

'God will soon show us whether this was a wise decision or not,' she said when she had regained some control over herself. 'But it shall be as you wish. You will have to pray with humility about this change and not let anything go to your head. Remember that what I give you can just as easily be taken away in an instant. For I am still your abbess.'

'Yes, Mother, for now you are my abbess,' said Cecilia Rosa with feigned humility so that the concealed warning in her words would not sound like a threat. Then she bowed her head and left. When she closed the door to Mother Rikissa's rooms, she made an effort not to slam it. But silently to herself she hissed, *for now, you witch*.

When Queen Cecilia Blanca came to visit this time she brought her firstborn son Erik with her, and she was obviously pregnant again. The meeting of the two Cecilias was more poignant than ever, because they were both now mothers. Cecilia Blanca also brought tidings of both her son Magnus and of Arn Magnusson.

Her son Magnus was a plucky lad who climbed trees and fell off horses, but he never injured himself. Birger Brosa claimed that he could already see in the boy that he would be such a good shot with a bow and arrow that only one man would be able to match him; there was no doubt about his fathers identity.

According to the latest news from Varnhem, Arn Magnusson was in good health and still carrying out his calling in Jerusalem, among bishops and kings. To Cecilia Blanca this meant that his life was not in danger, for among bishops and kings there were no terrible foes. She could both be happy about this and thank Our Lady for Her high protection.

To Cecilia Blanca's question about whether Rikissa were still behaving herself Cecilia Rosa replied in the affirmative, but also explained in no uncertain terms that this state of calm might soon be at an end. For there was a big problem and great danger.

But about this matter she would prefer to speak alone with the queen.

They went upstairs in the *hospitium* and lay down on the bed where they had said goodbye on the last night they had both been captives at Gudhem. Now they once again took each other's hands and lay silent for a while, musing and staring up at the ceiling.

'Well?' said Cecilia Blanca at last. 'What is it that only my ears should hear?'

'I need silver money.'

'How much and for what purpose? Of all that you lack here at Gudhem, the need for silver money is probably something that seems the least important,' said Cecilia Blanca, surprised.

'Our simple *yconomus*, whom I will soon be replacing, by the way, would say two handfuls of silver. That will be enough for a long journey to the south of the Frankish kingdom for two. I should think that a hundred Sverker coins would be sufficient. I beg you sincerely for this, and I will pay you back someday,' said Cecilia Rosa.

'You and Ulvhilde aren't planning to run away, are you? I don't want that, I don't want to lose my dearest friend! And remember that we're not old yet, and that half your penance has already been served,' the queen replied uneasily.

'No, I'm not asking for my own sake or for Ulvhilde,' said Cecilia Rosa with a little laugh, since she couldn't help thinking of herself and Ulvhilde wandering on foot, holding hands all the way to France.

'Do you swear it?' asked the queen dubiously.

'Yes, I swear it.'

'But you can't tell me what this matter involves?'

'No, I don't want to, dear Cecilia Blanca. Perhaps someone will come and tell you that this money was used for a grave sin, and malicious tongues will try to involve you in this sin. But if you know nothing about it, then you are without sin. That's what I thought, anyway,' said Cecilia Rosa.

They lay silent for a while as Cecilia Blanca thought it over. But then she giggled and promised to take the money from her own travelling funds, since the amount was so small. But she reserved the right to be told someday what this sin entailed; so that she was innocent of any involvement, although she was providing the money. At least she wanted to find out eventually, when it was all over.

Cecilia Rosa promised to tell her at some later time.

Because the second matter that Cecilia Rosa wanted to discuss dealt with Ulvhilde, she thought it would be better if all three of them spoke together. So they got up from the bed, kissed each other, and went down to the queen's table and her attendants.

On this first evening of her visit Cecilia Blanca had decided that Rikissa would be allowed to stay behind the walls, since it seemed to her such a bother to hold a banquet for her

211

queen. In this way the dear friends and Ulvhilde could spend a much more amusing evening together. The queen had minstrels in her retinue, and they performed merrily as the feast was consumed. There were only women in the hall; the queen's guards had to remain outside the *hospitium*, taking their own repast in their tents as best they could. For as Cecilia Blanca said, she had learned quickly as queen that men were bothersome to have at table. They talked so loudly, got so drunk, and had to show off if they were in the presence of too many women and maidens, with no king or jarl.

But all the women were now eating and drinking like men, whom they mimicked with the greatest mischief. For example, the queen could still perform a number of tricks she had played when she was to be scourged at Gudhem, belching and breaking wind thunderously. Which she now repeated as she stretched and scratched her bottom and behind her ears as some men were in the habit of doing. All the women had a good laugh at this.

When all the food was consumed, they kept some mead on the table and Cecilia Blanca sent all her ladies-in-waiting to bed so that she and her friends at Gudhem could more easily converse about serious matters. For the queen understood the need for secrecy, since what concerned Ulvhilde Emundsdotter could become quite serious.

Cecilia Rosa began. At the time when Ulvhilde came to Gudhem there was great unrest in the country; all three of them remembered that. And as the blessed Fru Helena Stenkilsdotter made them all realize, a woman was unwise to run like a goose after friends and enemies when war could turn everything upside down in the blink of an eye.

Now all of Ulvhilde's kinsmen were dead on the fields of blood outside Bjälbo and in the battles that followed, when the Folkungs and Eriks were victorious. That was when a message came to Gudhem that for Cecilia Rosa and her dear

212

friend Cecilia Blanca had been like the loveliest dream. But Ulvhilde belonged to those for whom the fields of blood were the blackest of all nightmares.

Since then it was as though everyone had forgotten about Ulvhilde here at Gudhem. There was no one to ask after her, and no one could plead her cause or demand her rights. And even if it was hard to know what payment had been made on Ulvhilde's behalf during the bloody mess that existed back then, it was inconceivable that Rikissa would have cast out a relation out of hand.

But now was the time to settle accounts, Cecilia Rosa concluded, reaching for her tankard of mead.

The queen said, 'Now, as your queen but above all as your dearest friend, I would like to know what exactly you have in mind.'

'It's very simple,' said Cecilia Rosa, collecting herself as she drank calmly. 'Ulvhilde's father died. Then her little brother and her mother inherited. But later her brother died on the field of blood. After her mother died too . . .'

'Ulvhilde was the sole heir!' said the queen. 'As I understand the law, that is true. Ulvhilde, what was the name of the estate they burned down?'

'Ulfshem,' said Ulvhilde in terror, for what was now being discussed was something she hadn't heard even from her dear friend Cecilia Rosa.

'Folkungs now live there. They took over Ulfshem as a prize of victory. I know the people who live there,' said the queen pensively. 'But in this matter we have to proceed cautiously, dear friends. Very cautiously, since we want to win. The law is clear, it cannot be anyone but Ulvhilde who inherits Ulfshem. But laws are one thing, and men's conceptions of what is right and reasonable are not always the same. I can't promise you anything for certain, but it will please me greatly to try and create order in this matter. I will first speak with Torgny Lagman

213

in Eastern Götaland. He is also a Folkung and is close to us. Then I will talk to Birger Brosa, and when I'm done with these two I will take my case to the king. You both have your queen's word on this!'

Ulvhilde looked as though she'd been struck by lightning. She sat there completely pale, straight-backed, and suddenly stone-cold sober. For even if she wasn't as cunning as her two older friends, she could see that what the queen had said might mean that her life could be changed as if by magic.

Her next thought was that in that case she would have to leave her dear Cecilia Rosa, and then the tears came.

'I refuse to leave you here alone with that witch Rikissa, especially now that Sister Leonore . . .' she sniffled, but was immediately interrupted by Cecilia Rosa, who laid a warning finger across her lips. She quickly moved to Ulvhilde's side at the table and took the girl in her arms.

'Hush, hush, my dear little friend,' Cecilia Rosa whispered to her. 'Remember that I was separated from my dear Cecilia Blanca once in the same way, and here we now sit, the dearest of friends. Remember too that when we see each other on the outside we'll be younger than Sister Leonore is now. And by the way, don't say anything else about this matter to your queen.'

Cecilia Blanca cleared her throat and rolled her eyes as if to show that she might already have understood too much. Then she excused herself and went into her own rooms on the ground floor to 'fetch a few trinkets', as she said.

While she was gone Cecilia Rosa stroked Ulvhilde's hair as the young girl continued to cry.

'I know what you're feeling now, Ulvhilde,' whispered Cecilia Rosa. 'I have felt the same. The day I understood that Cecilia Blanca would leave this Godforsaken place, I wept with joy for her sake but also with sorrow because I would be alone for a time which then seemed like an eternity. But the days no longer seem endless, Ulvhilde. I can now see that my penance will one day end.'

'But if you're left alone with the witch . . .' Ulvhilde sniffled.

'I'll be all right. I can manage. If you think about our secret here at Gudhem, the one only you and I and Sister Leonore know about, isn't it a miracle of God that love is so strong? And isn't it just as wondrous what Our Lady can do for someone who never loses faith and hope?'

Ulvhilde seemed to take some solace from this. She wiped away her tears with the back of her hand and pluckily poured a little more mead for herself, although she had already drunk more than enough.

Cecilia Blanca returned with long strides and slammed a leather purse down on the table. From the sound it was clear what the leather purse contained.

'Two handfuls, approximately,' Cecilia Blanca said with a laugh. 'Whatever wily female plans you have, dear friends, make damned sure you succeed!'

At first the other two were shocked by their queen's audacious manly speech. Then all three women burst into uncontrollable laughter.

They hid the leather purse with the hundred silver *pennings* in a crevice in the cloister wall out by the gardens and described the spot exactly for Sister Leonore. They sewed the necessary garments piece by piece and let Sister Leonore herself hide them where she pleased outside the walls.

And when the summer was winding toward its end, Brother Lucien again made visits to Gudhem because he thought that there were important things about the harvesting, and about how to handle the fresh herbs, which Sister Leonore had not yet fully grasped.

This time he brought along a little book that he had made

215

himself, in which most of what he knew could be read. And he gave this book to Cecilia Rosa along with a greeting. Though he never spoke to her, he wanted to thank her for keeping their secret. It was not easy to read everything in the little book; Sister Leonore had to carry questions between the giver and the receiver a few times until most of it had been explained.

One evening when the summer was approaching harvest time, when the apples had begun to turn sweet, when the moon reddened in the evening and the black earth smelled of moist ripeness, and it was now obvious in what blessed condition Sister Leonore found herself, Cecilia Rosa and Ulvhilde accompanied her to the back gate that led out to the gardens. All three of them knew where the keys were hidden.

They opened the little wooden gate very carefully, because it was a bit creaky. Out there in the moonlight Brother Lucien was waiting in his new worldly clothes. In his arms he had a bundle of clothes that Sister Leonore would wear all the way to the south of France, if they could make it that far before she had to give birth.

Hastily the three women embraced one another. They blessed each other but none of them cried. And so Sister Leonore vanished into the moonlight; Cecilia Rosa closed the little wooden gate quietly and carefully, and Ulvhilde silently locked it. They went back to the *vestiarium* and continued their work as if nothing had happened, as if Sister Leonore had only left them a little earlier than normal this evening, even though there was still much sewing to be done.

But Sister Leonore had left them forever. And afterwards there was much grumbling and many harsh words. But for Cecilia Rosa her absence left a great emptiness, since she both feared and hoped that for the second time she would soon be alone at Gudhem.

SEVEN

Autumn and winter were the time for rest and healing in the Holy Land. The land itself, like many of its warring inhabitants, seemed to be recovering from its wounds during this time when enemy armies could make no headway. The roads around Jerusalem turned into mud; wagons that were too heavy got stuck, and on the bare and windswept hills outside the holy city there was often thick, slushy snow. Together with the violent wind it would make any enemy siege more miserable for the besiegers than for the besieged inside.

In Gaza it often rained, but the weather could also be sunny and cool, like the Nordic summers. Snow had never been seen there.

The autumn and winter days following the remarkable, miraculous victory at Mont Gisard were at first filled with two tasks that were of greater concern for fortress master Arn de Gothia than all the everyday work. First, he had a hundred Mameluke prisoners who were more or less battered; and second, he had almost thirty wounded knights and sergeants in the north wing of the fortress.

Two of the captives were men who could not be locked in with the others in one of Gaza's grain stores. They were

217

Saladin's younger brother Fahkr and the emir Moussa. Arn had them quartered in private rooms, and he ate the midday meal with them every day instead of with his knights down in the *refectorium* by the fortress courtyard. He knew that this behaviour prompted some amazement among his close brothers, but he had not explained to them how important Fahkr was.

In all of Outremer and the surrounding lands, everyone acted in the same way when it came to prisoners, whether they were followers of the Prophet or Christians or something else. Important prisoners like Fahkr and emir Moussa were exchanged or released when ransomed. Prisoners who could not be exchanged were usually beheaded.

The captives in Gaza were mostly Mamelukes. The simplest thing would have been to find out which of them had earned their freedom and were rewarded with property, and which of them were still slaves. The result would be either death or, in the best case, the position of master of a whole region in one of Saladin's many lands.

Those who were still slaves ought to be beheaded at once. They were just as worthless as prisoners as Templar knights were, since they could never be ransomed. Besides, it was unhealthy to keep too many prisoners in close quarters, because they could easily spread disease. Killing them was the most hygienic solution, and also the wisest in terms of economical administration.

Prince Fahkr ibn Ayyub al Fahdi, which was his full name, would bring a ransom greater than anyone had ever been able to demand for a Saracen, since he was Saladin's brother. Even emir Moussa should be worth a good price.

To the amazement of both Fahkr and Moussa, Arn had quite a different suggestion. He wanted to propose that Saladin pay a ransom for every prisoner of the same price; 500 besants in gold, equivalent to about 78 ounces. Fahkr objected that most of the prisoners were not even worth one gold besant, and that he considered it an insult to make such a proposal. Arn then explained that he actually meant 500 besants for *each* prisoner, including Fahkr and Moussa themselves.

To this they were speechless. They didn't know whether to feel offended that this Al Ghouti – infidel though he was, yet considered among the believers to be the foremost of all Franks – had set the same price on them as on their slaves. Or whether Al Ghouti's proposal indicated that he didn't intend to extort an unreasonable price from Saladin to release his own brother. The possibility that a Templar knight might have no head for business never entered their minds.

They discussed this question and made slow headway when they ate together once a day. Nothing that Arn served them was unclean food, and cold fresh water was the only drink at mealtime. When they were left alone in Arn's quarters they had access to the Holy Koran.

Even though Arn treated his two prisoners with such great respect that they could have been guests, there was no doubt that they were prisoners. It made them both naturally circumspect during the conversations of the first few days.

But Arn wondered somewhat about their reluctance either to speak their opinions straight out or offer clear counterproposals, and the fourth time they sat down together for dinner he seemed to be losing patience.

'I don't understand you,' he said with a resigned gesture. 'What is it that is unclear between us? My faith tells me to show kindness toward the vanquished. I would be able to speak a great deal on this topic, although I don't want to force you to listen to a faith that is not yours, especially not now when you are not free men. But your own faith says the same thing. Consider the words of the Prophet, peace be with him, and his own words to you: "When you meet unbelievers in battle, let your sword fall over their heads until you have forced them to their knees; take then the survivors captive. Then will come the time when you shall set them free, in good faith or in exchange for ransom, so that the burdens of war are lightened. This is what you have to observe." Well? If I now tell you that my belief is the same?'

'It is your generosity we cannot understand,' muttered Fahkr self-consciously. 'You know very well that five hundred besants in gold for my freedom is a price that can only arouse ridicule.'

'I know that,' said Arn. 'If you were my only prisoner, I might suggest to your brother to pay fifty thousand besants. But what of the other prisoners? Should I leave them to our Saracen executioners? What is a man's life worth, Fahkr? Is your life worth so much more than that of every other man?'

'The man who claims such a thing is boasting and at the same time blaspheming against God. Before God one man's life is the same as another man's life. That is why the Holy Koran declares that life is inviolable,' replied Fahkr quietly.

'Perfectly true,' said Arn, sounding pleased. 'And Jesus Christ says the same thing. Let us not dispute this matter anymore; we actually have other things to talk about that demand more thought. So I would like Saladin to pay me fifty thousand besants in gold for *all* the prisoners, the two of you as well as all the others. Could you, Moussa, take this message to your lord?'

'You're releasing me and sending me as a messenger?' asked Moussa, astonished.

'Yes, I can't imagine a better messenger to take my demands to Saladin. Just as I cannot believe that you would seek only your own freedom and flee from this task. We have vessels that sail to Alexandria every other day, which you may or may not know. Or would I be sending you in the wrong direction? Should you travel to Damascus instead?'

'Damascus would be a much more difficult journey, but

it doesn't matter in the least,' said Moussa. 'From any city in Saladin's realm I can get the message to him the same day. Alexandria is closer and easier.'

'From any city at all . . . on the same day?' Arn wondered. 'It is said that you can do that, but how is it possible?'

'Simple. We have doves that fly with the messages. Doves always find their way home. If you take doves that were born in Damascus and move them in a cage to Alexandria or Baghdad or Mecca, they will fly straight home when you release them. You only have to wrap a letter around one of their feet.'

'What an ingenious way to make use of them!' Arn exclaimed, obviously impressed. 'So from here I could speak with my Grand Master in Jerusalem, where I believe he is now, in only an hour, or however long it takes for a dove to fly there?'

'Yes indeed, if you had such doves and someone to take good care of them,' muttered Moussa with an expression as if he thought the conversation was taking an irrelevant turn.

'How strange . . .' Arn mused, but then regained his composure. 'Then let's do it! You sail to Alexandria with one of our own ships tomorrow. Don't worry about the men accompanying you. I grant you safe passage, and the crew is mostly Egyptian anyway. You'll also be taking some of the injured prisoners with you. But let's talk about something else now.'

'Yes, let's do that,' Fahkr agreed. 'For there is certainly much else to talk about. I beseeched my brother Saladin to stay here outside Gaza and lay siege to the city. But he wouldn't listen to me. Imagine how different things would be now if we had stayed.'

'Yes, at the very least I would have been the one who was dead,' Arn agreed. 'You would have had half your army left, and you would be sitting here as the rulers of Gaza. But He who sees all and He who hears all, as you would say, willed a different outcome. He wanted the Knights Templar to be victorious at Mont Gisard even though we were only two hundred against several thousand. This was proved by virtue of the fact that it happened; it was His will.'

'Were you only two hundred?' Moussa burst out. 'That's astounding! I was there myself . . . we thought you were at least a thousand knights. Only two hundred . . . ?'

'Yes, that's true. I know because I led the attack myself,' said Arn. 'So instead of dying here in Gaza as I was sure I would, I won a victory that was truly a miracle of the Lord. Do you understand now why I didn't want to boast or behave with arrogance and cruelty toward the conquered?'

It was true for both believers and unbelievers that he who was granted God's grace so miraculously could not boast and imagine that he had done it all on his own. Such an overweening attitude was a sin which God would punish harshly, regardless of whether one understood God in the words of the Prophet or in the words of Jesus Christ.

They were in full agreement on the necessity for restraint after such a victory. On the other hand, what they could discuss even more heatedly, now that the sensitive matter of ransom of the prisoners had been clarified, was the question of God's will or man's sin.

Everything would have been different if Saladin had stayed in Gaza with his army and taken the city – that much was clear. But why did God then punish Saladin for showing leniency toward both Gaza and Al Ghouti himself? He had spared Al Ghouti and shortly thereafter God let Saladin suffer his greatest defeat at the hands of this very man. So what was God's intention?

All three of them brooded a long time over this question. Finally the emir Moussa said that it might be that God was sternly reminding His most beloved servant Saladin that in *jihad* there was no room for any man's personal wishes. In *jihad* one could not spare a city of infidels because one had a personal debt to a specific individual. For emir Moussa was, like Fahkr, convinced that Gaza would have been taken by force if its commander had not been Al Ghouti, to whom Saladin owed a personal debt. The defeat at Mont Gisard was God's punishment for that sin.

Arn not surprisingly held an entirely different view. He thought that the victory at Mont Gisard showed that God had protected those of his believers who stood closest to Him, for He had favoured the Christians in such a way that it could only be explained as divine intervention. Gaza had been spared because Saladin wanted a greater prize, and the siege force outside Ashkelon had been too small. Instead of heading directly toward Jerusalem, Saladin had allowed his once unconquerable army to disperse to plunder. The fog had favoured the side that had the smaller force to lead at Mont Gisard. And as if this were not enough, Arn and his brothers had had the improbable good luck to ride blindly to the precise spot where the Mameluke cavalry would pass. And as if this were still not enough, the attack by the Knights Templar came exactly at the spot where the enemy had the most difficulty both defending themselves and regrouping to counterattack.

All this in a single context was too much to be explained away as mere luck or skill. On the contrary, it was proof that the belief in Jesus Christ was the true path, and that Muhammad, peace be unto him, was a prophet inspired by God but not the messenger for the one truth. For how could the miracle at Mont Gisard otherwise be explained?

Emir Moussa ventured another explanation. When God saw how the faithful were on their way to crush the Christians, who were nevertheless human beings like any other human beings, then God had turned his back on all of them. After that, human errors and not God's will had prevailed.

For the the faithful had demonstrably committed a long series of mistakes, just as Al Ghouti had enumerated. The errors

223

were due mostly to arrogance, the fact that they believed victory was assured long before the first real battle was fought. Such arrogance was always punished in every war, in ways both small and large. He who had war as his profession and was old enough must have seen a thousand idiotic decisions and another thousand lucky ones that determined the difference between life and death. These things always happened. And wasn't it boastful to believe that God always participated in every little battle that His children fought? Yes, for otherwise God would not have much else to do other than rush from one war to another and from one battle to the next. So as far as Mont Gisard was concerned, a combination of human pride and the usual fortunes of war might be the simplest explanation.

Neither Arn nor Fahkr would agree to that. Fahkr thought that it was blasphemy to believe that God would turn His back on His warriors during *jihad*. And Arn thought that if war was being waged close to God's Grave, then He would not choose to be busy somewhere else.

And so they were back to the question of whose set of beliefs represented the true faith. No one would yield on that point, and Fahkr, who was an expert negotiator, then led the discussion to the only point on which they could agree. They could not know whether God punished those who in His name advanced in *jihad* toward Jerusalem, or if He was protecting those who in His name defended Jerusalem. If they did not know whether God was showing mercy or doling out punishment, then they could not say whether the message of the Prophet, peace be unto him, was the true one, or whether it was the message that came from Jesus Christ, peace be unto him as well.

Arn's fortress master brother Siegfried de Turenne, whose name in his own language was spelled Thüringen, was one of the Knights Templar who was wounded at Mont Gisard. Arn had convinced him to seek treatment for his wounds in Gaza, but he hadn't explained why he thought there would be better care in Gaza than in Siegfried's own fortress Castel Arnald up in the Ramle region.

What Arn had not told his brother was that the doctors at the fortress in Gaza were Saracens. Some among the Templar knights found it outrageous to employ Saracen doctors. It was mostly the new brothers who held such views, and it was the same among the worldly Franks in Outremer. Those who had just arrived usually held the view that all Saracens should be killed with impunity as soon as they were discovered. Even Arn had entertained such simplistic beliefs when he served his first year in the white mantle. But that was long ago, and Arn, like most brothers who had long served in the Holy Land, had learned that Saracen doctors were able to heal more than twice as many wounded as Frankish doctors did. More experienced brothers usually joked that if one fine day you lay wounded on the battlefield, the safest doctor to treat you was one from Damascus, the next safest no doctor at all, and the surely fatal one was Frankish.

Naturally there was a difference between what belonged to this world and what was faith. Some fortress masters and high brothers would probably agree, based on their own experience, that Saracen doctors were more skilled. Yet they still wouldn't rely on the unbelievers because that would be considered sinful.

Arn used to joke about such opinions, saying that it was truly odd for a man to be allowed to live because of his sin and die as punishment for his purity of faith. Going to Paradise because you died on the battlefield was one thing, but going there because you had neglected your health in the sickbed was hardly the same.

As Arn had instinctively felt, Brother Siegfried belonged

225

to those who because of their faith would rely only on unskilled doctors. But Siegfried was brought to Gaza on a stretcher, and at that moment he was in no condition to raise objections. An arrow had bored through his shoulder and shoulder blade, and a lance had penetrated deep into his left thigh. A Frankish doctor might have done something that would have cost him both his arm and his leg.

Initially Siegfried had strongly criticized Arn for his trick of leaving him in unclean hands. But the two doctors Utman ibn Khattab and Abd al-Malik had first succeeded in removing the arrow point despite the fact that it had penetrated all the way into the shoulder blade. Then using various herbal drinks they had quickly brought down the fever caused by the wound and thoroughly cleansed the opening with brandy, which burned like fire but also purified the wound. After only ten days Siegfried noticed how his wound was starting to heal, and soon he could move his arm, although the doctors immediately tried to stop him and in broken Frankish admonished him to lie still.

As Siegfried grew noticeably better he also began to observe with greater interest the huge differences that existed between Gaza and his own fortress when it came to treating the wounded. The first big difference he noticed was that here in Gaza the wounded lay high up in the fortress, cool and dry, and each bed was far away from its neighbour so that the wounded could hardly speak with one another. The cool air was no cause for concern, for each of the patients were bedded in both linen and pelts. The fact that this would have any importance for the healing of wounds was hard to believe, but it was pleasant to lie in clean bed linen.

All the arrow slots were furnished with wooden shutters to keep out the wind and rain, which seemed an unnecessary bother. If they had done as they did elsewhere, the wounded would have been kept down below in a grain storage chamber. But the Saracen doctors clearly insisted on keeping plenty of fresh air and a low temperature in the *infirmatorium* itself. This was not the first time Siegfried had been wounded, so he could compare this treatment to previous experiences.

Besides the temperature and ventilation, the big difference was in the absence of prayers in connection with the treatment, which was also quite minimal for most of the wounded brothers. After the Saracen doctors had washed and dressed the wounds, they mostly let the men rest; they didn't continually come running with new poultices, warming cow manure and other things that a wounded man might usually expect. On rare occasions the doctors would cauterize the wounds with red-hot irons, if the evil could not be washed away with the searing brandy. When such things were to be done, Arn de Gothia himself would come up with some sergeants in tow who would hold down the unfortunate patient while he was treated with the glowing iron.

But Arn also visited the wounded every day to observe a brief moment of prayer with them. Then he would go from bed to bed along with one of the doctors and translate his recommendations and opinions. All this was extremely foreign behaviour, and at first Siegfried de Turenne had looked on medicine in Gaza with great suspicion. But reason also had a say in the matter, and it wasn't easy to deny. Of the many wounded who came to Gaza after Mont Gisard, only one had died, but he'd had deep wounds in his abdomen, and it was well known that there was no remedy for such a grievous condition. But there was no denying the fact that the *infirmatorium* was emptied little by little, and that most of the wounded, even two who'd had their wounds burned with red-hot irons, would be able to go back into service. According to Siegfried's experience, half of the brothers who were treated for wounds in battle would usually die. And of the half that survived, many would be cripples. Here in Gaza the infidel doctors had only had one death, and it was a hopeless case. That fact could not be ignored. So it would be foolish not to try and employ Saracen doctors also at home in Castel Arnald as soon as possible. This was not an easy decision for Brother Siegfried to make. But if he had refused to accept what he saw with his own eyes, he would have sinned against wounded brothers, and that would have been even worse.

Doctor Abd al-Malik was one of Arn's oldest friends in Outremer. They had met when Arn was a shy and childish 18-year-old and new in service at the Knights Templar fortress of Tortosa far up the coast. It was Abd al-Malik who at Arn's stubborn insistence had given him his first lessons in Arabic, which then continued for two years before Arn was posted elsewhere.

The Holy Koran was naturally the best of all texts for this purpose, since it was written in consummate prose, which Abd al-Malik always explained by saying that it was God's own pure language given directly to human beings with only one Messenger, peace be unto him, as intermediary. But Arn explained that the Koran had come to be the standard for all written Arabic and thus had been perfected after the fact, since all had to sing in the same manner.

They could argue about such things because it did not trouble either of them that they didn't share the same belief. And Abd al-Malik was a man who refused to be upset by someone else's belief. He had worked for Seljuk Turks, for Byzantine Christians, for the Shia Caliphate in Cairo, and for the Sunna Caliphate in Baghdad; he worked wherever the payment was best. When he and Arn met again in Jerusalem just before Arn was to take over his new command in Gaza, they had quickly come to an amicable agreement, although not merely for the sake of old friendship. Arn had not hesitated to offer a princely salary for Abd al-Malik's services, because he knew how many lives of Templar knights such a wage would save. Looking at it that way, it was no great expense. Healing an experienced Templar knight and getting him back up on his horse was infinitely less expensive than training a newly arrived whelp from scratch.

In those days there was no wealthier order in the world, and there were those who thought that the Knights Templar had more gold in their coffers than the king of France and the king of England combined. Presumably that was true.

Gaza was thus not only a fortified city and the last outpost in the south to combat the threat of Egyptian invasions. Gaza was also a trading city, one of the eight ports of the Knights Templar along the coast up to Turkey. The harbour at Gaza also had a special advantage because, unlike the harbour in Acre, for example, it was ruled only by the Knights Templar. This meant, among other things, that they were able to maintain constant trade with Alexandria, war or no war.

But Gaza also traded with Venice and Genoa and sometimes with Pisa. And the Knights Templar had their own trading fleet with hundreds of ships that were constantly sailing the Mediterranean. Because Gaza had two Bedouin tribes at its disposal, from there they could also link Venice with Tiberias just as easily as Pisa with Mecca.

Of the goods that the Knights Templar sold to Franks, Germans and Britons, Portuguese and Castilians, sugar was the most important commodity. Sugar was coveted at the tables of many princes in those lands from which the Crusaders came; it was worth its weight in pure silver. The immense wealth that passed through the hands of Gaza's customs master and all his scribes might have tempted ordinary men to enrich themselves.

During Arn's long sojourn in the service of the Knights Templar, however, such a breach had never been discovered.

He recalled only one instance when someone's white mantle was taken away because a gold coin was discovered on him, which the unfortunate had explained by saying that it was an amulet for good luck – which it demonstrably was not, since it brought only misfortune upon its wrongful owner.

As a fortress master Arn had the right to five horses, while an ordinary brother had the right to four. But Arn had refrained from acquiring the extra horse because for a long time he'd been so set on obeying his vow of poverty that not even the sight of 50,000 besants in gold could entice him. And all the brothers he had known up till now were the same way.

On the other hand, it was a relief for Arn to get rid of all hundred Egyptian prisoners, just as he felt both a sense of relief and of loss when he followed emir Moussa and Fahkr aboard the waiting ship bound for Alexandria. Moussa had come back to Gaza in person with Saladin's ransom. They parted as friends and joked a bit that it would be a pleasure, at least for Fahkr and Moussa, to be able to hold Arn prisoner the next time they saw each other. Arn had a good laugh at that and pointed out that in that case it would have to be either a very brief or very long imprisonment, because unfortunately no gold besants would be paid for him. Such talk was pleasant enough for those who could not see into the future.

But none of them could have imagined in their wildest dreams what He who sees all and He who hears all had in store for them.

By the time Siegfried de Turenne's wounds had healed enough that he could walk and ride somewhat, he was eager to try his weapons again. Concerning that matter he turned to Arn, because he found it best to begin by practicing with a friend of the same rank.

They went down to the weapons master's armoury in the

courtyard of the fortress and selected the weapons they thought it wise to start with: sword and shield.

The practice weapons were the same as those they used in battle, but with blunt edges, not sharpened. The shields were likewise the same shape and weight as battle shields, but unpainted and with an extra-thick layer of soft leather so that they could withstand more blows.

As soon as the two walked outside in the raked sand on the practice field, Siegfried de Turenne attacked Arn with furious power, as if it were important to practice at full strength from the first instant. Arn parried him with a laugh and slipped away effortlessly; then he lowered his sword, shook his head, and explained that this was no way to exercise a wounded arm and thigh; it would only lead to more pain. Then he began aiming blows at Siegfried's shield side, now low and now high, using slow, obvious moves as he studied his friend, who was having more and more trouble raising and lowering his shield with his injured arm.

Then Arn changed his practice moves to go in close and pull back, back and forth, so that Siegfried had to lunge and retreat, stretching his injured thigh each time.

Soon, though, Arn stopped the practice, saying that it was still obvious where his wounds were located, but it would be unwise to proceed any further just now. Yet it looked as if Siegfried was on his way to becoming the same fit man he'd been before Mont Gisard. At first Siegfried wouldn't hear of stopping, because he believed that pain was something a Templar knight should be able to endure; it made a man stronger and tougher. Arn thought that this was true for men who were well, but it didn't apply to the wounded, and he would order Siegfried bound to his bed if he heard any more such nonsense. Even though they were brothers of the same rank, they were now in Arn's domain, so he could forbid Siegfried to practice with anyone but himself in the future. They turned in their weapons in spite of Siegfried's complaints, and then they went to the church to sing the *None*.

After the *None* on Thursdays Arn held a *majlis* outside the eastern wall of the fortress, where he decided disputes and judged criminals together with the learned physician Utman ibn Khattab. He invited Siegfried to come along and watch, as it might be interesting for a fortress master from the north to see the different sort of problems that required adjudication down here in the south. One condition, however, was that Siegfried had to wear his full Templar garb with mantle and sword.

Siegfried went along to the court mostly out of curiosity. But he also tried to convince himself to go there with an open mind, not to be too hasty in his judgment of anything that at first might seem foreign or repugnant. He reminded himself how the odd customs of Gaza still produced very good results when it came to the skill of the Saracen physicians.

But at first he saw only what seemed to him a tasteless spectacle. It was like a mockery of all things holy when not only God's Word but also the Koran were brought out and laid on a table before the tribune, where he sat together with Arn and the Saracen doctor named Utman ibn Khattab. A large crowd of people had gathered round a square marked off by ropes and guarded by black-clad sergeants with lances and swords. The proceedings began with Arn reciting the Pater Noster; only a small number of the onlookers seemed able to follow along. But then Utman ibn Khattab recited a prayer in the language of the infidels, and most of the listeners knelt and bowed their foreheads to the ground. When that was done, Arn declared that the first case should be called, and a Palestinian peasant from one of Gaza's villages stepped forward with a woman, her hands bound behind her back, and another woman at her side. He pushed the bound woman down in the sand before him. The second woman, who was wearing a veil over her face, he shoved behind his back as he bowed to the three judges. Then he raised his right arm and rattled off a long prayer, or perhaps it was a homage to Arn. To Siegfried it was merely gibberish.

Then the Palestinian peasant began to state his case clearly, and Arn translated in a whisper to Siegfried so that he could follow along with the argument.

The bound and humiliated woman was the peasant's wife. He had refrained from the right given to him by the true faith to kill her for her adultery. This leniency was entirely due to the fact that he wanted to respect the law within Gaza, which he, like everyone in his village, had sworn to obey so that they might have security in their lives. But now he had caught his wife in a grave sin, and as a witness he had brought along an honest woman who was his neighbour in the village.

Then Arn interrupted the monotonous lamentation and asked the honest woman to step forward, which she did as silence sank over the audience. Arn asked whether what her neighbour had said was true, and she confirmed it. He asked her to place her hand on the Holy Koran and swear before God that she might burn in Hell if she swore falsely, and then she had to repeat the accusation. She obeyed, but she was already trembling as she held out her hand to the Koran, and she placed it very gingerly as if afraid she might be burned. But she repeated the accusation word for word as was asked of her. Arn then asked her to step back and leaned over to Utman ibn Khattab, who made a quick whispered comment that Siegfried could neither hear nor understand, but he saw that the other two finally nodded in agreement as if they had reached a decision.

Arn stood up and recited a text from the scripture of the infidels, which Siegfried could not understand until Arn translated it to Frankish. And Siegfried found that they were astonishing words, for the gist of it was that four witnesses were required to prove adultery. And if it was not proven, then no man or woman could speak of it. Here a man had produced only one witness, which gave him no right to accuse his wife.

After this explanation Arn drew his dagger and strode over to the bound woman as a gasp of fright went through the crowd. But he did not do what some had feared. Instead he cut off the rope binding her hands and declared that she was free.

Then he did something that surprised Siegfried even more. He announced in both Arabic and Frankish that the woman who had sworn to the sin of adultery had sworn falsely, and that she would be punished. Henceforth she would have to serve the wrongly accused woman for one year, or leave the village. And if she did not obey, she would receive the punishment reserved for a perjurer, which was death.

And the man who had brought forth one person to bear false witness would now, as prescribed by the law of the Holy Koran, be taken away and given eighty lashes.

When Arn had pronounced his judgment, everyone stood as if petrified at first. Then two sergeants came forward and seized the man to be whipped and dragged him away to turn him over to Gaza's Saracen provost marshals. The two women retreated horror-stricken back into the crowd. When all three were out of sight, a loud roar of conflicting voices broke out, and it was evident that there were people both for and against the judgment. Siegfried gazed out over the crowd and noticed a group of elderly men with long beards and white turbans, whom he surmised must be some sort of infidel clergymen. He guessed from their calm conversation and nods of agreement that they must have found the odd judgment to be both wise and just.

The next case involved a dispute about a horse, a case that was now called out for the second time since the judges had set aside the case until the horse was presented. Now it was brought forward into the empty square beyond the cordon by two men who seemed to be having a hard time holding the horse by the bridle. The case proved to be simple in that both made claim on the horse and likewise accused the other of horse thievery.

Arn asked them both to swear on the Holy Koran that they were telling the truth, and they did so, taking turns holding the horse, which the audience found extremely comical. But neither of them hesitated to swear the oath. And there was nothing to indicate that either one had sworn falsely, although one of them had to be a perjurer.

Arn had another muttered discussion with his Saracen assessors and then reached behind him to signal to one of his guards. He whispered an order which Siegfried could easily hear, to call out the butchers from the slaughterhouse and a cart.

Then Arn stood up and spoke first in the incomprehensible language and then in Frankish so that Siegfried and the others could understand. It was sad to see when someone bore false witness, Arn explained. Today a man had forsworn his soul and would burn in Hell for the sake of a broken-down horse.

There could be only one verdict, he warned, drawing his sword and raising it high as if to make an exaggerated downward stroke. Both the men who laid claim to the horse looked equally terrified, but it was hard to tell which of them was the perjurer.

Arn watched them for a moment with his sword raised, then he turned slightly and swung with the sword in only one hand, severing the horse's head. He jumped quickly away so as not to be kicked by its death throes or drenched by the blood spurting in all directions. Then he calmly wiped off his sword with a rag taken from under his tunic and slid it back into its scabbard, raising his hand to put a stop to all the noise from the crowd.

The horse now had to be divided into two pieces of equal size, he explained. That meant that the man who was a liar would get half a horse in payment. But his punishment from God would be all the more severe.

One man would get only half a horse even though he told the truth. His payment would be all the greater from God.

The slaughterhouse butchers brought their cart and loaded up both the horse and the horse's head, strewed sand over the blood, and quickly took the cart away, bowing to Arn.

Then followed a number of disputes that were completely without interest to Siegfried, mostly dealing with money. Arn and his Saracen judges most often reached a compromise, except for one time when they caught one of the disputants in a lie. He was taken away for whipping.

The last case of the day was, as far as Siegfried could gather from all the whispering and curious looks from the spectators, something out of the ordinary. A young Bedouin woman without a veil and a young Bedouin man in beautiful clothes stepped forward. They asked for two things: first was asylum in Gaza and protection from their vengeful parents. The second was that they might have permission to be united as man and wife before God by a *kadi* from the believers of Gaza.

Arn explained at once that their first request was granted the moment it was spoken. They both had asylum in Gaza.

As to the second request he had another long, whispered discussion with Utman ibn Khattab; both of them seemed concerned, because they were frowning and shaking their heads as they talked. It was obviously not an easy question.

Finally Arn stood up and raised his right hand for quiet, and the noise subsided at once. Everyone waited with bated breath to hear his verdict.

'You, Aisha, named after the wife of the Prophet, peace be unto him, are a Banu Qays, and you, Ali, named after a holy man whom some call caliph, are a Banu Anaza. Both of you are from different tribes in Gaza, and you obey the Knights Templar and myself. But it is not that simple, since your kinsmen are enemies, and it would lead to war if I allowed you to be united before God. For that reason you cannot be granted what you asked for at this moment. But this matter is not concluded, on that you have my word. Go now in peace and enjoy Gaza's asylum!'

When Siegfried heard the Frankish translation, which Arn delivered this time as he had all the others, he was astonished at how a brother in the divine order of the Knights Templar could sink to such depths as to take up the petty problems of these savages, such as whether or not they might marry. But he found Arn's dignity admirable under such circumstances, and he had truly not failed to notice the respect with which both believers and infidel Saracens had accepted all the judgments.

In the next few hours he did not have much time to discuss everything that had filled his head, because they first had to go to vespers and then to the *refectorium*. There they ate together with all the other knights in the same part of the hall, but silence was enforced during the meal.

Between the evening meal and *completorium* and the time following with wine and the giving of orders for the next day, they did have plenty of time to converse.

Because Siegfried was unsure of what he actually thought about the matters, he preferred at first to speak mostly about the authority of the judges, as if for the sake of argument he wholly accepted this form of justice, in which slaves were treated as Christian human beings. He was even more amazed when Arn explained that it was the Saracen Utman ibn Khattab who was the actual judge, because unlike Arn he had long experience in such work. This was especially true when the *sharia* was to be interpreted – the law of the infidels.

The fact that Arn behaved as if he were the judge was nothing but play-acting, but it was necessary, and Utman ibn Khattab had no difficulty understanding that. Gaza did belong to the Knights Templar, and they had to make clear to everyone in Gaza who held the power.

Siegfried admitted that it made a big difference if one had so many infidel subjects as Arn did here in Gaza. For instance, he knew very little about the Bedouins.

Arn asked if he would like to meet some Bedouins, because Arn was going to do exactly that the next day; it had to do with the young runaways, who had in full collusion committed a bride-robbery.

Siegfried found it unseemly that Arn as the fortress master should get involved in such a trivial argument over how the infidels paired off. But Arn assured him that it was definitely not a triviality, and this would become clear to Siegfried if he accompanied him on the next day's visit.

Mostly out of curiosity Siegfried agreed to go along.

As they rode out the next day to visit one of the Bedouin camps, Siegfried protested that they were riding alone, without the escort of a single squadron. After all, they were two knights of fortress master rank, and many a Saracen would love to show off their severed heads on the point of a lance as he rode in among his own kinsmen.

That was assuredly true, Arn admitted. And it was not entirely unlikely that on some unfortunate day both their heads might be conveyed in that manner. The Saracens especially seemed to love seeing the heads of Templar knights on the points of lances, whether it had to do with their beards or something else. Worldly Franks were clean-shaven, after all, and their heads probably looked less amusing on the tip of a lance.

Siegfried had strict objections to this lighthearted way of thinking. The beard of a Templar knight had nothing to do with the matter; it was simply that Templar knights were justifiably the most feared enemies of the Saracens.

Arn dropped this discussion at once. But he did insist that they ride without an escort.

It took them only an hour to ride at a leisurely pace to the place north of Gaza where the Banu Anaza tribe had its camp of black tents. When they were within view, a force of about twenty men jumped into the saddle and rode toward them at full speed, wildly shouting, with their lances and swords drawn to attack.

Siegfried blanched a bit but drew his sword when he saw that Arn did so.

'Can you ride at full speed, at least for a short distance?' Arn asked with an expression on his face that seemed unreasonably cheerful in the face of storming Saracen riders of such superior numbers. Siegfried nodded grimly.

'Then follow me, brother, but for God's sake don't strike at any of them!' ordered Arn, spurring his horse to a full gallop and heading straight towards the Bedouin camp as if in counterattack. After hesitating briefly, Siegfried followed him, swinging his sword above his head the same way as Arn.

When they met the Bedouin warriors they wheeled around on both sides of them so that it looked as though both the Templar knights and the Bedouin defenders were now attacking the camp together. They rode up toward the biggest tent, where an elderly man with a long gray beard and black clothing awaited them. Arn pulled up his horse right in front of the old man, hopped off his mount, and greeted everyone around him with his sword, whispering to Siegfried to do the same. The Bedouin riders walked their horses around them in a big circle and greeted them with their weapons.

Then Arn slipped his sword into its scabbard, Siegfried

did the same, and the Bedouin riders turned off towards the camp.

Arn now greeted the old man heartily and introduced his brother. They were invited into the tent, where they were immediately served cold water before sitting down on piles of multicoloured mats and pillows.

Siegfried didn't understand a word of the conversation that took place between Arn and the old man, who he guessed was the chief of the Bedouins. But he saw that they both spoke to each other with the greatest respect; they kept repeating each other's words as if every polite phrase had to be turned inside out a few times before they could continue. But soon the old man grew agitated and angry, and Arn seemed almost humbly to retreat and start coaxing him to calm down. After a while the old man seemed to grow pensive, muttering and sighing as he pulled on his beard.

Suddenly Arn got up and began taking his leave; he seemed to be met with friendly but insistent protests. Siegfried got up as well in support of Arn, and the friendly protests, which seemed to be about eating before they left, gradually faded. They said farewell by taking the old man by both hands and bowing, something that Siegfried did with some reluctance. But he found it wisest when on foreign ground to do as his brother Arn did.

When they rode off almost the same ceremonies were conducted as when they arrived; the Bedouin warriors rode some distance at their sides with weapons drawn, but suddenly they all turned and raced back to their camp.

Arn and Siegfried then slowed their horses to a leisurely walk, and Arn began telling him what it had all been about.

First, they couldn't come to a Bedouin camp unannounced escorted by a squadron, because that would be showing either cowardice or hostile intent. However, a man who rode into the camp without protection was both courageous and a man with honest intentions. That's why they had been met by the warlike yet friendly show of welcome.

These Bedouins did indeed belong to Gaza, at least as far as the bookkeepers of the Christians and Knights Templar viewed the matter. But in the Bedouins' own world it was inconceivable that a Bedouin could be the slave of anyone, and it was also said that Bedouins could never be kept imprisoned like other men, but would die if robbed of their freedom. Viewing them as slaves of Gaza was an almost childish conceit; if they even suspected such an attitude, their camp would have vanished into the desert. In the Saracen world the Bedouins themselves were the epitome of a people who were unconquerable and eternally free.

It was really all a question of a mutual pact of security and business. As long as the Bedouins had their camps within the borders of Gaza, they were protected from all enemies among the Saracens. In return the Bedouins protected the caravan traffic to and from Tiberias transporting sugar and building materials, as well as to and from Mecca carrying spices, aromatic oils, and bluestone.

The tribe they had just visited was that of the bride-robber's, the young man named Ali. Bride-robbery sometimes occurred if young Bedouins were in disagreement with their parents. But those couples that ran away, because it was more a case of running away rather than actual abduction of the bride, had to submit to being banished from both their tribes; if they lived with the man they would be attacked by the woman's tribe, and vice versa. It was a matter of honour.

Unfortunately the two Bedouin tribes had been enemies since ancient times – no one any longer remembered why – and their truce applied only as long as they remained within the borders of Gaza.

What Arn had proposed to the old chieftain was to let the two runaways be married according to the rules, and that this marriage would signify the same as peace among all of Gaza's Bedouins. The old man, who was Ali's uncle, had said that he didn't believe that would be possible, since the enmity was far too deeply entrenched. Yet he would not oppose such a peace arrangement if the other side agreed to it, which he doubted. The small hope that did exist was due to the fact that both tribes had profited a great deal by pitching their camps within the borders of Gaza and concluding an agreement with the Knights Templar.

For a long time Siegfried was made quiet and thoughtful by what he had heard. The benefits for the business of the Knights Templar that came from the caravan traffic was easy to understand; all transport through the deserts would be impossible without the Bedouin caravans.

And as far as the economy of these savages was concerned, it was easy to see the number of Mameluke weapons and artfully decorated saddles that were to be found in the camp they had just visited. The tribe had probably never had such rich plunder as they found after the battle of Mont Gisard.

No, sighed Arn. They probably had not, and they no doubt wished for the victory of the Knights Templar against the Mamelukes more than the reverse, simply for that reason. Defeated Templar knights were worthless as prisoners and never carried any valuables on their person.

Siegfried was amazed that his brother Arn, who was younger than him, hadn't spent many more years in the Holy Land than he had, and yet he'd been able to learn all these foreign ways: the animal-like sounds that comprised the language of the Saracens, as well as their barbaric customs.

Arn replied that he had always been interested in new knowledge, ever since he was a little boy at the monastery. In the cloister as a child he had mostly sought out knowledge from philosophy and books, but there wasn't much of that in the Holy Land. Here he had instead sought practical knowledge, all the things that might be useful to know in war and business, which was often the same thing. And as for his complaints about the barbarians, Arn joked shamelessly, surely the Saracen doctors weren't so bad, were they? Siegfried would be as good a warrior after his injuries at Mont Gisard as he had been before.

Siegfried opened his mouth to object, but he changed his mind. He had heard so much that he wanted to work things out for himself before he got into any new discussions with his younger brother, who was far too well informed.

The next day Arn rode out to the Bedouins of the Banu Qays tribe south of Gaza. Their camp was pitched where the hills met the huge beach near the road to Al Arish. He was gone for a whole day, but returned in time for *completorium*. During the evening wine afterward he reported the good news. Gaza's Bedouins were going to make peace.

As springtime approached, the *infirmatorium* in Gaza's fortress was gradually emptied until only two knights remained. One of them would be lame for the rest of his life, and Arn gave him a position with the weapons master as a smith.

A couple of weeks earlier Siegfried de Turenne had returned to his fortress, Castel Arnald, completely recovered, as evidenced by his latest practice ride and rounds with the sword in Gaza.

Spring was a time to make preparations before a more hectic period began, since trade by sea was always cut back in the wintertime, because of possible danger to the ships from storms.

Arn divided his time between bookkeeping for the customs master, Koran studies conducted with the Arabian doctors, riding practice, and taking care of his horses. Since Siegfried had left, Arn spent the most time with his beloved Arabian horse Khamsiin. Other brothers probably thought that he was overdoing things in that respect, because he talked to his horse in Arabic, using intonation and gestures as if the horse could understand his every word.

The unusual thing was not the expression of love for a good horse; every Templar knight could understand that. But horses were the most susceptible to the enemy's arrows, and yet the fortress master's steed had managed to survive as long as it had. That was with the horse he rode closest to the enemy's archers, when he led the Templars' light cavalry, the Turcopoles, against the enemy mounted archers. He rode the Frankish stallion Ardent, for whom he clearly did not feel the same personal affection, in the heavy armoured attacks.

With the arrival of spring more ships came to Gaza, now and then with a load of newly recruited riders and sergeants. It was always the same pitiable scene when the pale men hobbled ashore, their legs wobbly after their many weeks at sea. These loads of troops usually came all the way from Marseille or Montpellier.

Arn and his weapons master took turns holding welcome ceremonies for sergeants and brand-new knights, for now almost any newcomer could be dubbed a knight over in the preceptories of France without any preceding probationary year as a sergeant. This meant that they received a number of tenderfeet, who were allowed to wear the white mantle and then had to be treated as fully accepted brothers. This required a good deal of conciliatory mediation, for the tenderfeet often had an exaggerated notion of themselves, their courage and ability. Even worse, their idea of what these more or less imaginary characteristics could be used for seldom corresponded to reality.

Easier to handle in this regard were the new sergeants, who were often older and rawer types with greater experience in war, but lacking the nobility required to become a knight.

In the first shipload of seasick sergeants, who had clearly had an especially nasty last week at sea, there were two men who during the formation for the welcome ceremony in the courtyard of the fortress showed not the slightest sign that the journey had done them any harm. They were both very tall, one with flaming red hair, the other very blond with a beard that would have looked good on any Templar knight. The Saracens often felt greater fear of knights with blond beards than of those with black ones.

The two men stood side by side, conversing merrily in the midst of the crowd of more or less stooping comrades with green faces. These two immediately aroused Arn's curiosity. When he perused the list of names he was given by the ship's captain, he could only guess at a name that might be fitting for one of the two, a name that awakened vague memories of the cloister in him.

'Sergeants in our order, which of you is Tanguy de Bréton?' he yelled, and the red-haired man at once raised his hand in confirmation.

'And you next to him, what's your name?' Arn asked, pointing at the red-haired man's comrade, who had to be something other than a Breton.

'My name now Aral d'Austin,' replied the blond man with the long hair, in heavily accented Frankish.

'And where is Austin?' Arn asked, puzzled.

'It not where, it is my other name cannot say Frankish,' said the blond in broken Frankish.

'Well, what is your name in your own language then?' Arn went on, amused.

'My name in my own language is Harald Øysteinsson,' said the blond in Norse, which seemed to render the high Templar knight speechless.

Arn searched his memory for the Nordic words to say that this was the first time in the Holy Land that he had met a kinsman from the North, but the words did not come to him, because when he wasn't thinking in Frankish it was in Latin or Arabic.

He gave up the attempt and instead gave his usual stern welcome speech to the newcomers and introduced the sergeant of the fortress, who would now see to arranging their quarters and registering the new men. But on the way from there he hastily whispered to the fortress sergeant to send that Aral d'Austin to the *parlatorium* when everything else was finished.

After *Sext* was sung the Norwegian, who like other Norwegians had suffered no ill effects from a little jaunt across the sea, came in to Arn, looking abashed and with his hair now cropped short. It was evident how much he hated losing his beautiful thick hair. Arn pointed to a chair and the man sat down, but not with the usual speed of those who had lived long among the Knights Templar.

'Tell me now, my kinsman . . . ,' he began, having trouble with the Nordic words that he was trying to think/work out in advance. 'Who are you, who is your father, and to which clan in Norway do you belong?'

The other stared at him, at first not understanding him; it took a few moments before he realized that Arn was speaking Norse. Then he burst into a long, sad tale about who he was. At first Arn had a hard time following along, but soon his old language seemed to seep back into his head and slowly filled it with understanding.

Young Harald was the son of Øystein Møyla, who in turn was the son of King Øystein Haraldsson. But more than a year ago the Birch-Legs, as his clan and their kinsmen were called, had lost a decisive battle at Re-i-Ramnes outside Tønsberg in southern Norway. King Øystein, Harald's father, had been killed, and things had looked bleak for all the Birch-Legs. Many had moved to Western Götaland where they had friends. But as King Øystein's son, Harald had found that he could not escape the seekers of vengeance unless he travelled very far away. And if he had to flee death anyway, why not seek death somewhere else and die for a greater cause than just being his father's son?

'Who is the king of Western Götaland now, do you know?' asked Arn, full of excitement that he struggled hard not to show.

'The king there has been Knut Eriksson for a long time, and he is close to us Birch-Legs, as is his jarl, the Folkung Birger Brosa. These two good men are our closest kinsmen in Western Götaland. But tell me, knight, who are you and what is your great interest in me?'

'My name is Arn Magnusson and I am from the Folkung clan; my father's brother is the jarl Birger Brosa. My dear friend since we were children is Knut Eriksson,' said Arn feeling a sudden strong emotion that he had a hard time concealing. 'When God led your path to our austere brotherhood he led you in any case to a kinsman.'

'You sound more like a Dane when you speak rather than someone from Western Götaland,' Harald noted dubiously.

'That's true. For many years as a child I lived with the Danes in the *Vitae Schola* cloister; I've forgotten what it's called in the vernacular. But you can be assured that what I said was true. I am a Templar knight, as you see, and we do not lie. But why did they give you a black rather than a white mantle?'

'There was something about having to have a father who was a knight. A great deal of discussion about that. My explanation that my father was not a knight but a king did not seem to make much of an impression.'

'In that case, you were done an injustice, kinsman. But let's look at the good side of this error, for I need a sergeant and you need a kinsman in a world that is very far from Norway. Wearing a black mantle you will learn more and live longer than if you'd been given a white one. There's only one thing you have to keep in mind. Even though we Folkungs and you Birch-Legs are kinsmen in the North, you are a sergeant and I a fortress master here in the Holy Land. I am like a jarl, and you are like a retainer; you must never imagine or pretend otherwise, even though you and I speak the same language.'

'Such is the lot of someone who is forced to flee his own country,' said Harald sadly. 'But it could have been worse. And if I had to choose between serving a man of Frankish lineage and a man of the Folkung clan, the choice would not be hard.'

'Well spoken, kinsman,' said Arn, standing up as a sign that the meeting was over.

When the summer approached and with it the time for war, much effort was spent organizing the new sergeants and knights in Gaza. As far as the knights were concerned, they worked most on getting the newcomers to adapt to the tactics of the cavalry and the command signs. They also needed to drill discipline into them, which was very strict. A knight who on his own authority left a formation risked being divested of his white mantle in disgrace. The only case in which the Rule permitted such a digression was if it were done to save a Christian's life. And that would have to be proven afterwards.

Most of the new men, who had become knights largely because of their lineage more than anything else, were quite used to riding horses, so that part of the exercise was the easiest and the most pleasant.

Worse was having to stand and sweat through all the practice with weapons in hand. On that point almost all the new tenderfeet were so awkward that they would soon needlessly die if they did not quickly realize that the belief they had previously entertained – that they were better than others with a sword, battle-axe, lance, and shield – was of no merit whatsoever here among the Templar knights. The newcomers had to learn this honest truth before they could start to learn their skills anew. Out of necessity, all the older teachers were harsh on the tenderfeet at first. The bodies of the new recruits were soon covered with black-and-blue marks and hurt so badly when they tried to sleep at night that they truly deserved their nickname of tenderfeet.

Harald Øysteinsson was a warrior as wild as he was wretched. At first he had picked out a sword that was much too heavy, and with it he stormed toward Arn like a Viking berserker with no wit or sense. Arn struck him to the ground, kicked him to the ground, and knocked him to the ground with his shield. He also hacked at his upper arms and thighs with his blunted sword, which didn't go through his chain mail but left bruises nevertheless.

And yet Harald had a hard time restraining himself. There was nothing wrong with his courage and bravery. The problem was that he fought like a Viking, and if he continued to do that he wouldn't live long in the Holy Land. He was stubborn too, but the more Arn punished his body with blows from the flat or the edge of his sword, the more furious he became when he attacked again. All the others who acted that way usually softened quickly both in mind and body, stopping to think and ask what they were doing wrong. But not young Harald.

Arn let the abuse continue for a week in the hope that Harald would grow wiser. But when that didn't help, he was forced to try and make his kinsman listen to reason.

'Don't you understand?' he appealed as they came out of vespers and had a free hour before the evening meal. As they walked together along one of Gaza's piers, Arn explained. 'It will mean the death of you if you don't banish all the old techniques you've learned and start over from the beginning.'

'It's probably not my ability with a sword that's the problem,' Harald muttered morosely.

'No?' Arn said, truly astonished. 'Then why is it that your body is aching from your neck to your shins, and yet you never hit me even once with your wild slashing?'

'Because I've met a swordsman that even the gods themselves could not defeat; against every other man it's different. I have killed many men. That's one thing I know for sure.'

'As long as you realize that you will be killed quicker than you can imagine,' said Arn dryly. 'You're too slow. The Saracens' swords are lighter than ours, just as sharp as ours, and very quick. And by the way, you're wrong when it comes to my skill. There are five of us here in Gaza who are exceptionally skilled, but three of the knights are better than I am.'

'I don't believe it. That can't be so!' Harald objected hotly.

'Good!' said Arn. 'Then tomorrow you'll have a chance to fight with Guy de Carcassonne, the day after with Sergio de Livorne, and then with Ernesto de Navarra, who is the best of all of us here in Gaza. And if you can still move your arms and legs after that, you can come back to me, because by then the medicine will have convinced you.'

That medicine bit hard. After three days of fighting against the best swordsmen in Gaza, Harald couldn't raise an arm without pain or take a step without staggering. Not a single time during these three days with the best of the best had he landed a blow or even come close to doing so. He said that it was like trying to fight in a nightmare in which he was stuck in boat tar.

Arn found to his satisfaction that he had finally broken the stubborn Norwegian's inflexible resolve.

Now they could start afresh. First he took Harald to the armoury and selected a lighter sword that would be more suitable. He tried as kindly as possible to explain that it was never the weight of a sword that was decisive, but rather how well it sat in the hand of the man who wielded the weapon.

Then Arn let Harald lick his wounds for two days as a spectator, while he himself practiced with Ernesto de Navarra, the best of them all.

The two knight-brothers alternated between fighting in earnest and then repeating the same moves slowly so that the young tenderfoot could observe and learn. It was very strong medicine for Harald, for when the knights Arn and Ernesto went at each other with full force and at full speed, it was often hard for the eye to follow along in the whirling and flashing stream of blows and parries. It seemed as though the combatants were equal, yet Brother Ernesto seemed to be the one who connected more often.

What most astonished Harald was that when the two knights were fighting at full force, their blows were so hard that any man would have fallen to the ground in pain. But they both seemed able to withstand anything at all.

When one of them was struck he did not change expression, but took a step backward and bowed as a compliment, only to go on the attack himself in the next instant.

So young Harald's journey to the world of a different kind of war had finally begun. When he once again faced Arn, they were able to practice move for move, drilling each little step and gesture until Harald could do them automatically. And soon Harald felt that he was changing, as if he saw the first small glint of light from the other world where such men as Arn and Ernesto lived. He became determined to reach that other world himself.

The next test for Harald was that his lord opined that he could not ride. Naturally he had been riding horses for his whole life like all the other people in the North. But there was a big difference between riding and merely sitting on a horse, as Arn Magnusson explained. Like all dwellers in the North, Harald was also convinced that horses were of no use in war, that one should ride to the battlefield and there dismount and tie up the horse before rallying and rushing at the enemy on the nearest field.

At first he was offended that Arn objected that as a warrior Harald was no good on a horse, but he went on to say that foot soldiers were important too. It took some time before Harald realized that this was actually true, that the foot soldiers were as important for success as the cavalry was.

When they proceeded to archery practice Harald was filled with renewed hope, because he had never met his match as an archer. Every Birch-Leg back home knew this, and their enemies even more so.

But when he shot against Arn Magnusson he soon felt annihilated, as if the breath went out of him and all hope was quenched.

Arn thought afterwards that he may have waited too long to tell young Harald the truth, and that he had let his sergeant come close to despair before deigning to encourage him.

Young Harald had not even noticed how his archery contest with Arn had attracted both knights and sergeants as a furtive audience. They all pretended to have something to do in the vicinity, even though they really wanted to study the new sergeant who could shoot almost as well as the man whom even the Turks referred to as unsurpassed.

'Now I will tell you something that might cheer you up,' said Arn at last as they went to put away their bows and arrows in the armoury on their fifth day of practice. 'You are truly the best archer I have ever seen here in the Holy Land. Where did you learn your skill?'

'I hunted squirrels a lot as a child,' replied Harald before his thoughts caught up with his words and his face suddenly brightened. 'Did you say that I was good? But you shoot better than I do every time, and so do all the others.'

'No,' said Arn, his expression both amused and a bit mysterious. He turned suddenly to two knight-brothers passing

252

by and explained that his young squire had little faith in himself when it came to archery because he had lost to his lord. The two broke out laughing and slapped young Harald encouragingly on the back before they walked away, still laughing.

'Now I shall tell you the truth,' said Arn with a smile. 'I am not as bad with a bow as I am on horseback or with a lance and sword. The truth is that I shoot better than any Templar knight in the Holy Land. I say this only because it is true; a Templar knight may not boast. Your ability will be a great joy to us, and perhaps more than once it will save your own life and those of others too.'

Harald Øysteinsson's first opportunity to save his life with his bow came soon. The summer had not progressed very far before the Templar knights in Gaza were summoned to the north with full forces, which meant both heavy and light cavalry and archers afoot.

Saladin had perhaps learned something from the great defeat at Mont Gisard. This was how he viewed defeats, merely as something from which to learn for next time, and not at all as a sign that God had abandoned either him or *jihad*.

That spring he had gone into the northern part of the Holy Land with a small army of mixed Syrian and Egyptian soldiers. He had defeated King Baldwin IV far up near Banyas and then plundered Galilee and southern Lebanon and burned all the crops he could. Now in the summer he had returned with what was thought to be the same army. But that was an erroneous assumption on the part of the Christians and it would cost them dearly.

The king had mobilized a new secular army, but it was too weak to meet Saladin on its own. So he had turned to the Grand Master of the Knights Templar and obtained a promise of full support.

For Harald Øysteinsson this meant a hard march lasting ten days, alternately walking and riding on any available spare horse through a land that was completely unfamiliar and in heat that seemed to him inhuman.

When the battle finally began, it was like Ragnarök, the Twilight of the Gods. He found himself in a sea of fast Saracen riders galloping forward, each one of whom was harder to hit than a squirrel. And yet it soon felt as though there was no sense in shooting, for no matter how many men Harald hit, new ones kept coming in wave upon wave. He soon realized that he was in the midst of a defeat, but he didn't know that it was one of the greatest catastrophes that had ever befallen both the Knights Templar and the Christian secular army in the Holy Land.

For Arn the defeat was clearer and easier to understand, and therefore even more bitter.

In upper Galilee between the River Jordan and the River Litani, the Templars had their first skirmish with Saladin's forces. They were on their way to join up with the royal army, which under Baldwin IV's leadership was busy neutralizing a small band of plunderers on their way back from the coast of Lebanon.

The Grand Master Odo de Saint Amand may have misunderstood the situation. Perhaps he thought that the royal army was already engaged with Saladin's main force and that the riders now appearing before the Templar knights were merely plunderers separated from the main force, or a small group intended only to disrupt or delay the Templars.

However, the truth was precisely the opposite. While the royal Christian army was occupied with a small company, Saladin led his main force around and past them to cut off the Templar knights, who were on the way to provide relief.

Afterwards it was as clear as water what Odo de Saint Amand should have done. He should have refrained from attacking; at all costs he should have tried to unite his knights, his infantry, and his Turcopoles with Baldwin IV's army. And if that had not succeeded, he should have taken a stand. There was one thing he absolutely should *not* have done, and that was to send out the whole heavy cavalry of knights for a single decisive attack.

But that was what he did, and neither Arn nor any other Templar knight ever had a chance to ask him why.

Afterwards Arn thought that he may have had a better view from his high position up on the right flank than Odo de Saint Amand had. Arn and his light, fast mounted archers stayed up high and beside the advancing main force so that they could cut off attack by enemies who rode with the same equipment as they did. From up there Arn had clearly seen that what they were about to meet was an infinitely superior army bearing Saladin's own flags.

When Odo de Saint Amand far below formed the heavy cavalry to a frontal assault, Arn at first thought that it was a stratagem of war, a way to create doubt in the enemy and gain time to save the foot soldiers. His despair was all the greater when he saw that the black-and-white flag of the Grand Master's *confanonier* was raised and lowered three times as a sign for an all-out attack. He sat as if paralysed up on his hill, surrounded by his Turkish riders, who also could not believe their eyes. The main force of the Templar knights was riding straight to their deaths.

When the heavy Templar knights came closer to the light Syrian cavalry, the enemy simply retreated and pretended to flee to the rear in the typical Saracen manner. Soon the assault by the knights was stopped even though they had not made contact with anything, and then they were caught unprotected and surrounded.

The Turkish riders near Arn shook their heads and threw out their arms to show that the battle was now over as far as they were concerned. If the army of which they were a part lost its entire heavy cavalry, the Turcopoles had nothing to protect but their own lives. And so they fled, leaving Arn alone with a few Christian riders.

He waited briefly to see whether any Templar knights had survived and were trying to fight their way out of the trap. When he noticed a group of ten men attempting to head back in the direction of their own foot soldiers, reserve horses, and supplies, he attacked at once along with the few men who were still with him. The only thing he could hope for was to create a distraction so that the fleeing knights could take shelter behind the infantry and archers.

His hopeless attack with a handful of terrified men against a force a thousand times greater at least had the effect of creating a momentary confusion among the pursuers, who were soon pointing and calling his name from every direction. With that he and his little group became the target of the pursuers, and it was not hard to understand why. After Mont Gisard anyone who could bring Al Ghouti's head on his lance to Saladin would surely be richly rewarded.

Soon he was riding all alone, because the men who at first had followed him turned off and fled toward the remnants of their own army and foot soldiers. Arn swung abruptly in the other direction in a wide arc away from his own forces and towards a hillside where he would be stuck in an obvious trap. When he saw that all his own men had taken cover, he gave up and stopped. He couldn't go any farther anyway; the slopes before him were too steep.

When the attackers saw his predicament they reined in their horses and walked them slowly toward him with their bows half raised. They surrounded him, laughing, almost as if wanting to draw out the pleasure of the moment.

Then a high emir came galloping up, pushed through his own ranks, pointed at Arn and began shouting various orders.

All the Syrian and Egyptian riders greeted him with their bows raised over their heads before they wheeled their horses around and vanished in a cloud of dust.

At first Arn sat there thinking that he had witnessed a miracle of God, but his reason told him quite clearly that there was no question of anything like that. They had spared his life, it was that simple. Whether it had to do with Saladin or something else it was impossible to know. Right now there were more important questions to worry about.

He shook off the sense of calm, which he had mustered while waiting for death, and rode fast down toward the remaining portion of their own forces. Of the knights that had survived, almost all of them were wounded in one way or another. There were now about twenty reserve horses, the same number of pack horses, and a hundred archers on foot. Arn's Turcopoles had all fled. They fought for money, not to die unnecessarily for Christians. They intended either to win or to flee.

The defeat was great. More than three hundred knights were lost, more than Arn had ever heard of in any other battle. But right now the important thing was to think clearly and save whatever could be saved. He was the highest-ranking of all the surviving knight-brothers, and he took command at once.

Before they all rushed off they had to hold a brief council, so he gathered three of the least wounded brothers around him. The first question was why Saladin's army hadn't finished off the attack now that they had succeeded in what they had always wanted; to separate the Christians' infantry from their cavalry. The answer must be that they were on their way to engage in battle with King Baldwin's army and planned to wipe it out first, before they returned to finish here. So there was no time to waste; if possible, they had to reunite with the king's army before all was lost.

They hastened to remove all the equipment and supplies

from the reserve horses so as to load their wounded instead. All the spare horses were to be ridden by the oldest sergeants and archers, while the younger ones had to run along beside the pitiful remnants of the army of knights that now set its course toward the River Litani. Arn's thought was that Baldwin's army surely was hard pressed, and their only salvation was to make it across the river.

But King Baldwin's army was already beaten and had dispersed into small fleeing groups that were being caught up by superior pursuers, one group after another. The king himself and his bodyguards, however, had managed to make it across the river. That made the situation even worse for all the stragglers, including the depleted and suffering force that Arn was leading.

As his men and horses were attempting to cross the river, Arn gathered the best archers around him on the riverbank – Harald Øysteinsson among them – to try to hold the enemy's mounted archers and lancers at a distance while foot soldiers, horses, and wounded knight-brothers waded across the river in a bloodied and desperate contingent.

They shot arrows until they were all gone, then flung off their weapons and shields and cast themselves into the river, Arn and Harald bringing up the rear. But they were the only two to survive among those who came last. They both were able to dive down and let the current in the middle of the river take them a good way downstream before they staggered ashore, panting.

There was only time for a brief respite on the other side while they attempted to establish order once again. Feeling an unexpected sense of joy in this desperate situation, Arn saw his stallion Khamsiin come galloping up to him in the midst of the confusion.

Riders and foot soldiers from the Hospitallers had come to their rescue on the other side of the Litani, and they led the defeated group of Templar knights to the fortress of Beaufort, which was only about an hour away. Many men from the royal army had also taken refuge there.

Soon the fortress was surrounded by Saladin's forces, but that was no cause for alarm because Beaufort was one of the impregnable fortresses.

The Hospitallers of St John were no friends of the Templars, though Arn did not know why, only that there was always tension between the two orders. It often happened that if the Hospitallers were in a battle, the Templars would stay out of it, and vice versa. This time the Hospitallers had not participated with more than a symbolic force, while their main force remained in safety behind the walls of Beaufort.

The nickname the Templars had for the Hospitaller Order was the black Samaritans, which referred both to their black mantles with the white cross and to the fact that they had originated as a hospital offering free medical care. But since there were now many wounded to take care of, not a word of affront was heard among the rescued and wounded Templar knights who had involuntarily become the guests of their rival order.

It was a hard first night with many wounded to look after at the fortress of Beaufort. Exhausted and red-eyed from lack of sleep and with a paralysing sorrow within him, Arn forced himself to take a walk around the walls of the fortress to observe and learn. Beaufort was situated at a high elevation. He could see the glittering sea in the west, the Bekaa Valley in the north, and snow-clad mountains in the east. The high location of the fortress made it impossible even to imagine how an enemy could build siege towers outside on the slopes to get over those walls. The steep cliffs all around would make it equally impossible to drag catapults into position. Standing outside the walls and screaming insults, as the enemy soldiers were now doing, was meaningless. Not even a very long siege would have any effect, because the fortress was supplied by its own spring and had cisterns that were so overfilled that they had to release water into an artificial stream toward the west. The grain magazine was always full and held enough to support five hundred men for a year.

One drawback was possibly that the steep cliffs outside made it impossible to strike back at a besieger with surprise cavalry attacks. Right now there were more than three hundred knights inside the fortress and an equal number of sergeants. That was a force that on a flat battlefield would quickly have obliterated the vituperators that now camped outside the walls. Had they known what a large force was inside the fortress they would surely have been less audacious. But that was the thing about fortresses: they always contained a secret. Were there only twenty defenders inside? Or a thousand? More than once a superior enemy had passed by fortresses without attacking because they had miscalculated the size of the garrison. The opposite had also occurred. As in this case, the enemy thought they were besieging an almost empty fortress and let themselves be lulled into a false sense of security. Then they were crushed in the first assault.

Arn went to take care of Khamsiin again, brushing the horse and speaking to him about his great sorrow. For the third time he examined every inch of his steed's body to assure himself that there was no hidden arrow-wound. But Khamsiin proved to be as uninjured as his master, with only a few scratches, the sort that they both had learned to live with.

After tending to Khamsiin he proceeded to the sergeants' quarters, speaking with the wounded and praying. After prayers he took Harald Øysteinsson up on the walls to teach him how a fortress functioned.

As they walked along the breastwork on the eastern wall, they discovered a grisly procession on its way up to the fortress. There were several squadrons of Mameluke cavalry slowly working their way up the slopes. On their raised lances they each bore a bloody head, and almost all the heads had beards.

They stood as if petrified, without saying a word, without showing on their faces what they were feeling. This was hard for Harald Øysteinsson, but he made a great effort to behave in the same apparently unmoved manner as his lord.

The triumphant Mamelukes lined up in row after row below the eastern wall and shook their bloody lances so that the beards on the severed heads flapped up and down. One of them rode up in front of the others and raised his voice in something that sounded to Harald like a prayer, a lament, and a victory cry all at the same time.

'What is he saying?' Harald whispered, his mouth dry.

'He says that he thanks God the Almighty that the indignity of Mont Gisard is now eradicated, that what happened yesterday at Marj Ayyoun is more than sufficient redress, that we will all have our heads skewered in this way, and more such talk,' said Arn without expression.

Just then Beaufort's weapons master came hurrying up onto the wall along with several Hospitallers. The weapons master shouted orders not to shoot at the enemy, and the sergeants who had already begun to fumble for their bows and crossbows laid down their arms.

'Why can't we shoot?' asked Harald. 'Shouldn't some of them have to die so we can put an end to their bluster?'

'Yes,' said Arn in the same toneless way he had spoken before. 'The one riding in front should die. You can see by the blue silk band around his right arm that he is their commander, and he's the one who is proclaiming that he's the great conqueror, God's favourite, and other blasphemy. He should be the first to die, but not before we have sung *None*.'

'Shouldn't we take revenge rather than sing hymns?' Harald muttered with ill-concealed impatience.

'Yes, it might seem so,' replied Arn. 'But above all we must not act prematurely. You see that they have lined up at what they think is a safe distance from arrows and –'

'But I can –'

'Hush! Don't interrupt me. Remember that you are a sergeant. Yes, I know that you could hit him from here. So could I. But the braggart down there doesn't know that. We're not in charge here at the Hospitallers' fortress. Their weapons master gave orders for no one to shoot, and that was a wise thing to do.'

'Why was that so wise? How long do we have to put up with this blasphemous display?'

'Until after we have sung *None*, I said. Then the sun will be low in the west; the men down there will have the sun in their eyes and won't see our arrows until it's too late. The Hospitallers' weapons master was wise because those of us up here must not show our despair or shoot wasted arrows that will provoke only laughter. We certainly don't want to goad on their merriment. That's why he gave the order.'

Arn took his sergeant over to the weapons master, who was still up on the walls. He greeted the man very courteously and requested permission to kill some of the Mamelukes that afternoon, although no one would loose an arrow before then.

Only reluctantly did the weapons master give his permission, since he thought that the enemy would stay at a safe distance for at least that long.

Arn bowed humbly and requested furthermore that he and his sergeant might borrow bows from the armoury, since they had lost their own when they crossed the River Litani. He also asked that they be allowed to practice with the bows down in the courtyard before it was time.

Perhaps there was something in the earnestness of Arn's

manner, or perhaps it was the black edge of his mantle that showed his high rank, but the Hospitallers' weapons master suddenly changed both his tone of voice and bearing as he granted Arn everything that he had asked.

A while later Arn and Harald tried out various bows in the armoury and took two each along with a large quiver of arrows out to the courtyard; there they set up two hay bales as targets. They practiced resolutely until they found the bows that suited them best and learned how high above the target they had to aim. The knights among the Hospitallers came to watch their desperate guests attempt a feat that was far too difficult, at first acting somewhat superior in both speech and manner. But they soon fell silent when they saw what the tall brother and his sergeant could do.

When the sun was the correct height that afternoon and they had sung the hymns they had to sing with the Hospitaller brothers in the big fortress church, Arn took some of his Templar knight-brothers and Harald up on the walls. He asked them to walk back and forth a few times to show themselves. As he had hoped, the white mantles up on the walls incited the enemy down below, and the soldiers again raised their lances with the severed heads of the knights' brothers. Hooting and taunting, they took up where they had left off earlier before they tired of all the commotion, since it had not prompted even one vain shot from above.

The Templar knights stood silent and grave, in full view up on the walls, as the scornful enemy dared come ever closer. Soon the Templars could recognize some of their brothers who were now in Paradise. Siegfried de Turenne was one of them. Ernesto de Navarra, the great swordsman, was among them too.

Once more the emir who yelled loudest about God's protection and the great victory at Marj Ayyoun rode up in front of the others with his bloody trophy raised before him.

'He's the one we'll take first,' said Arn. 'We'll both shoot at him, you high and I low. When he's dead we'll see how many of the others we can hit.'

Harald nodded sombrely as he drew his bow, raised it, and glanced at Arn, who was also now raising his drawn bow. They stood like silhouettes against the sun, and the shadows of their bodies concealed the shiny tips of their arrows.

'You go first,' Arn commanded.

The emir down below was just moving on from a long tirade of boasting to invoking God anew. He had leaned his head back and was singing a prayer as loudly as he could.

Then an arrow slammed into his open mouth and out through the back of his neck, and another arrow struck him low in the chest where the ribs divide. He fell soundlessly from his horse.

Before the men around him understood what had happened, another four of them fell, skewered by arrows, and a tumult arose as they all tried to withdraw at the same time. A shower of arrows then landed in their midst, for now all the archers up on the breastwork had orders to take their best shot. More than ten Mamelukes fell due to their boastful pride and their willingness to mock the defeated.

Afterwards Harald reaped much praise from both the Templars and the Hospitallers for taking the first shot and shutting the mouth of the worst of the blusterers in the best imaginable way. That arrow-shot would live long in the memory of all.

Harald admitted to Arn that he had struck too high, that his intention had been to put the arrow somewhere below the man's chin. Arn said that there was no reason to admit that miss to anyone else. In any case it looked as though God had steered the arrow straight into the blasphemer's mouth. The pranks of the Mamelukes were now over, and that was the important thing. When their own dead lay before the walls they would surely lose their desire for further taunting.

And so it was. The Mamelukes withdrew and waited for the dark of night so they could fetch their dead. The next morning they were gone.

At the request of Count Raymond III of Tripoli, who was also among the defeated behind the walls, the master of the Hospitallers' fortress at Beaufort had refrained from inviting Arn to the evening wine and bread after *completorium*. It was well known that Count Raymond detested the Templars.

But when the master of the fortress heard how his brother in rank from the Templars had shut up the boisterous foes outside the walls, he found it unreasonable not to invite Arn for wine and bread that same evening.

Arn arrived unsuspecting, although he knew that Count Raymond was the foremost among the secular knights in Outremer; but he knew nothing about the count's hatred of the Templars.

What he noticed first that evening when he entered the master's own rooms in the northeastern part of the fortress was that the count was the only one among both the secular and ecclesiastical knights who refused to greet him.

When all had sat down and blessed the bread and wine, the mood was tense. They ate and drank for a while in silence, until Count Raymond in derisive terms asked what the madmen had intended at Marj Ayyoun.

Arn was the only one in the room who did not understand what the count meant by 'the madmen', so he didn't think that the question was directed at him. But he soon noticed that everyone was staring at him and waiting for an answer. Then he spoke the truth, that he hadn't understood the question, if it indeed was directed at him.

Count Raymond then asked Arn, in a sarcastically polite tone of voice, if he would relate what had happened to the

Templar knights who had been expected to rescue a royal army in great difficulty.

Arn told him briefly and bluntly about the mistakes that had led the Templar knights into death. He added that he had seen it all, because at the crucial moment he was high up on one flank and perhaps had been able to see what his Grand Master unfortunately could not when he gave the last command of his life.

The Hospitallers in the room bowed their heads in prayer, for they could imagine better than anyone what had happened. They too were known for their sometimes foolhardy attacks.

But Count Raymond was not for an instant moved by the tragic tale. In a loud voice and without the slightest courtesy he began describing the Templars as madmen who would lead an army to its doom on one occasion only to be victorious the next; they would really be better off without them. The knights were reckless fools, friends of the condemned Assassins, uneducated louts who knew nothing about Saracens and who through their ignorance might lead the entire Christian population of Outremer to their deaths.

He was a tall and very powerful man with long blond hair that had begun to turn gray. His language was coarse and harsh, and he spoke Frankish with the accent of a native Frank, those that were called *subars*. It was said that a *subar* resembled the cactus fruit the word described, prickly on the outside but deliciously sweet inside. Yet their speech could be hard to understand for newly arrived Franks because they used many of their own words and many words that were Saracen.

Arn did not reply to the count's insults because he had not the slightest idea how to handle the uncomfortable situation in which he now found himself. He was a guest of the Hospitallers, but a guest of necessity. And he had never before heard such affronts spoken about the Templars. For the sake of his honour a Templar knight could draw his weapon, but the Rule also forbade any Templar knight from killing or mistreating a Christian. The punishment was the loss of his mantle. So Arn could not defend himself with his sword. Nor with words.

Yet his submissive silence did not put a stop to Count Raymond, who had lost a stepson in the battle and was in despair like all the others in the room over the crushing defeat. The presence of an odious young Templar knight at the same table provoked his wrath.

As if to put Arn in his place once and for all, he repeated some of the last things he had said about the filthy brutes who didn't even know what the Koran was, and understood the Saracens even less.

At last a bright idea entered Arn's head. He raised his wine glass to Count Raymond and spoke the language of the Saracens to him.

'In the name of the Merciful and Compassionate, honoured Count Raymond, bear in mind the words of the Lord as we now drink together: *And from the fruits of the date palm and the grapevine you shall extract both wine and healthful sustenance; in this there is certainly a message to him who employs his reason.*'

Arn sipped his wine slowly, set his Syrian wine glass carefully on the table, and looked at Count Raymond without rancour, but without lowering his gaze.

'Were those really the words of the Koran? About drinking wine?' asked Count Raymond after a long, tense silence in the room.

'Yes, indeed,' replied Arn quietly. 'They are from the 16th *sura*, the 67th verse, and it bears thinking about. In the previous verse it does say that milk is preferable. But it does bear thinking about.'

Count Raymond sat in silence for a moment, gazing intently at Arn, before he suddenly asked a question in Arabic.

'Where, Templar knight, did you learn the language of the unbelievers? I learned it during ten years of captivity in Aleppo, but surely you have not been a captive, have you?'

'No, I have not, as you may well understand,' replied Arn in the same language. 'I learned from those who worked for us among the believers. The fact that I, unlike yourself, am forbidden to submit to captivity was made quite evident from what we saw today outside the walls. It pains me, count, that you speak so ill of my dead brothers. They died for God, they died for the Holy Land and for God's Grave. But they also died for you and yours.'

'Who is this Templar knight?' Count Raymond then asked in Frankish. His question seemed to be directed at the weapons master of the Hospitallers.

'That, Count Raymond,' said the weapons master, 'is the victor of Mont Gisard, when two hundred Templar knights conquered three thousand Mamelukes. That is the man whom the Saracens call Al Ghouti. With all respect, count, I would therefore like to ask you, as long as you are our guest, to pay more attention to your language.'

Everyone now looked at Count Raymond without saying a word. He was the master of Tripoli and the foremost knight of the Franks, used to commanding any table at which he sat. The predicament he now found himself in was an unfamiliar one for him. But he was a man with great experience of both his own and others' mistakes, and he decided to repair as quickly as possible the unnecessary dilemma that he had precipitated.

'I have been an ass here this evening,' he said with a sigh followed by a smile. 'The only redeeming feature I possess as an ass, however, is that unlike other asses I know when I've made a mistake. I shall now do something that I have never done in my life.'

With these words he got up and strode across the room

to Arn, pulled him to his feet and embraced him. Then he fell to his knees to beg forgiveness.

Arn blushed and stammered that it was not right for a worldly man to humble himself so before a Templar knight.

In this odd way a long friendship was begun between two men who in many respects stood far apart, but who both stood closer to the Saracens than did other Christians.

That evening they were soon left alone in the three rooms of the Hospitallers' fortress master. Count Raymond had taken a seat next to Arn and insisted that they both speak only Arabic so that all the others would be shut out of their conversation, which was his initial intention. Once they were left alone, which had also been his intention, and he ordered more wine as if he were at home in one of his own fortresses, Count Raymond still wanted to continue their conversation in Arabic. For as he said, the walls had ears everywhere in Outremer, and some of what he had to tell Arn might be called treason by malicious people.

And people of malice now held the power in the Kingdom of Jerusalem, which could lead to the greatest defeat. Not a defeat like the recent one at Marj Ayyoun; that was only one of a thousand battles waged over many years, and the Saracens and Christians had each won about an equal number. Raymond himself had been victorious more than a hundred times, but had lost almost as often.

Worst of all the malicious people was the king's mother, Agnes de Courtenay, who now had insinuated herself into the court in Jerusalem and actually had become the one who had the greatest say in matters. Her various lovers were those who acquired power. They were all newly arrived tenderfeet, and behaved as one did at a royal court in Paris or Rome; they dressed in the courtly manner and divided their time between instigating base intrigues and committing unmentionable sins with small boys from the slave market. Agnes de Courtenay's latest lover was a fop named Lusignan, and he was scheming to get the king's sister Sibylla married off to a younger brother named Guy. If that happened, little brother Lusignan could soon become king of Jerusalem. The days of the young but leprous Baldwin IV were numbered.

For Arn these were mostly incomprehensible matters that Count Raymond began complaining about more and more loudly as he drank, and urged Arn to drink more too. It was another world, a world in which God did not exist, where God's Grave was guarded not by devoted believers but by intriguers and those who consorted with donkeys and slave boys. It was like looking down into Hell, as it was said that the Prophet, peace be unto him, had to do when he climbed up the ladder to Heaven from the rock beneath the Temple of the Lord.

When Count Raymond eventually realized that he was blurting out too many things that the childlike but honest young Templar knight did not understand, he switched to discussing the latest lost battle at Marj Ayyoun.

They soon agreed, now that no one could hear them, that it was not so much their own mistakes as Saladin's cunning that had turned the tide against them. Either Saladin had had extraordinary good luck, as the Templar knights had experienced at Mont Gisard, or with uncanny skill he had done everything right. He must have planned the whole thing in advance, for when he attacked earlier in the spring he had only had a small army, and now he had come with a force five times as strong. The Christians had not realized this until it was too late. So his victory was fully justified.

Even though the wine had now gone to Arn's head, he tried to argue against the idea of a justified victory for the enemy, but he could offer no valid objections. On the contrary, after a few more glasses he had to agree with the count's conclusion; so he changed the subject out of sheer embarrassment. He asked Count Raymond why he hated the Knights Templar.

Count Raymond retreated a bit and told him that there were a few Templar knights, including Arn, or Al Ghouti rather, whom he did admire. Foremost among them was Arnoldo de Torroja, Jerusalem's Master. If God would ever involve Himself in a good way in the situation in the Holy Land, then Arnoldo de Torroja should be the next Grand Master. By now Odo de Saint Amand was either dead or taken captive, which in the case of Templar knights was usually the same as death. According to Count Raymond, Arnoldo de Torroja was one of the few high Templars who grasped the sole important issue for a Christian future in Outremer. They would have to make peace with Saladin. They had to divide Jerusalem, no matter how painful it might be, so that all pilgrims, even Jews, had equal right to the city's holy places.

There was only one alternative to that: continued war with Saladin until he gained complete victory and took Jerusalem by force. But as the royal court in Jerusalem now looked, with only schemers and dilettantes, there was not much hope.

Besides, the Knights Templar, whose power had to be acknowledged no matter what one thought of them otherwise, had many exceptionally incompetent and immoral friends. Worst among them was the inveterate rascal Reynald de Châtillon, who had recently insinuated himself into the court by marrying Stéphanie de Milly, the daughter of the Grand Master, and with that he had gained the two fortresses, Kerak and Montreal. This had given him the support of the Knights Templar.

The villains were gathering like hungry vultures around the court in Jerusalem. A scoundrel equally as dangerous as Reynald de Châtillon was one Gérard de Ridefort. Arn would remember that name; he was a friend of the Knights Templar and just as dangerous as the Assassins.

Gérard had arrived as an ordinary adventurer among all the others who came by ship to Tripoli. He had taken service with Count Raymond, and at first all had seemed to go well. In a moment of weakness Count Raymond had promised Gérard the first suitable heiress to be his in marriage, and a certain Lucia had been mentioned. But it so happened that a merchant from Pisa then offered Count Raymond Lucia's weight in gold if he would be allowed to marry the heiress. And since she was a rather plump young lady, it was impossible for Count Raymond to refuse such an offer. The ungrateful Gérard was furious, claiming that his honour had been sullied, and he refused to wait for the next suitable heiress. Instead he had joined the Knights Templar and sworn to take revenge on Count Raymond.

Arn then cautiously interjected, and this was the first time he had said a word in a while, that this was the most peculiar reason he had ever heard for joining the Templar order.

Count Raymond continued to talk all night until the sun came up and dazzled their eyes. Arn's head was spinning, as much from the wine as from Count Raymond's vast knowledge of all the things that were wrong in the Holy Land.

Arn recalled having once drunk too much ale at a banquet when he was very young; the next day he felt ill and had a searing headache. He had managed to forget that feeling, but this morning was a harsh reminder of what it meant to drink too much.

A week later Arn and his sergeant Harald were riding alone along the coast toward Gaza. They had transferred all their wounded from Beaufort to the Templar quarters in Saint-Jean d'Acre, the city that others called Akko or merely Acre. There Arn had ordered larger and safer transport for all the surviving and more or less battered sergeants south to Gaza; he wanted to get his wounded men under Saracen care as soon as possible. He and Harald now rode together, planning to arrive in advance.

They didn't talk much on the way. They had left Gaza in a large contingent with forty knights and a hundred sergeants. Only two knights and fifty-three sergeants were returning. Among the brothers who were now in Paradise were five of six of the best Templar knights Arn had ever known. Under such circumstances there was neither joy nor relief in having survived, merely a feeling of inconceivable injustice.

Harald Øysteinsson tried on one occasion to jest that as a Birch-Leg he was experienced in defeat, and that this experience had been put to good use in the Holy Land, although the outcome was not at all as he had hoped.

Arn neither smiled nor replied.

They stopped in Ashkelon and took lodging in the Knights Templar quarter, where they separated for the night, since knights and sergeants never slept in the same lodgings, except in the field. Arn nevertheless did not spend the night sleeping, but rather on his knees in the knights' chapel before the image of the Virgin Mary. He did not ask Her for protection or for his own safety. Instead he asked Her to protect his beloved Cecilia and their child, whether it was a son or a daughter. And he beseeched Her for an answer, for the grace to understand, for the wisdom to distinguish between true and false. For much of what Count Raymond had told him when he was drunk and despairing and angry had stayed in his mind, and he could not free himself of such thoughts.

If it was true that the Virgin Mary gave him an answer the very next day, then Her answer was cruel. Or, as Count Raymond would have said with a thundering laugh, it was a brutally frank answer to come from God's Mother.

Because when they had not much longer to go to reach Gaza and were approaching the Bedouin camp of the Banu Anaza, they could see from afar that something was terribly wrong.

No warriors came riding out to meet them. Among the black tents lay women, children, and elders with their foreheads pressed to the sand in prayer. Up on a hill by the camp, three worldly Frankish knights were making ready to attack.

Arn spurred Khamsiin to top speed and stormed into the camp with sand flying, leaving Harald far behind. The sound of thundering hooves made the praying Bedouins huddle even closer to the ground in fright, because they did not see who was coming.

Arn walked Khamsiin among the black-clad people, whom he could not identify from his position on horseback. Then they cautiously began to look up. Some of the Bedouin women suddenly raised their long, ululating cry of welcome and they all stood up, praising God that He had sent Al Ghouti at the last moment.

An older woman began waving her hand rhythmically and soon everyone in the camp fell into the song of welcome: Al Ghouti, Al Ghouti, Al Ghouti!

He found the elder of the tribe with the long beard, the man named Ibrahim after the forefather of all peoples, no matter how they prayed to God.

Arn was careful to dismount from Khamsiin before he took the old man's hands in greeting.

'What has happened, Ibrahim?' he asked. 'Where are all of Banu Anaza's warriors, and what do those *franji* up on the hill want?'

'God is great who sent you, Al Ghouti, therefore I thank Him more than you,' replied the old man in relief. 'Our men are out on a raid in Sinai. There is war there and no truce we need to respect. We have shelter here and needed no defence, or so we thought. But these *franji* came from the north, from Ashkelon, and they spoke to us and said that we should pray for the last time. They intend to kill us all, if I understood them right.'

'I can't ask you to forgive them because they know not what they do, but I can certainly drive them away!' replied Arn, bowing to Ibrahim. Then he jumped up on Khamsiin and rode at a good clip toward the three Franks up on the hill.

As he came nearer he slowed down to study them. They were undoubtedly newly arrived tenderfeet, all three; they had a great deal of colour and ornamentation on their mantles, and they wore the newest type of helmet that encased the whole head and scarcely left a small cross-shaped slit for the eyes. Reluctantly they now took off their helmets and did not seem glad to see a Christian.

'Who are you three, where do you come from, and what is this supposed to mean?' Arn shouted in his practiced tone of command.

'Who are you, Christian, who dresses like a Saracen?' asked the Frank in the middle. 'You're interrupting our holy mission, so we must ask you kindly to step aside before we turn unfriendly.'

Arn did not reply for a moment, since he was praying silently for the lives of the three fools. Then he swept aside his mantle so that his surcoat with the red cross was visible.

'I am a Templar knight,' he said in a restrained manner. 'I am Arn de Gothia and I am the master of Gaza. You three are now in Gaza's territory. What you see down there are Bedouins who belong to Gaza, our property. Fortunately for you, all the warriors in camp are out on business or at work for me, otherwise you would be dead. Now I repeat my question: who are you three Christians and where do you come from?'

They said that they came from Provence, that they had come with their count to Ashkelon along with many others, that they were out on their first day of patrol in the Holy Land, and that they had been fortunate to find Saracens whom they intended to send immediately to Hell. They had

275

namely taken the cross, all three, and therefore it was their duty according to God.

'According to the Holy Father in Rome, in any case,' Arn corrected them sarcastically. 'But we Templar knights are the Holy Father's army; we obey only him. So the closest you are now to your pope is the commander of Gaza, and I am that man. Enough of this. I bid you welcome to the Holy Land, may God stand by you. But now I *order* you to return to Ashkelon without delay, or wherever you may wish to go. But you must leave Gaza's territory, where you now find yourselves.'

The three knights showed absolutely no sign of obeying. They insisted that they had a holy duty to kill Saracens, that they had taken the cross, that they were intending to begin their holy mission right here and now, and other such nonsense. They clearly had no idea what a Templar knight was, and they didn't seem to realize that the black border along the mail protecting Khamsiin's hindquarters meant that they were talking to a high brother. They were like madmen.

Arn tried to explain that they could not carry out this imagined holy mission to kill women, children, and old people, since there was a Templar knight in their way. They had to accept that they were at a serious disadvantage.

This they did not understand at all; on the contrary, they thought that they were three against one and that it might be enjoyable to fight off a Saracen-lover before they completed their blessed mission to slaughter the village.

Arn patiently begged them to reconsider. Since they were only three, it would be foolish to attack a Templar knight. If they returned to Ashkelon and asked those who had been in the Holy Land longer, they would surely be told the same.

But they wouldn't listen to reason. Arn gave up and rode rapidly down the hill to position Khamsiin directly in front of the camp. There he demonstratively drew his sword, raised it to the sun three times, lowered it and kissed it, and then began his obligatory prayers.

Old Ibrahim labouriously trudged through the sand to reach him from one direction while Harald came on horseback from another. Arn explained first in Arabic and then in Norse what in the worst case might happen if the three crazy men up on the hill refused to be sensible. Ibrahim hurried off at once, while Harald stationed his horse next to Arn's and cockily drew his sword.

'You have to move back, you'll just be in the way,' said Arn in a low voice without looking at Harald.

'Never shall I abandon a kinsman who finds himself at a disadvantage. You can't make me do so, jarl that you are!' Harald protested vehemently.

'You will be killed at once and I don't want that to happen,' said Arn without taking his eyes off the three Frankish knights. They had now knelt down to pray before their attack; the fools were apparently serious. But Harald didn't make the slightest attempt to move away.

'I'm telling you once and for all that you must obey my order,' said Arn in a louder voice. 'They're going to attack with lances, and you'll be killed at once if you're nearby. You *must* move your horse away now. If there is a fight on foot, then you may assist me. If you can find a bow and arrows in any of the tents, use them. But you may not ride against Franks!'

'But you don't have a lance!' Harald objected in despair.

'No, but I have Khamsiin, and I can fight like the Saracens, which these three have probably never encountered. So go now and at least look for a bow and arrows so that you can be of some use!'

Arn had given this last order in a very stern tone. Harald obeyed and trotted toward the tents just as old Ibrahim came back, out of breath and stumbling in the sand, holding a bundle in his hands. When he reached Arn he had to catch his breath for a moment. The three Franks up on the hill were now putting on their helmets with plumes in beautiful colours.

'God is truly great,' the old man puffed as he began to unwrap his bundle. 'But His ways are inscrutable to men. From time immemorial we of the Banu Anaza have taken care of this sword. It was the sword that the holy Ali ibn Abi Talib lost when he was martyred outside Kufa. It has been our duty to pass this sword down from father to son until our saviour came, he who would save the faithful. It is you who are that man, Al Ghouti! The one who fights with a soul so pure and for a cause so holy as you now intend to do can never lose with this sword in hand. It was written that you should have it!'

Beseeching him and with trembling hands the old man held out an ancient and clearly dull sword toward Arn. Despite the gravity of the moment, he couldn't help but laugh.

'I doubt that I am the right man, my dear friend Ibrahim,' he said. 'And believe me, my sword is just as holy as yours. It is also, if you'll pardon me saying so, somewhat sharper.'

The old man would not yield; he continued to offer the sword, trembling all the more with the effort.

Then a shadow slipped into Arn's thoughts. The Rule forbade any Templar knight from killing or even wounding a Christian. His own sword was blessed before God in the church at Varnhem; it could never be raised in sin for then he, as he himself had sworn, would be smitten to the ground.

He reached down his shield arm and grabbed the old sword, weighed it tentatively in his hand, and ran his finger along its blunt edge. The three Franks now lowered their lances and began galloping in tight formation toward Arn. He had to decide at once.

'Look here, Ibrahim!' he said, handing him his own sword.

'Stick this sword in the sand before your tent, and pray before the cross you see there. I shall use your sword and we shall see how great God is!'

In the next instant he spurred Khamsiin, who had already begun to quiver with eagerness, and dashed straight ahead toward the lances of the three Franks. Ibrahim ran back to his tent, stumbling in the sand, to do with Arn's sword as he had been asked.

Harald had not found any bow, no matter how much he searched, and now he stood as if paralysed, watching what was happening. His jarl was dashing with sword in hand straight for three attacking knights with lances lowered.

In the following moments he came to fully appreciate his jarl's words, which he had thought contemptuous, when Arn said that no Norwegian was any good on a horse.

Anyone at all, even Harald, could now see that Arn Magnusson's horse was much faster than those of the others. Up to the last second it looked as though Arn was really intending to fall like a fool with his head down into the three lances rushing toward him. But just beyond their reach he turned sharply to the right so that Khamsiin bolted almost horizontally in the turn and the three knights missed. When they pulled up and looked around as best they could through the narrow slits in their helmets, Arn had already circled and struck the first man with a blow across the neck. The Frankish knight collapsed at once, dropped his lance and shield and fell slowly, sliding lifelessly off his horse. By then the second knight had Arn upon him. He tried to defend himself with his shield as the third knight, who now had his comrade in the way, had to manoeuvre around to take a new angle of attack.

Arn hacked his nearest foe's horse straight across the small of its back so that the steed collapsed paralysed when its hind legs failed. When the knight then lost his balance he

279

was struck by Arn's sword straight across his face through the helmet's eye slit. He too fell.

Now only two men were left on their horses out there, Arn and the third Frank. It looked as though Arn then wanted to negotiate with the man and convince him to surrender. Instead the knight once again lowered his lance and went on the attack. Instantly his head was tossed through the air, still in its helmet, and fell with a dull thud to the ground followed by the body, spurting blood. Arn seemed very surprised and reined in his horse. He ran his fingers over the edge of the sword, testing it, shook his head, and then walked Khamsiin over to the second of the three Frankish knights, who was not dead. He got down from Khamsiin and went over to help the fallen man to his feet. The bewildered knight took Arn's hand and stood up. Arn helped him wriggle out of his helmet. The man's face was bloody but he did not seem seriously injured.

Arn turned to see to the first man he had knocked to the ground, but as he did the man he had just helped up drew his sword and ran it full force into the belly of Khamsiin.

Khamsiin reared up screaming in fear and cast himself about while wildly bucking and kicking his hind legs. The sword was buried in his flesh almost to the hilt. Arn stood as if petrified for a second, then he ran toward the villain who sank to his knees and held up his hands before his face, pleading for mercy. But he found none.

Then everything that had to be done was done at once. Arn went to get his own sword after sticking the holy Saracen sword under his belt. He called Khamsiin to him using loving and soothing words. Despite his terror and rolling eyes the stallion came staggering toward his master, the Frankish sword jolting up and down with each step. Arn caressed the animal, kissed him, and then took two steps to the side behind him, turned around suddenly and as if in a fury of despair sliced off Khamsiin's head with a single blow.

Then he numbly dropped his sword to the ground and walked away from the camp, his face white, and sat down by himself.

Women and children now came rushing from all directions and began quickly digging in the sand. Some began folding up the tents, and others rounded up the camels, goats, and horses. Harald did not understand everything that was going on. He definitely didn't want to disturb his jarl right now, and he knew he could not be of any assistance.

The old man went to get Arn's sword where he had dropped it, wiped it off, and then walked with slow but deliberate steps toward Arn. Harald was quite sure that he should not interfere.

When Ibrahim came up to Arn he was sitting motionless with an absent look on his face and holding the holy sword of Islam in his hand. Ibrahim was a Bedouin and could understand Arn's grief. He sat down next to him without saying a word. If necessary he was prepared to sit there for two days and two nights without speaking. According to custom, Arn was the one who must speak the first words.

'Ibrahim, I know that I must speak first,' said Arn, in torment. 'Such is your custom, but it might just as well have been my Rule, about which you are fortunately unaware. The sword you gave me is truly remarkable.'

'It belongs to you now, Al Ghouti. You were our saviour. Thus it was written and thus it has now been proven by what happened.'

'No, Ibrahim, that is not the case. Do I have the right to ask you for a favour?'

'Yes, Al Ghouti. And whatever you ask, if it is within human power or the power of all of Banu Anaza, I shall fulfil your wish,' Ibrahim whispered with his face bowed to the ground.

'Then take this sword and ride with it to the one to whom

it belongs. Go to Yussuf ibn Ayyub Salah al-Din, the one we call in our simple language Saladin. Give him this sword. Tell him that it was written so, that Al Ghouti has said so.'

Ibrahim silently accepted the sword which Arn now carefully handed to him. They sat for a while next to each other, staring out over the sand dunes toward the sea. Arn's sorrow was so great that it seemed to create a shroud of coldness around him, and Ibrahim was a man particularly well suited to understand the cause, at least so he believed. But he was only half right.

'Al Ghouti, you are now the friend of Banu Anaza forever,' said Ibrahim after a pause that could have been long or short, because for Arn time hardly existed anymore. 'The favour you asked of me was too small, although I shall see that it is done. Let us now do what has to be done. We Bedouins bury horses such as Khamsiin. He was a great warrior, almost like one of our horses. Come!'

The old man persuaded Arn to stand up and follow him. When they approached the camp everything was almost packed up and loaded onto camels. The three dead Franks, like their horses, had vanished somewhere beneath the sand. But all the women, children, and old people of the camp stood solemnly gathered around a grave in the sand, and a short distance away stood a bewildered Harald.

The ceremonies were brief, for horses as well as for men. The Bedouins' belief, as it was spoken in the prayer of their leader Ibrahim, was that Khamsiin would now run forever among wide green fields with plenty of cool water. Arn's prayer was similar, although he murmured the words silently to himself, since he knew that he was now committing blasphemy. But Khamsiin had been his friend since he was a boy, and Khamsiin was the only one for whose sake Arn had ever blasphemed in his life. So great was his grief that at the moment Arn preferred the belief of the Bedouins.

In his mind he could see Khamsiin in full gallop with his tail raised high and his mane fluttering, racing across the green fields of Paradise.

Then they all set off toward Gaza. Three Franks from Ashkelon had died in Banu Anaza's camp. Because of this the new camp had to be pitched right next to Gaza, and if that was not safe enough, then inside the city walls.

The Bedouins' women and children were just as skilled at riding camels and horses as any Saracen man, and they knew how to keep all the animals with them in a close group.

Harald rode next to Arn, who had borrowed a somewhat unruly horse that seemed to be giving him trouble. But Harald did not dare say anything to his jarl on the short ride to Gaza. He never could have imagined a man such as Arn Magnusson weeping like a child, and he felt much embarrassment at seeing this weakness, especially as it was displayed before un-Christian savages. But they in turn seemed not in the least surprised at the knight's childish sorrow over a horse. Their faces were as if carved in leather, immobile, showing no expression of either sorrow or joy, fear or relief.

They were Bedouins. But about such people Harald knew hardly more than any Norseman.

When they reached Gaza, Arn silently pointed out a spot where the Bedouins could pitch their camp near the city wall, but on the north side so that the smells from the city would not bother the camp since the wind was from the west. He got off his borrowed horse and began to unfasten Khamsiin's harness and saddle. But then Ibrahim rode quickly up to him, hopped nimbly from his horse, and took Arn by the hands.

'Al Ghouti, our friend, you must now know one thing!' he stammered, out of breath. 'Our tribesmen, Banu Anaza, own the best horses in all of Arabia; that is known to all. But no one, not even sultans or caliphs, has ever been able to buy such a horse. We only give them away when we have found an exceptional reason to do so. The young stallion you just rode from our camp has hardly been broken to the saddle, as you surely noticed. He has no true master. He was intended for my son since his blood is the purest of any steed; he is our best. You must take him, because what you asked as a favour from me was too little, and so I must make you this gift.'

'Ibrahim, you can't . . .' Arn began, but could not go on. He bowed his head in tears. Ibrahim then embraced him like a father and stroked his back and neck to console him.

'I certainly can, Al Ghouti. I am the eldest of Banu Anaza, and no one may contradict me. Not even you may contradict me, for until now you have been my guest. You can't insult your host by refusing his gift!'

'That is true,' said Arn and took a deep breath, wiping his tears with the back of his hand. 'Before my own people I seem weak as a woman and possibly a fool for showing such grief for a horse. But you are a Bedouin, Ibrahim. You know that this grief will never pass, and only to someone like you can I admit such a thing. Your gift is very great, and you will have my gratitude as long as I live.'

'You shall also have a mare,' Ibrahim smiled slyly, and made a sign. Leading the mare forward was Aisha, the young woman whose love for Ali ibn Qays from the other Bedouin clan had prompted Arn to negotiate a peace between tribes.

The gesture was well planned by Ibrahim. For according to custom Arn could not refuse a gift from Aisha, the one he had made happy through his powers, and the one who bore the name of the most beloved wife of the Prophet, peace be unto him.

EIGHT

Over the course of a few years Cecilia Rosa's life at Gudhem had fundamentally changed. The affairs of the convent had undergone such a transformation that it was difficult for anyone to grasp. Despite the fact that few new properties had been donated to the cloister in recent years, Gudhem's income had doubled. Cecilia Rosa explained time after time that it all had to do with order and discipline. Well, that was not the only explanation, she admitted if Mother Rikissa or someone else prodded her with more persistent questions. They had also raised a number of their prices. A Folkung mantle from Gudhem now cost three times as much as when they first began making them. But just as Brother Lucien once predicted, the mantles were now selling at a steady pace; the garments didn't disappear in a single week like they did before. This meant that it was also easier to plan the work; some of the novices could always sit and work in the *vestiarium* without rushing or doing the sewing in a careless fashion. The pelts that were required for the most expensive mantles could only be purchased in the spring and at only a few marketplaces. If they planned wrong, as they'd some-times done before, then they might be left without enough pelts and far too many orders. As it was now, the fur supply never ran out, and the work flowed evenly and yet brought in so much silver that Gudhem's coffers would have been overflowing if Mother Rikissa hadn't ordered so much stonework from the Frankish and English stonemasons. In that way Gudhem's increasing wealth was also made visible to the eye. The tower of the church had been finished and now held an English bell with a lovely sound; the walls around the cloister's inner sanctum were finished, as well as the pillared vault all the way around the arcade.

Next to the sacristy two big new rooms had been built of stone to form a separate building. This was Cecilia Rosa's realm, where she reigned among the account books and silver coffers. In the outermost room wooden shelves had been built for her with hundreds of cubbyholes where all of Gudhem's donation documents were stored in a strict order which only Cecilia Rosa had mastered. If Mother Rikissa came to ask about some property or other and its value or rent payments, Cecilia Rosa could without hesitation go and fetch the letter of donation and read it aloud. Then she would search in the books until she found the date of the last rent payment, how much was paid per bushel and when, and the date the next payment was due. When payments were late she wrote letters that Mother Rikissa had to sign and stamp with the seal of the abbess. The letter was sent to the bishop located nearest to the delinquent tenant, and soon thereafter minions were sent out to collect the rent, either with friendly reminders or stern fists. Not the tiniest fish ever slipped through Cecilia Rosa's net.

She was not unaware of the power that the position of *yconoma* had given her. Mother Rikissa could ask about matters large and small and obtain the answers she had the right to demand, but she could never make any important decisions without first going to the *yconoma*, not if it pertained to Gudhem's business affairs. And without its business transactions Gudhem could not survive.

So for this reason it did not surprise Cecilia Rosa that Mother Rikissa did not now treat her with the same condescension or cruelty that she had done in the beginning. They had both found a way to relate to each other that would not disrupt either the business dealings or the divine order at Gudhem.

The more at ease Cecilia Rosa felt in handling the bookkeeping and abacus, the more time she began to have free for other things. She spent this extra time with Ulvhilde in the gardens, when it was the season, or in the *vestiarium* sewing and talking, sometimes far into the night.

A long time had passed without any solution being found for the matter of Ulvhilde's inheritance. During her visits Cecilia Blanca had seemed a bit evasive, saying merely that everything would undoubtedly work out, although nothing could be done about it in a trice. The hope that had been ignited in Ulvhilde's heart seemed to have been extinguished, and she seemed reconciled to the situation.

Mother Rikissa and Cecilia Rosa had found a *modus vivendi* in which they had as little as possible to do with each other. And so Cecilia Rosa was utterly unprepared when Mother Rikissa asked her to come to the abbess's private rooms for a talk about what they never talked about, as she mysteriously described the reason for her summons.

For some time now Mother Rikissa had been using the scourge on herself, and she always slept in a horsehair shift. It was something that Cecilia Rosa had noticed in passing although she didn't give it much thought. Women in the convent sometimes got such notions, and it was nothing new or odd.

When they now met, Mother Rikissa seemed shrunken, smaller somehow. Her eyes were red-rimmed from lack of

287

sleep, and she kept on rubbing her hands together as if she almost wanted to humble herself and literally bowed to Cecilia Rosa.

In a weak voice she explained that she was seeking forgiveness, both from the Virgin Mary and from the person whom she had treated most harshly in life. She was earnestly searching her heart, she said, for the evil that had taken up residence inside her without her knowledge. Now she entertained a slight hope that this was possible, since she believed she could feel that the Mother of God was about to have mercy on her.

But the question was whether Cecilia Rosa could do the same. All that time Cecilia Rosa had spent in the *carcer* and all the lashes with the scourge she had received, Mother Rikissa would gladly take upon herself now, even in double and triple measure, if she could only achieve atonement.

She told Cecilia Rosa that even as a girl she had suffered from her ugliness; she was well aware that God had not created her as some tender virgin praised in the songs of knights. Her clan was of royal lineage, but her father was not wealthy, and this had meant that Rikissa would probably never marry, because her dowry would not be sufficient.

Her mother had consoled her by saying that God had a plan for everything, and that a girl who was not created for the bridal bed had no doubt been created for a higher calling. God's kingdom was where Rikissa should turn. Since her father knew old King Sverker well, they had worked out that Rikissa was particularly suited to take charge of a new convent that the Sverker clan planned to establish in Gudhem. Once both the king and her father had decided her fate she naturally had nothing to say about it. The very year after she finished her time as a novice she became abbess. God knew then how inexperienced she was and terrified of the great responsibility. Some of the severity she had shown toward

Cecilia Rosa in the beginning could probably be explained by the fact that there was a war going on outside in those days. The Folkungs and the Eriks were fighting a hard battle against the Sverker side. It was unjust, of course, that Cecilia Rosa, who had been so young and delicate, had been forced to carry the yoke of war on her shoulders even inside the cloister, where war had no place. It was unfair and it was wrong. Mother Rikissa acknowledged that the sin was her own as she bowed her head as if to weep.

During Rikissa's long confession Cecilia Rosa had felt a flood of emotion that she never could have imagined. She felt sorry for the abbess, sympathizing with the plight of the ugly girl and picturing how both noblemen and ordinary men must have laughed behind her back. They surely must have pointed out even then how oddly like a witch Rikissa was, just as Cecilia Rosa and Ulvhilde and Cecilia Blanca had later done. It must have been very difficult for the young Rikissa, filled with the same hopes and dreams as other maidens her age, slowly but inexorably to realize that she was doomed to a different life, a life she had not wished for at all.

And it was also unfair, Cecilia Rosa thought. For no woman or man could choose her own appearance; the best-looking fathers and mothers could have the ugliest children, and vice versa. Whatever God's intention for creating Rikissa in the image of a witch, at least it was not her own fault.

'That is a sad story you have told me, Mother,' she finally began cautiously. 'But it is true that your sin was a grave one; I have felt it on my own skin and through many a bitter winter night. But God is good and merciful, and anyone who regrets her sin as you do shall not be lost. My forgiveness is of only minor importance, my wounds have healed long ago, and the cold has long since left the marrow of my bones. You must seek God's forgiveness, Mother. How could I, insignificant sinner that I am, take precedence over God in such a matter?'

'So you will not forgive me?' Mother Rikissa sobbed, leaning forward as if in pain and twisting so that a rattling sound betrayed the cilice she wore under her woollen clothes.

'There is nothing I would rather do, Mother,' replied Cecilia Rosa, relieved that she had actually managed to wriggle out of this dilemma. 'The day that you are convinced of God's forgiveness, come to me, and together with great joy we shall offer a prayer of thanksgiving for His grace.'

Mother Rikissa slowly straightened up from her hunched position and nodded thoughtfully, as if she had found Cecilia Rosa's words proper and worthy of consideration, even though she had not received the forgiveness she had sought. She wiped her eyes as if she had actually shed a few tears, and sighed deeply. Then she began to speak about all the trouble that had been caused by the two who had run off from Gudhem and Varnhem. Both she and the elderly Father Henri had been harshly taken to task by the archbishop for this grave sin, which it had been their responsibility to prevent.

But Mother Rikissa had not had anything to say in her defence, since she had known nothing about what had gone on behind her back. Now, so long afterwards, couldn't dear Cecilia Rosa show some mercy and explain the truth of the matter? Cecilia Rosa turned to ice inside. She scrutinized Mother Rikissa and thought she could see the serpent eyes of the Devil, for the pupils in those red-rimmed eyes had turned to slits. They looked like the eyes of a snake or perhaps a goat, didn't they?

'No, Mother Rikissa,' she replied stonily. 'About this matter I know no more than you. How would I, a sinful penitent, come to know anything about what a monk and a nun were planning?'

She got up and left without saying anything more, and

without first kissing Mother Rikissa's hand. She kept her temper under control until she had closed the doors on her and come out into the lovely arcade. There the roses now twined their way up all the pillars as a constant greeting from Sister Leonore, of whom nothing had been heard, nor of Brother Lucien. And since nothing was heard about punishment and penance or excommunication, that was good news. By now they were probably both in southern France, happy with their child and without sin.

Cecilia Rosa walked slowly past all the climbing roses in the arcade, smelling the red ones and caressing the odourless white ones. All the roses seemed to send greetings from Sister Leonore and the happy land of Occitania. Yet a cold shiver went through Cecilia Rosa although it was a warm summer night.

She had been sitting in the presence of the Serpent herself. The serpent had spoken as sweetly as a lamb, and for a moment she had made Cecilia Rosa believe that the Serpent was indeed a lamb. What great misfortune and what a terrible punishment might have resulted if she had given in to that siren song.

In every phase of life, it was important to try and think like a man of power, or at least like Cecilia Blanca.

There was one thing that had happened in recent weeks that might offer an explanation for Mother Rikissa's penitence, or rather her fruitless attempt to lure Cecilia Rosa into betraying herself as the worst sort of sinner against the peace of the cloister. A message had come from Queen Cecilia Blanca saying that she would not come alone to Gudhem on her next visit. She would bring the jarl Birger Brosa with her.

This was fateful news. The jarl was not a man who would travel to the convent to waste his valuable time speaking with some poor penitent woman, even if he had shown Cecilia

Rosa his support. If the jarl came, there was something important afoot.

Cecilia Rosa also suspected this when she received the message. Nowadays Mother Rikissa could not keep such an imminent event to herself. The *yconoma* had to know well in advance what sort of hospitality was expected from Gudhem, so that she could send her men to purchase all the sorts of food that would normally not be eaten at Gudhem. The rules naturally forbade all men and women who had dedicated their lives to God from eating four-footed animals. But for jarls there were certainly no such rules. Nor did such rules apply in all cloisters. It was well known that the Burgundian monks at Varnhem, under Father Henri's supervision with his clear consent, had created the best cuisine in the North. Birger Brosa could come to Varnhem unannounced and still dine better than at any of his own tables. But when it came to Gudhem, he was more prudent.

Yet whatever Birger Brosa had on his mind, it was not something that Cecilia Rosa worried about beforehand. She had nothing special to hope for except that eventually her long penance would come to an end. Until that time, no king or jarl could do anything at all for her except try to keep Mother Rikissa, if not obedient to the nurture and admonition of the Lord, then at least within the discipline of the secular authorities. And unlike Mother Rikissa, Cecilia Rosa had nothing to fear from the jarl and the queen. For her it was only a matter of sweet anticipation as she waited for her dear friend Cecilia Blanca's visit, which this time would be much different.

The jarl arrived with a great retinue. He was already quite well-fed and content because for safety's sake he had stayed up at Varnhem for a day and a night before he and the queen continued the short distance to Gudhem.

Horses' hooves clattered on the new cobblestones outside the walls, and men spoke in loud, rough voices. A great din arose from the tent posts, ropes and windlasses as the camp for the jarl's men was raised; the tension inside Gudhem grew with each unfamiliar sound. But Cecilia Rosa, who could now go out to the *hospitium* without asking Mother Rikissa's permission, sat inside with her books and her goose quill, finishing up all the bookkeeping occasioned by the state visit. It felt good not to rush off to see the queen, whose visit cheered her heart each year; instead she would first conclude her work, as a good toiler in God's garden. She believed that enjoyment and rest were the rewards for good work. And that was a belief that she would take with her one day, to her life outside Gudhem. For now so much of her penance had been served that she could see the end of it, and she had cautiously begun to imagine what her life might be like in the future. But she couldn't be very specific in her daydreaming, because one thing was not at all clear.

It had been several years since any news had come from Varnhem and Father Henri about Arn Magnusson. The only thing she knew for certain was that he was not dead, for according to what Father Henri had told Cecilia Blanca, Arn had now risen to the high rank of a Templar knight. If he had fallen in the holy war, masses would have been read for his soul all over the Cistercian world. So she knew that he was among the living, but nothing more.

However, tidings of Arn were the first thing Birger Brosa spoke of when she went out to the *hospitium*, embraced Cecilia Blanca, and then bowed her head to the jarl. She didn't dare embrace him because her years in the cloister had begun to take a deep toll on her, although she was not aware of it.

When they had said their greetings and the jarl had received his desired tankard of ale, he sat down comfortably at the table, pulling up one leg as was his wont. Then he gave

Cecilia Blanca a sly look as she sat down and arranged her skirts.

'So, my dear kinswoman Cecilia,' he said with a smile, stalling a bit to pique her curiosity even more. 'The queen and I have a great deal to say to you. Some news is of great import and other news may be of lesser interest. But I think you would like to hear first the latest news about Arn Magnusson. He is now one of the great victors of the Knights Templar, and recently he won a huge battle at a place called Mont Grisar, at least that's what I thought Father Henri said. It was no ordinary battle. Fifty thousand Saracens fell, and he himself led ten thousand knights, riding in the vanguard. May God preserve such a warrior so that we have him home soon. We Folkungs hope for this as much as you do, Cecilia!'

Cecilia Rosa at once bowed her head in a prayer of thanksgiving and soon the tears were streaming down her cheeks. Birger Brosa and Cecilia Blanca let her weep but exchanged a meaningful glance.

'Shall we switch to another topic that also warrants our attention?' asked the jarl after a while, again smiling broadly. Cecilia Rosa nodded and dried her tears. But she smiled at Cecilia Blanca as if neither words nor silent cloister signs were needed to explain the joy that the news from Varnhem had brought her.

'Well, I thought I'd speak with you about Ulvhilde Emundsdotter, because that matter has not been easy to resolve,' the jarl went on when he thought Cecilia Rosa had collected herself sufficiently.

Then he calmly explained, point by point and in good order, how various difficulties had arisen and what he had tried to do about them.

First and foremost he wanted to say that it was quite true that Ulvhilde had the law of Western Götaland on her side. About that, three *lagmän* were in agreement. Ulfshem had been Ulvhilde's childhood home. As her mother and her brother had been killed, she was indeed the rightful heiress to Ulfshem.

And yet the matter had not been quite so simple. For King Knut Eriksson had been no friend of her father, Emund One-Hand. On the contrary, when the issue of the inheritance had been brought up, the king had vehemently declared that if he could kill Emund again every single day, then he would be supremely happy to do so. Emund was a king-killer and worse because in an ignominious and cowardly fashion he had slain Saint Erik, King Knut's father. And why, King Knut had then asked, should he feel the slightest mercy toward the evil Emund's offspring?

Because the law required it, Birger Brosa had then tried to explain. The law was above all other power; the law was the basis on which a country was built, and no king could object to that.

But the difficulties were not limited to the king's intractable stance. Ulfshem had been burned to the ground. Then it had been given to some Folkungs who had served well in the victory on the fields of blood. Now living at Ulfshem were Sigurd Folkesson and his two unmarried sons. Their mother had died in childbed, and for some reason Folkesson had never remarried.

These Folkungs could claim that they had been given Ulfshem by royal bequest and that they had then built up everything from the ground.

Here, to his considerable surprise, the jarl was interrupted by Cecilia Rosa who almost audaciously pointed out that the land was worth much more than any buildings.

The jarl frowned at being corrected in this way, but since the only witness was the queen he chose to ignore the affront. Instead of being annoyed he praised Cecilia Rosa for her shrewd business sense.

In any case, this matter had been gone over time and time again. There was more than one way to get out of this fox-burrow.

One way was with silver. Another way was by marriage. For if Ulvhilde agreed to be betrothed to one of Sigurd's sons, there would be no impediment to her assuming more than half ownership of Ulfshem. She had to have something as a dowry, after all.

Here Cecilia Rosa looked as if she wanted to say something, but she refrained.

The second possibility, the jarl went on as he held up his forefinger with a smile so as not to be interrupted again, was to buy out the Folkungs now living at Ulfshem.

As Cecilia Rosa surely understood, he and Cecilia Blanca had not wanted to have this discussion in Ulvhilde's presence; that was the only reason she had not yet been invited over to the *hospitium*.

They wanted to know what Cecilia Rosa thought of this, and whether they could agree on a wise solution so they could then summon Ulvhilde. What was Cecilia Rosa's opinion? She was the one who knew Ulvhilde best. Should they seek the expensive solution and buy out the Folkungs, or could they simply arrange for her to marry into the Folkung clan?

Cecilia Rosa thought that this dilemma could be settled in the twinkling of an eye. In a better world in which Ulvhilde had not had all those nearest and dearest to her killed in a war, her father would have long ago made the best match he could for her. But as things now stood, Ulvhilde had no such constraints. Cecilia Rosa was sure that she would go along with whatever her two sole friends proposed for her, in consultation with the jarl. But rushing to force Ulvhilde into a bridal bed might just as well lead to her unhappiness as to her happiness.

After thinking for a while, Cecilia Rosa suggested that it would be best if Ulvhilde were simply allowed to travel home to her family estate without any betrothal promises. While Birger Brosa arranged for new land for the Folkung Sigurd and his two sons, they could stay and help Ulvhilde settle in as mistress of the estate. For it was no easy matter to learn such responsibilities, since she had spent the greater part of her life in singing hymns, gardening, and doing needlework.

After a brief pause he nodded his agreement and asked Cecilia Rosa to go to the cloister and fetch Ulvhilde.

Before leaving she was reminded by Cecilia Blanca that this would be the last time Ulvhilde walked through the gate of Gudhem, for they would take her along on their journey north in a day or two. So, she added, if there was any suitable Sverker mantle, it would be best to bring it along at once. The jarl would surely have nothing against paying for such a gift. And if he made a fuss about this small expense, Cecilia Blanca would pay for it herself. She and Birger Brosa had a good laugh at that.

Her cheeks red and her heart pounding, Cecilia Rosa hurried into the cloister and off to the *vestiarium*, where at this hour she expected to find Ulvhilde. But she wasn't there. Cecilia Rosa quickly selected a very lovely blood-red Sverker mantle with gold and silk threads adorning the embroidered black griffin on the back. She folded it up under her arm, and hurried off to find Ulvhilde. She suddenly felt a great sense of unease.

And as if guided by this foreboding she did not stop to look in places where she should have looked first, but went straight to Mother Rikissa's own rooms. There she found them both on their knees and weeping. As if to console the young woman Mother Rikissa had placed her arm around Ulvhilde's shoulders, which were shaking with sobs. What Cecilia Rosa had feared most was about to happen or in the worst case had already happened, despite all her warnings to Ulvhilde.

'Don't let yourself be led astray, Ulvhilde!' she shouted, running over to them and brusquely snatching Ulvhilde from Mother Rikissa's clawlike grip. She embraced her and stroked her trembling back as she fumbled with the red mantle.

Mother Rikissa then stood up, hissing with her red-rimmed eyes flashing. She began screaming wildly that no one had the right to interrupt confession. Then she tried to seize Ulvhilde's arms to pull her away.

With a strength that did not seem her own, Cecilia Rosa separated her weeping friend from the witch and then held up the red mantle as protection between them. Both quieted down, surprised to see the large, blood-red garment.

Cecilia Rosa promptly draped the Sverker mantle over Ulvhilde's shoulders, as if it were an iron shield against Mother Rikissa's evil.

'Now you must get hold of yourself, Rikissa!' she said, again displaying a force that she would not have believed she possessed. 'She is your slave no longer, not your poor maiden Ulvhilde among the novices without silver or clan. Here stands Ulvhilde of Ulfshem, and you two, God be praised, shall never see each other again!'

In the sudden silence that descended upon both Ulvhilde and Mother Rikissa, Cecilia Rosa quickly pulled Ulvhilde out the door of Mother Rikissa's rooms without even a word of farewell. They hurried the short distance down the arcade and right out through the big gate.

Panting as if they had run a race, they stopped outside beneath the stone image showing Adam and Eve as they were cast out of Paradise.

'I warned you over and over again, I told you how the serpent could turn herself into a lamb,' Cecilia Rosa said at last.

'I . . . felt . . . so . . . sorry for her!' Ulvhilde sobbed.

'Maybe you *should* feel sorry for her, but it doesn't diminish her evil. What did you tell her? You didn't confess about . . . ?' Cecilia Rosa asked cautiously, greatly concerned.

'She got me to cry over her misfortune, she got me to forgive her,' Ulvhilde whispered.

'And then you were supposed to confess!'

'Yes, then she wanted to hear my confession, but you appeared as if sent by Our Lady. Forgive me, my dearest, but I was very close to committing a great stupidity,' Ulvhilde said, shamefaced and with her eyes on the ground.

'I think you're right; I think Our Lady, in her mercy, sent me at exactly the right moment. The mantle you now wear would have been ripped from you at once and you would have withered away inside Gudhem forever if you told her the truth about Sister Leonore. Let us pray and thank Our Lady!'

They both dropped to their knees outside the gate of the cloister Ulvhilde had now left for the very last time. Ulvhilde had to stop herself from asking any questions, for only now did she truly come to her senses and begin to understand what a treasure Cecilia Rosa had draped over her shoulders. They prayed for a long time, offering words of deep and sincere thanksgiving to the Virgin Mary for the forgiveness of their sins – the sins that had almost cast them both into perdition and might have pulled the queen down with them. For the rest of their lives they would be convinced that the Virgin Mary had sent a miraculous salvation at the last moment. The witch had truly cast a spell over Ulvhilde, who had come close to putting her head in the noose.

Then they stood up and embraced and kissed each other. Ulvhilde now had her wits about her and began caressing the soft red garment, wondering what it could mean.

Cecilia Rosa then explained that it was time for Ulvhilde to journey home. The mantle was a gift from either the jarl or the queen, but it certainly was not Ulvhilde's only possession, for Ulfshem was now hers, free and clear.

As they walked in reverent silence the short distance to the *hospitium* where their benefactors waited, Ulvhilde tried with all her might to understand what had just happened.

A moment ago she had not owned more than the clothes on her back, and strictly speaking not even those. The clothes she had once worn when she arrived at Gudhem were a child's clothing, long since outgrown and by now discarded or sold. She had not needed to fetch a single possession before she walked out the gate of Gudhem.

It was impossible to comprehend this sudden leap to the precious red mantle and becoming the mistress of Ulfshem. She needed more time to ponder it.

Cecilia Rosa and Ulvhilde both looked pale but no more distressed than their benefactors might have expected when they both entered the banquet hall in the *hospitium*, where roast-turners and ale-fetchers had already begun their work. But the jarl, who had jumped up roguishly to receive the new mistress of Ulfshem with a deep, courtly bow, saw at once that something was amiss.

Hence the feast began strangely since Cecilia Rosa and Ulvhilde had to report about Mother Rikissa's last enraged attempt to bring misfortune down on their heads. The jarl now heard for the first time the story of how the three conspirators had assisted the runaway monk and nun. At first he grew pensive because he understood quite well, without being very knowledgeable about the rules of the church, that in life the happiness and welfare of everyone hung by a fragile thread. However, it was his firm conviction that the danger was now past. He reminded them that there were only four people in the whole country who knew the truth about the runaways from the cloister. The queen and Cecilia Rosa would certainly guard the secret well. As would Ulvhilde, especially if she married into the Folkung clan – there the two Cecilias gave him a stern look – especially, he quickly altered his statement, because she would be concerned about the peace and happiness of her friends. And for his own part, he added with a broad grin, he had no intention of casting the country into ferment and war just for the sake of a runaway monk.

For that had been Rikissa's intention, he explained, instantly turning more serious. For her it was about more than taking revenge on two maidens who displeased her. She was the one, after all, who had almost succeeded in having Arn Magnusson excommunicated. Her actions had caused much trouble for Knut Eriksson, who at that time was not yet acclaimed king by everyone. If Rikissa, as she now intended, had managed to get Queen Cecilia Blanca excommunicated for the escape from the cloister – since she had aided the crime by financing it – her sons could not inherit the crown, and then war would be inevitable. That was the way Rikissa thought. Had she succeeded she certainly would have dredged up good reasons to rejoice for the rest of her earthly life, and on her way to Hell, where her path would undoubtedly lead in the end.

But now there was even more reason to celebrate, he went on in a merrier mood. And he raised his tankard to all three of them in a very courtly manner.

Slowly but surely they all grew more lively as they ate and drank, joking about Cecilia Rosa's and Ulvhilde's usual meagre fare, which had kept them young and fresh; the ample food of freedom and wealth probably had a worse effect on anyone who wanted to live a long time. They gorged on veal and lamb and even sampled some wine, but drank mostly ale, of which there was an inexhaustible supply.

As could be expected, the two Cecilias and Ulvhilde gave up long before Birger Brosa, who like many Folkungs was known for his hearty appetite. His grandfather had been Folke the Fat, after all, the mighty jarl.

In fact, Birger Brosa stopped eating his meat, his sweetened turnips, and beans earlier than he would have done in the company of men. Eventually he found it strange to continue eating while the other three looked at him with growing impatience. After all, it was over tankards of ale after the meal that they could usually talk most comfortably, at least until they were too drunk. And Birger Brosa had several matters he wanted to discuss.

When he noticed that the two Cecilias and Ulvhilde had begun using their silent language and giggling at him, he pushed away his plate. Then he filled his tankard, stuck his knife in his belt, and wiped his mouth. Pulling one leg up under him, he set his tankard on his knee as was his habit. He had more to tell that would probably be considered important, he declared solemnly, taking another large gulp as he waited for the silence he knew would ensue.

It had been a great nuisance that the Sverkers held most of the cloisters, and until now all the convents in the country, he began. Such an arrangement could not be allowed to stand; therefore he had endowed a new convent that would soon be consecrated. It was called Riseberga and was situated in the forest of Nordanskog northeast of Arnäs, in darkest Svealand. But they shouldn't worry too much about that, he quickly added when he saw his listeners grimace at the word Svealand. Now they were on their way to becoming a unified kingdom under King Knut. The important thing for the clans was to act together, marry each other, and if necessary go into cloisters together rather than attempt to wage war with each other. The latter course had been tried since time immemorial without success.

Riseberga convent would soon be open, but two things were still lacking. One was an abbess of either the Erik or Folkung clan, and at the moment they were searching through the nuns of the land high and low to find someone suitable. If that proved unsuccessful, they would have to take a novice, but it was preferable for the abbess to be a nun who had already taken her vows, someone who was well versed in everything that needed to be done in a convent.

The second thing they needed was a good *yconomus*. Birger Brosa had heard from many quarters that Gudhem managed its business affairs better than all the convents in the land, and the one who took care of these affairs was not a man, however difficult that might be to believe.

Here he was interrupted by the two Cecilias, both sounding resentful. One thought that she had informed her jarl of this long ago, and one thought that the *yconomus* they'd had previously at Gudhem may indeed have been a man but he was a fool.

Feigning alarm Birger Brosa retreated behind his ale tankard before explaining with charming merriment that he was well aware of the situation; he simply liked to jest. But back to serious matters, he wanted Cecilia Rosa to take on the position as *yconomus* at Riseberga cloister.

Yconoma, Cecilia Rosa corrected him, pretending her feelings were hurt.

The only problem, Birger Brosa went on, was that it would take time before he could get Cecilia Rosa out of Gudhem and arrange for her to be driven up to Riseberga. A letter had to be signed and sealed by the archbishop, and other details had to be arranged. Meanwhile Cecilia Rosa would be alone with Rikissa at Gudhem, without friends or witnesses, and that thought did not sit easy with them.

Cecilia Rosa agreed with his assessment. If Mother Rikissa understood that she would soon be forced to take care of

Gudhem's affairs on her own, she might resort to any manner of conniving. There was no limit to that woman's evil.

But if the abbess didn't know what was in the works, then her desire to keep the cloister's affairs in order would probably be stronger than to try new tricks with the horsehair, confessions, and feigned weeping. Especially so soon after the failed attempt she had just made. Right now she was probably in bed, without the horsehair to be sure, gnashing her teeth with hatred.

Ulvhilde was convinced that Mother Rikissa actually used witchcraft, that she could rob a person of her will and make her confess to anything at all, as if it were God's intention and not the Devil's. Against such sorcery there was no protection; Ulvhilde had found that out herself when despite everything she had been close to yielding to Mother Rikissa's evil persuasion.

Cecilia Blanca interrupted her to say that this was something that could be easily resolved. What Cecilia Rosa should do was to wait a few days, then seek out Rikissa alone and pretend to forgive her. She should pray with the abbess a few times and thank God that He had forgiven His sinful Rikissa.

Naturally that would be to lie and dissemble before God. But God must be wise enough to see the necessity of this sacrifice. Cecilia Rosa could later pray for grace once she was alone with God up in Riseberga.

Furthermore, Cecilia Blanca went on, Birger Brosa must keep secret his plans for bringing an *yconoma* to Riseberga; even better, she should get someone else to spread false rumours about the matter. Anything at all was permissible in the fight with the Devil.

The result of such carefully planned smoke screens would be that one day a convoy would come and fetch Cecilia Rosa with no advance notice whatsoever. Cecilia Rosa must then walk straight out through the gate, just as she herself and Ulvhilde had done, without even saying goodbye. And the witch would be left helpless to intervene.

They all found Cecilia Blanca's suggestions to be wise. And so it was decided. Surely that was also God's will. For why should He want to punish Cecilia Rosa more, and why should He want to help Rikissa in her evil?

It wasn't God who helped Mother Rikissa, it was someone else, Cecilia Rosa said pensively. But she would pray to Our Lady for protection every night. Since Our Lady had protected both her and her beloved Arn for so many years, surely She would continue to do so now.

When young Ulvhilde Emundsdotter rode out from Gudhem to her new life in freedom, it was just before Olsmas. That was the time between the old and the new harvests, so barns and storehouses were empty but hay-making was in full swing.

She rode together with the queen, at the head of the procession and just behind the jarl and the riders who carried flags with the Folkung lion and the three crowns. Behind the queen and Ulvhilde followed a strong contingent of more than thirty men on horseback who mostly wore blue, even though Ulvhilde was not alone with her red mantle.

Wherever the retinue passed on the road to Skara, all work stopped in the fields and men and women would come over to the side of the road, kneel down, and pray God to preserve the peace, the jarl, and Queen Cecilia Blanca.

Ulvhilde had not been on a horse since she was a child. Even though it was said that riding was something that anyone could do, because it was God's plan that the animals should serve humanity, she soon found that riding was not the most pleasant way to travel for the one who was in the saddle. The whole time she had to keep squirming to try and change position; the blood would stop flowing in her leg or her knee chafed against the saddle. As a child she had ridden in a normal saddle with one leg on each side of the horse, but now she and Cecilia Blanca rode as was proper for high-born women with both legs on the same side of the horse. It was both more difficult and more painful.

And yet the nuisance of the saddle was a minor annoyance that was mostly blocked by all her other senses. The air was cool and delightful to breathe, and Ulvhilde kept filling her lungs and holding her breath, as if she didn't want to exhale the sensation of freedom.

They rode across fields and through oak forests, past many rivers and glittering streams, until they came up onto Billingen Mountain. There the forest grew denser and the ranks of soldiers were rearranged so that half of the men rode on ahead, in front of the jarl and the queen. There was nothing to worry about, Cecilia Blanca explained to Ulvhilde. There had been peace in the land for a long time, but men always liked to behave as though they were expecting to have to draw their swords.

The forest did not look very threatening in Ulvhilde's eyes; it was mostly tall oaks and beeches, and the light filtered down in shimmering colours through the high crowns of the trees. They saw some deer in the distance, moving cautiously away among the trees.

Ulvhilde never could have imagined that the world outside would be so beautiful and inviting. She was twenty-two years old now, a woman in the prime of life who long ago should have had children – something that she had believed she would never have the chance to do, since she had viewed her life as staying in the convent until the end of the road.

She had a feeling that the happiness she felt right now could not last, that freedom would have other aspects that would prove more difficult and challenging. But when she rode out on these first days with her back to Gudhem, knowing she would never have to return, she pushed aside everything but the joy she felt. It seemed almost too much for her heart; sometimes it even hurt when she took a deep breath. She felt intoxicated with freedom, and nothing else really mattered just now.

They stopped for the night in Skara and slept in the royal castle. The jarl had something to take care of among the grim men who were waiting for him, and Queen Cecilia Blanca arranged for the women at the castle to bring new clothes to Ulvhilde. They bathed her, combed and brushed her hair, and dressed her in the softest green gown with a silver sash.

Ending up on the floor of the chamber where they were busy with this task was a sad little heap of undyed and brown woollen clothes, the garments that Ulvhilde had worn for as long as she could remember. One of the castle women took the clothes away to be burned.

Ulvhilde would always remember that moment when she saw her cloister clothes being carried out at arm's length, shabby and reeking and intended for the fire, not even good enough to be sold or given to the poor. Only then did she understand that she was not living in a dream, that she really was the person she saw in the highly polished mirror that one of the castle women, giggling and laughing, held up to her while another woman draped the red mantle over her shoulders in a particularly artful way.

The person she saw in the mirror had to be herself, since the mirror image did everything she did: raised an arm, straightened the silver clip in her hair, or fingered the soft mantle with the warm, blood-red colour. And yet it was not herself, because like Cecilia Rosa she had been marked by the simplicity of cloister life. Ulvhilde could suddenly envision her friend back at Gudhem with the same clarity she could see herself in the mirror.

Then a shadow fell across her great joy for the first time. It felt unfair to be happy about so much and to be so selfish when Cecilia Rosa had been left alone with the witch at Gudhem, and she still had long years ahead of her in that place.

During the banquet that evening Ulvhilde was sometimes so happy that despite feeling out of place and shy she laughed loudly at the coarse jests of the minstrels and men of the retinue. Yet sometimes she was so sad at the thought of her dearest friend that the queen had to console her. The queen struck a deep chord with Ulvhilde when she said that the most difficult part of their journey was now at an end. Once they had been three young friends at Gudhem, and for a long time it seemed as if they had all been forsaken by everyone else. But they had stuck together, they had never betrayed their friendship, and they had endured.

Now two of them were free, and they should be happy about that rather than grieving for the third friend. Cecilia Rosa would also be free one day; that time was no longer so far off. And the feeling of friendship that Ulvhilde and Cecilia Blanca had for Cecilia Rosa would never fade, would it? The three of them still had half of their lives to enjoy their liberty.

Cecilia Blanca did not choose to mention Ulvhilde's beauty in her words of consolation or joy. The queen wisely thought that at present such things were outside Ulvhilde's realm of comprehension, given her cloister soul.

In time Ulvhilde would finally begin to understand that she had been transformed as if overnight from a cloister maiden about whom no one cared in the least to one of the most desired maidens in the kingdom. She was beautiful and rich and a friend of the queen. Ulfshem was no paltry estate, and Ulvhilde would soon rule over it single-handedly, without a surly father or argumentative kinsmen trying to manoeuvre her into one bridal bed or another. Ulvhilde was a much freer woman than she could ever imagine.

The next day they continued to the shore of Lake Vättern, where a small black boat that had been given the odd name of *The Serpent* awaited them. The boatswains were tall and blond, and from their language it was apparent that they were all Norwegians. They were among the king's personal retainers because, as was well known, King Knut had mainly Norsemen guarding his life out in the castle at Näs. Some of these Norsemen were friends from the king's long exile as a child; others had arrived in later years when the kinsmen of both the Folkungs and Eriks in Norway had found many reasons to flee their country. Norway had been severely ravaged by the war for the king's crown, the same as had occurred in Western Götaland, Eastern Götaland, and Svealand for more than a hundred years.

It was an unusually warm summer evening with no breeze at all when the entourage arrived at the royal boat harbour on Lake Vättern. There the jarl and the queen, along with Ulvhilde, separated from the mounted retinue that would return to Skara. They climbed down into the small black boat to be rowed across the still water all the way to the castle of Näs on the island of Visingsö. It was so far away that it could not even be seen in the distance.

The jarl sat alone in the bow because he had some things to think about and said he wanted to be left in peace. The queen and Ulvhilde sat in the stern next to the helmsman, who seemed to be the chief of the Norsemen.

Ulvhilde's heart pounded as the boat set sail, and the huge Norsemen expertly propelled their oars through the placid water. She couldn't remember ever being in a boat as a child, although it must have occurred. She sat spellbound, following the eddies of the oars in the dark water and breathing in the smell of tar, leather, and sweat. From the shore they were leaving behind came the song of a nightingale that could be heard far out over the water; oars and leather creaked, and ripples formed at the stern of the boat with each powerful stroke of the oars as the eight Norsemen rowed, making it seem effortless.

Ulvhilde was a little scared and took Cecilia Blanca's hand. When they were some distance out, which did not take long, she pictured herself riding in a tiny hazelnut shell over a vast black abyss.

After a while she nervously asked Cecilia Blanca if there was any chance of getting lost on such a great body of water. Cecilia Blanca had no chance to reply before the helmsman behind them, who had heard her question, repeated it loudly to his eight oarsmen. They all laughed so heartily that two of them doubled over. It was a while before their merriment subsided.

'We Norsemen have sailed on bigger seas than Lake Vättern,' an oarsman then explained to Ulvhilde. 'And one thing I can promise you, we will not get lost on little Vättern, which is only a small lake. That would hardly be fitting for us Norsemen.'

In the twilight when it began to grow cool, Cecilia Blanca and Ulvhilde wrapped their mantles tighter as they approached the castle that stood at the southern tip of Visingsö. Steep slopes extended straight up toward the castle's two ominous towers and the high wall between them. On one of the towers was a large flag with gold on it, which Ulvhilde guessed must be the three crowns.

She was frightened by the dark menace of the fortress but also by the thought that she would soon stand before her father's killer, King Knut. She had not given that matter any thought until now, as if she wanted to cling as long as possible to what was good about her newfound freedom. She would gladly have refrained from meeting King Knut at all, but she realized that it was too late as the boat pushed up onto the shore with a mighty lurch and everyone prepared to climb out.

As if Cecilia Blanca had read her friend's thoughts she then gave Ulvhilde's hand a little squeeze and whispered that there was no cause to worry.

The king himself had come down to the beach to receive his queen and his jarl along with, as he only now seemed to remember, his young Sverker guest.

He first greeted his jarl and his queen with all the courtliness that could be desired. Then he turned to Ulvhilde and looked thoughtfully at the young woman. Full of trepidation and shyness she lowered her gaze. What he saw, however, was instantly to his liking, which surprised everyone except his wife. He took a step toward Ulvhilde, placed his hand under her chin to tip up her face, and looked at her with an expression that was far removed from hatred. It was clear to everyone that he was pleased by what he saw.

But his words of greeting to Ulvhilde surprised even Birger Brosa.

'We bid you welcome to our castle, Ulvhilde Emundsdotter. What was once between us and your father is now buried, because that was war and now we have peace. So you should know that it is a joy for us to greet you as the mistress of Ulfshem. You are safe among friends here as our guest.'

His gaze lingered on Ulvhilde before he suddenly offered her his arm and then took the queen under his other arm. He then escorted them both past all the others up toward the castle.

Ulvhilde's time at Näs was brief, but for her it felt long because there were a thousand details she had to learn regarding matters about which she had not the slightest knowledge. Eating was not just eating, but a pastime as full

311

of rules as at Gudhem, although these new rules called for the opposite sort of behaviour. The same was true of speaking and greeting people. At Gudhem Ulvhilde had learned never to speak unless spoken to and always to be the first to greet someone. Here at Näs it was just the opposite, except when it came to the king, the queen, and the jarl. So there was much embarrassment associated with such seemingly trivial things. Ulvhilde created a stir the first days when she offered a friendly greeting to stable boys and roast-turners as well as the queen's chambermaids before they greeted her. Even more difficult was learning to be first to speak, since it seemed to be an ingrained habit to wait with bowed head until she was addressed.

Freedom was not merely something that existed like air and water. It was something one had to learn.

During this time Cecilia Blanca often thought of a swallow she had found as a girl at home in the courtyard of her father's farm. The swallow lay on the ground chirping piti-fully when Cecilia Blanca picked it up, but quieting down when she warmed it between her cupped hands. She placed the swallow in a birchbark box which she lined with the softest wool, and for two nights she slept with the little bird beside her. On the second morning she got up early, carried the bird out to the courtyard and flung it straight up in the air. With a sharp cry to greet its newfound freedom the bird instantly flew high up toward the sky and disappeared. She had never understood why she knew how to make the bird fly again, she had simply sensed it was the right thing to do.

In a similar manner she now looked at Ulvhilde, who unlike herself and Cecilia Rosa had come to Gudhem as a child rather than a maiden; she couldn't have been older than eleven. So all the rules of the evil convent world had perme-ated her mind so completely, that out in the free world she was as helpless as the swallow on the ground. She didn't even understand that she was beautiful. Ulvhilde belonged to the side of the Sverker clan of which Kol and Boleslav were chieftains; women and maidens on that side of the clan often looked like Ulvhilde, with black hair and brown eyes, slightly slanted. But Ulvhilde was unaware of her own beauty.

Cecilia Blanca had not mentioned the current situation at Ulfshem, whence she would soon accompany Ulvhilde despite the fact that the king grumbled about the journey. But leaving Ulvhilde alone in the clutches of a Folkung who was going to be evicted along with his two lustful sons was out of the question. She knew the two men slightly. The older son was named Folke, and he was of such a hot temper that it would undoubtedly shorten his life; his tongue could prove the bane of his existence. The younger son's name was Jon, and he had gone to school with his kinsman Torgny Lagman. He was soft-spoken in a way that indicated things hadn't been easy for him as the younger brother of a future soldier. Folke, as brothers will do, had practiced much of his fighting skills on his younger and weaker brother.

Cecilia Blanca pondered what would happen to a woman who was as beautiful and rich as Ulvhilde, and yet so innocent, when she landed among men who wanted to possess her for more than two reasons. Wouldn't it be like releasing a lamb to the wolves at Ulfshem?

Cautiously the queen attempted to speak with Ulvhilde about what she might expect. She insisted that they ride together every day, for no matter how much Ulvhilde complained of her sore buttocks, she had to be able to ride a horse. During their rides Cecilia Blanca tried to revive the conversations the three of them had had at Gudhem when they occasionally touched on the love that Cecilia Rosa felt for her Arn, or when they had made plans to rescue Sister Leonore and the monk Lucien. But it was as if Ulvhilde shrunk from such

313

conversations in fright, pretending to be more interested in saddles and the various gaits of horses than in love and men.

She seemed more receptive when together they spent an enjoyable time each day with Cecilia Blanca's two sons, who were now five and three years old. The love between mother and child seemed to interest Ulvhilde considerably more than that between man and woman, although of course the first could not exist without the latter.

Just after Larsmas, when the hay-making was over in both Western and Eastern Götaland, Cecilia Blanca and Ulvhilde rode up to Ulfshem with some retainers. They sailed with the Norsemen up to Alvastra, and from there they rode along the great highway toward Bjälbo and further toward Linköping, where they would find Ulfshem halfway in between.

Ulvhilde had grown more accustomed to the saddle and didn't complain much, although it was a two-day ride. The closer they came to Ulfshem, the more silent and self-conscious she seemed to become.

When they spied the estate Ulvhilde recognized it at once, since the new buildings had been built exactly where the old ones had stood and were of similar design. The huge ash trees on the property were the same as during her childhood, but many other things seemed smaller than she remembered.

They were expected, of course, because a queen did not pay a visit without sending word in advance. When their retinue came within sight there was suddenly a great deal of activity at Ulfshem; servants, guards, and slaves lined up in the courtyard to receive and greet them, bringing out the first bread to break with the guests before they came inside.

Cecilia Blanca was a sharp-eyed woman. She saw at once what most people would have seen sooner or later, with the possible exception of the innocent Ulvhilde. Herr Sigurd Folkesson and his two sons Folke and Jon, who stood beside

314

him, seemed to Cecilia Blanca's eyes to transform the closer she and Ulvhilde came to the courtyard.

If the Folkungs from a distance had looked unwilling or almost hostile in their bearing, they now tempered their stance and made an effort not to show their astonishment when they saw Ulvhilde wearing the magnificent mantle of their enemies as she climbed down from her horse.

Herr Sigurd and his eldest son Folke hurried over to assist Cecilia Blanca and Ulvhilde as they dismounted to receive the welcoming bread.

Even though Sigurd and his sons would be richly compensated and would be able to acquire estates larger than Ulfshem for some of the silver which Birger Brosa had looted during his crusade, there was still the matter of honour. No one could think that it was honourable for Folkungs to have to move for the sake of a pitiful little maiden from the Sverker clan.

But Ulvhilde was not what they had been expecting. For men seldom imagine the enemy's women to be beauties.

Sigurd Folkesson may have thought about greeting them with harsh words, but could do little more than stammer and hem and haw as he bade them welcome, while his two sons mostly gaped, unable to take their eyes off Ulvhilde.

When the confused welcome speech seemed to be over, Cecilia Blanca sought to rescue Ulvhilde from her embarrassment by saying the words required in response. But Ulvhilde spoke first.

'I greet you Folkungs, Sigurd Folkesson, Folke and Jon, with joy as I return to my childhood home,' Ulvhilde began without the least hint of shyness. Her voice was calm and clear. 'What was once between us Sverkers and Folkungs has now been buried, because that was war and now we have peace. So you shall know that it is a pleasure for me to welcome you to Ulfshem and that I feel happy to have you as my friends and guests.'

Her words made such a strong impression that all the Folkungs were speechless. Then Ulvhilde held out her arm to Sigurd Folkesson so that he could lead her into the main building on her property. The eldest son Folke eventually realized that he should offer the queen his arm.

As they entered Ulfshem through the large double gate made of oak, Cecilia Blanca smiled with relief; at the same time she was rather amused. The worthy words with which Ulvhilde had surprised her Folkung guests had been borrowed shamelessly from the king. It was almost word for word what King Knut had said to greet Ulvhilde as a guest at Näs not so long ago.

Ulvhilde was a quick learner, as were all who were forced to live in cloisters, thought the queen. But it didn't help much to be swift to learn; one also needed good sense in order to use what one learned. And that was what Ulvhilde had now shown in a manner as powerful as it was surprising.

The swallow flew, rising steadily on small, swift wings toward the sky.

NINE

If it was really God's will for the Christians to lose the Holy Land, then He had assigned them such a long and winding road to the great defeat at Saladin's hands that in each small decisive event it became almost impossible to discern His will.

If that was the case, then the first big step toward the catastrophe was the Christians' defeat by Saladin at Marj Ayyoun in the year of grace 1179.

As Count Raymond III of Tripoli told Arn when their friendship began, and when they together tried to drown their sorrow at the fortress of Beaufort belonging to the Hospitallers, the defeat at Marj Ayyoun could of course be viewed as merely one in an endless series of battles over almost a hundred years. No side could count on winning every time; for that they were altogether too susceptible to the whims of fate, to weather and wind, reinforcements that did or did not arrive in time, wise and foolish decisions on both sides, and for those who seriously claimed that this was the decisive factor, to God's ever-inscrutable will. No matter how they tried to explain their fortunes in war, and how much they prayed to the same God, each side would inevitably lose some battles and win others.

But among the knights from King Baldwin IV's army who were captured at Marj Ayyoun was one of the foremost in the ruling class of barons in Outremer, Baldwin d'Ibelin. For a man of Baldwin d'Ibelin's position to fall into captivity was naturally mortifying and costly, but it was not a mortal blow.

However, Saladin was the warrior of that era who was more meticulous than any other in obtaining information about the enemy; nothing that had to do with power in Antioch, Tripoli, or Jerusalem escaped Saladin's attention.

For that reason he knew to set a high price for the release of Baldwin d'Ibelin. He demanded the dizzying sum of 150,000 besants in gold, the highest ransom ever demanded from either side in the almost hundred-year war.

What Saladin knew, and what determined his price, was that Baldwin d'Ibelin was probably going to be the next king of Jerusalem. The leprous King Baldwin IV's days were numbered, and the reigning monarch had already failed once in his attempt to arrange the succession to the throne by marrying his sister Sibylla off to William Longsword. This Longsword had soon died, presumably from one of the shameful diseases that ravaged the court of Jerusalem, although people called it consumption.

After William Longsword's death, Sibylla gave birth to a son whom she named after her brother, King Baldwin. But she was in love with Baldwin d'Ibelin, and the king had nothing at all against such an alliance. The Ibelin family was one of the most respected among the land-owning gentry in Outremer, and the marriage between Sibylla and Baldwin d'Ibelin would strengthen the position of the court and diminish the opposition to the worldly landowners in the Holy Land.

Unfortunately for Baldwin d'Ibelin, Saladin was fully informed of this. And since he could claim that in essence he had a king in captivity, he demanded a king's ransom.

But 150,000 besants in gold was more than the combined

assets of the entire Ibelin family, and in this part of the world there was only one man who might put up such a fortune, and that was Emperor Manuel of Constantinople.

Baldwin d'Ibelin sued for his freedom from Saladin by swearing on his honour either to borrow the sum or to return to captivity. Saladin, who had no occasion to doubt the word of a respected knight, agreed to the proposal, and Baldwin d'Ibelin travelled to Constantinople to attempt to persuade the Byzantine emperor to lend him the money.

Emperor Manuel found it rather convenient to have a claim on the next king of Jerusalem for the rest of his life by making an admittedly large contribution. So he lent Baldwin all the gold he needed, and the latter sailed off for Outremer and paid Saladin. Then he was able to return to Jerusalem to report the good news about his freedom and once again resume his love affair with Sibylla.

But Emperor Manuel, Saladin, and Baldwin d'Ibelin himself had not reckoned with the women at the court of Jerusalem and their attitude toward men with large debts. The mother of both the king and his sister Sibylla, the constantly scheming Agnes de Courtenay, had little difficulty in convincing her daughter of the folly of such a relationship burdened by a debt of 150,000 besants in gold.

One of Agnes de Courtenay's many lovers was a crusader knight who had never exchanged sword blows with the enemy but preferred exercises in bed. His name was Amalrik de Lusignan. Even though he was no warrior he was not slow in seeing the opportunities in the play for power at court. To Agnes he began praising his younger brother Guy, who was said to be a handsome man as well as quite a passable lover.

So while Baldwin d'Ibelin went to Constantinople to see Emperor Manuel, Amalrik de Lusignan was in France to fetch his brother Guy.

When Baldwin d'Ibelin, after many trials, returned to

Jerusalem, he found that Sibylla had transferred her affections to the newly arrived Guy de Lusignan.

The difference between having Guy de Lusignan rather than Baldwin d'Ibelin as king of Jerusalem would have been like darkness versus light or fire versus water. Without realizing it himself, Saladin had shortened the path to his ultimate victory.

As far as the Knights Templar were concerned, the defeat at Marj Ayyoun was also of great significance, since Grand Master Odo de Saint Amand was one of the survivors and was taken prisoner after the battle. Normally all Hospitallers and Templars were beheaded as soon as they landed in captivity. Their Rule forbade them to be ransomed, so they had no financial value as prisoners. They were also the Christians' best knights, and from Saladin's point of view they were better off beheaded than exchanged for Saracen prisoners, which was the other possibility besides ransom.

With a Grand Master, however, Saladin thought the situation was different. The Grand Masters of both the Hospitallers and Templars held all power in their hands; their brothers in the order had to obey their decisions, without question. A Grand Master might be valuable if they could convince him to cooperate.

But Saladin got nowhere with Odo de Saint Amand. The Grand Master referred merely to the Rule, which forbade ransoms for Templar knights, and so Odo de Saint Amand's captivity in Damascus was brief. Within a year he was dead, though no one knew the cause.

It was most likely that the new Grand Master of the Templar order would be Arnoldo de Torroja, who held the next highest position as Jerusalem's Master.

Because power in the Holy Land was divided among the court in Jerusalem, the two spiritual orders of knights, and the barons and landowners, it was of great importance who became Grand Master, and what sort of warrior, spiritual leader, and negotiator he was. It was even more important, of course, that he held a conciliatory attitude towards the Saracens, for the sake of peace in the Holy Land.

Arnoldo de Torroja had made a long career as a member of the Knights Templar in Aragon and Provence before he came to the Holy Land. He was much more of a businessman and wielder of power than his warlike predecessor Odo de Saint Amand.

Looking at these potential power shifts from Saladin's point of view, the royal power in Jerusalem seemed on its way to landing in the clutches of an ignorant adventurer who would be little threat on the battlefield. And the mighty Order of the Knights Templar had in Arnoldo de Torroja acquired a leader who was more a man of compromise and negotiation than his predecessor, who was more like Count Raymond of Tripoli.

For Arn de Gothia, master of Gaza, Arnoldo de Torroja's elevation to Grand Master had a more immediate effect. Arn was summoned to Jerusalem in order to assume without delay the office of Jerusalem's Master.

For the two Cistercian monks, Father Louis and Brother Pietro, who at this time arrived at the centre of the world as the special envoys of the Holy Father in Rome, their encounter with Jerusalem was a mixture of violent disappointments and pleasant surprises. But almost nothing was as they had expected.

Like all newly arrived Franks, secular or ecclesiastical, they'd imagined the City of Cities to be a wonderfully peaceful place with streets of gold and white marble. What they found was an indescribable tumult of teeming crowds and jabbered languages and narrow streets filled mostly with garbage. Like all Cistercians they had an image of their military brother organization the Knights Templar as a group of uneducated roughnecks who could scarcely spell their way through the

Pater Noster in Latin. What they found first was Jerusalem's Master, who addressed them in Latin. And almost immediately they all fell into an interesting discourse about Aristotle while waiting for the Grand Master whom they had come to meet in person.

The rooms of Jerusalem's Master reminded them a good deal of a Cistercian monastery. There was none of the worldly and sometimes ungodly ostentation which they had seen at other places in the Templars' quarter of the city. Instead there was a long arcade with a view over the city, much like a part of every Cistercian cloister, and all the walls were white and without sinful pictures. Their host served them an excellent meal despite the fact that there was nothing that originated from four-footed animals or other items that Cistercians could not eat.

Father Louis was a clear-sighted man, schooled from a very young age by the best teachers in the Cistercians at Cîteaux; for many years he had been the Cistercian order's envoy from the Holy Father. So he was rather amazed how little he actually knew about the so-called Jerusalem's Master, a title that seemed to Father Louis utterly grotesque in its presumption, and so ill-suited to the man he assumed he would meet. They had told him that Arn de Gothia was a warrior of especially high repute, that he was the victor of the battle of Mont Gisard, when the Templars despite great inferiority in numbers had defeated Saladin himself. So Father Louis had probably expected someone comparable to the Roman commander Belisarius, in any case a military man who could barely speak of anything besides war. But if it were not for a number of white scars on the face and hands of this Arn de Gothia, Father Louis would have thought from his gentle demeanour and conciliatory manner of speaking that he was no different from a brother of Cîteaux. He couldn't help plying Arn a bit with questions, and thought that he better understood at least one side of the matter when he learned that this Templar knight had actually been brought up in a cloister. Then it was like seeing the dream of blessed Saint Bernard fully realized: the warrior in the Holy War who was at the same time a monk. Father Louis had never imagined that he would ever encounter this dream in the flesh.

Nor could he avoid noticing that his host ate only bread and drank only water despite all the other food and drink that were on the table, provided for the pleasure of his guests. This high Templar knight was thus doing penance for something. But no matter how much Father Louis wanted to learn more about the matter, this first meeting was hardly the right time to inquire. He was the envoy of the Holy Father, and had brought a papal bull that might not be readily accepted. Besides, these Templar knights were known for their pride; the man who was Grand Master, whom they would soon meet, apparently viewed himself as next in rank only to the Holy Father himself. Which meant that the so-called Jerusalem's Master would be considered no less than an archbishop. It would be reasonable to assume that such men did not view an abbé as possessing any great power. Nor could they be expected to understand the position of an abbé who worked directly under the Holy Father, acting as his advisor and envoy.

When the Grand Master himself at long last joined their meeting, all remnants of the meal had been cleared away and they were having a pleasant discussion about the divisions of philosophy into knowledge, learning, and faith. They were also talking about ideas as something that always had to be manifested in material objects; they could not exist solely in the higher pure spheres. This was precisely the sort of conversation that Father Louis never would have imagined having with a Templar knight.

Arnoldo de Torroja apologized for his tardiness by saying that he had been summoned by the king of Jerusalem.

He also told them that he and Arn de Gothia would need to leave soon to meet with the king again. However, he did not want to allow the entire first evening to pass without meeting his Cistercian guests and hearing about their mission. According to Father Louis's first impression, this Grand Master was a man like those he might have met among the emperor's ambassadors in Rome, a full-fledged diplomat and negotiator. So he was no coarse Roman Belisarius either.

Father Louis thought it was a little awkward to proceed at once to the sensitive topic they had come to discuss, but his hosts did not leave him much choice. It would not be proper to do nothing but chat about superfluous matters at their first meeting, and then return the next day to present solemn decrees.

So he explained the matter directly and without any unnecessary digressions. His two hosts listened attentively, without interrupting and without revealing their thoughts by any change in expression.

Archbishop William of Tyrus had travelled from the Holy Land to the Third Lateran Council in Rome, and there he had presented serious charges against both the Knights Templar and the Hospitallers.

According to Archbishop William, the Knights Templar were in certain respects consistently counteracting the Holy Roman Church. If anyone was excommunicated in the Holy Land, he could be buried by the Knights Templar. And before his death he could even be admitted into their order. If a bishop imposed an interdict upon a whole city so that all the sinners were removed from the care of the Church, then the Knights Templar could send their own priests to take care of all churchly services. All these abuses, which gave the impression that the power of the Church was weak or even ridiculous, arose from the fact that the Knights Templar did not answer to any bishop and thus could not be excommunicated

324

or even punished by the patriarch of Jerusalem. What made the situation especially serious, of course, was the fact that both Templars and Hospitallers accepted payment for these services. The Third Lateran Council and the Holy Father Alexander III had therefore decided that all such business transactions must cease immediately. However, Archbishop William had found no hearing for his proposal that various punishments should be imposed on the two orders of knights for these offences against the Church, which had supremacy over all people on the earth.

Father Louis brought with him a papal bull affixed with the Pope's seal. He now took it out and laid it on the empty table before them. There in writing stood all that he had just explained. He now needed to know what answer he should take back to the Holy Father.

'Say that the Order of the Knights Templar from the moment we received word from the Holy Father, shall yield to his edict,' replied Arnoldo de Torroja gently. 'This is valid from the moment that I, the Grand Master, pronounced our submission. We shall see to it that this new order is implemented as soon as possible. It may take time, but we do not intend to cause any unnecessary delays. Our decision is already in effect because I have pronounced it so, and I don't think that my friend and brother Arn de Gothia has any different view in this matter, do you, Arn?'

'No, absolutely not,' replied Arn in the same calm tone. 'We Knights Templar conduct all sorts of business, and business is important to support the expense of an ongoing and costly war. I will gladly tell you more of this matter tomorrow, Father Louis. But to conduct business transactions relating to ecclesiastical matters conflicts with our rules and is called simony. Personally I view the business you spoke of, Father, as simony. So I can fully understand both Archbishop William's charges and the decision of the Holy Father.'

'But then I don't understand . . .' said Father Louis, as relieved by the swift acceptance of the decision as he was astonished by it. 'Why did this sin occur if you both so clearly take exception to it?'

'Our previous Grand Master Odo de Saint Amand, now blessed in Paradise, had a different perspective on these matters than the two of us,' replied Arnoldo de Torroja.

'But couldn't you as highly-placed brothers have criticized your Grand Master for this shameful act if you were so against it?' asked Father Louis in amazement.

He was met only by meditative smiles from the two men, but received no answer.

Arn summoned a knight and instructed him to show Father Louis and Brother Pietro, who had not said a word during the conversation, to their lodgings. Then he excused himself by saying that the king wanted to see both the Grand Master and Jerusalem's Master at once. He assured them that on the following day he would be a better host. With that the Grand Master rose and blessed his two spiritual guests, to both the surprise and resentment of Father Louis.

The two Cistercians were led to their quarters for the night, but not without an initial blunder, since they were first led to a room intended for worldly guests with Saracen tile patterns and fountains. But then they were guided to the proper lodgings and were each given a whitewashed cell of the same type they normally occupied.

Arnoldo de Torroja and Arn hastened together to the king's night quarters. They had little opportunity to talk about the papal bull on the way, but they were still agreed on the matter. It would be a drain on their income, yet it was good to be freed of this business which they both regarded as extremely dubious. So much the better then that they had been given direct instruction from the Holy Father himself to throw in the face of all those who might be displeased.

The king's private rooms were small and dim, because he was unable to move or see very well. He awaited them sitting on his curtained throne, where he sat behind blue muslin so that from the outside he was visible only as a shadow. It was whispered that he had now lost both his hands.

In the room there was only one servant, a huge Nubian who was both deaf and dumb and sat on some cushions next to the wall with his gaze fixed on his half-concealed lord so that he could intervene at the slightest sign, which only he and the king understood.

Arnoldo de Torroja and Arn entered, walking side by side, and bowed to the king without a word. Then they sat down on two Egyptian leather stools before the unusual throne. The king spoke to them in a rather high-pitched voice; he was only in his twenties.

'I'm pleased that the two foremost brothers of the Knights Templar have heeded my summons,' he began and then broke off coughing and made a sign that his guests didn't understand. The Nubian slave rushed over and arranged something behind the blue curtain though they couldn't see what he did. They waited in silence.

'Although I'm farther from my death than some people both believe and hope,' the king went on, 'I have no lack of troubles. You are both the backbone in the defence of the Holy Land, the Templar knights, and I wish to discuss two matters with you with no other ears present. So I shall speak in a language that in other circumstances I would have phrased in better terms. Is that all right with you, Templar knights?'

'Absolutely splendid, Sire,' replied Arnoldo de Torroja.

'Good,' said the king, then coughed briefly again but made no sign to his slave and continued at once. 'The first question deals with the new patriarch of Jerusalem. The second question is about our military situation. I would like to take up the question about the patriarch first. Soon a new patriarch will be appointed, since Amalrik de Nesle is dying. It seems to be a matter for the church, but if I understand my mother Agnes correctly, it is actually more her concern, or rather mine. We have two candidates: Heraclius, archbishop of Caesarea, and William, archbishop of Tyrus. Let us weigh the arguments for and against each. I have understood that William is the enemy of the Knights Templar, but he is a godly man whose honour no one doubts. Heraclius is, if I may be quite honest now that no one can hear us, a rogue of a type that is rather common here in our land, a gone-astray choir boy or the like, and he is also known for his sinful life. And he is my mother's lover, one of many, naturally. But he doesn't seem to be your enemy; on the contrary. As you see, there are many less noble weights in the balance trays that we have before us. What is your opinion in this matter?'

It was obvious that Arnoldo de Torroja should answer, and equally obvious that he had a hard time replying with complete candour. And so he launched into a long harangue about life, God's inscrutable will, and other things that merely meant that he was talking as he tried to work out what he should actually say. Arn was astonished by the unfortunate young king, who in spite of his frail voice exuded such an unusual power and decisiveness. And yet he suffered from an illness that meant he would soon die, and it caused him always to hide himself from whoever was in his presence.

'So, to sum up,' said Arnoldo de Torroja, finally coming to a conclusion. 'It's a good thing for the Knights Templar to have a patriarch who is our friend, and a bad thing to have one who is our enemy. At the same time it's a good thing for the kingdom of Jerusalem to have a man of honour and faith as the supreme guardian over the True Cross and God's Grave. And a sin to have a sinner in the same responsible post.

What God might think in this matter is of course not hard to surmise.'

'Assuredly, but now it's a matter of a higher power than God, namely my mother Agnes,' replied the king dryly. 'I know that it's actually the council of all the archbishops in the Holy Land that will decide and vote on this matter. But nowadays many of these men of God are easy to buy. So the decision is de facto mine, or yours and mine, or my mother's. What I want to know is whether you Templar knights are absolutely opposed to one or the other of these two. Well?'

'A sinner who is well-disposed toward us or an honest man of God who is against us, that is no easy choice, Sire,' replied Arnoldo de Torroja evasively. Had he been able to see into the future he would have said something else with all his might.

'Fine,' said the king with a sigh. 'Then it looks like we'll have a very unusual man as patriarch, since you're leaving the decision to my mother. If God is as good as you Templars say, He will undoubtedly send His bolts of lightning against this man every time he approaches a slave boy or a married woman, or an ass for that matter. So! The second thing I wanted to talk about was the situation in the war. In this case everyone lies to me, as you may well understand; it sometimes takes me a year to grasp what has happened and not happened. For example, regarding what really happened at my only victory in the wars that I myself have waged. First I was the great victor at Mont Gisard; there were reliable witnesses who saw Saint George riding above me in a cloud and other such foolishness. Now I know that it was you, Arn de Gothia, who was the victor. Am I not right in this?'

'The truth is . . .' Arn replied hesitantly, since he had received a direct question from the king and Arnoldo de Torroja could not answer in his stead, 'that the Templar knights in that battle conquered three or four thousand of Saladin's best troops. It is also true that Jerusalem's secular army defeated five hundred.'

'Is that your answer, Arn de Gothia?'

'Yes, Sire.'

'And who led the Templar knights in that battle?'

'I did, with God's help, Sire.'

'Good. That's what I thought. An advantage with some Templars, and you are clearly one of them, Arn de Gothia, is that they answer truthfully. I gladly would live my final years in that manner, but that will hardly be granted me. So! Tell me briefly something about the military situation!'

'It's a complicated situation, Sire –' Arnoldo de Torroja began but was instantly cut off by the king.

'Forgive me, dear Grand Master, but Jerusalem's Master is at the moment the order's highest military commander, is he not?'

'Yes, Sire, that is true,' replied Arnoldo de Torroja.

'Good!' said the king with an audible sigh. 'God, if only I had such men as you around me, men who speak the truth. Then it is no doubt proper that I ask this question of Arn de Gothia, my dear Grand Master, without violating all your numerous rules and honour and glory?'

'That is fully in order, Sire,' said Arnoldo de Torroja some-what tensely.

'Now then!' the king said, peremptorily.

'The situation can be described as follows, Sire,' Arn began uncertainly. 'We have the absolute worst opponent in Christendom against us now, worse than Zenki, worse than Nur al-Din. Saladin has largely united all the Saracens against us, and he is a skilled military leader. He has lost once, when Your Majesty won at Mont Gisard. Otherwise he has won every significant battle. We have to reinforce the Christian side in all of Outremer, otherwise we are defeated, or will be locked inside fortresses and cities, and we can't stay there indefinitely. That's the situation.'

'Do you share this opinion, Grand Master?' the king asked harshly.

'Yes, Sire. The situation is just as Jerusalem's Master has described it. We must have reinforcements from our home countries. Saladin is something entirely different from what we've had to deal with previously.'

'Well! Then so it shall be. We shall send an envoy to our homelands, to the emperor of Germany, the king of England, and the king of France. Would you be so kind as to participate in this mission, Grand Master?'

'Yes, Sire.'

'Even if Grand Master Roger des Moulins from the Hospitallers is also included?'

'Yes, Sire. Roger des Moulins is an extraordinary man.'

'And with the new patriarch of Jerusalem, even if he turns out to be someone with whom you should be cautious in the night?'

'Yes, Sire.'

'Well, that's excellent. So it shall be. One more question: who is the best commander of all the secular knights in Outremer?'

'Count Raymond of Tripoli and then Baldwin d'Ibelin, Sire,' replied Arnoldo de Torroja quickly.

'And who is the worst?' the king shot back with equal speed. 'Could it possibly be my sister's dear husband Guy de Lusignan?'

'To compare Guy de Lusignan with either of the two men I mentioned would be like comparing David and Goliath, Sire,' said Arnoldo de Torroja with a slightly ironic bow. This made the king pensive and silent for a moment.

'So you think that Guy de Lusignan would beat Count Raymond, Grand Master?' he asked in amusement when he was finished thinking.

'I didn't say that, Sire. As the Scripture says, Goliath was the greatest warrior and David merely an inexperienced boy. Without God's intervention Goliath would win in a thousand out of a thousand battles against David. If God supports Guy de Lusignan as much as he supported David, then Guy de Lusignan would of course be invincible.'

'But if God turns his back, what then?' asked the king with a little coughing laugh.

'Then the battle would be over quicker than you could blink, Sire,' said Arnoldo de Torroja with a friendly bow.

'Grand Master and Jerusalem's Master,' said the king, coughing again and giving a signal that made his Nubian slave hurry over to his side. 'With men such as yourselves I would wish to speak longer. However, my health prevents me, so I bid you both God's peace and good night.'

They got up from their soft leather stools, bowed, and exchanged uneasy glances as the wheezing and gurgling sounds continued behind the muslin curtain that concealed the king. They turned and retreated tactfully from the room.

To his considerable surprise Father Louis was awakened in good time before *Lauds* by Arn de Gothia, who had come in person to fetch him and Brother Pietro for the morning song in the Temple of Solomon. The two Cistercians were led by their knight companion through a labyrinthine system of corridors and halls and up a dark staircase until they suddenly emerged in the midst of the huge church with the silver cupola. It was already filled with Templar knights and sergeants who were silently assembling around the walls of the round sanctuary. No one arrived late. When it was time almost a hundred Templar knights and more than twice as many black-clad sergeants stood along the walls.

Father Louis took great pleasure in the morning song; impressed by the gravity with which these men of war sang, and by the fact that they sang so well. This was another thing he had not anticipated.

After *Lauds* in the Temple of Solomon, Arn de Gothia took his guests with him on the usual tour that all new visitors to Jerusalem expected. He explained in passing that it was best to take the tour early in the morning before the crowds of pilgrims grew too great.

They went back across the entire Templar area and past the Temple of the Lord with the gold cupola, which Arn thought they could leave until last since no pilgrims were allowed inside on this day, which was set aside for cleaning and repairs. They went out through the Golden Port and up on Golgotha, which was still free of both tradesmen and visitors. At the site where the Lord suffered and died on His cross for their sins, the three prayed long and fervently.

Then Arn took his visitors in through the Stefan Gate so that they emerged up on the Via Dolorosa. Reverently they followed the Lord's last path of suffering through the gradually awakening city all the way to the Church of the Holy Sepulchre, which was still closed and guarded by four sergeants of the Templar order. The sergeants opened the church at once to make way for Jerusalem's Master and his visiting clergymen.

The church was beautiful to see from the outside with its simple vault of the type that Father Louis and even Arn and Brother Pietro were familiar with from the cloisters where they grew up. But inside the church was littered and in disarray because so many different religious factions had to share it.

There was a corner glaring with gold and a multitude of colours and brash paintings that Father Louis recognized as the style of the heretical Byzantine church; there were other styles that he did not recognize. Arn explained, as if in passing, that it was the rule in Jerusalem that Christians of

333

every sort should have access to the Holy Grave. For him this fact did not seem odd in the least.

When they walked down the stone steps in the dark, damp crypt of Saint Helena, however, they were all filled with such a great solemnity that they began to shiver; even Arn seemed affected as much as his visitors. They knelt down before the stone slab and prayed in silence; none of them wanted to be the first to stop. Here was the heart of Christianity, here was the very place that had cost so much blood over so many years, God's Grave.

Father Louis was so overwhelmed by this first visit to God's Grave that afterwards he could not remember how long they were down there, what he had actually experienced, or what visions he had seen. But they seemed to have been there for a long time, because when they exited through the main door of the church into the blinding sunlight, they were met by a muttering, ill-humoured crowd that had been kept at a distance by the four sergeants and not allowed inside. The muttering subsided quickly when they saw that it was Jerusalem's Master himself coming out of the church with his ecclesiastical guests.

On their return through the city Arn chose another and more worldly route which went from the Jaffa Gate straight through the bazaars to the Knights Templar quarter. Strong foreign odours from spices, raw meat, poultry of various kinds, burnt leather, fabrics, and metal prickled the noses of the visitors. Father Louis thought at first that all these foreign people speaking incomprehensible languages were unbelievers, but Arn explained that they were almost all Christians, although from societies that had been in Outremer long before the Crusaders had arrived. They were Syrians, Copts, Armenians, Maronites, and many others that Father Louis had hardly heard of. Arn told him that there was a cruel history associated with all these Christians. For when the first Crusaders came they had not understood, like Father Louis and Brother Pietro, that these people were kinsmen of the faith. Since their appearance did not distinguish them from Turks and Saracens, they had been killed by Christian zealots in almost the same numbers as the unbelievers. But that evil time was long past.

When they finally visited the empty Temple of the Lord inside the Templars' quarter, they prayed at the rock where Abraham was said to have offered to sacrifice Isaac, and where Jesus Christ as a child had been consecrated to God.

After they prayed, Arn took his guests around the very beautiful sanctuary, and Father Louis had to admit that it was beautiful, despite all the foreign decoration. Arn read without difficulty the texts of the unbelievers which were inlaid in silver and gold along the walls. To Father Louis's question of why these ungodly texts had not been destroyed, Arn replied apparently unconcerned that most people did not consider them texts, since Christians usually could not read the language of the Koran and hence viewed them as meaningless decorations. And to those who could read them, he added, the content of most of the texts was such that it agreed very well with the true religion, since the unbelievers praised God in many respects in the same way as Christians did.

Father Louis was upset at first when he heard Arn so wantonly speaking heresy, but he held his tongue, thinking that there was probably a great difference between Christians who had lived a long time in the Holy Land and those who like himself were making their first visit.

It was already time to sing *Ters*, and they had to hurry a little so as not to arrive late to the Temple of Solomon. Afterwards they went back up to the rooms which were delegated to Jerusalem's Master. A big crowd of visitors was already waiting; judging by the diverse clothing they wore, they could be anything from knights in the Holy Land to unbeliever craftsmen and merchants. Arn de Gothia excused himself, saying that he had a good deal of work to do that could not wait any longer, but that he would see his Cistercian guests again after they had sung *Sext*.

So they met again a few hours later, and Arn then took his visitors out into the pillared arcade which resembled that in a Cistercian cloister. There he had them served with cold drinks made from something called lemons. Arn still drank only water.

Now Father Louis had a reason to ask Arn whether he was doing penance, and he received a cautiously affirmative reply. But realizing that he might be expected to explain the matter in more detail, Arn told him that it involved something that he would prefer to confess only to his dearest father confessor in life. His name was Henri and he was the abbé in the faraway West Gothic cloister of Varnhem. Then Father Louis lit up and told him that he knew this abbé quite well, since they had met several times in Cîteaux at chapter meetings. Father Henri had told him many interesting things about Christianizing the wild Gothic people. Imagine that the world could be so small! So they had a mutual friend, which was completely unexpected.

For Arn it was like hearing a greeting from home, and for a moment he turned thoughtful as he sank into reminiscences from both Varnhem and *Vitae Schola* in Denmark and the sins for which he'd had to do penance; the worst of them, no matter how hard it was to believe, was that he had loved Cecilia, his betrothed.

Father Louis had no difficulty in persuading Arn to recount what had happened to him in life from the time he met his father confessor Henri until now, so many years later, he was here in Jerusalem as a Templar knight. Nor did Father Louis, who was a practiced tender of souls, have any trouble hearing the underlying tone of sorrow in Arn's account. He then offered to take his old confessor's place, since he was the closest person to Father Henri that Arn could expect to find in the Holy Land. Arn agreed after a brief hesitation, and Brother Pietro went to fetch his abbé's confession stole and then left them alone in the vaulted arcade.

'Well, my son?' asked Father Louis after he had blessed Arn before confession.

'Forgive me, Father, for I have sinned,' Arn began with a deep sigh as if to take a running start at his affliction. 'I have sinned gravely against our Rule; that is the same thing as if you, Father, had sinned against the cloister rules. I have also kept my sin secret and thereby aggravated it, and the worst thing is that I have found a way to defend my actions.'

'Then you will have to tell me more concretely what it involves if I am to understand and be able to advise you or absolve you,' replied Father Louis.

'I killed a Christian, and it was done in malice; that is one sin,' Arn began hesitantly. 'The second is that I then rightly should have been stripped of my mantle, and in the best case be set to tend to the latrines for two years; in the worst case to leave our order. But because I kept my sin secret, I rose in the ranks within our order and now hold one of our highest positions, for which I am unfit.'

'Is it a striving for power that drove you to commit this sin?' asked Father Louis with concern. He saw a very troublesome case before him in terms of deciding on a penance.

'No, Father, I can honestly say that it is not,' Arn replied without hesitation. 'As you have understood, men like me, to some degree, and especially men like Arnoldo de Torroja, hold great power in our order. That's why it's important which men assume these positions, because the presence of all Christendom in the Holy Land may depend on it. Arnoldo de Torroja is a better Grand Master and I'm a better

Jerusalem's Master than many other men. But not because we are purer in our faith than others, not because we are greater spiritual leaders or better at leading many knights in battle than others might be. We are better in these positions because we belong to those Templar knights who seek peace rather than war. Yet those who seek war are leading us to our downfall.'

'So you're defending your sin by saying that it protects the Holy Land?' asked Father Louis with scarcely noticeable sarcasm which in any case went right over Arn's head.

'Yes, Father, that is what I see if I try to look deep into my conscience,' he said.

'Tell me, my son,' Father Louis went on after a moment, 'how many men have you killed during your time as a knight?'

'That's impossible to say, Father. No fewer than five hundred, no more than fifteen hundred, I should think. I never know what happens when a lance or an arrow hits its mark; I have been struck eight times by arrows so badly that eight Saracens may think they have killed me.'

'Among these men you killed, were more than one Christian?'

'Yes, undoubtedly. Just as there are Saracens who fight on our side, there are Christians on the other side. But that is not the same thing. The Rule does not forbid us to shoot at our enemies with arrows or strike them with swords or ride against them with lances, and we can't stop and ask about our enemy's faith every time we raise a weapon.'

'So what was it about the Christian you killed that made his death more sinful than that of other Christians you may have killed?' asked Father Louis, clearly baffled.

'One of our most important rules of honour goes like this,' replied Arn with a hint of sadness in his voice: '*When you draw your sword – do not think about who you must kill. Think about who you should spare.* I have tried to live according to that rule, and it was in my thoughts when I confronted the three foolish new arrivals who for the sake of their own pleasure intended to attack and kill defenceless women, children, and old men who were under the protection of the city of Gaza. I was the master of Gaza then.'

'Surely you must have had the right to defend your wards even from Christians. Didn't you?' asked Father Louis, relieved.

'Yes, most certainly. And I did try to spare two of the knights. The fact that they died anyway is not my sin; that is something that can easily occur when riding with drawn weapons against one another. But with the third knight it was worse. First I spared him as I wished and should have done. He rewarded me by killing my horse right before my eyes. Then I killed him at once and in anger.'

'That was bad, of course,' sighed Father Louis, who saw the hope for a simple solution vanish. 'You killed a Christian man for the sake of a horse?'

'Yes, Father, that is my sin.'

'That was bad, truly bad,' Father Louis nodded sadly. 'But tell me one thing that I perhaps do not understand. Aren't horses particularly important for you knights?'

'A horse can be a closer friend to a knight than his friends among other knights,' said Arn sadly. 'To your ears, Father, this may sound strange or even blasphemous, but I can only tell you the honest truth. My life depends on my horse and our camaraderie. With a lesser horse than the one that was killed before my eyes, I would certainly have fallen in battle long ago. That horse saved my life more times than I can count, and we had been friends ever since I was young and he was young. We lived a long warrior life together.'

Father Louis felt strangely moved by this childish declaration of love for an animal. But from his brief sojourn in the centre of the world, he had already understood that many things were different here; some things that were sins back home might not be found sinful here, and vice versa. So he did not want to be hasty, and he asked Arn for time to think over what he had heard until the next day. In the meantime Arn should again seek God in his heart and pray for forgiveness for his sin. With that they parted. Arn, moving as if carrying a heavy burden, had to go and take care of matters that could no longer wait.

Father Louis remained out in the arcade, pondering with a certain satisfaction the interesting problem that had now been handed to him. Father Louis enjoyed cracking hard nuts.

The men who were indeed Christians had been about to murder women and children – Father Louis was not aware that the women and children were Bedouins, since Arn had not mentioned it, because he did not find that fact significant in the same way a newcomer would.

But God would hardly want to protect such criminals, Father Louis went on. The fact that God put a Templar knight in the way of the criminals was no cause for surprise. Two of them had undoubtedly received the punishment they deserved. So far, no problem.

But to kill a Christian man for the sake of a soulless horse, and in a fit of anger at that? Perhaps Father Louis might better understand the problem if he tried like the philosopher to weigh the usefulness of such action that God might have placed in the balance trays.

If he accepted Arn de Gothia's account about the horse, and clearly he had to do so, then the horse would have been pleasing to God because it had helped its master kill hundreds of God's enemies. So wouldn't the horse be worth just as much as a mediocre worldly man who had taken the cross and journeyed to the Holy Land for both noble and less noble purposes?

Theologically the answer would obviously be no. However, by killing that particular horse the criminal had actually damaged God's cause in the Holy Land just as much as if he had killed a knight. This sin had to be weighed in the balance trays. Add to that the fact that the criminal intended to murder innocent women and children solely for the sake of his own enjoyment. It was easy to understand that God had sent His punishment in the form of a Templar knight against such a sinner.

That was the objective side of the matter. But greater difficulties arose when one approached the subjective side. Arn de Gothia knew the Rule and he had broken it. He was no ignorant sinner; he was educated and he spoke perfect Latin with an amusing Burgundian accent that reminded Father Louis of his friend Father Henri, which was no surprise. It was impossible to escape the fact that Arn de Gothia's sin was great, and it could not be diminished by pointing to a lack of understanding.

But this time there was a third side to the issue. Father Louis had been secretly dispatched as the Holy Father's informant in Jerusalem. The Holy Father had a big problem on his hands because all the men of the church in the Holy Land were constantly reporting complaints against one another. They demanded that the others be excommunicated, or they requested that certain orders of excommunication be lifted; they accused each other of all sorts of sins, and unquestionably often lied in doing so. It was a particularly vexing problem because the Holy Land had more bishops and archbishops than other countries. And it had become almost impossible to sit there in Rome and try to dissect what was true and what was not in all these counter-accusations. So Father Louis had been given the assignment by the Holy Father to serve as the Holy See's eyes and ears in Jerusalem, but preferably without revealing his role to anyone.

In this case he had to ask himself what would be best in terms of this task he had been assigned: to retain Arn de Gothia as Jerusalem's Master in the Holy Father's own blessed army, or to replace him with some boorish and ignorant man?

This question seemed easy to answer. It would serve the holy mission best if Arn de Gothia received forgiveness for his sins and continued as host for Father Louis. In view of the much greater task ordered by the Holy Father, even the sin of having killed a Christian villain paled in comparison. Arn de Gothia would receive forgiveness for his sins the very next day, but Father Louis would also describe this interesting dilemma in his first letter to the Holy Father himself, so that he could give the absolution his papal blessing. With that the problem could be dismissed for good.

When Arn met Father Louis at the same place in the arcade just before *Lauds* the next morning, he was given absolution in the name of the Father, the Son, and the Holy Virgin. But just as they knelt to pray together in thanksgiving, Father Louis was disturbed by a great wailing in the midst of the pre-dawn silence. He had heard the sound before but had not yet asked what it was.

Arn, who saw his concern, calmed him by telling him that it was only the *muezzin* of the unbelievers calling his faithful to morning prayer by assuring them that God was great. Father Louis was then completely distracted in his prayers when he realized that the enemy unbelievers seemed to assume that it was the most natural thing in the world to hold their blasphemous prayers in the midst of God's most holy city. But at the moment he did not want to address that problem.

Arn thanked God for His grace. Yet he did not seem so overwhelmed or even surprised that he had so easily received absolution for such a grave sin, and with only a week's penance on bread and water.

In the past, Arn's spiritual father Henri had seemed to forgive serious sins of that type with equal nonchalance. This was now the second time that Arn had received absolution of sin after having killed a Christian man. The first time, when Father Henri had forgiven him, Arn had been very young, hardly more than a child. Back then he had been consumed by fear, and because of his lack of experience when he defended himself against two peasants who were trying to kill him, he ended up slaying them both. It was explained to him that the sin could be forgiven because it had been the fault of those who were killed, and the Virgin Mary had intervened to save a young maiden's love. There were other details that Arn could now hardly remember, but he had indeed been forgiven.

The only sin that hadn't been quickly forgiven in his life was still the one that was reckoned the greatest: the fact that he had loved his betrothed Cecilia in the flesh only a short time before such a deed would have had God's blessing. For that sin Arn had done almost twenty years of penance. But still he had never honestly been able to understand why this particular sin had been the one out of many that could not be forgiven.

Nor had he been able to understand God's intention in sending him so far away to the Holy Land. He had killed many men, that was true. But could that have really been God's sole purpose?

The new patriarch of Jerusalem, who held the highest position in Roman Christendom after the Holy Father himself, was a man who effortlessly exceeded his own evil reputation. The patriarch's palace stood adjacent to the royal palace and was soon known throughout Jerusalem as the place where they had turned night into day. One of his most notorious lovers was soon called the Patriarchess, and people spat after her covered litter whenever she came to visit the holy city. The king's mother Agnes de Courtenay did not object that her lover the patriarch had other women, simply because she also had other men.

Exactly how the appointment of the new patriarch had come about remained forever unclear. Archbishop William of Tyrus was believed to be the obvious successor to the high position by all who understood anything about the struggle for ecclesiastical power. But he had not merely lost the fight with the sinful fornicator Heraclius when it came to the patriarchal throne. He also had to endure the ignominy of being excommunicated almost immediately after his painful loss, supposedly because of a long series of alleged sins which he had not committed, as surely as the new patriarch Heraclius had done far worse.

Archbishop William of Tyrus, whom history made forever infamous even as it decorously drew a veil over the misdeeds of Heraclius, had to demean himself further by making the long, uncomfortable journey to Rome to persuade the Holy Father to rescind the excommunication. In everyone's opinion, it was quite certain that he would be successful in his mission. At the same time many, including Heraclius himself, assumed that the knowledgeable and ecclesiastically skilful Archbishop William would no doubt be able to reveal certain things that would threaten the new patriarch's position in Jerusalem.

Unfortunately for the Holy Land, William was poisoned shortly after his arrival in Rome, and the documents he had been carrying disappeared without a trace.

Hence Heraclius had now secured the throne for himself as Jerusalem's patriarch. Not even Saladin understood how well this situation would play right into his hands.

The cease-fire that was in effect at the time of William of Tyrus's murder was now broken, and for the most common of reasons. Reynald de Châtillon could not restrain himself when he saw all the richly loaded caravans travelling between Mecca and Damascus that passed by his fortress of Kerak in Oultrejourdain. He resumed his plundering raids.

It was soon demonstrated that the deathly ill king in Jerusalem could not control his vassal Reynald, and thus war with Saladin was inevitable.

Saladin then crossed the River Jordan above the Sea of Galilee and began to plunder his way south through Galilee in the hope of luring the Christian army into a decisive battle.

Because Guy de Lusignan, the fool with the flowing locks, was now married to the king's sister, he was legally the successor to the throne. That meant he was also the supreme commander of the royal army, which he would have to lead against Saladin himself for the first time. His task was not an easy one. It wouldn't have been easy even for Count Raymond of Tripoli, who put himself and his knights under Guy's command, more or less reluctantly, just as the Templars and Hospitallers joined in with a large number of knights.

The Grand Master of the Templar Order had entrusted the command over all Templar knights to his friend Arn de Gothia. The Hospitallers were led by Grand Master Roger des Moulins.

When the Christian and Saracen forces had their first hostile encounter in the Galilee, the irresolute Guy de Lusignan was plied with contradictory advice from all sides.

Arn de Gothia, who again had authority to make use of his Bedouin scouts, said that he was sure that they could see only a small part of the enemy forces, and that an attack would thus be foolhardy and exactly what Saladin was hoping for. If, on the other hand, they held their position and took up a defensive posture, then the light Arabian cavalry would have a hard time attacking. Or, if they did attack out of impatience, they would be quickly defeated, because the Christians had come to rely increasingly on many footsoldiers

345

with longbows. They could send swarms of arrows a long distance, in such numbers that the sky would grow dark. A light Arabian cavalry that rode in under such a black cloud of arrows would be annihilated before it reached the front lines.

Some of the worldly barons and Guy's own brother Amalrik de Lusignan, who had become the highest commander of the royal army next to Guy himself, advocated an immediate attack with all the cavalry, since the enemy seemed clearly inferior in numbers. Guy's mother-in-law's brother, Joscelyn de Courtenay, had also been given a high post in the royal army, and he too wanted to attack at once.

The Grand Master of the Hospitallers, Roger des Moulins, would have been expected to disagree with whatever plan the Templars promoted, as expected. But since he and Arn de Gothia had had a private discussion, he was leaning toward the opinion that an attack would be foolhardy. There was a great danger, he thought, that they might be lured into the same trap as at Marj Ayyoun.

In this situation the unreliable courtier Guy de Lusignan could not make up his mind in favour of one plan or the other.

Over time the test of strength ran out into the sand, so that neither side won. Saladin failed in his attempt to persuade all the Christians' heavy cavalry to rush out to seize the first small quarry so that he could then lure them into the waiting trap. On the other hand, he had no plans at all to carry out the reverse tactic, to attack a well-armoured Christian army with light cavalry.

As far as Saladin was concerned, this war that did not happen was of little consequence. No one was threatening Saladin's position of power in either Cairo or Damascus; he had no angry prince to whom he needed to justify a failed war. And he reckoned that eventually new opportunities would present themselves.

For Guy de Lusignan the situation was much worse. By the time Saladin at last retreated without a decisive battle, because he could no longer provision his army, the Galilee had been plundered anew.

Home at the court in Jerusalem, Guy de Lusignan had a hard time defending himself against all those who had been part of the abortive siege and claimed they knew exactly how they could have defeated Saladin if only Guy had not been so stupid as to rely on cowardly Templars and Hospitallers. Guy had everyone against him; even his mother-in-law Agnes appeared to have acquired the knowledge of an experienced battlefield commander.

King Baldwin IV was now completely blind from leprosy and could no longer move. Nor could he defend himself from the lamentations that rose up around him. Guy de Lusignan was an indecisive and cowardly bungler, and it would be a disaster to have such a man as king.

Something had to be done, and time was short because death was breathing down the leprous king's neck. He appointed his sister Sibylla's six-year-old son, also named Baldwin, as successor to the throne. And he made Guy de Lusignan the count of Ashkelon and Jaffa, but with the condition that the count must live in Ashkelon and not make life miserable at the court in Jerusalem by his presence. With much gnashing of teeth and many harsh words, Guy de Lusignan moved to Ashkelon, taking with him Sibylla and her sickly son.

Because the six-year-old prince regent was so clearly in ill health that it was evident to all. The king's stratagem of making the boy the successor to the throne was therefore mostly intended as a manoeuvre to prevent Guy de Lusignan from seizing power.

It was now in God's hands as to which of the two would die first, the twenty-four-year-old King Baldwin or his six-year-old namesake.

Father Louis had been forced to wait for several months before a suitable occasion arose when the Grand Master of the Knights Templar, Arnoldo de Torroja, and Jerusalem's Master Arn de Gothia could meet with him in Jerusalem at the same time. They were most often out travelling, the Grand Master because he had to make all the difficult decisions within the order from Christian Armenia in the north to Gaza in the south, and Arn de Gothia because as commander-in-chief he constantly had to visit the various fortresses of the order.

But Father Louis wanted to find a time when he could meet with them both, and in a situation of relative peace and quiet. The nature of his mission was such that it would weigh very heavily upon the shoulders of a single man, and two heads were always better than one. It could not be helped that his secret would be betrayed when he presented the matter; then it would be revealed that he was not some old monk on a pilgrimage but actually the Holy Father's special envoy and informant.

He thought that Arn de Gothia may have already realized the truth, since the hospitality lavished on Father Louis in Jerusalem was far beyond what was normal. Father Louis had been allowed to take lodgings in the Templar quarter instead of resorting to the nearby Cistercian cloister on the Mount of Olives; so he was literally living in the heart of power, as every secret informant would prefer.

If Arn de Gothia had understood the real nature of Father Louis's mission in the holy city, then it was no wonder that he extended the utmost hospitality. But Father Louis was unsure of how much Arn actually knew, for the strange knight seemed to have become quite attached to him. He often sought out Father Louis to have long conversations on both ecclesiastical and secular topics, much as he would have sought out his old confessor, Father Henri, in the faraway cloister in Western Götaland whose name Father Louis had forgotten.

Out of old habit Arnoldo de Torroja and Arn de Gothia now sat down with their guest out in the arcade in the twilight after *completorium*. They began to joke about the city's mixture of holy and less holy odours and sounds, so that the tone of the conversation was at first indecorously merry and not appropriate to what Father Louis wished to discuss.

Yet when he saw the two high Templars sitting next to each other he was also deeply moved. Outwardly they were very different from each other: one tall with dark eyes and black hair and beard, mercurial in his temperament, jocular and witty like a man at any of the greatest courts in the world. The other was blond with an almost white beard and pale blue eyes, his figure almost slight in contrast to the stocky de Torroja, his demeanour thoughtful and many of his comments brusquely gruff. So they were like the symbol of the immiscible: the fiery south and the cold north, yet both equally devoted to the cause, possessing no personal property, with no other reasons for waging war than to defend Christianity and God's Grave. Saint Bernard must be laughing in Heaven upon seeing these two together, thought Father Louis. It would be impossible to get any closer than this in the material world to Bernard's dream of the new knight-hood that would sacrifice everything for God.

Then there was the side of the matter that Father Louis had the hardest time understanding. Both these men were experienced in courtly and spiritual matters. If their beards were shaved and their warlike white mantle with the red cross was replaced with a monk's white habit, they would be able to sit quite naturally in any arcade in any cloister together with Father Henri.

Yet there was something inexplicable that set them apart. These men were among the best warriors in the world. They were fearsome on the battlefield; everyone who understood military questions could testify to that. And yet they presented these kindly looks, these cautious smiles, and this quiet speech. That, precisely that, was probably the clearest manifestation of blessed Saint Bernard's vision.

In order to put a stop to the light-hearted tone of the conversation in which they were engaged, Father Louis fell silent and said a short prayer with his head bowed. The other two instantly took the hint and unconsciously settled in to listen. Both knights fell silent.

Now was the time for Father Louis to speak.

He began by telling them the truth, that he was the special envoy of the Holy Father. He explained that all the Cistercians who had come and gone since the first monk he had brought with him, Pietro de Siena, had all travelled to Rome, taking letters directly to the Holy Father.

Both of his listeners remained stone-faced as he spoke; it was impossible to tell whether they had already guessed the secret or whether it was unexpected news to them.

Naturally letters came back in reply from the Holy Father and his chancellery in Rome. And a particularly unpleasant matter had now come to light. The patriarch of Jerusalem, Heraclius, had a man in his service named Pleidion who was apparently a runaway servant from the heretical church in Constantinople. Exactly what sort of work this Pleidion did for Heraclius was not entirely possible to ascertain; he seemed to take care of a multitude of tasks, especially in connection with the unmentionable nightly activities that often took place at the patriarch's palace.

Only now did Father Louis's account cause both listeners to raise their eyebrows in mild surprise, whether it was because of the news itself about Pleidion or because Father Louis had managed to learn what this less than reputable individual was up to.

Father Louis now came to the unpleasant part. Archbishop William of Tyrus had been poisoned to death when he was in Rome, just before he was to have an audience with the Holy Father. It had long been known that this death was murder; the evidence found in the dead man's room as well as the colour of his face when he was discovered had told its tale all too well.

But now they knew who had visited him during the hour before he died. It was none other than Pleidion. That also explained the mysterious disappearance of all the documents that Archbishop William had brought with him to present at his audience with the Pope.

As far as the Holy See was concerned, there was no longer any doubt about the truth of this matter. Heraclius's minion Pleidion had been given the assignment to murder Archbishop William of Tyrus.

Some research had been done into the background of this Heraclius. He was born in Auvergne around 1130 to a family of meagre means; he had served as a singer in the village church, but otherwise had not been consecrated as either a priest or a monk, which might explain why the man couldn't speak Latin. He had come with the mobs of adventurers to the Holy Land but preferred to use lies and deceit rather than to fight to gain favour. Father Louis did not have all the details about Heraclius's path to power, but he had basically acquired influence through the many lovers he had bedded. The most important one, of course, was the king's mother, Agnes de Courtenay. But her predecessor, Pasque de Riveri, the woman called 'Madame la Patriarchesse', had surely meant a great deal for the man's ascent to the second highest ecclesiastical office in the world.

Summa summarum. The patriarch of Jerusalem was a deceiver and a poisoner.

There Father Louis concluded his account without mentioning anything about the Holy Father's decision in the matter.

'What you have told us, Father,' said Arnoldo de Torroja, 'is most disquieting. Something of this man's evil talents was known to both me and Brother Arn. But the awful truth that he ordered the venerable William of Tyrus poisoned is an utter surprise to us. And that, of course, brings me to the obvious question. Why are you telling us this now, and what do you, or your exalted principal, want us to do with this knowledge?'

'It is my task simply to convey this information, but you may not share it with anyone outside the rank that you both hold,' said Father Louis tensely, because he found this part of his instructions difficult to impart. 'If someone succeeds Arn de Gothia, you Arnoldo shall inform his successor of this matter. And the same applies to you, Arn de Gothia.'

'Is this the express will of the Holy Father?' asked Arnoldo de Torroja.

'Yes it is, and for that reason I now deliver to you this papal bull,' replied Father Louis. He opened his mantle and took out a parchment roll bearing two great papal seals, placing it on the empty table between them.

The two Templar knights bowed their heads as a sign of submission. Arnoldo de Torroja took the bull and stuffed it inside his mantle. Then they sat in silence for a while.

'As you no doubt understand, Father, we shall obey to the letter these orders from the Holy See,' said Arnoldo de Torroja. 'But might we be permitted to ask further questions regarding this matter?'

'Yes, in the name of God, you may,' replied Father Louis,

crossing himself. 'But since I have already surmised what you intend to ask, I shall give my answer at once. You are both wondering why the Holy Father doesn't clap the iron gloves on this man. Isn't that what you wanted to know?'

'That's exactly what we would like to know, if it is permitted,' Arnoldo de Torroja confirmed. 'Many of us have realized that Heraclius is a deceiver. Everyone knows that he lives a life that does not befit a man of the Church. Our Lord knows that he is a shameful presence in Jerusalem. But his position is such that the only one who might bring about his downfall is the Holy Father himself. So? Why not excommunicate this deceiver and poisoner?'

'Because the Holy Father and his highest advisors have concluded that excommunication of Heraclius would damage the Holy Roman Church far beyond the injury that it has already suffered. The deceiver's path to Hell is short, judged in human terms. He is sixty-seven years old. If he is excommunicated now, then the entire Christian world would know that the Holy Land had a poisoner, deceiver, and whoremonger as its patriarch. The damage caused by such knowledge spreading throughout Christendom would be irreparable. So for the sake of the Church and the Holy Land . . . well, you understand.'

The two Templars both crossed themselves as they reflected on what Father Louis had said. They nodded in gloomy silence as a sign that they agreed and that they had no further questions or objections.

'Well, that was the matter of the poisoner . . .' said Father Louis in a lighter tone, as if he were almost jesting about this serious topic. 'Now we come to the next question. No, don't look so alarmed. This is a completely different matter, and there is no papal bull to present but instead certain quandaries to discuss. It's my task to try to reach clarity. If I may, I'll get right to the point.'

'By all means, Father,' replied Arnoldo de Torroja, sweeping his hand over the table as if he expected some little demon to appear. 'By now both Brother Arn and I are prepared for anything. Well?'

'This involves certain peculiar customs here in Jerusalem,' Father Louis began somewhat uncertainly because he didn't know how to present his problem in both a polite and resolute way. 'I understand that you permit unbelievers to pray within your jurisdiction in Jerusalem. In fact, they are allowed to announce quite loudly to the entire neighbourhood when they intend to commence their ungodly prayers. Isn't that so?'

'Yes, that's true. So it is,' replied Arn when Arnoldo de Torroja gestured that he should handle this problem. 'You see, there are thousands of times more Saracens than Christians here in Outremer. Even if we could kill them all, it wouldn't be wise, because then we would starve to death. We have not owned the Holy Land for more than a hundred years, but our intention is to remain here forever, is it not?'

'Yes, one could put it that way,' Father Louis agreed, waiting for more details.

'Some Christians fight on the side of the Saracens,' Arn explained. 'And many unbelievers fight on our side. The war is not Allah against God, because God is the same for everyone. The war is between good and evil. Many of our trading partners, caravan merchants, and those we hire to conduct espionage are unbelievers, just as are many of our physicians. To demand their conversion while they are working for us would be like going out in the fields and telling the Palestinian peasants to let themselves be baptized. Impossible and futile.

'Or let's look at another matter: our trade with Mosul, for example, which has not yet been incorporated into Saladin's empire. It takes two weeks by caravan between

Mosul and Saint-Jean d'Acre, which is the most important export harbour for textiles from Mosul – what we call muslin. There in Saint-Jean d'Acre the merchants from Mosul have a *caravanserai*, with their own places of prayer and their own mosque and minaret from which the hour of prayer is announced. They also have their own tavern for eating and drinking, in accordance with their dietary laws. If we want to break off all trade with Mosul and also cast the Turkish atabeq there into the arms of Saladin, then we should forcibly shave off the merchants' beards and baptize them with much kicking and screaming. We don't consider that doing so would be in the best interests of the Holy Land.'

'But is it good for the Holy Land to have unbelieving ungodliness in the midst of the holiest of cities?' asked Father Louis dubiously.

'Yes, it is!' Arn retorted. 'You, Father, know as well as I do that God's pure teaching is ours. You are prepared to die for His pure teaching, and I have sworn to do so whenever it is demanded of me. We know what is the truth. Unfortunately nine-tenths of the people here in Outremer do not understand this. But if we are cast out by Saladin or any of his successors, how would it look here in a hundred years? In three hundred years? In eight hundred years?'

'So you think that the truth will prevail in the end?' Father Louis asked, showing an unexpected glint of mirth in the midst of this deeply serious conversation.

'Yes, that is what I believe,' said Arn. 'We can hold the Holy Land by the sword, but not indefinitely. We won't have truly won until we no longer need the sword. People of all kinds seem to have an equally strong aversion to being converted by force. The wiser course of action is to attempt a gradual conversion through trade, conversation, prayers, good preachers, and other peaceful means.'

'So to conquer the ungodliness we must permit it,' Father

Louis pondered. 'If such words had come from a runaway monk in Burgundy, I might have regarded his vision as childish, since he would know nothing of the power of the sword. But if you two, who know more about the sword than any other Christians, are of this opinion . . . And by the way, is this your opinion too, Grand Master?'

'Yes,' said Arnoldo de Torroja. 'I may have tried to explain the matter less succinctly than my friend Arn. But in summary I would have said the same thing.'

In the year of grace 1184, three years before God's angry judgment descended upon the Christians in the Holy Land, the Grand Master of the Hospitallers, Roger des Moulins, and the Grand Master of the Knights Templar, Arnoldo de Torroja, set off together with the patriarch of Jerusalem, Heraclius, on a long journey. Their purpose was to try to persuade the emperor of Germany as well as the kings of France and England to lead new crusades and send new armies so that they could defend the Holy Land against Saladin.

It is unknown whether Arnoldo de Torroja warned his high brother in the Hospitallers of the scorpion who was their travelling companion, Heraclius.

On the other hand it *is* known that their journey brought in a good deal of money, especially from the king of England, who viewed it as an opportunity to make amends for the murder of the bishop Thomas Becket by donating a vast sum as an indulgence. But money was not the greatest need, particularly for the Order of the Knights Templar, which was richer than the kings of England and France put together. What they needed instead was understanding in their homelands because the situation at this time was genuinely difficult. Saladin was unlike any of his predecessors. What they needed above all were reinforcements with plenty of soldiers.

But it was as though people in the homelands had long ago gotten used to the idea that the Christian world owned the Holy Land. To take up the cross and ride off to liberate a country that had long been liberated did not seem the most urgent task in life to the faithful.

There were still those who, like the majority of crusaders in the past century, considered travelling to the Holy Land to get rich on plunder, but it was well known that few would realize such wealth. The Holy Land was now owned by local barons who had little sympathy for the wishes of newly arrived crusaders to get rich at the cost of their Christian brothers.

The envoys from the Holy Land may have managed to procure some funding, but they were unable to convince the German emperor to lead a mighty new army that could have evened out the balance with Saladin. Nor did the English or French kings come forward, since they were both competing for the same lands and considered it unwise to go off on a holy mission. If one of them did so, the other would be quick to snatch the kingdom left behind without its sovereign. It seems only natural that Arnoldo de Torroja must have been highly suspicious of the deceiver, poisoner, and patriarch of Jerusalem during this long journey. Especially since they both knew where each other stood in the larger context. Arnoldo de Torroja was among those accused of cowardice by his opponents at the court in Jerusalem, since he had many times openly admitted that negotiations and a fair compromise with Saladin would be wiser than eternal war.

Heraclius reckoned himself on the side of courage and principles; he counted as his friends Agnes de Courtenay, her brother Joscelyn de Courtenay, and to some extent also the man banished from succeeding to the throne, Guy de Lusignan, and his ambitious wife Sibylla.

No matter how wary Arnoldo de Torroja should have been

to travel in the company of a poisoner, he ended up dying of poison during the journey anyway. He was buried in Rome.

At that time only three men in the whole world could suspect, or more than suspect, what had happened. The first was the new Pope Lucius III, who surely must have obtained enough information about the matter from the papal archives thanks to obliging sources. The second was Jerusalem's Master Arn de Gothia, who in the absence of a new Grand Master was for a time the highest authority in the Order of the Knights Templar. The third was Father Louis.

Heraclius had now not only poisoned an archbishop, but also a Grand Master in God's Holy Army.

But no matter whether the news was good or bad, it travelled slowly during those years, especially in the autumn when shipping trade was often held to a minimum. Arn heard about the murder of his Grand Master directly from Father Louis when one of his constantly travelling Cistercians arrived from Rome after a very difficult passage.

They were both crushed by the news. In his despair, Arn at first claimed loudly that now more than ever the poisoner deserved to be excommunicated. But Father Louis sadly pointed out that the matter would probably prove even more troublesome than that. If Lucius III were to excommunicate Heraclius for the earlier poisoning, about which there was great certainty, then he would at the same time reveal his predecessor Alexander III as far too fallible. It was not credible that the new Holy Father would choose such a path.

Then how many murders by poison would it take to provoke such action! asked Arn, disconsolately. He received no answer.

Should a murderer, a whoremonger, a deceiver – a pure misfortune for the entire Holy Land – be granted even greater protection the more despicable the crimes he committed?

He got no answer to that question either. But they did

pray together a great deal during those days, since they shared a heavy secret.

They both had plenty of work in which to drown their sorrows. With Arn's help Father Louis had managed to insinuate himself into the court in Jerusalem. There he could walk around looking quite unobtrusive although he kept his ear to the ground.

Arn, as the highest authority among the Knights Templar, had taken on the double task of minding the business transactions of Jerusalem as well as the affairs of the entire order. Although the latter task consisted mostly of signing documents and attaching his seal, all this work still demanded a great deal of both time and energy.

When winter arrived the following year, King Baldwin IV summoned the entire High Council in Outremer to announce his last wishes. This meant that every baron of importance in the Holy Land as well as the county of Tripoli and the principality of Antioch had to put in an appearance. The only Christian ruler in Oultrejourdain, Reynald de Châtillon, also had to travel to Jerusalem. It took some time for all of them to gather, and while waiting Arn felt more or less relegated to the role of an innkeeper. The Order of the Knights Templar owned the most guest rooms and the largest halls in Jerusalem, so every coronation was always concluded with a grand banquet on the premises owned by the Templars. The royal palace would never have been big enough.

The day before the king was to announce his last wishes, Arn arranged for the customary large feast to be held in the knights' hall of the Templar quarters, which was located on the same high floor as his own rooms. But there were special entrances to the knights' hall via a broad stone staircase leading from the western wall, so that worldly guests would not disturb the peace on their way in and out. This was wisely arranged, Arn realized, when he saw the number of loud and in many instances already drunken guests proceeding up the stairs.

The knights' hall was decorated with the flags and colours of the Knights Templar, and in the middle above the long table, where the king's place was situated, hung the flags captured from Saladin at Mont Gisard. Otherwise the decor of the hall was austere, with white walls and black wooden tables.

At the long table the royal family sat in the seats of honour in the middle, surrounded by the landowners and barons who were closest to them. On either end of the table, two smaller tables jutted out, and at one of them sat, as usual, men from Antioch and Tripoli with Prince Bohemund and Count Raymond in the middle.

At the second table facing them sat Templars and Hospitallers. At that table a departure from tradition was visible, since Arn had arranged for exactly the same number of Hospitallers as Templars in alternating seats, with him and the Grand Master of the Hospitallers, Roger des Moulins, in the middle. It was a change that drew everyone's attention, since the Templars had previously always indicated that in their house the Hospitallers were not the most highly regarded guests.

Arn explained this break with custom to Roger des Moulins by saying that he'd never understood the feeling of unfriendly competition that existed toward the Hospitaller brothers. Besides, the one time he had been their guest at the fortress of Beaufort, he'd been treated extremely well by his hosts and received generous support when he needed to move his injured men from there. He may have presented these innocent reasons for his demonstratively friendly gesture toward the Hospitallers because he wanted their Grand Master to choose whether to take the next, larger step toward moving the two orders closer to each other.

Solidarity between the Christians' best knights had now become more important than ever.

Just as Arn had hoped, Roger des Moulins seized the opportunity to have a serious discussion with Arn as they ate the lamb and vegetables and drank the wine. At the same time, they looked as though they were having the most innocent conversation, as befitted a banquet table.

Roger des Moulins pointed to the royal seats beneath Saladin's captured flags at the long table and said bluntly that there sat the men, and especially the women, who bore the blame for the downfall of the Holy Land. As a sign that he was right, just then the patriarch Heraclius staggered up from his seat. With his wine glass sloshing, he babbled cheerfully as he moved to the king's empty seat and plopped down there unabashed, right next to his former lover Agnes de Courtenay.

The two high brothers exchanged a knowing glance of distaste. After that Arn immediately took up Roger des Moulins' ideas about a rapprochement between them. For his part, he thought that the two spiritual orders of knights would be forced to assume increasing responsibility for the Holy Land, since things were in such disarray at the royal court. This meant they would have to see to putting aside everything that was less important, including any minor disputes between the orders.

Roger des Moulins agreed to this at once. He went even further by proposing that they should call a meeting of the highest brothers of the Hospitallers and Templars. When they agreed on this decisive step, Arn put to him a furtive question about Arnoldo de Torroja's untimely death in Verona.

Roger des Moulins seemed surprised by the sudden shift in topic; at first he hesitated to speak and gave Arn a long, searching look. Then he said straight out that he and Arnoldo had been in agreement about most things concerning the future of the Holy Land, which they had discussed during that journey, including putting aside old disputes. But Heraclius had continually interrupted them with the most childish comments, claiming that anyone who hesitated to annihilate all the Saracens was a coward. And even worse, the ungodly whoremonger had actually had the nerve to say that Roger des Moulins and Arnoldo de Torroja were both standing in the way of God's will. And he hoped that they as traitors and blasphemers might soon depart this world.

Since Arnoldo de Torroja did indeed leave this world shortly thereafter, and in a manner that hardly indicated God's will, Roger des Moulins from then on had been very circumspect about what he ate and drank in the presence of the arch-sinner Heraclius. He had his own suspicions. So he now asked Arn whether he knew anything that might cast some light on these suspicions.

A vow of silence had been imposed on Arn directly from the Holy Father, but he found a way to reply without actually answering.

'My lips are sealed,' he said.

Roger des Moulins nodded and had no more questions.

The next day all the guests were gathered again in the same knights' hall, some quite red-eyed and foul-smelling after the long night of drinking. They were there to hear King Baldwin IV's last wishes.

They all rose in the hall when the king was carried in inside a small covered litter that seemed big enough only for a child. The king had by now lost both arms and legs and was completely blind.

The litter with the king was placed on the huge throne that had been carried into the hall before him, and next to him was placed the royal crown.

The king began to speak in a faint voice, presumably

mostly to show that he could still talk and had use of all his faculties. But soon one of the court scribes stepped forward to read aloud what the king wanted to say and what he had already composed in writing and affixed with the royal seal.

'The successor to the throne will henceforth be the king's sister Sibylla's son Baldwin,' began the scribe.

'As he is only seven years old at present, Count Raymond of Tripoli is hereby appointed as regent for the Holy Land, until the boy comes of age in his tenth year. As modest thanks for Count Raymond's services as regent, the city of Beirut will be incorporated into his County of Tripoli.

'The boy, Prince Regent Baldwin, will be raised and cared for until the day of his coming of age by the king's uncle, Joscelyn de Courtenay. If the crown prince should die before he reaches the age of ten, a new successor will be appointed jointly by the Holy Father in Rome, the Emperor of the Holy German-Roman Empire, the King of France, and the King of England.

'In such a case, until such date as a new successor should be appointed by these four, Raymond of Tripoli would continue to act as regent in the Holy Land.

'In particular it is decreed that Guy de Lusignan under no circumstances should ever become either regent or successor to the throne.'

The king now demanded of all that they step forward and before God swear an oath to comply with this last royal decree.

Everyone in the hall took this oath with a light heart and without any sign of displeasure. Count Raymond himself swore this oath, as did his good friend Prince Bohemund of Antioch; Roger des Moulins swore on behalf of all the Hospitallers, while Arn de Gothia swore on behalf of all the Templars.

Some of the others, such as the patriarch Heraclius, the

king's mother Agnes de Courtenay, her lover Amalrik de Lusignan, and the king's uncle Joscelyn de Courtenay, made less of a show about taking the oath. But at last all had sworn before God to obey King Baldwin IV's last wishes. For the last time the small litter with the king's stunted body and the flickering flame of his life was carried out of their sight. As most people in the hall surmised with a good deal of dejection and tears, they would not encounter their brave little king again until his funeral in the Church of the Holy Sepulchre.

The guests now made their way out of the Templars' great hall amidst a swelling murmur of voices. All of a sudden Raymond strode over to Arn and, to the amazement of everyone around, pressed his hand heartily and requested hospitality for the night for himself and also for others whom he intended to summon. Arn immediately agreed to his request and said that all Count Raymond's friends would be received as his own.

Thus it was that two quite different groups gathered that evening in Jerusalem to discuss far into the night the situation that had now arisen. The mood was gloomy in the king's palace. Agnes de Courtenay at first had been so incensed that she could hardly speak, and the patriarch Heraclius paced the rooms, bellowing like an enraged bull though claiming divine despair.

The mood was considerably more optimistic in the rooms belonging to Jerusalem's Master. Count Raymond had summoned the Hospitallers' Grand Master Roger des Moulins, Prince Bohemund of Antioch, and the d'Ibelin brothers. Without Count Raymond having to ask, Arn saw to it that a good quantity of wine was brought in for the new allies, now united by their oath to the king.

They were all agreed that this was a turning point. Here was a golden opportunity to save the Holy Land and to limit the power of Agnes de Courtenay, as well as the perpetrator of unmentionable sins, Heraclius, and their notorious criminal friend, Reynald de Châtillon. They all now sat in the royal palace gnashing their teeth along with Agnes de Courtenay's brother, the incompetent military commander Joscelyn.

According to Count Raymond, much could be accomplished at once. First, he had to negotiate a new truce with Saladin, giving as justification the paltry winter rains, which would lead to poor harvests for both believers and unbelievers alike. And this time the plunderer Reynald de Châtillon could only acquiesce.

Looking ahead a bit, the king would undoubtedly soon be dead. But his sickly nephew and successor to the throne might not live long either, since he was clearly suffering from the after-effects of the sinful life at court. Children who were born into such illnesses seldom lived to the age of ten, if they even survived their own birth.

And if the Pope, the German emperor, and the constantly bickering kings of England and France could not agree on a new successor, power would remain with the regent, Count Raymond for a long time.

So it looked as though the brave little king in his litter had managed to save the Holy Land after all; it was his last accomplishment in this life.

On that night in Jerusalem there was no other apparent possibility, no cloud in the sky despite the fact that all the men among Arn's guests were far more experienced in the struggle for power than he was. Not even Agnes de Courtenay or her treacherous brother Joscelyn could do much to counter the unanimous oath given before God by the High Council.

For almost an hour they tried to imagine what possible or impossible intrigues the evil woman, her patriarch lover, and incompetent brother might dream up in their desperate situation. But Outremer's most experienced knights could see no way out for her and her cronies.

Therefore they turned to the wine, which always runs more lightly down merry throats than gloomy ones, and the guests spent the rest of the night telling wild tales.

Prince Bohemund of Antioch knew everything about the man who more than anyone else threatened the peace: Reynald de Châtillon. Reynald was a man who carried destruction within him, like the genie in the bottle, Bohemund recounted. Reynald had come to Antioch from somewhere in France. He took service with Prince Bohemund's father and proved himself so skilled on the battlefield that after only a few years he was rewarded with the hand of Bohemund's sister Constance in marriage.

A wise man of normal ambition would have stopped there: prince of Antioch, wealthy and protected. But not Reynald, whose appetite had grown to insatiable proportions.

He wanted to go out on expeditions of conquest and plunder but did not have the money to do so, so he ordered the patriarch Aimery de Limoges to be bound naked to a stake under the blazing sun and smeared with honey. After a while the patriarch could no longer stand the bees and the sun, and he agreed to lend the rogue Reynald all the money he demanded.

With the funds of a war chest, all he needed then was to locate good plunder. And Reynald chose Cyprus, which was a province in the realm of the Byzantine emperor Manual Komnenos. Cyprus was harried more cruelly than ever before by Reynald de Châtillon. He had the noses of all Christian priests cut off and ordered all the nuns to be raped; he plundered all the churches, destroyed all the harvests, and returned to Antioch with riches. But not with honour.

Emperor Manual Komnenos flew into a rage and sent the entire Byzantine army against Antioch. It was of course unthinkable for Antioch to go to war with the emperor for the sake of a single fool, no matter that he was married to one of the princesses.

Strangely enough Reynald gained the emperor's forgiveness by returning all the plundered goods still in his possession.

But he had not learned from his experience, and only two years later he set out on a new plundering expedition against the Armenian and Syrian Christians, who naturally did not expect to be attacked by fellow believers. There was ample rich booty to be had. And many Christians ended up dead.

Heavily loaded with loot on his way home to Antioch, Reynald was captured by Majd al-Din of Aleppo. And finally he landed where he belonged, in one of Aleppo's dungeons.

Since everyone agreed that it was much safer to leave him there, and nobody would ransom the criminal, the story should rightfully have ended happily there.

Prince Bohemund now paused in his account, toasted his friend Count Raymond ironically, and explained that the rest was actually Raymond's fault.

Count Raymond laughed and shook his head, ordered more wine which Arn supplied at once, and said that assigning the blame was probably both right and wrong.

It all happened during the war ten years before, he told them. Saladin was still far from uniting the Saracens, and in that respect it was important to throw as many poles into the spokes of his wheels as possible. At that time, in 1175, Saladin had an army outside the walls of Aleppo and another one outside Homs. The problem was to ensure that the two cities did not fall into his hands. Count Raymond had therefore sent his army from Tripoli to break the siege at Homs, forcing Saladin to release his grip on Aleppo and rush toward Homs. In this way Aleppo was spared Saladin's power for several years.

So far everything had gone as they had hoped, Count Raymond said with an exaggerated sigh. But Gumushlekin of Aleppo now wanted to show his goodwill toward the Christians and decided to release a number of prisoners. He couldn't have done the Christians a greater disservice. Or a greater favour to Saladin, for that matter. Among the prisoners that were now released were Reynald de Châtillon and Agnes de Courtenay's incompetent brother Joscelyn!

The guests now doubled over with laughter when they heard what a misguided favour the atabeq of Aleppo had done his Christian friends.

Well, they all knew the rest of the story, Count Raymond went on. The now impoverished Reynald de Châtillon, deeply despised by all honourable men, accompanied Joscelyn de Courtenay to Jerusalem, and everything soon fell into their undeserving hands. First King Amalrik died, so that Baldwin IV became king, although still a child. Then his mother returned to the court, after years of being forbidden to show her face there, for reasons known to everyone. Her brother Joscelyn soon came into favour, and Reynald was able with the evil Agnes's help to find a rich widow, namely Stéphanie de Milly of Kerak and Montreal in Oultrejourdain. And so the villain was a fortress master and wealthy once again!

The only question was: Who had benefited more from this play of caprices in life, the Devil or Saladin?

Both had reaped equal benefits, they all were quick to agree.

Furthermore the conspirators gathered in the Templar quarter believed on that night that they now had Reynald under control. Fortunately the sickly King Baldwin had mustered the strength to intervene against Reynald's constant breaches of every peace agreement, and Guy de Lusignan, during his brief time as regent, had shown himself to be utterly incompetent. Count Raymond, much enlivened, assured them that with him as regent things would be very different in Jerusalem.

Now that they were speaking of incompetents, the question remained where Gérard de Ridefort had gone. Arn replied that the blessed Grand Master, Arnoldo de Torroja, had made Brother Gérard the fortress master of Chastel-Blanc.

Count Raymond then frowned and opined that that was a rather elevated position for someone with so little time in service. Arn agreed, but explained that as he understood the matter, it was the price Arnoldo de Torroja had been willing to pay to keep Gérard de Ridefort as far from Jerusalem as possible. Gérard was thought to have acquired some unsuitable friends at court, and it might be wise to keep him away from such people.

The lively conversation continued until it began to grow light outside, and that night it looked as though the Holy Land could be saved from the misfortune that bunglers, arch-sinners, and intriguers had done their best to bring about. King Baldwin IV died soon afterwards, as everyone had expected. Count Raymond then took up his office as regent of Jerusalem. Soon peace prevailed in the Holy Land, pilgrims began to stream in anew, and with them came the longed-for income.

It truly did look as though everything had taken a turn for the better.

Then the new Grand Master of the Order of the Knights Templar, Gérard de Ridefort, came ashore at Saint-Jean d'Acre. He came by ship from Rome, where the Knights Templar had convoked a *concilium* with a sufficient number of high brothers present, including the Master of Rome and the Master of Paris.

From Rome Gérard de Ridefort had brought with him the group of new high brothers who would now take over the leadership of the Knights Templar in the Holy Land. They rode to Jerusalem at once.

Jerusalem's Master Arn de Gothia was informed about his high-ranking guests only a few hours in advance. He had a few words with Father Louis about the misfortune that had befallen them, then he prayed for a long time in his inner sanctum, which was like a cell in a Cistercian cloister. But otherwise he had no time to do much except make the necessary preparations for the arrival of the Grand Master in Jerusalem.

When the Grand Master and his lofty retinue, with almost all the knights bearing a black band around their horse's side armour and their mantles, arrived at Jerusalem they were received by two files of white-clad knights who stood lined up all the way from the Damascus Gate to the Templar quarter. There large torches burned at the entrance and the banquet tables were waiting in the great knights' hall.

Arn de Gothia, who greeted them outside the grand staircase, fell to his knees and bowed his head before he took the Grand Master's horse by the reins to show that he was no more than a stable boy for Gérard de Ridefort. It was thus prescribed by the Rule.

Gérard de Ridefort was in a radiant mood, pleased with his reception. He settled into his seat in the king's place at the table in the knights' hall and at once allowed himself and his high brothers to be served. He spoke loudly and at great length about how delightful it was to be back in Jerusalem.

Arn, on the other hand, was not in such a good mood and was having a hard time concealing his feelings. What seemed worst to him was not that he had to obey the slightest gesture of a man whom everyone described as illiterate, vengeful, and unworthy, and who had not served half the time that Arn had served as a Templar knight. The worst thing was that the Knights Templar now had a Grand Master who was a sworn enemy of the regent, Count Raymond. With that the clouds of unrest began gathering again over the Holy Land.

After the meal when most of the guests had been shown to their quarters, the Grand Master ordered Arn and another two men whom Arn did not know to accompany him to his private rooms. Gérard de Ridefort was still in a very good mood, almost as if he were looking forward with special joy to the rapid changes he now intended to implement.

He sat down with pleasure in Arn's normal seat, pressed his splayed fingertips against each other, and regarded the three men for a moment in silence. They all remained standing.

'Tell me, Arn de Gothia . . . that is what you are called; is it not? Tell me, you and Arnoldo de Torroja were very close, I understand?' he said at last, in a voice that was so deliberately smooth that the hatred was quite audible.

'Yes, Grand Master, that is true,' replied Arn.

'And one might assume that was why he elevated you to Jerusalem's Master?' asked the Grand Master, cheerfully raising his eyebrows as if he had just had a bright idea.

'Yes, Grand Master, that may have played a role. A Grand Master in our order appoints whomever he likes,' said Arn.

'Good! A very good answer,' said the Grand Master with satisfaction. 'What pleased my predecessor in that respect will also please me. Here next to you stands James de Mailly. He has served as fortress master at Cressing in England. As you can see, he wears a fortress master's mantle.'

'Yes, Grand Master,' said Arn without expression.

'Then I propose that the two of you exchange mantles; you look to be about the same size!' commanded the Grand Master, his tone still cheerful.

As was the custom of the Knights Templar, they had eaten with their mantles fastened around their necks, so that it took only a moment's work to bow to the Grand Master as a sign of submission and exchange mantles and thus rank and position in the Order of the Knights Templar.

'So, now you're a fortress master again!' said Gérard de Ridefort with satisfaction. 'It pleased your friend Arnoldo to send me off up to the fortress of Chastel-Blanc. What would you say if you were to take over my old post?'

'As you command, so shall I obey, Grand Master. But I would rather take over my old post as fortress master in Gaza,' replied Arn in a low but steady voice.

'Gaza!' the Grand Master burst out, amused. 'That's merely an out-of-the-way speck compared with Chastel-Blanc. But if that is your wish, I shall grant it. When can you leave Jerusalem?'

'Whenever is convenient for you, Grand Master.'

'Good! Shall we say tomorrow after *Lauds*?'

'As you command, Grand Master.'

'Excellent, then you can go. Jerusalem's Master and I have a number of important affairs to discuss. I bless you and wish you good night.'

The Grand Master turned away from Arn as if he expected the man to vanish into thin air. But Arn remained where he was. Then the Grand Master feigned surprise at finding him still there, and waved his hand as if to inquire the reason.

'It is my duty to report one thing to you, Grand Master, a fact that I may not convey to anyone but you and whoever is Jerusalem's Master, and that is now Brother James.'

'If Arnoldo gave you such instructions, I waive them immediately. A living Grand Master takes precedence over a dead one. So what does this concern?' asked Gérard de Ridefort with clear scorn in his voice.

'The instructions come not from Arnoldo but from the Holy Father in Rome,' replied Arn in a low voice, careful not to respond to the derisive tone.

For the first time the new Grand Master's excessive self-assurance faltered. He gave Arn a doubtful look before he realized that Arn was serious, and then nodded to the third brother to leave the room.

Arn went to the archive located several rooms away and fetched the papal bull describing the fact that the patriarch Heraclius was an assassin, and also how this secret must be preserved. When he returned he unrolled the text and placed it on the table before the Grand Master, bowed, and took a step back.

The Grand Master glanced at the bull, recognizing the papal seal; he also realized that he could not read the text because it was in Latin. He therefore had no choice; he had to humble himself and ask Arn to read it and translate, which Arn did without showing a hint of surprise.

Both the Grand Master and his new Jerusalem's Master James de Mailly lost their good humour immediately when they heard the bad news. Heraclius was the man who had campaigned harder than anyone in the Church for Gérard de Ridefort to become Grand Master. As a result the new Grand Master now owed a debt of gratitude to a known poisoner.

Arn was waved away, and he left the Grand Master at once after giving a deep bow. It was with an unexpected feeling of relief that Arn now went to seek lodging for the night among the guest rooms, for it had struck him that he had only a little more than a year left of his penance. He would soon have served nineteen of the twenty years that he had sworn to complete in the Order of the Knights Templar.

This was a new and foreign thought for him. Until the precise moment when he had been dismissed by the new Grand Master Gérard de Ridefort and for the last time walked through the high-ceilinged halls in the quarters of the Knights Templar in Jerusalem, he had avoided counting the years, months, and days. Possibly because it was more than likely that he would be sent to Paradise by the enemy long before he had managed to serve his twenty years.

But now there was only a year left, and a peace accord was in place for the next several years with Saladin. There was no war on the horizon in the coming year. So he might survive after all; he might at last travel home.

Never before had he felt such a strong longing for home. At the start of his time in the Holy Land the twenty years had seemed such an eternity that it was impossible to imagine himself living beyond that point. And in recent years he had been much too busy with his blessed work as Jerusalem's Master to imagine another life for himself. On that evening, not long ago, he had sat in the rooms where Gérard de Ridefort now ruled, discussing the future of the Holy Land with Count Raymond, Prince Bohemund, Roger des Moulins, and the d'Ibelin brothers. On that evening all the power in the Holy Land and Outremer was together in the same room, and the future had looked bright. Together they had been able to conclude peace with Saladin.

Now the entire chessboard had been overturned. Gérard de Ridefort was a mortal enemy of the regent Count Raymond. All plans to bring the Templars and the Hospitallers closer together would now probably come to naught. As if he felt some warning about the future, Arn sensed that he was seeing only the beginning of evil changes that were in store for the entire Holy Land.

When he returned to Gaza he could at least look forward to seeing his Norwegian kinsman Harald Øysteinsson, who by this time was heartily tired of singing hymns and sweating all day long in a remote fortress in the baking sun. The little that Harald had seen of war in the Holy Land had not been to his liking; the tedious daily life time in a fortress during peacetime must seem even worse.

Arn then realized that as fortress master he would be able to order the brothers and sergeants who could swim and dive to continue practicing those skills. If Gaza's harbour was ever blockaded by an enemy fleet and the city was simultaneously under siege, the ability to swim at night through the enemy blockade would be of great importance. Since Arn himself and Harald were the only ones who could really swim and dive, this new exercise would be more for their own private pleasure than any serious preparation for war. The Rule forbade them to practice together on Gaza's jetties, since no Templar knight could show himself undressed before another brother, nor could anyone swim solely for the sake of pleasure. So they would have to take turns swimming, but their enjoyment in partaking of this alleged practice for war would surely be considerably greater than its military usefulness to the Knights Templar.

Some years earlier Arn would never have dreamed of twisting and turning the Rule so wantonly. But now that he felt his remaining time in service to be more of a waiting period than a holy duty, he surrendered much of the gravity that had previously marked his behaviour. He and Harald began to speak of travelling together; as fortress master Arn could relieve Harald at any time from his duties as sergeant. They agreed that such a long journey to the North was something they would prefer to do together.

Yet it was difficult to imagine how they would get together enough funds for the journey. During his almost twenty years of being personally penniless Arn was no longer accustomed to thinking of money as a problem. On reflection, however, he found that he could certainly borrow enough travelling money from one of the worldly knights he knew. In the worst case, he and Harald might have to go into service for a year or so, for instance in Tripoli or Antioch, before they could afford to leave.

Once they began talking about the journey, it made them long for home even more. They dreamed of regions they had long ago pushed out of their minds; they saw faces from the past and in the silence heard their own language. To Arn a special image from what had once been his home grew stronger than everything else. Each night he saw Cecilia, each night he prayed to God's Mother to protect Cecilia and his unknown child.

Occasionally he received news from travellers going between Gaza and Jerusalem, and his feeling was reinforced that everything was sliding downhill when it came to the Holy Land. Now in Jerusalem no prayers were permitted except by Christians, and no Saracen doctors or Jews could work for either the Templar knights or the worldly ones. The enmity between Hospitallers and Templars had grown worse than ever, since the two Grand Masters refused to speak to each other. And the Knights Templar seemed to be doing whatever they could to sabotage the peace that the regent, Count Raymond, was trying his best to maintain. One warning sign was that the Knights Templar had come to be close friends with the caravan plunderer Reynald de Châtillon of Kerak. As Arn understood the situation, it was probably only a matter of time before that man would venture out on new plundering raids. When he did the peace with Saladin would be broken, and that was what the Knights Templar clearly wanted to happen.

But nowadays Arn was thinking about his journey home and was more interested in counting his remaining days in the Order of the Knights Templar than he was concerned about the black clouds he saw looming over the eastern horizon of the Holy Land. In his own mind he defended this attitude by thinking that he could no longer do any useful work since God had taken away all his power within the Order. Nor could he blame himself for his new indifference.

During this uneventful year in Gaza he devoted more hours than necessary every day to riding his Arabian horses, the stallion Ibn Anaza and the mare Umm Anaza. They were the only property permitted to him; if he found the right buyer they would pay for both his and Harald's trip home to the North several times over. But he had no intention of voluntarily relinquishing these two horses, because he judged them to be the best steeds he had ever seen, much less ridden. Ibn Anaza and Umm Anaza would definitely come home with him to Western Götaland.

Western Götaland. He said the name of his country to himself now and then, as if to get used to it again.

When he had ten months left of his service, a rider came with urgent news from the Grand Master in Jerusalem. Arn de Gothia was to ride immediately to Ashkelon with thirty knights to serve as part of an important escort.

Obviously he obeyed at once, and arrived with his knights in Ashkelon that same afternoon.

What had happened was momentous but not unexpected. The child king Baldwin V had died in the care of his uncle, Joscelyn de Courtenay, and the body now had to be accompanied to Jerusalem along with the funeral guests Guy de Lusignan and Sibylla, the apparently not very sad mother of the child.

On the road between Ashkelon and Jerusalem Arn had already realized that the import of the journey was much greater than grieving for and burying a child. There was a power shift in the making.

Two days later in Jerusalem, when Joscelyn de Courtenay proclaimed his niece Sibylla as successor to the throne, the plans of the conspirators of the coup were made clear.

In the Templars' quarter where Arn was now living in the guest rooms for the lower knights, he met a dejected Father Louis, who told him everything that had happened.

First Joscelyn de Courtenay had come rushing to Jerusalem. There he met with the regent, Count Raymond, and told him about the death of the child king Baldwin. He suggested to Raymond that he summon the high council of barons to meet in Tiberias instead of in Jerusalem. In this way they could avoid interference from the Grand Master of the Templars, Gérard de Ridefort, who did not feel bound by any oath to obey King Baldwin IV's last will, and the patriarch Heraclius, who also tried to get his fingers in everything.

Count Raymond had thus let himself be duped into leaving Jerusalem. At that point Reynald de Châtillon came thundering into the city with scores of knights from Kerak; then Joscelyn de Courtenay at once proclaimed his niece Sibylla the next successor to the throne. This would mean, if the plan were carried out, that the incompetent Guy de Lusignan could soon be King of Jerusalem and the Holy Land. Count Raymond, the d'Ibelin brothers, and all the others who could have prevented such a move had been lured away from Jerusalem. All the gates and walls around the city were guarded by the Knights Templar, so no enemy of the conspirators could slip into the city. It seemed that nothing could stop the evil that was about to befall the Holy Land.

The only one who made any attempt to avert this calamity in the following days was the Grand Master of the Hospitallers, Roger des Moulins. He refused to betray the oath he had given before God to the late King Baldwin IV. The patriarch Heraclius, however, did not feel bound by any oath, and the Grand Master of the Templars, Gérard de Ridefort, pointed out that he himself had never sworn such an oath; the promise that a dismissed Jerusalem's Master had made on his behalf could not be considered valid.

The coronation took place in the Church of the Holy Sepulchre. First the caravan plunderer Reynald de Châtillon gave a powerful speech in which he claimed that Sibylla was in truth the rightful successor to the throne, since she was the daughter of King Amalrik, the sister of King Baldwin IV, and the mother of the deceased King Baldwin V. Then the patriarch Heraclius crowned Sibylla. She in turn took the crown and placed it on the head of her husband, Guy de Lusignan, and then placed the sceptre in his hand.

As everyone was filing out of the Church of the Holy Sepulchre to go to the customary banquet in the Templars' quarter, Gérard de Ridefort shouted out his joy. With God's help he had finally taken his great and absolutely glorious revenge on Count Raymond, who now sat far off in Tiberias and could do nothing but gnash his teeth.

Arn was present during the coronation because he had been entrusted with the responsibility for the guards that would protect the lives of the new king and queen. He found this to be a bitter task, since he viewed those he protected as perjurers who would drive the Holy Land to its doom. He steeled himself with the thought that his remaining time in the Holy Land was only seven months.

To add to Arn's bitterness, Grand Master Gérard de Ridefort called him over to assure him that he did not bear a grudge. On the contrary, the Grand Master said that there was much that he did not know when he so hastily relieved Arn of his command of Jerusalem. He had now learned that Arn was a great warrior, the best archer and rider, and also the victor of Mont Gisard. So now he wanted to make amends to some extent by giving Arn the honoured assignment of becoming commander of the royal guard.

Arn felt insulted, but he didn't show it. He began counting the days until the 4th of July, 1187; it was on that day twenty years earlier that he had sworn obedience, poverty, and chastity for the length of his penance.

What he saw during his brief time as commander of the royal guard did not surprise him in the least. Guy de Lusignan and his wife Sibylla carried on the same indecent nighttime activities as did the patriarch Heraclius, Sibylla's mother Agnes, and her uncle Joscelyn de Courtenay.

Earlier in his service Arn would have probably wept to see all power in the Holy Land gathered in the hands of these sinners from the abyss. Now he felt more resigned, as if he had already become reconciled to the idea that God's punishment could only be one: the loss of the Holy Land and Jerusalem.

Toward the end of the year, as expected, Reynald de Châtillon broke the truce with Saladin and plundered the largest ever caravan to be attacked on its way between Mecca and Damascus. It was not hard to understand that Saladin was furious; one of the travellers who had landed in the dungeon of the fortress of Kerak was his sister. Soon the rumour reached Jerusalem that Saladin had sworn to God to kill Reynald with his own hands.

When Saladin's negotiator came to King Guy de Lusignan to demand reparations for the breach of the peace agreement and the immediate release of the prisoners, Guy could promise nothing. He regretted that he had no power over Reynald de Châtillon.

With that there was no salvation from the coming war.

Prince Bohemund of Antioch, however, quickly concluded peace between Antiochia and Saladin. Count Raymond did the same for both his County of Tripoli and his wife Escheva's lands around Tiberias in the Galilee. Neither Bohemund nor Raymond considered that they had any responsibility for what the demented court in Jerusalem might do, and they soon informed Saladin of this fact.

Now a civil war amongst the Christians seemed imminent. Gérard de Ridefort persuaded King Guy to send an army to Tiberias to humble Count Raymond once and for all.

However, at the last minute Balian d'Ibelin managed to convince the king to listen to reason. Civil war would be the same as death, because they would soon be in a full-scale war with Saladin. What was needed now, argued Balian d'Ibelin, was reconciliation with Count Raymond; he offered to serve as the envoy and go to Tiberias to negotiate.

Appointed as negotiators were the two Grand Masters, Gérard de Ridefort and Roger des Moulins, Balian d'Ibelin, and Bishop Josias of Tyrus. A few knights from the Hospitallers and the Templars would escort them, including Arn de Gothia.

Meanwhile, Count Raymond in Tiberias had a difficult dilemma. As if to test the viability of the peace accord between them, Saladin sent his son al Afdal with a request to be allowed to send a large scouting party for one day through Galilee. Count Raymond agreed to this, under the condition that the force would ride into the region at sunrise and be out by sundown. So it was agreed.

At the same time Count Raymond sent riders to warn the approaching negotiation group not to end up in the clutches of the enemy force.

Outside Nazareth, Count Raymond's messengers encountered the negotiators and issued the warning. They were thanked kindly for the warning by the Grand Master of the Templars, Gérard de Ridefort, but his gratitude was not for the reasons they would have guessed.

Gérard de Ridefort now thought that this was a brilliant opportunity to defeat one of Saladin's forces. He sent a message to the fortress of La Fève, where the new Jerusalem's Master James de Mailly was located with ninety Templar knights. In the city of Nazareth they were able to scrape together an additional forty knights and some foot soldiers. And as they rode out from Nazareth to search for al Afdal and his Syrian riders, Gérard de Ridefort stirred up the residents of Nazareth to follow after them on foot, for he assured them that now there would be much rich booty to plunder.

Bishop Josias of Tyrus wisely stopped in Nazareth, since he didn't think he was qualified to proceed any farther unless negotiations were to be conducted. He would never regret that decision.

A Christian force of a hundred and forty armoured knights, of which the majority were Templars, accompanied by about a hundred foot soldiers, made a rather imposing presence. But when they encountered the enemy at Cresson's springs as expected and gazed down the slopes, they at first couldn't believe their eyes. Down there by the springs they now saw seven thousand Mameluke lancers and Syrian mounted archers watering their horses.

It might all come down to simple arithmetic and nothing more. If they were a hundred and forty knights, of which most were Templars and Hospitallers, under favourable conditions they might be able to take on seven hundred Mamelukes and Syrian archers. Seven hundred, but not seven thousand.

The Grand Master of the Hospitallers, Roger des Moulins, therefore calmly counselled retreat. The Templars' military commander James de Mailly was of the same opinion.

But Grand Master Gérard de Ridefort was absolutely opposed. He flew into a rage and called the others cowards. He insulted James de Mailly by saying that he was much too concerned about the safety of his blond head to risk it before God. He said that Roger des Moulins was an unworthy Grand Master, and he made other claims of this sort.

Arn, who now had too low a position to be consulted, sat a short distance away on his Frankish stallion Ardent, but not so far that he couldn't follow the heated argument. To him it was clear that Gérard de Ridefort must be insane. An attack in broad daylight against such an overwhelming force could only end in death, especially since the enemy had already noticed the danger and had begun mounting their horses to form ranks.

But Gérard de Ridefort was unrelenting. He was going to attack. With that the Hospitallers and the others were forced to follow, for honour left them no choice.

When they were arrayed in battle order, Gérard called Arn over and asked him to ride as *confanonier*, since that task required an especially bold and skilled horseman. This meant that Arn was to ride next to the Grand Master and carry the flag of the Knights Templar. At the same time he would function as the Grand Master's shield, ready at any moment to sacrifice his life to protect the highest brother in the Order. The Grand Master and the flag were the last that should be lost in battle.

Arn was aware of several emotions, but fear was not the strongest as he formed up with his other brothers in a straight line of attack. His strongest feeling was disappointment. He had come so close to freedom. Now he would have to die for the whim of a fool; his death would be just as meaningless as that of all the others in the Holy Land who had fallen because they were subordinate to insane or incompetent leaders. For the first time in Arn's life his mind was filled with the thought of flight. But then he remembered his oath, which applied for another two months. His life was finite but his oath was eternal.

The Grand Master gave him the order to attack; he raised and lowered the flag three times, and then the hundred and forty knights thundered without hesitation straight down the slope toward death.

But Gérard de Ridefort rode somewhat more slowly than all the others, and since Arn had to follow beside him, he too lagged behind. Just as the first knights crashed into the sea of Mameluke cavalry, Gérard de Ridefort turned sharply to the right and Arn followed with his shield raised against the arrows that were now whizzing around them. Arn felt himself being hit by many arrows, and some of them penetrated his chain mail. Gérard de Ridefort then completed his turn and rode with Arn and the flag away from the attack he himself had instigated.

Not a single one of the Hospitallers or Templars survived the attack at Cresson's springs. Among the fallen were Roger des Moulins and James de Mailly.

Some of the worldly knights they had scraped together up in Nazareth were taken prisoner for future ransom demands. The inhabitants of Nazareth who had come along on foot, lured by Gérard de Ridefort's promise of rich plunder, were quickly captured; with their hands tied behind their backs they were dragged off to the nearest slave market.

That afternoon, just before sundown, Count Raymond saw from his ramparts in Tiberias how al Afdal's forces, exactly as agreed, were making their way across the River Jordan to leave Galilee before the end of the day.

In the vanguard of the Saracen army rode the Mameluke lancers. They carried over a hundred bearded heads on their raised lances.

This sight was a stronger argument than any that a negotiating group could have presented to persuade Raymond. He could not be a traitor; he had to renounce his truce with Saladin and, no matter how much it stung, swear allegiance to King Guy de Lusignan. He had no other choice, but he had never been forced to make a more bitter decision.

When Saladin attacked in earnest later that summer, he came with the largest army he had ever assembled, over thirty thousand riders. He was now determined to resolve this war once and for all.

The news reached Arn down in Gaza, where he had retreated to obtain Saracen medical care for the arrow wounds he had suffered at Cresson's springs. King Guy had now proclaimed *arrière-ban*, which meant that all men with battle experience were now called up to serve under the banners of the Holy Land.

Hospitallers and Templars emptied every fortress of knights and left behind only a few officers and sergeants to take care of maintenance and handle the defence from the walls.

Among the men that Arn left in Gaza was Harald Øysteinsson, since he believed that such a good archer was worth ten times as much on the walls when there were so few defenders.

He had no warning about what was about to happen. With the *arrière-ban* that was now in force, the Hospitallers and Templars alone would have a force of almost two thousand men. To that were added perhaps four thousand secular knights and between ten and twenty thousand archers and footsoldiers. In Arn's experience no Saracens, no matter how many, could defeat such a force. He was more worried that the large army would be lured away by one of Saladin's diversionary tactics, and that then they might lose some of the cities that they had left with only meagre defences.

He couldn't imagine that the foolhardy Gérard de Ridefort would repeat the same mistake that he'd made at Cresson's springs. Gérard de Ridefort could give orders to the Knights Templar, but he could not make the decisions for the entire Christian army.

When Arn reached Saint-Jean d'Acre with his sixty-four knights and barely a hundred sergeants from Gaza, he had less than a week left in the service of the Knights Templar. He dwelled very little on that fact, since he could not terminate his service in the middle of a war. But he thought that after the war, towards autumn when the rain would drive Saladin back across the River Jordan, then he could begin his journey home. Western Götaland, he said again and again in his childhood tongue, as if savouring the unfamiliar words.

The enormous assembly of forces at Saint-Jean d'Acre became a vast army encampment in the summer heat. Inside the fortress a war council was being held, at which a bewildered King Guy as usual found himself surrounded on all sides by men who hated one another.

The Grand Master of the Hospitallers contradicted everything that Gérard de Ridefort said. Count Raymond contradicted everything that both these Grand Masters claimed. And patriarch Heraclius contradicted everyone.

Count Raymond's ideas at first garnered the most approval among those present. It was now the hottest time of the year, he pointed out. Saladin had broken into Galilee with a larger army than ever before and badly ravaged the land. But with so many horses and riders he had to keep supplying them with water, animal fodder, and food shipments from various directions. If Saladin did not meet with resistance at once, which was clearly his hope, his army would be gradually worn down by their own impatience and the heat, as so often happened with the Saracens.

The Christian side could afford to bide its time in peace and quiet, well provisioned inside the cities, and attack just as the Saracens gave up and were on their way home. Then they would be able to prevail. The price was all the plundering they would have to endure in the meantime, but that was not too high a price if for once they were able to defeat Saladin.

It surprised no one that Gérard de Ridefort immediately offered another opinion, nor that he began calling Count Raymond a traitor, friend of the Saracens, and treaty maker with Saladin. Not even King Guy was impressed by such reckless outbursts.

On the other hand, the patriarch Heraclius won King Guy's

ear when he said that they had to attack at once. What Count Raymond had proposed would seem the wisest course, so they should surprise the enemy by acting in a way that did not seem as wise.

In addition, Heraclius now carried the True Cross. And when, he asked dramatically, had the Christians lost a battle when they were carrying the True Cross? Never, he answered himself.

It was a sin to doubt victory when in the company of the True Cross. By winning a quick victory, all those who had sinned by doubting could then purify themselves.

Therefore the best course of action and the one most pleasing to God would be if they attacked at once and won.

Unfortunately, Heraclius went on, his health did not permit him to bear the True Cross into battle himself. But he would have no qualms about assigning that task to the Bishop of Caesarea; the main thing was that the most holy of relics was brought along to guaranteed victory.

So in the last days of June in the year of grace 1187, the Christian army set off toward Galilee to meet Saladin during the hottest time of the year. They travelled for two days until they reached the springs at Sephoria, where there was plenty of water and forage. There they received word that Saladin had taken the city of Tiberias and now was besieging the fortress itself.

Tiberias was Count Raymond's city, and his wife Escheva was in the fortress. In the Christian army at Sephoria were Escheva's three sons, who now appealed for immediate aid to be sent to their mother. The king seemed prepared to grant their request.

Then Count Raymond took the floor. It was so quiet that even Gérard de Ridefort did not speak or interfere in any way.

'Sire,' Count Raymond began calmly, but in a loud voice so that everyone could hear. 'Tiberias is my city. In the fortress is my wife Escheva and my treasure chest. I am the one who has the most to lose if the fortress falls. So you must truly take my words seriously, Sire, when I say that we should not attack Tiberias. Here at Sephoria we can defend ourselves well, and we have ample water supplies. Here our foot-soldiers and archers can do great damage to attacking Saracens. But if we proceed toward Tiberias, we will be beaten. I know that on the way there we'll find not a drop of water and no forage; that land is a desert this time of year. Even if Saladin takes my fortress and tears down the walls, in any case he cannot hold it. And I will build the walls back up. If he takes my wife then I will ransom her. That much we can afford to lose. But if we march on Tiberias now in the summer heat, we will lose the Holy Land.'

Count Raymond's words made a great impression. For the moment they convinced one and all, and King Guy decided that they should hold their ground at Sephoria.

But that night Gérard de Ridefort visited King Guy in his tent and told him that Raymond was a traitor, in a secret pact with Saladin, and that they should therefore ignore his advice. In fact, here was an opportunity for King Guy to win a decisive victory against Saladin himself, for the Holy Land had never before brought such a large army against the Saracens. Besides, they were carrying the True Cross, so victory was promised by God. What Raymond wanted was merely to rob King Guy of the honour of defeating Saladin. Besides, he was envious because he had lost the power of regent when Guy became king. He might be conspiring to take the crown in any case, and that's why he sought to prevent Guy from winning this war.

King Guy believed Gérard de Ridefort. If he'd at least had the wits to order the army to move against Tiberias at night, history might have turned out differently. But he wanted to get a night's sleep first, he said.

At dawn the next day the great Christian army set off, marching on Tiberias.

First rode the Hospitallers, in the middle the secular army, and in the rear the Knights Templar, where the demands would be greatest.

Gérard de Ridefort had forbidden the Templars from bringing along the light Turkish cavalry, since he considered it ungodly to employ such soldiers. So Arn, like all the other brothers, rode as armoured knights with a few footsoldiers around them to protect the horses. They had to attire both themselves and the horses in all the heavy, hot armour right from the start.

When faced with an armoured Christian army on the approach, the Saracens always acted the same way. They sent out swarms of light cavalry to ride in close to the enemy columns and shoot arrows at them; then they would turn with their fast horses and vanish. After that a new wave would come. This began early in the morning.

The Templar knights had orders not to break formation for any reason. They could not shoot back because they no longer had any light cavalry on their flanks, since that had been declared ungodly by the Grand Master. Within a few hours all the Templar knights had been struck by arrows; their wounds may have been mostly minor, but they could be quite painful in the heat.

It was a very hot day with desert winds from the south. And as Count Raymond had said, there was not a drop of water along the entire route. From dawn to sunset the Christians had to plod through an unceasing gauntlet of attacking light cavalry. At first they carried their dead with them, but soon they had to start leaving the bodies where they fell.

Toward evening they neared Tiberias and saw the lake shining in the sunset. Count Raymond tried to persuade the king that they should attack at once and fight their way to the water before it grew dark. If after such a terrible day without water they waited all night without water as well, they would be defeated when the sun rose.

Gérard de Ridefort thought instead that they would fight much better if they got some sleep. And King Guy, who admitted that he felt rather tired, thought this sounded sensible, so he gave the order to pitch camp for the night.

By the slopes near the village of Hattin, where two small peaks among the low hills were called the Horns of Hattin, the Christians pitched their camp so that they could, as they believed, at least cool off and get some sleep before the next day's decisive battle.

When the sun went down and it was the hour of prayer for the Saracen army, which was now within sight of the exhausted Christians, Saladin thanked God near the lakeshore for the gift he had been given. Up there by the Horns of Hattin was the entire Christian army in an untenable position – all the Hospitaller knights and almost all the Templar knights, the Christian king and his closest officers. God had served up the final victory on a golden platter. All that remained for Saladin to do was to thank Him and then carry out the duty required of His faithful.

That duty began with setting fire to the dry summer grasses south of the Horns of Hattin. The Christian encampment was soon enveloped in choking smoke that made impossible any thought of a night's rest before the final battle.

In the morning at first light the Christians found themselves completely surrounded. Saladin's army made no move to attack, for they had time on their side. The longer the Christians waited, the weaker they would become. The sun climbed mercilessly, and still King Guy could not make a decision.

Count Raymond was among the first to mount his horse.

He walked it about the encampment until he came to the Templars' section; there he found his way to Arn and proposed that Arn take some men and follow him in a breakout. Arn politely declined, saying that he was sworn by oath until the conclusion of this very day and could not break his word before God. They said farewell, and Arn wished Raymond all luck and said that he would pray for a successful assault.

And he did pray.

Count Raymond ordered his weary knights to mount their horses and gave a brief speech, exhorting them to action and explaining that they would now risk all on a single attempt. If the breakout failed they would die, that was true. But so would everyone who remained at the Horns of Hattin.

When that was said he lined up his forces in a narrow wedge-shaped phalanx instead of advancing across a broad front. Then he gave the signal to attack and stormed down toward the compact mass of enemy soldiers who were standing with their backs to all the water in the Sea of Galilee, as if they were guarding it.

In response to Raymond's charge the Saracens opened their ranks so that a wide avenue was formed, into which Count Raymond and his knights vanished. Then the Saracens closed up ranks behind them.

Not until much later could the Christians see, from up by the Horns of Hattin, Count Raymond and his knights disappearing far in the distance, with no one pursuing them. Saladin had spared him.

Gérard de Ridefort then flew into a rage. He gave a long speech about traitors and ordered all his Templar knights to mount up.

Now there was much shouting and commotion among the Saracens when they saw the Templar knights, still at least seven hundred in number, making ready to attack. No Saracen had ever seen such a huge force of Templar knights before.

And they all knew that it was now that the battle would be decided; now was the moment of truth.

Were these white demons impossible to defeat? Or were they human beings like everyone else, and like all soldiers would be suffering from a day without water?

When the Hospitallers saw that the Templars were getting ready to attack, they did the same, and then King Guy gave orders for the royal army to mount up as well.

But Gérard de Ridefort did not wait for the others; he stormed down the hills in advance with his entire force of knights. The enemy instantly drew back so that the mighty blow the Christians had intended never fell upon them. Then the knights had to try to turn around, heavy and slow. By then the water was within sight, which disturbed their horses greatly. They attempted to make their way back into the hills, but on the way up they met the Hospitallers rushing down. The Hospitaller attack was now brought to a halt, and there was a devastating chaos of Templar knights and Hospitallers facing in opposite directions.

Then the Mameluke lancers attacked from the rear with full force.

Gérard de Ridefort lost half of his knights in this foolhardy sortie. The Hospitallers' losses were even greater.

After that they sought to gather all the Christian forces in a common attack. But by then some of the footsoldiers who had lost their wits tore off their helmets and began running toward the water with their arms outspread. They drew many others with them, and so a horde of footsoldiers ran to their deaths. They were easily struck down by the mounted Egyptian lancers.

The second attack by the knights was better than the first, but they had only covered half the distance to the water before they were forced to turn around. When they regrouped around the king's tent, two thirds of the Christians were gone.

Now Saladin launched his full-scale attack.

Arn had lost his horse, which was felled by an arrow through the neck, and he could no longer see clearly what was happening around him. The last thing he remembered was that he and several brothers who had also lost their horses were making a stand with their backs to each other, completely surrounded by Syrian footsoldiers. He recalled striking many of them with his sword or with his battle hammer that he held in his left hand. He had lost his shield when his horse fell.

He never knew how he was struck to the ground, or by whom.

The Templars and Hospitallers who were taken alive during the last hour at the Horns of Hattin, when the Frankish army finally collapsed, were all given water to drink. Then they were lined up on their knees before Saladin's pavilion down by the shore.

They were given water to drink not out of mercy but so that they could speak. The beheadings began down by the shore, and the Saracens were gradually working their way up to finish by the victory pavilion in a couple of hours.

The surviving brothers numbered 246 Templar knights and about the same of Hospitallers. That meant that the two orders were now as good as wiped out in the Holy Land.

Saladin wept with joy and thanked God as he watched the beheadings begin. God had been inconceivably good to him. Both of the fearsome orders had now been defeated, because those who were one by one losing their heads were the last. Their almost empty fortresses would fall like ripe fruit. The road to Jerusalem finally lay open to him.

The secular knights who had been captured were treated as usual in a completely different way. After Saladin had enjoyed for a while the sight of Templars and Hospitallers being decapitated, he went back inside his victory pavilion.

There his most notable captives had been invited in, among them the unfortunate Guy de Lusignan and Saladin's most hated foe, Reynald de Châtillon, who sat beside the king. Next to him sat the Grand Master of the Knights Templar, Gérard de Ridefort, who might not prove to be a very valuable captive. But Saladin could not be sure. Faced with death, men who had previously shown themselves to be brave and honourable could change in the most pitiful way.

One of the high-born and valuable Frankish captives could expect no mercy. Saladin had sworn to God that with his own hands he would kill Reynald de Châtillon, and he did so now with his sword. He reassured the other prisoners at once that they would not be treated in the same way. He gave them all water to drink, handing it to them himself.

Outside, many Saracen soldiers had gathered to watch the beheadings and were celebrating the occasion. A group of Sufi scholars from Cairo had been following Saladin's army because they imagined that they would be able to convert Christians to the true faith. As a cruel joke some emirs had agreed to let the Sufis make an attempt with the fighting monks, the Hospitallers and Templars.

So now these men of faith, not entirely happy with their task, were allowed to go from Templar to Hospitaller and ask if he was ready to renounce the false Christian beliefs and convert to Islam if his life was spared. Each time the Sufis received the same defiant answer, and then they had to perform the beheading themselves. This led to much merriment among the spectators, since they seldom managed to sever the head with one blow. Instead the learned defenders of the faith mostly had to hack away at the poor knight's neck. Each time a beheading was finally successful, the spectators cheered. Otherwise the soldiers laughed and shouted, voicing their jocular disapproval and offering advice.

From the water he received Arn revived enough that he

understood what was about to happen. But his face was covered in blood and he could see only out of one eye, so he had a hard time knowing what exactly was happening farther down the line.

But he was not very interested in any of that. He prayed and prepared to deliver up his soul to God. With all the strength he could muster he asked God: What can be the meaning of this? For it was July 4, 1187. On precisely this day twenty years ago he had sworn the oath to the Knights Templar. From sundown on this day he would be free. What was God's intention in letting him live until the last hour in service and then taking his life? And why let him live until precisely this day, when Christendom was defeated in the Holy Land?

Arn caught himself being selfish. He was not alone in dying, and the last hour of life ought to be used for better thoughts than directing accusatory questions at God. Now that he was finished with his own life he should instead be praying for Cecilia and the child who would soon be fatherless.

When the sweating group of blood-soaked and distressed Sufi scholars reached Arn, they asked him dejectedly if he was ready to renounce his false beliefs and convert to the true faith if he might be allowed to live. Their manner of asking indicated that they had little hope for his conversion, and they had not even tried to ensure that he understood.

Defiantly Arn then raised his bowed head and spoke to them in the language of the Prophet, peace be unto him:

'In the name of the Most Benevolent, Ever-Merciful, hear the words from your own Holy Koran, the third *sura* and the fifty-fifth verse,' he began, taking a deep breath so that he could continue, as the men around him fell silent in astonishment.

'And God said,' he continued in a voice that barely managed to form the words, '"O Jesus! I will take thee and raise thee to Myself and clear thee of the falsehoods of those who blaspheme; I will make those who follow thee superior to those who reject faith, to the Day of Resurrection: Then shall ye all return unto me, and I will judge between you of the matters wherein ye dispute."'

Arn closed his eyes and leaned forward in anticipation of the sword striking his neck. But the Sufis around him had become as if paralysed at hearing God's own words from one of their worst enemies. At the same time a high emir stepped forward and called out that they had found Al Ghouti.

Even though Arn's face was so heavily battered that nobody would have recognized him, they all knew that only one foe was known for his ability to quote so purely and clearly God's own words.

And Saladin had given them all strict instructions that if Al Ghouti were found among the living, under no circumstances was he to be treated as a captive, but rather as an honoured guest.

TEN

When the sun went down on the last day of Cecilia Rosa's twenty-year penance, she was sitting by one of the fish ponds at Riseberga all by herself. It was a warm evening with no breeze just after Persmas, when the summer was just about to pass its zenith, and when the hay-making would soon begin down in Western Götaland, but not yet up here in Nordanskog.

She had been to mass twice, and she had gone to Holy Communion, filled with the thought that on this day, with the help of Our Lady, she would have completed the time that had seemed never-ending when she was first sentenced. She would finally be free.

But not yet. For when the hour of freedom struck it was as though nothing had changed; there was not the slightest sign that anything was different. Everything was the same as usual, just like on any summer day.

She realized that she may have had childish notions, that Arn, whose hour of freedom must have struck at the same time as hers, would immediately come riding towards her out of nowhere, although he would have a very long journey ahead of him. Those who knew about such things said that it could take a year to travel to or from Jerusalem.

Maybe she had also pushed aside all thoughts of this singular moment of happiness because deep in her heart she knew that it would feel just like this. It was nothing special. She was now thirty-seven years old and owned nothing except the clothes on her back. As far as she knew, her father was sitting at home in Husaby paralysed by a stroke, impoverished, and utterly dependent on the Folkungs at Arnäs for whatever income he received. She would not bring him much joy by coming home and demanding to be supported.

She had no interest in going to Arnäs. Her sister Katarina was the mistress there, and since it was Katarina's fault that Cecilia Rosa ended up doing twenty years of penance in the convent, a meeting between the sisters would not be welcomed by either of them.

She could go to Näs on Visingö to be the guest of Cecilia Blanca, and she would surely also be welcome for a time at Ulfshem with Ulvhilde. But it was one thing for friends to visit each other when they could offer the same hospitality in return. It was another matter to arrive homeless.

As if struck by a sudden bright idea, she tore off the wimple around her head that she had grown used to wearing for twenty long years. In all that time she had been forced to ignore her hair. Now she shook out her tresses and ran her fingers through the tangles so that her hair hung free. According to the rules it was much too long, but she had managed to evade the most recent two of the six haircuts required per year.

She leaned forward and tried to see her reflection in the surface of the pond. But twilight had already fallen and she could barely see her face and the red hair. The image she saw was probably more the way she remembered herself from her youth than the way she actually looked now. As at every other convent, there were no mirrors at Riseberga.

She awkwardly ran her hands over her body the way a

free woman had a right to do; she even attempted to run them over her breasts and hips since as of this evening that would no longer be a breach of the rules. But the touch of her hands did not tell her much. She was thirty-seven years old but not yet free; that was the only thing she could say for certain.

Now that she thought about it, even freedom seemed enclosed by both fences and walls. Birger Brosa had decided that she could continue as *yconoma* at Riseberga as long as she wanted; when she heard him say that it had sounded like a mere pleasantry. But now in the first hour of her freedom, as she tried to examine what that friendly statement had implied, it seemed more likely that she would continue the same work that she had been doing in recent years.

But not in entirely the same way. She decided that she no longer intended to cover her hair with a wimple, and that she no longer needed to sing either *Lauds* or *Matins* or take part in *completorium*. In this way she would gain a good deal of extra time to work. And starting today she would be able to go to the marketplaces and make purchases herself; that suddenly seemed to her the greatest change of all. She had the right to mix with other people, and she could speak with anyone she cared to address; she was no longer burdened with sin and punishment.

Most of all she wanted to go to Bjälbo to see her son Magnus. But that was a meeting that she had imagined with equal parts longing and trepidation.

In the view of many people, but above all in the eyes of the church, Magnus had been born in sin and shame. Birger Brosa had taken him in as an infant and brought him into the clan as a legitimate heir when approved by the *ting*. Then he had raised the boy as his own child. But all too many tongues knew how he had been admitted to the clan by the *ting*, and the gossip had reached Magnus himself, first as furtive hints, then from those who spoke more boldly and in anger.

On the verge of becoming a man, Magnus had begun to realize the truth. Then he took Birger Brosa aside and demanded to be told how things stood. Birger Brosa had seen no other option than to tell him the unvarnished truth. For a time Magnus had gone about like a recluse, sullen and taciturn, as if his secure life as the jarl's son had been smashed to bits. During that time Birger Brosa decided not to bother the boy, since he thought that things would change soon enough and curiosity would replace disappointment.

And so it was. After a while Magnus sought out his foster father and began to ask the first questions about Arn Magnusson. As Birger Brosa recounted to Cecilia Rosa, he may have exaggerated a bit when he described Arn as the best swordsman ever seen in Western Götaland and an archer with few equals. Birger Brosa excused himself by saying that this was not entirely untrue. The memory still lived on about how young Arn, hardly more than a boy, had vanquished the huge Sverker giant Emund Ulvbane at the *ting* of all Goths in Axevalla. It had been like the story of David and Goliath in the Holy Scriptures, and yet not the same, because Arn proved to be so much better with a sword than Emund, who lost his hand instead of his life because young Arn chose to spare him.

When Magnus felt himself free to ask older kinsmen about this event, he met many who had actually been present at Axevalla, or at least claimed they had. Yet they could still embellish the story with the most outrageous details.

Since young Magnus at an early age had shown himself to be a much better shot with a bow than other boys, he now suspected that it was because his father was such an excellent archer. He began to practice far more than was necessary, neglecting other aspects of his education. He also

400

went to Birger Brosa and told him that if his father did not come home alive from the Holy Land, then he would not take the surname Birgersson after Birger Brosa. Nor would he choose Arnsson. Instead he would call himself Magnus Månesköld, and he had painted with his own hand a little silver half-moon above the Folkung lion on his shield.

It was Birger Brosa's opinion that since such a long time had already passed, it would be best if mother and son did not meet until Cecilia Rosa's penance was completed. It would be better for the boy's soul to meet his mother as a free woman than as a cloister servant who still had years of penance left to serve. Cecilia had no objection to that proposal. But now the time had come when she was free and no longer a penitent servant. Now she feared this meeting more than she ever would have thought. She began to worry about things that she had never considered before: Was she old and ugly? Were her clothes too plain? If young Magnus had such big dreams about his father, wasn't there a greater danger that he would be disappointed when he saw his mother?

When the other women at Riseberga – six nuns, three novices, and eight lay-sisters – went to *completorium* that evening, Cecilia Rosa went instead to her bookkeeping chamber. Her first hour of freedom began with work.

That autumn Cecilia organised an expedition down to Gudhem to purchase all sorts of useful and lovely plants that could only travel in the fall so that they wouldn't die on the way. She also needed many things for sewing and dyeing cloth. All such matters had been worked out long ago at Gudhem, while Riseberga up in Nordanskog was only in the beginning stages of its operation. Because Cecilia Rosa would be bringing a great deal of silver along for payment, Birger Brosa had arranged for her to have armed horsemen accompany her south to Lake Vättern. Then Norwegian seafarers would take her across the water, and Folkung riders would again escort her from the lake to Gudhem.

She too travelled on horseback. Since she had been a good rider at the age of seventeen, it didn't take her long to regain her previous skill on horseback, although her body did ache.

As she approached Gudhem with her retinue, she stubbornly insisted on riding in front because she was an *yconoma* and used to making decisions. The armed horsemen were only her escort. But she was surprised at how mixed her feelings were. Gudhem was situated in a beautiful location, and it was lovely to see even at a distance. In the middle of autumn like this, many roses were still blooming along the walls; they were the kind she would try to buy for the beautification of Riseberga, along with other flowering plants.

There was no place on earth she had hated as much as Gudhem; that much was true without a doubt. But what a remarkable difference there was in approaching Mother Rikissa's realm as a free woman rather than as one who had to obey her every demand.

Cecilia Rosa told herself that she was here strictly for business and to obtain the best for Riseberga. There was no reason to seek out a quarrel with Mother Rikissa or to make a special effort to show the abbess that her power had been broken. As she rode down the last gravelled lane toward Gudhem, Cecilia Rosa imagined behaving toward Rikissa as if they were now equals: the abbess from Gudhem and the *yconoma* from Riseberga, who were going to transact business to the best of their ability and nothing more. But she did scowl a bit when she recalled Mother Rikissa's lack of understanding when it came to business dealings.

But nothing came of her imagined encounter with the abbess. Mother Rikissa lay dying, and Bishop Örjan from Växjö had been called to the deathbed to hear her confession and give her extreme unction.

Upon hearing this news, Cecilia Rosa at first considered leaving Gudhem. But the journey had been long and difficult, and life in both Gudhem and Riseberga would go on long after everyone who now lived there was dead. So she changed her mind and took lodging in the *hospitium*, where she and her companions were welcomed as if they were any other travellers.

Early that evening the bishop, whom she did not know, came to see Cecilia Rosa and asked her to accompany him into the cloister to visit the abbess one last time. Mother Rikissa herself had requested this last favour from Cecilia Rosa.

To refuse the last wish of someone who was dying when it would be so easy to comply was of course out of the question. Reluctantly Cecilia Rosa followed Bishop Örjan to Mother Rikissa's deathbed. Her reluctance was not on account of death, as she had seen much of that in the convent, where many old women came to live out their last days and then die. Her reluctance was because of the emotions she feared she would discover in her heart when faced with Mother Rikissa's death. To exult over her death would be a difficult sin to forgive. But what other emotions could she feel for a person who was evil incarnate?

With the bishop lamenting and praying at her side, Cecilia Rosa entered Mother Rikissa's innermost sanctum. The abbess lay there with the covers pulled up to her chin and with a candle burning on either side of the bed. She was very pale, as if the Grim Reaper were already squeezing her heart with his cold skeletal hand. Her eyes were half shut.

Cecilia Rosa and the bishop fell at once to their knees beside the bed and said the obligatory prayers. When they finished praying, Mother Rikissa opened her eyes a little. Suddenly she stuck a claw-like hand out from under the covers and grabbed Cecilia Rosa by the back of the neck with a strength that was not at all like that of someone who was dying.

'Cecilia Rosa, God has called you here in this hour so that you will forgive me,' she snarled, and her strong grip relaxed a bit around Cecilia Rosa's neck.

For a brief moment Cecilia Rosa felt the same icy terror that she had always associated with this evil woman. But then she collected herself and removed without undue firmness Mother Rikissa's hand from her neck.

'What is it that you want me to forgive you, Mother?' she asked, her tone betraying no emotion.

'My sins, and mostly my sins against you,' whispered Mother Rikissa as if she had suddenly lost most of her surprising strength.

'Like when you whipped me for sins that you knew I hadn't committed? Have you confessed to that evil?' Cecilia Rosa asked coldly.

'Yes, I have confessed these sins to Bishop Örjan who is at your side,' replied Mother Rikissa.

'Like when you tried to kill me by keeping me in the *carcer* in the wintertime with only a blanket? Did you confess to that too?' Cecilia Rosa went on.

'Yes, I have . . . confessed to that too,' said Mother Rikissa. But then Cecilia Rosa couldn't help noticing how Bishop Örjan, still on his knees at her side, made a restless movement. She glanced at him at once and couldn't avoid seeing his look of surprise.

'You're not lying to me on your own deathbed after you've confessed and received extreme unction, are you, Mother Rikissa?' Cecilia Rosa asked in a soft tone, though she felt as hard as iron inside. In Mother Rikissa's red glowing eyes she again saw the slitted pupils of the goat.

'I have confessed to all that you have asked me about. Now I want to have your forgiveness and your prayers before

404

my long journey, for my sins are not insignificant,' Mother Rikissa whispered.

'Have you also confessed to trying to kill Cecilia Blanca in the *carcer* during the hard winter months?' Cecilia Rosa continued implacably.

'You're torturing me . . . show some mercy to me on my deathbed,' Mother Rikissa panted. But she spoke in such a way that Cecilia Rosa had the impression it was all a sham.

'Have you or have you not confessed that you tried to take my life and Cecilia Blanca's by using the *carcer*?' Cecilia Rosa asked, because she had no intention of yielding. 'Poor sinner that I am, I cannot forgive such sins if I don't know that they have already been confessed. You understand that, don't you, Mother?'

'Yes, I have confessed these grave sins to Bishop Örjan,' Mother Rikissa said then, but this time without panting or whispering. Instead some impatience could be heard in her voice.

'That is your dilemma, Mother Rikissa,' said Cecilia Rosa coldly. 'Either you're lying to me now when you say that you have confessed this to Bishop Örjan. And then of course I cannot forgive you. Or else you have actually confessed to these mortal sins, for it is a mortal sin to attempt to take a Christian's life, even worse if you are in service to God's Mother. If you have indeed confessed these mortal sins, then Bishop Örjan could not forgive you. And lastly, who am I, a poor sinful penitent under your whip for so many years, to forgive that which even the bishop and God Himself cannot forgive?!'

With these words Cecilia Rosa stood up abruptly as if she knew what was about to happen. Mother Rikissa twisted violently in the bed and once again reached out her hands for Cecilia Rosa as if trying to grab her around the neck. This caused the blanket to fall off her, and a revolting stench spread through the room.

'I damn you, Cecilia Rosa!' shrieked Mother Rikissa, displaying strength that seemed to come out of nowhere. Her red eyes were now wide open, and Cecilia Rosa thought she could clearly see the slitted pupils of the goat.

'I curse you and your indecent liar of a friend Cecilia Blanca. May you both burn in Hell, and may you suffer the punishment of war for your sins, and may your kinsmen die with you in the fire that shall now come!'

With these words Mother Rikissa fell back as though she had lost all strength. Her black hair, which had begun to turn gray, had slipped out from under her wimple. Out of the corner of her mouth ran a narrow stream of blood which looked completely black.

Bishop Örjan then cautiously put his arm around Cecilia Rosa's shoulders and led her out, closing the door after her. Then he returned to the abbess as if he found it necessary to try to have a few more words with the dying woman before it was too late for her to repent, too late to confess.

Mother Rikissa died that night. The next day she was buried beneath the flagstones in the arcade, and her seal as abbess was broken in two and placed beside her. Cecilia Rosa attended the funeral, although reluctantly. But she didn't think she had much choice. On the one hand she found it unreasonable to pray for someone so evil and stand there feigning grief with all the others. She could not imagine anything more meaningless than rattling off prayers for the inveterate sinner who had lied during confession on her own deathbed.

On the other hand there was a concern that had to do with the secular life. She had no idea who this Bishop Örjan from Växjö was; she had never even heard that there was a bishop in Växjö. But there had to be a reason why this unknown and insignificant bishop had been called to Mother Rikissa's deathbed. First, he had to be of the Sverker clan, perhaps closely related to Mother Rikissa. Second, he now had knowledge of Mother Rikissa's last wishes, and that was surely of some importance. With the last words she uttered in her life, as Cecilia Rosa had heard, Mother Rikissa had threatened to plunge them all into fire and war. What she meant by those words probably only Bishop Örjan knew. So it would undoubtedly be wise to stay close to this Örjan as long as possible, in order to discover if possible at least part of the secret he now held.

The other reason for staying for the funeral was more practical. Cecilia Rosa and her increasingly impatient companions had travelled far so that she could conduct business. It would be best to conclude these matters now and not have to travel back home in the spring.

Bishop Örjan was a tall, thin man with a neck like a crane and a bobbing Adam's apple. He stammered a bit when he talked. Cecilia Rosa thought she could tell immediately that he was not very bright, although she reproached herself for such a hasty judgment, since a person's appearance did not necessarily match his inner qualities.

But her preconceived opinion turned out to be correct, for when she innocently suggested that she and some of her companions along with the bishop and some of his companions should drink a grave ale together in the *hospitium* before they parted, he was quick to find this a very good suggestion.

As the only woman in the *hospitium*, she naturally led the bishop to the table, and of course he grew more talkative the more he drank. At first he complained that he, as a member of the Sverker clan, had been able to win only the new bishopric in Växjö. All the new promotions of importance in the church were now going to those who were either Folkungs or Eriks or related to them in some way.

With that Cecilia Rosa had learned her first important bit of information.

It wasn't long before the bishop expressed concern as he enquired whether Cecilia Rosa – who, as far as he knew, had been close to Queen Cecilia Blanca during her time at Gudhem – knew exactly when Cecilia Blanca had taken her convent vows before Mother Rikissa.

With that Cecilia Rosa had acquired her second important piece of information, but now her blood turned to ice.

She tried not to let on, she tried to pour more ale down her throat and giggle a little when she replied, but then she told him the truth: that Cecilia Blanca had never taken any convent vows. On the contrary, the two of them had promised each other never to do so, and they had lived as close friends for many years at Gudhem.

Bishop Örjan then fell silent as he pondered this news for a moment. Then he said that naturally he couldn't break the confidentiality of the confession, but he could say something about what Mother Rikissa had written in her last will, which he had promised before God to send to the Holy Father in Rome. In that document it said that Queen Cecilia Blanca had taken convent vows at Gudhem.

To hide the fear that now came over Cecilia Rosa, she served Bishop Örjan more ale to give herself time to think. He drank it down in one gulp.

She had now obtained her third important piece of information.

Shouldn't such a testament be sent to the archbishop as quickly as possible? she then asked as innocently as she could.

No, it shouldn't. For two reasons. First, the country's other archbishop Jon had recently been murdered in Sigtuna when the wild folk from across the Eastern Sea had plundered the town, so at the moment there was no archbishop. And if Mother Rikissa's testament was to go to Rome, then it would be an unnecessary detour for him to take it via Östra Aros. There he would have to wait for a new archbishop, who

408

would surely also be a Folkung, Bishop Örjan muttered crossly. So he now thought he would honour his oath to the dying abbess Rikissa by travelling south and handing over the testament to his Danish kinsman, Bishop Absalon in Lund.

With that Cecilia Rosa had now acquired her fourth important piece of information. At once she poured more ale for the bishop and giggled happily when he put his hand on her thigh, although she was repulsed.

Cecilia Rosa now realized that she knew all she needed to know, because nothing else was of any importance. So she attempted to do what she had quickly realized was a hopeless endeavour: to talk sense into this fool of a bishop.

First she cautiously pointed out that she and Cecilia Blanca had spent more than six years together at Gudhem as the closest and dearest of friends. It was hard to imagine that one of them would have done something as momentous as to take vows without telling the other.

The bishop then made a concerted effort to act dignified and stern while he was drunk, replying that the vows a person took before God, like everything that was said in confession, were to be forever kept secret from the rest of the world.

Cecilia Rosa feigned concern as she objected that the venerable bishop might not know how things were done in a convent. But it so happened that if anyone took the vows, she instantly became a novice. She then had to undergo a year of probation and was immediately separated from all novices and lay-sisters. If Cecilia Blanca truly had taken the vows, then wouldn't it have been noticed, if only by those within the convent?

To this the bishop slurred some vague reply that much was seen by God alone and that only He could look into the souls of human beings.

Since Cecilia Rosa could make no objection to that observation, she at once changed tactics. She herself had understood through Mother Rikissa's own words that the abbess had refrained from confessing her mortal sins before she departed this life. Surely a person who lied in such a situation could hardly be expected to tell the truth, especially when it concerned an outlandish assertion that the queen had taken the vows and then given birth to four children in sin. For wasn't that what this was all about?

Yes, that was indeed what this was about, admitted bishop Bengt in the middle of a yawn, but then he quickly changed his mind. No, it was all about the sin itself, he hastened to explain. The sin was at the heart of the matter. One couldn't take into account the fact that the sin in this particular case had certain consequences for the throne of the realm. Then he asked whether Cecilia Rosa might want to accompany him to Denmark. Of course there was some talk that bishops would no longer be able to marry before God, but there were simple solutions for getting around that problem. And he had plenty of silver, the bishop bragged ignorantly, so why not?

By now Cecilia Rosa had all the information she needed, but she also felt sullied and besmirched, as if the bishop had thrown filth on her.

She therefore excused herself by saying that for female reasons that she could not mention she had to withdraw at once. When he then tried to fumble after her she quickly slipped away, since she was not nearly as drunk as he was.

When she at last emerged into the fresh air she vomited. And all night long she prayed, unable to sleep because she knew that her sins were many. Using deception she had seduced a bishop, she had even let him touch her sinfully, and all this she had done in order to fool him into saying what he didn't want to say.

All this caused her shame. But she felt most ashamed that the touch of this scarcely honourable man had instantly ignited a longing that she had always tried to suppress. He had made her picture once again in her mind the last time Arn had come riding into the courtyard. It seemed an almost unforgivable sin that her pure love could have been inflamed by such an evil man.

The second matter that she had to take care of at Gudhem was much easier than the first. She bought all the plants and sewing materials she needed from a confused prioress who without Cecilia Rosa's friendly advice would have been cheated badly in these deals. Gudhem was once again a house of the Virgin Mary, and for that reason it was owed the greatest reverence.

But Cecilia Rosa also thought that if she had remained at Gudhem she would be very careful about where she set her feet in the arcade. Mother Rikissa was not in Paradise, after all. Perhaps she was lying in her grave with her malicious red eyes gleaming beneath the flagstones in the arcade. She might be ready to spring up like a wolf and swallow any of those she hated, for hatred had been her strongest force in earthly life.

On her way home to Riseberga, Cecilia Rosa had to stop for a few days, as planned, with Cecilia Blanca at Näs. When she reached the king's harbour on the shore of Lake Vättern, her impatient companions began muttering as they loaded all the strange items she had brought from Gudhem into the sinister-looking black longboat. The mere sight of the vessel made Cecilia Rosa turn pale. Out on Vättern the waves were high with whitecaps foaming at their tops. The first autumn storm was moving in.

She asked her way among rough sailors who seemed to be Norwegians until she stood before the one who appeared to be their leader. He greeted her courteously and said that his name was Styrbjørn Haraldsson, and that it would be a pleasure for him to sail a woman who was the friend of the queen out to Näs. Cecilia Rosa anxiously asked whether it was advisable to venture out on the water in a storm. He smiled in reply and shook his head, saying that such questions made him long for home, but that his loyalty to King Knut unfortunately prevented his return. Then without another word he took her by the hand and led her out onto the wharf, where his men were about to cast off. They put in place a wide plank for Cecilia Rosa to board the boat, tossed her purchases from Gudhem on deck, and stowed the cargo securely. Then they shoved off with the oars and hoisted the sail.

The wind at once took hold of the rectangular sail, filling it out completely with sudden force. In the next instant the vessel was slung forward so that Cecilia Rosa, who had not managed to sit down, was thrown back into the arms of Styrbjørn. He immediately pressed her down into her place by the tiller and wrapped her up in rough blankets and sheepskins so that only the tip of her nose stuck out.

The storm roared around them and the waves surged against the planking. The longship leaned so much that Cecilia Rosa saw only dark clouds on one side; on the other side she thought she could look straight down into the menacing black waters of the agitated lake. For a moment she felt paralysed with fear.

None of these strange, burly men seemed the least bothered. They sat leaning against the side of the vessel that rose up toward the sky and seemed now and then to joke with each other as best they could in all the noise. They must know what they are doing, she reasoned desperately. When she glanced back at the man called Styrbjørn she saw that he was standing up with the wind tearing at his long hair, his legs wide apart in a confident stance and a happy grin spreading across his bearded face. He seemed to enjoy sailing.

She still couldn't help yelling out two questions to him; she wanted to know whether it was dangerous to venture out in a storm, and whether they were sure that someone was holding a protective hand over them all. She had to repeat the questions twice, each time a little louder, although Styrbjørn had leaned down toward her to hear what she was asking.

When Styrbjørn finally grasped what she wanted to know, he first threw back his head and gave a hearty bellow so that the storm once again tore at his long hair and blew it into his face. Then he leaned down and yelled to her that things had been worse earlier in the day when they were rowing *against* the wind to reach the harbour. Now they were sailing *with* the wind, and it was like a dance; they would be there within half an hour, no more.

And so it was. Cecilia Rosa saw the castle of Näs approaching at a dizzying speed, and all at once all the Norsemen rose as one man and sat down at the oars while Styrbjørn took down the sail. The men on the left side put their oars in the water first and drew them backward, while the men on the other side dug in their heels and rowed forward. It was as though a giant hand had tossed the whole vessel up into the wind, and it took only ten strokes or so before they came into the lee and the bow of the ship glided up on shore.

Witnessing the men's skill, as Cecilia Rosa did now, made her feel a bit ashamed of her worries at the start of the passage.

On the path up toward the castle, as Styrbjørn politely led her before the others, she begged him in somewhat veiled terms to forgive the fear she had expressed, because clearly there was no cause for alarm.

Styrbjørn merely gave her a friendly smile since he deemed her apology unnecessary, and he assured her that she was not the only woman from Western Götaland who had little understanding when it came to ships. Once, he told her, there was a young woman who actually asked if they might get lost on the way. At this he laughed boisterously, and Cecilia Rosa responded with a cautious smile, unsure what was so humourous about that woman's concern.

Soon thereafter Cecilia Blanca welcomed her dearest friend, as she told anyone within earshot. The queen was so happy and excited that her words tumbled out like the song of the lark in the springtime, impossible to stop. She summoned servants to stow away Cecilia Rosa's leather sacks containing spiny plants and pelts and sewing implements. Then she took Cecilia Rosa by the arm and hurried her through several gloomy halls to a great fireplace where she offered her mulled wine. She thought that was the best remedy after such a cold crossing.

Cecilia Rosa basked in the warmth of her friend's kindness and her eagerness to please, but she also fretted about the evil news that would soon have to be told. But it was not easy to broach the subject. The king and the jarl were up in Östra Aros to arrange for a new archbishop, since plunderers from across the Eastern Sea had killed the old one. Besides, the Estonians had burned down the whole town of Sigtuna, so the men had plenty to do, including new crusades and shipbuilding that needed to be done. The advantage, though, was that the two Cecilias now had Näs all to themselves, because when the king and jarl weren't around, the queen was in charge. Here they could talk all night and drink plenty of mulled wine!

For a little while Cecilia Rosa let herself be carried away by her friend's irresistible merriment and joy. It was true that they were now celebrating the hour when they could meet as free women at last; now all three of the friends from Gudhem were free.

At that point Cecilia Rosa thought of speaking about the topic that could not be ignored. But before she could say anything, Cecilia Blanca began recounting with shining eyes and little laughs how things had fared for little Ulvhilde – well, she wasn't so little anymore, since she was expecting her first child.

Just as Cecilia Blanca had supposed, the eldest son at Ulfshem, Folke, was not to Ulvhilde's taste at all, despite the fact that he was the one who at first had tried to court her. His aggressive manner had, as one might imagine, only destroyed his chances, but soon Ulvhilde had become more interested in the younger son, Jon. And since Jon could not impress Ulvhilde by waving about a sword and bow, he talked more about how a country must be built by laws, and other such things he had learned. He could also sing beautifully, and so it wasn't difficult to imagine how things would go. Their bridal ale would take place soon, which was fortunate considering that she was already expecting their first child.

At that news Cecilia Rosa had been more shocked than happy. Because expecting a child before the bridal ale was celebrated and the bedding completed, could cost young people dearly. She herself knew more about this harsh truth than did most others.

But Cecilia Rosa brushed aside her concern at once. These were new times. Whoever was to become archbishop would probably not want to make his first decision the excommunication of someone who had the protection of the king and the jarl. So Ulvhilde's minor sin would soon be blessed by God, and nothing more would be heard of it. She was very happy, their little friend, and freedom had embraced her with open arms.

Relieved to hear that Ulvhilde didn't seem to be in the danger Cecilia Rosa had at first imagined, she finally held up both hands to stop her friend's happy chatter and tell her the truth. She brought ominous tidings from Gudhem. Cecilia Blanca fell silent at once.

But they got off to a bad start. For when Cecilia Rosa took a deep breath and started by reporting solemnly that Mother Rikissa was now dead and buried, Cecilia Blanca clapped her hands and burst out in delighted laughter. Then she promptly crossed herself and raised her eyes heavenward, praying for forgiveness since it was a sin to rejoice at someone else's death. Afterwards she regained her cheerful demeanour and said that this was certainly not bad news.

Cecilia Rosa had to start over. But she didn't get very far into her story of the false confession and the abbess's testament that was supposed to be sent to Rome before Cecilia Blanca turned serious.

When Cecilia Rosa finished her account, they sat for a moment in silence. Because what was there actually to say about the lie itself? It was absurd to think that any unfortunate maiden who had been forced under Rikissa's scourge at Gudhem would consider taking her vows at that particular convent. It was even more unreasonable to expect that Cecilia Blanca, who had always longed to escape and return to her betrothed and her queen's crown, would renounce her own future and instead become Rikissa's slave. It was like saying that birds flew in water and fish swam in the sky.

They interrupted the conversation so that Cecilia Blanca could take her friend to say hello to her children before they continued their night together. They knew it would be a long one.

The queen's eldest son Erik was with his father up in Östra Aros, since he had much to learn about matters that were a king's concern. The other two sons and the daughter Brigida were fighting so wildly over a wooden horse that the maidservant couldn't stop them. When the two Cecilias came in, the children calmed down at once, but they stared with some amusement at Cecilia Rosa's odd clothing. After evening prayers the two Cecilias amazed the children by singing together a hymn that was lovelier than any ever sung at Näs. They evidently hadn't expected to hear such a heavenly song from their mother. They went to bed without a fuss, chirping with delight about this new song of their mother's.

As the two friends headed back to the fireplace, where more mulled wine awaited them, Cecilia Blanca explained in embarrassment that she hadn't done much singing during her freedom, because she thought she'd had enough of it at Gudhem. But when they sang together it was different; then she remembered their dear friendship instead of the chill mornings at dawn when, groggy with sleep, they would stumble across the cold floor to the miserable *Lauds*.

When they sat once again by the cosy fire, with no hostile ears to hear them and with wine in their hands, it was time to try and make sense of the situation.

Cecilia Blanca began by saying that Rikissa's intention was to make the Holy Father in Rome declare that King Knut of Western Götaland, Eastern Götaland, and Svealand, and the archbishopric of Östra Aros, was living in whoredom. That meant that little jarl Erik had been conceived in whoredom and could not inherit the crown, nor could any of her other sons.

It was no surprise that Rikissa wanted to send this message directly to the Holy Father in Rome. Nor that the message should go via Denmark, where the Sverkers had all their exiled kinsmen and where many of them had married close relatives of the king. The fire and the war that Rikissa had predicted on her deathbed was thus the war when the Sverkers would return to seize the king's crown. That was how Rikissa had imagined the outcome.

But her entire calculation was built upon a lie, Cecilia Rosa argued. What was written in her testament was not true. How such a document might be read in Rome was one matter, but when it was presented before a Swedish archbishop, the matter would be cast in a different light.

They now fell to brooding over whether the lie might actually prevail. They found it easier to understand the fact that Rikissa had given her soul to get revenge, even if it was a terrifying thought that any person could be so evil as to condemn herself to the eternal fire for the sake of revenge.

She probably looked on it as a sacrifice, Cecilia Rosa said; she sacrificed her soul to save her kinsmen. Like a mother or father who would give up their own lives for their child. The Cecilias could shudder at what Rikissa had done, but also understand it, especially since they'd had the misfortune to observe first hand the evil ways of Rikissa during her earthly life.

It was as if they suddenly felt a chill despite the warmth of the log fire. Cecilia Blanca got up, went over to her friend, kissed her, adjusted the pelts around her, and then went to arrange for some more wine.

When she came back, they tried to free themselves of Rikissa's evil spirit in the room. They consoled each other that at least they'd learned the news in good time, and that Birger Brosa would certainly be able to make use of this information. Then they tried to talk about other things.

Cecilia Rosa wondered a bit about Ulvhilde. She had hardly managed to set foot outside Gudhem before she was on the way to the bridal bed. She had even tried out that bed. Was this really a good thing? In her innocence hadn't she been delivered up like a lamb? She had only known two noblemen in her life of freedom, and now she was going to share the bed and position of one of them. Was that really such a good idea?

Cecilia Blanca thought that it was. She knew Jon, after all, and she had been quite sure that things would go the way they did, because she also knew Ulvhilde. Naturally it was a good union between Sverkers and Folkungs that no one could fault, but that was only one side of the matter. The other thing to take into account was that certain people seemed to be made for each other. Surely Cecilia Rosa and Arn had been like that. So it might well be the same for Ulvhilde and Jon Sigurdson. Cecilia Rosa would soon see for herself, because she had decided that at Christmas they would all get together for a big Christmas feast at Näs.

At these last words Cecilia Rosa grew so pensive that for a moment she almost forgot where she was. As if it were the most natural thing in the world, her friend the queen had invited everyone to a Christmas feast. And now that she had embarked on this new life, it *was* straightforward and natural. Cecilia Rosa was free; she could even decline the invitation if she wished, but she had no intention of doing so. Yet the mere possibility of declining, she thought, growing sleepy, was one of the strangest things about her new freedom.

She fell asleep with her glass in her hand, unused as she was to this particular aspect of the free life, the right to drink as much mulled wine as she liked.

Cecilia Blanca summoned some castle maids who carried her friend off to bed.

The next day brought a great change in Cecilia Rosa. The queen's maidservants took her to be bathed and scrubbed, but mostly they concentrated on her hair, which they untangled and brushed out, combed and clipped where it was rough and unevenly cut. Haircuts at the cloister were meant to keep the hair short, not to keep it beautiful, because it would never be displayed anyway.

Cecilia Blanca had thought a great deal about what new clothes she should give her friend. It was obvious to her that they couldn't be the most beautiful clothes; the leap from the loose brown or undyed garments of the convent to those of a mistress of a fortress would have been too great. Besides, she had understood without having to ask that Cecilia Rosa did not want to move to Näs merely as the queen's friend; she was much too headstrong for that. Cecilia Blanca grasped very well that her friend's dearest wish was that Arn Magnusson would return home. Whether this hope would be answered after all these years was impossible to know, but the chances were probably not very great. So that was not a good topic of conversation either. Time would take its course, and with it would come answers, whether one wanted to hear them or not.

Cecilia Blanca decided that Cecilia Rosa should continue her journey from Näs wearing a brown mantle as worn in the cloister by lay-sisters, but made of much softer lambs' wool. A mantle in her clan colours would have been much too sensitive an issue, because Cecilia Rosa actually belonged to the Pål clan, so she should have a green mantle. But she had always thought of herself as Arn Magnusson's bride and thus always pictured herself wearing a blue Folkung mantle. But the truth was that Cecilia Rosa's betrothal to Arn Magnusson, no matter how real it might be for her, was not valid in the Church. So a brown mantle in the cloister colour was the best choice for the time being.

On the other hand, surely a secular *yconoma*, who had been hired by the convent, would have the right to wear whatever worldly clothing she liked. So Cecilia Blanca also had a green dress sewn, because she thought that the green would go particularly well with Cecilia Rosa's red hair. Finally, as if to add a hint of her Folkung connection, she had exchanged Cecilia Rosa's black wimple for a blue one, the precise blue colour that she knew so well, which she could even make with her own hands.

It took a bit of persuasion to get Cecilia Rosa to dress in all this finery, and also to wear her red hair loose for a whole day without covering her head. It was a way of practicing for the future, according to Cecilia Blanca.

The queen realized, but perhaps too late, that this single day of practice might not be enough. For when evening approached she again took Cecilia Rosa to the maidservants' chamber to be dressed in the much more beautiful green dress, fastening a silver sash around her waist and a silver clasp in her hair. She explained that company was coming to supper that evening.

Then she took Cecilia Rosa to her own rooms, where there was a big polished mirror in which she could see herself from head to toe. Cecilia Blanca was all aquiver to see her friend's reaction.

When Cecilia Rosa looked at herself, at first she was struck dumb, and it was impossible to read in her face what she was thinking. But then she suddenly began to weep and had to sit down. Cecilia Blanca comforted her for a long while before she managed to find out what had caused this unexpected sadness.

She had turned old and ugly, Cecilia Rosa sobbed. This wasn't the way she remembered herself; this was somebody else who was old and ugly.

Cecilia Blanca consoled her with a kiss but then laughed out loud. She took her friend by the hand and led her back to the mirror so that they could both look at the same time.

'Now you can see both of us,' she said with feigned sternness. 'I have looked at you for many years without being able to see myself, just as you have seen me. Well, here I stand with my stomach sticking out and breasts that hang and a pudgy face, and there you stand next to me. The mirror cannot lie. It sees a beautiful woman who is only thirty-seven years old but looks younger, and it sees me, forty years old and looking my age. Time has not taken a toll on you as much as you think, dearest Cecilia Rosa.'

Cecilia Rosa stood in silence for a moment, staring at their reflections. Then she spun around, threw her arms around Cecilia Blanca, and begged her forgiveness. She was so unaccustomed to seeing herself and that was why she was shocked by her reflection. And she soon cheered up again.

But this unusual reaction on the part of her friend did not make Cecilia Blanca feel any less worried, because she now realized that she had saved one secret for far too long. And soon there would be little time left to keep silent about it.

The person who was coming to the evening banquet, riding from the north end of Visingö and travelling from Bjälbo, was Magnus Månesköld, Cecilia Rosa's son. The sole purpose of his visit was to meet his mother for the first time.

Cecilia Blanca realized that there were two possibilities. One was not to say anything and let mother and son get to know each other by themselves.

The other option was to tell her friend the truth right now, with all the uneasiness that might entail.

She asked Cecilia Rosa to sit down before the mirror and pretended that she was going to fix her hair. She fetched a brush and combs and began brushing her friend's hair, and kept on for a while, because it was very soothing. Then she said as if in passing, almost as if her thoughts were elsewhere, that oh, there was one more thing. Magnus Månesköld would be coming to tonight's supper. They could ride out to meet him if she liked.

Cecilia Rosa suddenly froze, and she stared at herself in the mirror for a long time. Tears glinted in her eyes without falling; but she said nothing. To hide her concern, Cecilia Blanca resumed brushing the lovely red hair, which was still a bit too short.

The storm had long since abated over Lake Vättern, and there were only a few clouds in the sky when the two of

422

them, without escort, rode to the north on the island of Visingö. They said little on the way, although Cecilia Blanca complimented her friend for how well she rode. Cecilia Rosa said something about the weather and the lovely evening.

In a clearing in the woods where the oaks had been cut down to make longboats years ago, they met three riders. All three of them wore Folkung mantles. The one riding in front was the youngest, and his hair shone red in the evening sun.

When the three men saw the queen and the woman riding next to her, they reined in their horses at once. The young red-haired man dismounted and began walking across the clearing.

Custom now demanded that Cecilia Rosa remain seated on her horse and calmly wait for the man to approach her, bow, and offer her his hand so that she could dismount safely from her saddle. Then they would greet each other.

Cecilia Rosa would undoubtedly have known this when she was seventeen years old, and she would have behaved as custom required. It was not certain that she would remember the custom after so many years in the cloister.

Nonetheless, as nimbly as if she were still seventeen, she leaped to the ground in a manner that was anything but courtly and rushed across the clearing, taking steps that were too long for her green dress, so that she stumbled a little.

When Magnus Månesköld saw this he also began to run, and they met in the middle of the clearing and embraced each other without a word.

Then they took each other by the shoulders so that they could look into each other's eyes. They looked like mirror images.

Magnus Månesköld had brown eyes and red hair; he was the only one in his adopted family who had such colouring.

They gazed at each other for a long time, but neither could say a word. Then Magnus dropped to his knees before her, took her right hand, and kissed it tenderly. This was the sign that he legally acknowledged his mother.

When he stood up he took her hand and slowly led her back to her horse. There he again knelt down as he handed her the horse's reins, held the stirrup, and bade her step on his back to get into the saddle, as custom demanded.

Not until she was well seated on her horse did he speak.

'I have had many thoughts and dreams about you, my Mother,' he said, somewhat embarrassed. 'Perhaps I thought that I might recognize you, but not with as much certainty as you and I did just now. And I never would have imagined, despite what my dear kinsman Birger Brosa told me, that it would be like seeing a sister rather than a mother. Would you therefore allow me the honour of escorting you to this evening's banquet, dear Mother?'

'That you may,' said Cecilia Rosa, smiling a bit at her son's formal way of speaking.

Magnus Månesköld was a young man with down on his cheeks who had not yet come close to the time when his kinsmen would begin to think of choosing a bride for him. But he was also a man who had grown up in the fortresses of power, so he knew to behave as custom demanded. He wore the Folkung mantle with the confidence that showed he understood its value, and its significance. When they approached Näs in the last rays of the setting sun he rode up beside his mother and said something about the evening chill as he hung his blue mantle over her shoulders. This was how he wanted to ride in with her to the king's castle at Näs. He said nothing of this to his mother, but she understood.

At the banquet he drank ale like a man, but not wine as the two Cecilias did. At the beginning of the evening he spoke with them mostly about what their imprisonment at Gudhem had been like, because he had never been able to imagine such a thing. Only now did he learn for sure that Gudhem was the place where he was born, and something about the circumstances.

But as both the Cecilias had expected would happen, and as they had discussed using the sign language that only they understood outside the cloister, Magnus Månesköld soon began to ask cautious questions about his father. He wanted to know the truth about Arn Magnusson's skill with the sword and bow. Cecilia Rosa answered his questions without reservation, for the fear she had felt only hours ago had now been replaced by a warm happiness. She explained that all the tales about him wielding the sword were something she had only heard others tell, although there were many stories. But once she had seen Arn Magnusson shoot with the bow at a banquet at Husaby royal estate, and he did so quite passably.

Just as Cecilia Blanca was signing behind the prodigal son's back what she thought he would ask next, he did wonder how good his father's skill had been.

'He hit a silver coin with two arrows from a distance of twenty-five paces,' Cecilia Rosa replied without blinking. 'At least I think it was twenty-five paces, but maybe it was twenty. The target was definitely a silver coin.'

At first young Magnus was absolutely dumbstruck. Then the tears welled up in his eyes, and he leaned over toward his mother and embraced her for a long time.

Behind his back Cecilia Blanca then asked in signs whether it was really a silver coin.

No doubt an unusually large silver coin, Cecilia Rosa signed back and then sank into the delightful warmth of her son's embrace. The way he smelled brought back a memory, something that reminded her of youth and love.

* * *

Just before Katarinamas, when the temperature already was so cold that it presaged a hard winter, Birger Brosa arrived on a hurried visit to Riseberga. He met with the prioress Beata only long enough so as not to appear impolite at the convent, which naturally belonged to the Virgin Mary, though he probably viewed it as his own property.

Above all he wanted to meet with the *yconoma*. Since the early cold made it difficult to sit comfortably outside, they had to sit together in her bookkeeping chamber, which she'd had built in the same manner as the one at Gudhem.

He spoke first about business, but with his thoughts clearly on another matter, since he continually kept mentioning his upcoming crusade to the east in the spring.

Then he commenced talking about what was really on his mind. There was still no abbess at Riseberga. If Cecilia Rosa now took her vows, she would at once be promoted to the position, based on her long experience of the cloister world. He had spoken with the new archbishop about the matter and there should be no obstacles to her becoming abbess. Impatiently he seemed to be demanding an immediate answer.

Cecilia Rosa felt faint and stunned by the news. She couldn't imagine that the jarl, who knew Queen Cecilia Blanca so well, could have the slightest belief that she would want to take the vows.

After she had collected herself and thought it over, she looked him straight in the eye and asked what was the real intention behind this question. She wasn't stupid, and no one in the entire realm was smarter than the jarl, so there must be some reason that weighed very heavily for him to make such an unexpected demand.

Then Birger Brosa gave her his familiar broad smile. He sat down comfortably with one leg drawn up under himself, clasped his hands around his knee, and looked at Cecilia

Rosa for a moment before he told her the reason, although not straight out.

'In truth you would be a jewel as one of the wives in the Folkung clan, Cecilia,' he began. 'In a way you are already, and that's why I've come to you with this solemn request.'

'Request?' Cecilia Rosa interrupted, terrified.

'Well, let's call it a question. Your knowledge in the handling of accounts and silver is probably matched only by Eskil's. Yes, Eskil is Arn's brother, and it is he who manages the affairs of the realm. You cannot be fooled with duplicitous words, so I will speak to you bluntly. We need an abbess who can counterbalance the false witness of another abbess. That is how things stand.'

'You could have told me as much when you first arrived, my dear jarl,' Cecilia Rosa protested. 'So the false witness of this liar was carried all the way to Rome?'

'Yes, it was carried all the way to Rome by hands that were all too willing,' replied Birger Brosa gloomily. 'Right now we may have refractory forces in the east that have to be crushed once and for all, but farther in the future we may have a great war facing us if things go wrong.'

'A great war with the Sverkers and Danes?'

'Yes, exactly.'

'Because King Knut's son Erik might be judged a bastard?'

'Yes, you understand it all.'

'And in Rome the words of the queen and myself count for naught against a letter from a lying abbess?'

'I assume that is so.'

'If I take the vows then it's the word of one abbess against another?'

'Yes, and you may save the country from war.'

At that Cecilia Rosa fell silent. She caught herself musing that she probably shouldn't have such a hasty conversation with a man like Birger Brosa, because he was said to have the best mind in the country. She needed to gain time to think this over.

'It's strange how God arranges things in this world and guides the path people take,' she began, the confidence of her words belying the confusion that she felt inside.

'Yes, it is truly strange,' Birger Brosa agreed when he could think of nothing else to say.

'Rikissa sold her soul to the Devil in order to plunge the country into war. Isn't that strange?'

'Yes, it is very strange,' Birger Brosa agreed, a bit impatiently.

'And now you want me to deliver up my soul to the Virgin Mary at the prime of my earthly life so that we can counter this sin?' Cecilia Rosa went on with an innocent expression.

'Though your words are harsh, you have grasped the situation most succinctly,' replied Birger Brosa.

'People will say that the new abbess was once long ago a maiden who hated Rikissa, who refused to forgive her even on her deathbed, and therefore her words are not worth water!' Cecilia Rosa burst out in a tone that astonished herself more than the jarl.

'You're thinking sharply but you are very stubborn, Cecilia Rosa,' he said after pondering for a moment. 'But you have an opportunity to save the country from war with a sacrifice which requires that you become an abbess. Riseberga will be your realm, and here you can rule as queen; it's not at all like being whipped by some Rikissa. What could you do with your life that would be better than to serve your kinsmen, your queen, and your king?'

'Now you're the one who is being stubborn, Birger Brosa. Would you like to know what I've been praying and hoping for every night for twenty years? Do you understand in your warrior's soul how long twenty years in a cage is? I'm speaking to you so boldly and frankly not merely because I feel despair

428

at what you're asking me to do, but because I know that you're fond of me and don't mind such blunt talk.'

'That's true, my dear Cecilia Rosa, that's true,' sighed the jarl, now in retreat.

Without a word Cecilia Rosa left him then and was gone for a while. When she returned she held a magnificent Folkung mantle in her hands. She turned it back and forth a few times so that the gold threads in the lion on the back flashed in the candlelight; she let him stroke the soft fur on the inside. He nodded his admiration but without saying a word.

'For two years I worked on this,' Cecilia Rosa explained. 'It has been like my dream. Now we have it here at Riseberga to examine and copy, because we are still far behind Gudhem in this art.'

'It is truly very beautiful,' said Birger Brosa pensively. 'I've never seen such a lovely blue colour and such a powerful lion.' He already sensed what Cecilia Rosa was going to say next.

'Do you understand, my dear kinsman, for whom I sewed this mantle?'

'Yes, and may God grant that you may drape it over Arn Magnusson's shoulders. I understand your dream, Cecilia Rosa. I probably understand better than you might believe what you were thinking during the years it took you to sew this mantle. But you must still listen to me and also understand. If Arn does not come soon, then I will buy this mantle from you for the day when Magnus Månesköld will drink his bridal ale, or the day when Erik Knutsson will be crowned, or whatever else may suit me. You cannot hope too long, Cecilia Rosa; you owe that much to your kinsmen.'

'Then let us now pray for Arn's speedy return,' said Cecilia Rosa, lowering her eyes.

Faced with such an exhortation there was no choice for either man or jarl, especially not in a convent, and in a convent he happened to own. Birger Brosa nodded that they should pray.

They knelt down together among the account books and abacuses and prayed for Arn Magnusson's salvation and swift return.

Cecilia Rosa prayed for the sake of her burning love, which had not faded in twenty years, and which she would rather die than relinquish.

The jarl prayed for a more complicated reason, but with equal sincerity. Yet he thought that if they couldn't arrange the matter of the succession to the throne as simply as pitting one abbess's oath against another's, then they would probably need all the good warriors they could muster on the Folkung side.

And as he had heard recently from blessed Father Henri at Varnhem, Arn Magnusson was a warrior by God's Grace in more than one respect. In the worst case, he would soon be needed at home.

ELEVEN

Arn was kept for two weeks at the Hamediyeh Hospital in Damascus before the doctors managed to stop the fever from his wounds. They believed it was God's providence that he recovered, because no one could live much longer with such a fever. From earlier battles he had more scars on his body than he could count, but he assumed they might be more than a hundred. Yet he had never been wounded so badly as at the Horns of Hattin.

He didn't remember much from the early stages of the battle. They had carried him away, cut off all his chain mail, and sewn up the worst of the wounds before they took him along with the wounded Syrians and Egyptians up into the hills where it was cooler. Arn and the other wounded soldiers had suffered greatly during the move, and most of them began bleeding again. But the doctors thought it would be even worse for them to remain in the heat among the flies and stench of corpses down below near Tiberias.

How Arn later came to Damascus he did not remember; by the time they moved him out of the field infirmary in the hills, a terrible fever had set in.

In Damascus the doctors had cut open some of his wounds,

tried to clean them, and then sewn them back up, although this time with greater precision than what had been done at the field hospital near Tiberias.

The worst wounds were a deep gash from a sword that had sliced through his chain mail and deep into his calf, and an axe-blow that had cracked his helmet diagonally above his left eye, ripping his eyebrow and the left side of his forehead. At first he hadn't been able to keep any food down, but vomited up everything they tried to force into him. And he suffered from a murderous headache so that the fogs of fever that began to seep into his mind actually came as a relief.

He didn't remember any pain to speak of, not even when they cauterized his leg wound with a red-hot iron.

When the fever finally broke, the first thing he discovered was that he could again see out of both eyes, for he remembered that he had been blind in the left eye.

His bed was on the second floor of the hospital in a lovely room with blue mosaics, looking straight out into the shadow of tall palms. Now and then the wind gently rustled the palm fronds, and down in the courtyard he could hear the sound of fountains.

The doctors treated him with cool courtesy in the beginning, doing their work as well as their professional skill permitted. Above Arn's bed hung a little picture in black and gold with Saladin's Arabic calligram, which clearly showed that Arn was worth more to the sultan living than dead, despite the whispers that he was one of the white demons with the red cross.

When the fever subsided and Arn could begin to speak coherently, the doctors' joy at his recovery was ever greater when they heard to their astonishment a Templar knight speaking God's language. As doctors in Damascus they did not know what at least half the emirs in the army knew about the man who was called Al Ghouti.

432

The most distinguished of all the doctors was named Moses ben Maimon; he had travelled up from Cairo where he had been Saladin's personal physician for many years. To Arn's ears his Arabic had a foreign sound, because he had been born in far-off Andalusia. Life in that region had been hard for the Jews, he told Arn at their first meeting. Arn was not surprised that Saladin's personal physician was a Jew, because he knew that the Caliph of Baghdad, the supreme leader of the Muslims, had many Jews in his service. And since his experience with Saracen doctors had shown him that they were all knowledgeable in the rules of both the faith and philosophy, he took care to ask about the significance of Jerusalem for the Jews. At that Moses ben Maimon raised his eyebrows in surprise and asked Arn what could make a Christian warrior take interest in such a thing. Arn told him about his meeting with the high rabbi from Baghdad and what it had led to, at least for as long as Arn held power in Jerusalem. If the Christians viewed God's Grave as a holy place in Jerusalem, he went on, and the Muslims had Abraham's rock where the Prophet, peace be unto him, had ascended to Heaven, then he could understand the power that these pilgrim sites had for the believers. But King David's temple? That was merely a building constructed by human beings and torn down by human beings; why would it be considered so holy?

Then the Jewish doctor patiently explained to Arn that Jerusalem was the only holy site of the Jews, and according to prophecy the Jews would return to reclaim their kingdom and build up the Temple anew. Arn gave a deep and sorrowful sigh, not for the sake of the Jews, he quickly pointed out when he saw his newfound friend look somewhat puzzled, but for the sake of Jerusalem. Soon Jerusalem would fall into Muslim hands, if it hadn't already happened. Then the Christians would spare no effort to take the city back. And if the Jews also got involved in the argument over Jerusalem, the war could go on for a thousand years or more.

Moses ben Maimon then went to get a little stool and sat down next to Arn's bed in order to continue this discussion in earnest, which suddenly seemed more important to him than anything else he had to do at the hospital.

He asked Arn to explain what he meant more clearly, and then recounted conversations he'd had with both Saladin and Count Raymond of Tripoli. Both of them – despite the fact that one was Muslim and the other Christian, each other's most dangerous foes on the battlefield – still seemed to reason the same way on this matter. The only way to bring an end to the eternal war would be to give equal rights to all pilgrims, no matter where their pilgrimage to the holy city was headed and regardless of whether they called it Al Quds or Jerusalem.

Or *Yerushalaim*, Moses ben Maimon added with a smile.

I agree, Arn said at once. These were the sorts of thoughts he had touched upon when he had given the rabbi from Baghdad permission for Jews to pray at the western wall. But back then he hadn't known the full extent of how sacred this wall was for Jews. The two men soon agreed that they ought to seek an occasion to speak with Saladin about this matter before he took the city.

Their friendship grew during the following weeks as Moses began to urge Arn to stand up and try to walk. The doctor's opinion was that he shouldn't wait either too short or too long a time to get back on his feet. In the first instance he risked tearing open the wound in his leg again, but if he delayed too long the leg might stiffen and grow weak.

At first they walked only a few turns around the garden among the palms and fountains and pools. It was easy to walk there, because the whole garden up to the roots of the palm trees was covered with mosaics. Soon Arn was allowed to borrow some clothes, and they could venture out on cautious promenades in the city. Since the great mosque stood only a stone's throw or two from the hospital, that was one of their first destinations. As infidels they were not allowed to enter the mosque itself, but they could go into the surrounding courtyard, where Moses showed him all the wonderful gold mosaics in the covered arcades. They clearly stemmed from the Christian era, while the Muslim patterns in black, white, and red in the marble floor were from the time of the Umayyads. Arn was astonished that all the Christian Byzantine art was allowed to remain untouched, since it depicted both people and saints, an art that most Muslims would regard as ungodly. And the great mosque was quite clearly a church, even though a minaret had been built beside it.

Moses ben Maimon pointed out that as far as he knew, it was the opposite in Jerusalem, where the two great mosques had now been churches for some time. It was practical, after all, he said with a hint of irony, to keep all such holy sites intact. Because as soon as somebody new conquered the structures, all they had to do was tear down the cross from the *cupola* and put up a crescent moon, or vice versa, depending on who won and who lost. It would be worse if they had to tear down the old holy sites every time and build new ones.

Because Arn knew nothing about the Jewish faith, this was one of their first major topics of discussion, and since he could read Arabic, Moses ben Maimon loaned him a book he had written himself entitled *Guide for the Perplexed*. Once Arn started to read the book, their conversations became endlessly long, for what Moses ben Maimon worked on most in his philosophy was to find the correct juncture between reason and faith, between the teachings of Aristotle and the pure faith, which many people believed to be free of reason and a revelation from God. Making these alleged opposites

435

mesh together seamlessly was the greatest task of philosophy, in his view.

With some difficulty Arn followed along in these lengthy arguments, for as he said, his mind had gone through a drought since the time in his youth when at least the ideas of Aristotle were with him every day. But he did agree that nothing could be more important than making faith reasonable. For the war in the Holy Land had shown with the power of an earthquake what blind, unreasoning faith would lead to. That so many men could walk across the trembling ground and say that they saw nothing and heard nothing was one of the great mysteries of the intellectual world.

Arn's scabs began to fall off, leaving angry red but healing scars; at the same time his friendship with the doctor and philosopher Moses ben Maimon grew, along with his ability to think of other things besides rules and obedience. He felt as though his body was not the only part of him undergoing the process of healing.

He may have cast himself with such hypnotic zeal into the world of the higher intellect because he wanted to push aside the gnawing knowledge of what was now happening outside in the rest of the world. But his unconscious effort to keep this knowledge at bay met with difficulties whenever others who were being cared for at the Hamediyeh Hospital had visitors. With jubilation they would announce that now Acre and Nablus had fallen, now Beirut or Jebail, now this or that fortress had been seized. It was not easy to be the only Christian when everyone around him reacted with such strong and boisterous joy at the influx of such news.

When Saladin's brother Fahkr came to visit Arn, all these reports from the outside world were soon confirmed, even though such matters were not the first things they discussed.

They were both moved by the meeting and immediately embraced each other as if they were brothers. Everyone in the beautiful garden who observed how they greeted each other was greatly surprised, for they recognized Saladin's brother.

The first thing that Fahkr reminded him of, which was unnecessary because Arn had thought about the matter several times already, was how they had joked when they parted in Gaza. That was back when Fahkr had been Arn's prisoner and was about to board the ship for Alexandria, and they had laughed about how amusing it would be if the roles of captive and guard were reversed. The present situation made them both think that God had seen fit to jest with them.

Arn pretended to be worried and upset that Fahkr might have complaints about the time he had spent as a prisoner in Gaza. Fahkr replied with the same feigned concern that his only objection was that he'd been forced to eat pig meat, which Arn heartily denied. And then they fell into each other's arms laughing again.

Then Fahkr turned serious for a moment and asked for Arn's word of honour that he would not try to escape or raise his weapon against anyone as long as he was Saladin's guest. If there was any rule against this, then they would unfortunately have to treat him more prudently. Arn explained that, first, there was no rule that forbade a Templar knight from keeping his sworn word, which he gave to Fahkr without protest; second, he could not be regarded as a Templar knight any longer since his time in service to the Order had expired on the evening after the battle at the Horns of Hattin.

Fahkr instantly turned serious and said that it must be seen as a sign from God that Arn's life was spared at the very moment that his time as a Templar knight ran out. Arn countered that if that was the case, he probably believed more in Saladin's mercy than in God's mercy, even though he no longer remembered exactly how things had gone.

Fahkr didn't reply, but hung a large gold medallion with

Saladin's monogram on it around Arn's neck. Then he took him by the arm and led him out to the street. Arn still felt a bit naked in his borrowed clothes, since he missed the weight of the chain mail. He was also bareheaded, and his short blond hair gleamed, making it impossible for him and Fahkr to walk along the street unnoticed. He seemed to arouse greater curiosity in the company of Fahkr than with Moses ben Maimon; as if it was more natural for a Jew and a Christian to walk together than for a Christian to walk with the sultan's brother.

A bit vexed by all this attention, Fahkr led Arn into the great bazaar located next to the mosque and bought a piece of fabric that Arn could wrap around his head a few times. Then Arn had to choose between some light Syrian mantles in the next stall; when he saw the blue colour of the Folkungs held out to him by an eager merchant, he made up his mind at once. Shortly after making these purchases it was as if Arn and Fahkr finally melted into the crowds among the stalls.

Now Fahkr led him through the winding alleys of the bazaar until they came to an opening leading to a courtyard, where there were piles of Christian weapons and shields and helmets. Fahkr explained that it was Saladin's express order that Arn should now select a new sword, preferably the most beautiful one he could find. As Saladin said, he owed Arn a costly sword. The merchant had separated all the Christian swords into two small piles and one giant one. In one of the two small piles lay all the articles of great value, swords that could have belonged to Christians of royal lineage, decorated with gold and precious stones. In the little pile next to it lay the swords that were considered the next finest, and in the large pile all those that were of lesser value.

Arn went straight over to the large pile and pulled out one Templar knight's sword after another and looked at the number marks. When he had found three swords with the proper size numbers, he compared them hastily and then handed one of them to Fahkr without hesitation.

Fahkr gazed with disappointment at the plain, unembellished sword and emphasized that Arn was passing up a fortune out of sheer stubbornness. Arn said that a sword was considered a treasure only by men who could not use it. A Templar knight's sword of the proper weight and size, such as the one he had just handed to him, was the only thing he would ever want to hang at his side. Fahkr tried to persuade him otherwise. Arn could choose the most expensive sword, sell it, and then buy the inexpensive one, which he could probably get for one or two dinars, and keep the difference. Arn snorted at this suggestion and said that it would hardly be honouring Saladin's gift to behave in such a manner.

But Fahkr wouldn't let him take the sword at once; instead he handed it to the merchant and whispered something that Arn didn't hear. Then they left the bazaar without the sword and made their way to Saladin's palace, where they would spend the evening and night. Perhaps Saladin himself would come home to Damascus tonight, and in that case Al Ghouti was one of the men he would want to see immediately; it was important to stay nearby, Fahkr explained.

Saladin's palace was located far from any of the larger buildings around the great mosque. It was a simple two-story house with few decorations, and if it hadn't been for the forbidding Mameluke guards outside the gate, nobody would have guessed that this was the sultan's residence. The rooms that they walked through were sparely furnished with rugs and cushions, while the walls were adorned only with beautifully painted quotations from the Koran, which Arn amused himself by reading and reciting as they walked past.

When they finally came to one of the rooms facing a long

balcony covered by an arcade, Fahkr served cold water and pomegranates and then sat down with an expression that was easy to understand. Now he wanted to turn to more serious matters.

What remained of the Christian reign in Palestine were Tyrus, Gaza, Ashkelon, Jerusalem, and a few fortresses, Fahkr told Arn with restrained triumph in his voice. First they would take Ashkelon and Gaza, and then it was Saladin's desire that Arn should accompany him. After that they would take Jerusalem itself, and Saladin also wanted to have Arn on hand as advisor when that time came. Saladin himself would convey this wish to Arn as soon as they met, so it would be wise for Arn to prepare his mind for what attitude he would take.

Arn replied sadly that of course he had known for a long time that things would go this way, and that the Christians had only themselves and, above all, their own sins to blame for this great misfortune. And indeed he was no longer bound by his oath to the Knights Templar. But it would be too much to ask that he join the side of his former enemy.

Fahkr tugged at his thin beard and replied pensively that Arn had probably misunderstood the sultan's wish. It was not a question of asking Arn to draw his sword against his own, but rather the opposite. A sufficient number of Christians had already been killed or driven from their homes in flight; that was not the issue any longer. But it would probably be best to allow Saladin to explain all this himself. Arn would, as he no doubt already had divined, still be released when the time was ripe, for Saladin had not spared Arn at the Horns of Hattin only to kill him later. Nor was Arn a prisoner for whom they could demand a ransom. But it would also be best if Arn spoke with Saladin in person about this. In the meantime they could discuss what Arn should do with his freedom.

Arn said that as far as he was concerned his twenty years of service in the Holy Land were at an end. If possible, he wanted to journey home to his own country as soon as that could be arranged. Yet he was concerned because even though he had indeed served the time bound by his oath, the Rule required that he be relieved of his duty by the Grand Master of the Order of the Knights Templar; otherwise he would be counted a deserter. And he had no idea how that could now be arranged.

Fahkr was apparently mightily amused by Arn's musings, and he explained that if Arn rubbed his thumb twice on the oil lamp in front of him, this wish could easily be granted.

Arn gave his Kurdish friend a dubious look and searched for an explanation for the jest in his eyes. But when Fahkr merely nodded stubbornly toward the oil lamp, Arn reached out and rubbed it with his thumb.

'See now, Aladdin, your wish is fulfilled!' shouted Fahkr happily. 'You shall have any document you want, signed and sealed by the Grand Master's own hand. For he is also our guest here in Damascus, although in somewhat less friendly circumstances than those rightfully vouchsafed to you. Simply write out your document, and the matter will be arranged at once!'

Arn didn't find it hard to believe that Gérard de Ridefort was a prisoner in Damascus, because he had never believed that the man would fight for God's Mother to his last drop of blood. But would he sign anything at all?

Smiling, Fahkr just shook his head and assured him that it would be so. And the sooner the better! He called a servant and ordered the proper writing implements to be brought from down in the bazaar. Then he promised Arn that he would be able to watch as the Grand Master signed his name.

A little while later a servant trudged upstairs with parchment and writing tools, and Fahkr left Arn alone to compose the document after having a small writing desk brought in. Then he went to spend some time in prayer and in preparation for the evening meal.

Arn sat for a while with the blank parchment in front of him and the quill pen in his hand, trying to see clearly both himself and the world's order at this extraordinary moment in time. He was to write his own document of release. And this was happening in the sultan's palace in Damascus, where he sat on soft cushions before a Syrian writing desk with his legs crossed and with a turban wrapped around his head.

Many times in recent years he had tried to imagine the end of his time as a Templar. But even in his wildest speculations he had never come close to the situation in which he now found himself.

Then he collected himself and with a steady hand quickly printed the text he knew well, since during his time as Jerusalem's Master he had composed numerous similar letters. He also added a sentence that occasionally appeared in such documents: that this knight, who was now leaving with great honour his service in God's Holy Army, the Order of the Knights Templar, was free to return to his previous life, yet whenever he found it suitable, he had the right to wear his Knights Templar garments displaying the rank he held at the time he left the Order.

He read through the text and recalled that Gérard de Ridefort did not know Latin, so he wrote down a translation into Frankish.

There was still room left on the page, and he couldn't resist the small pleasure of writing out the text a third time for the Grand Master, who was barely literate, this time in Arabic.

He sat for a moment, waving the document to dry the ink. He cast a glance outside at the sun, and saw that there were at least two hours left until the evening prayers for both Muslims and Christians. Just then Fahkr returned, glanced at the document, and picked it up with a laugh when he saw that there was an Arabic translation; he swiftly read through it and then picked up the quill pen to write in the vowel marks more clearly. It was really not a bad joke on His Holiness the Grand Master, he said with a smile as he took Arn by the arm and led him outside to the city once again. They had to walk only a few blocks before they came to the building where the most valuable Christian prisoners were held. It was larger and more expensively decorated than Saladin's own palace.

But there were guards here, of course, and an occasional locked door, even though it was difficult to see what an escaping Grand Master would do once he was on the streets of Damascus. Fahkr explained all the precautions as no more than an empty gesture, occasioned by the fact that the Grand Master and King Guy had both explained that an oath to unbelievers was not valid.

King Guy and Grand Master Gérard de Ridefort were locked up together in two magnificently furnished halls with furniture in the Christian style. They were sitting at a little carved Arabic table playing chess when Fahkr and Arn came in and the doors were demonstratively locked behind them.

Arn greeted them both without exaggerated courtliness and pointed out that it was against the Rule for Templar knights to play chess, but that he didn't intend to bother them for long. There was just a document he needed signed, and he handed it over with a bow and flourish to Gérard de Ridefort. Unexpectedly, the Grand Master seemed more abashed than angered by Arn's less than submissive manner of speech.

The Grand Master pretended to read the document and tried to frown as if he were pondering the contents. Then, as expected, he asked Arn what was the intention of this, and formulated the question so that the answer might explain the text, which he could not read at all. Arn carefully retrieved the parchment page, read the text aloud in Frankish, and then quickly explained that everything was in order since he had been sworn for only a specified time into the Order of the Knights Templar, which was not a rare occurrence.

Gérard de Ridefort now turned angry at last, muttering that he had absolutely no intention of signing such a document, and if the former Jerusalem's Master had plans to desert, then it was a matter between him and his conscience. He waved his hand as if to remove Arn from his sight and stared hard at the chessboard, pretending to contemplate his next move. King Guy said nothing, and merely looked in astonishment from the Grand Master in his Templar attire to Arn in his Saracen clothing.

Fahkr, who understood enough of the situation, went over to the door and knocked lightly on it. It was opened at once, and he merely whispered a few words before the door was again locked.

Then he went over to Arn and said in a low voice, as if he unconsciously believed that the other two men in the room might understand, that this would only take a few moments, but that it would go more smoothly with a different interpreter than Arn.

On his way out Arn met a Syrian, who judging by his clothing was a merchant, not a military man.

He didn't have to wait long outside the doors before Fahkr came out holding up the document, signed and stamped with the Grand Master's seal. He handed over Arn's release document with outstretched hand and a deep bow.

'What did you say to make him change his mind so fast?' Arn wondered as they made their way back toward the sultan's palace, where the crush had now increased with all the throngs on their way to evening prayers.

'Oh, nothing very serious,' replied Fahkr, as if discussing a mere trifle. 'Only that Saladin would appreciate a favour to a Templar knight whom he esteemed greatly. And that Saladin might perhaps be upset if this small favour could not be done for him, something like that.'

Arn could imagine a great number of ways to formulate such a request, but he had a feeling that Fahkr may have expressed himself a bit more harshly than he wanted to admit.

Just before evening prayers Saladin returned to Damascus at the head of one of his armies. He was cheered by people in the streets all the way to the great mosque, for now more than ever he deserved his title: al-Malik al-Nasir, the victorious king.

Ten thousand men and women prayed with him as the sun went down; there were so many that they filled the gigantic mosque as well as large parts of the courtyard outside.

After the prayers Saladin rode slowly and all alone through the crowds of people to his palace. To all his emirs and others who were waiting for him with a thousand missives, he had said that on this first evening in Damascus he wanted to be alone with his son and his brother; he had been in the field for two months now and had never had a moment to himself. No one found it hard to submit to those orders.

As Saladin, in a radiant mood, made his way through the palace, greeting and embracing all his friends and relatives, he seemed set on leaving all the affairs of state behind on this evening. And so he was all the more surprised, and for a moment even seemed a bit disturbed, to find himself suddenly eye to eye with Arn.

'The vanquished salutes you, victorious king,' Arn greeted him solemnly, and the happy murmur around them subsided at once. Saladin paused before he suddenly seemed to change his mind. He took two quick steps forward and embraced Arn and kissed him on both cheeks, which sent a ripple of whispers through the gathering.

'I greet you, Templar knight. It is perhaps you more than anyone else who has afforded me the victory,' Saladin replied, motioning for Arn to walk beside him to the banquet table.

Soon big platters were brought in with roast pigeons and quail, and tall carafes of gold and silver misted with ice-cold water.

Next to Saladin and Arn sat Saladin's son al Afdal, a slender young man with an intense gaze and sparse beard. He waited a long time before he bade leave to ask Arn about something.

He'd had the command of seven thousand horsemen at Cresson's springs the year before, and some of his emirs had said that Al Ghouti was the one who carried the flag of the Knights Templar. Was that true?

Arn was now reminded of the doomed attack which Gérard de Ridefort had forced them to make, a hundred forty knights against seven thousand, and of the ignominious flight in which he was forced to take part. He looked clearly embarrassed when he confirmed that he had indeed been there, and that it was he who carried the flag away in flight.

The young prince didn't seem very surprised to hear this, and he mentioned that he had given orders to all the emirs that Al Ghouti had to be taken alive. But what he could not understand, either at the time or later on, was how Christian knights could so deliberately ride to their deaths.

There was silence around the table as they all waited for Arn to reply; he flushed because he had no answer. He shrugged his shoulders and said that for his part it seemed just as foolhardy as it must have looked to al Afdal himself and his men down below. There was no logic in such an attack. At such an instance, faith and reason parted ways. Such things happened sometimes; he had seen Muslims do similar things, but perhaps never as extreme as this. He went on to say with an unmistakable expression of disapproval that it was Gérard de Ridefort who ordered the attack and then decided to flee as soon as he had sent all his subordinates to their death. Arn, as the *confanonier*, was then compelled to follow his highest leader, he added shamefaced.

In the embarrassed silence that now arose, Saladin pointed out that God had still guided the events to the best outcome. It was better for Arn and for himself that the Templar knight was captured at the Horns of Hattin and not before. Arn didn't understand just then what Saladin meant, but he had no desire to prolong this topic of conversation by asking.

Soon Saladin made it clear that he wanted to be left alone with his son, his brother, and Arn, and he was obeyed at once. When they were alone they went into another room and reclined comfortably among soft cushions with their ice-cold goblets of water. Arn wondered how they produced this delightful cold, but he didn't want to ask about such trifles now that they would undoubtedly be speaking of the gravest matters, although he could not predict what they might be.

'A man named Ibrahim ibn Anaza came to me once,' Saladin began slowly and contemplatively. 'He brought with him the most marvellous gift, the sword that we call the Sword of Islam, which had been lost for a long time. Do you understand what you did, Arn?'

'I know Ibrahim well; he is a friend,' replied Arn cautiously. 'He seemed to believe that I had earned this sword, but I was convinced that I was unworthy. So I sent the sword to you, Yussuf. Why, I can't really say, but it was a moment of great emotion, and something made me do what I did. I'm glad that old Ibrahim carried out my wish.'

'But you didn't understand what you did?' Saladin asked softly, and Arn noticed at once the tense silence that fell over the room.

'I felt that I was doing the right thing,' said Arn. 'A sword that is holy to Muslims is not for me to keep, but perhaps,

I thought, it should belong to you. I can't explain it any better than that. Perhaps God was guiding my action.'

'No doubt He was,' said Saladin with a smile. 'It's as if I would have sent you what you call the True Cross, which is now held in safety in this house. It was written that he who once recovered the Sword of Islam would unite all believers and conquer all the infidels.'

'If that is true,' Arn replied, somewhat shaken, 'I am not the one you have to thank, but God, who guided me with that sudden decision. I was merely His simple tool.'

'That may be, but I owe you a sword in any case, my friend. Isn't it odd how I seem to keep landing in your debt?'

'I have found a sword now, and you owe me nothing, Yussuf.'

'But I do. If I had sent you the so-called True Cross you probably wouldn't think you could free yourself from debt to me with the gift of even the most beautifully carved piece of wood. We'll talk about my debt later. I want to ask you a favour.'

'If I can in good conscience, I will do whatever favour you ask, as you well know, Yussuf. I am your prisoner and you can never get a ransom for me.'

'First, we will now take Ashkelon. Then Gaza, and after that Jerusalem. What I want is for you to be my advisor when that happens. Then you shall have your freedom and you shall not leave here unrewarded. That is what I ask of you.'

'What you're asking me to do is truly appalling, Yussuf. You're asking me to be a traitor,' Arn objected, and everyone could see his plight.

'It's not what you think,' Saladin said calmly. 'I don't need your help to kill Christians. As far as that matter goes, I have countless helping hands at the moment. But I recall something from our conversation that night, the first time I ended up indebted to you. You said something about a

448

Templar rule that I have often pondered: *"When you draw your sword – do not think of who you shall kill. Think of who you shall spare."* Do you understand now what I mean?'

'That is a good rule, but I feel only partially relieved. No, I don't entirely understand what you mean, Yussuf.'

'I have Jerusalem here in my hand!' Saladin exclaimed, holding up his fist before Arn's face. 'The city will fall when I want it to fall, and that will be after Ashkelon and Gaza. To win a victory is one thing, but to win a victory well is another. As to what is good and evil here, I must speak with someone other than my emirs, who are convinced that we must do as the Christians did.'

'Kill all the people and all the animals in the city and let nothing but the flies survive,' said Arn, bowing his head.

'What if it were the other way around?' Fahkr said, now joining the discussion for the first time, although without waiting for his older brother to ask his opinion. 'What if we were the ones who had taken Jerusalem from you almost a century ago, and what if we had ravaged the city the way you did? What would then be your reasoning in your camp outside the holy city, when you knew that you would soon be taking it back?'

'The most foolhardy kind,' said Arn with a grimace of distaste. 'Men such as your two captives, Gérard de Ridefort and Guy de Lusignan, would for once be in complete agreement. No one would speak against them. Not a single person would object when they claimed that now must come the hour of vengeance; now we must do even worse than the enemy did when they desecrated our city.'

'That is how we all reason, except my brother Yussuf,' said Fahkr. 'Can you persuade us that he is right when he says that vengeance is wrong?'

'The longing for vengeance is one of the strongest emotions in men,' said Arn, sounding resigned. 'Muslims and Christians are this way, perhaps Jews as well. The first argument against such reasoning is that one should behave with greater dignity than the enemy who acted in an ungodly way. But those who seek revenge don't care about that. The second argument is what I heard both from a Christian, Count Raymond, and from a Muslim, Yussuf: that the war will never end as long as all pilgrims do not have access to the holy city, including Jews. But those who seek revenge don't care about that either; they want to see blood flowing today, and they don't think about tomorrow.'

'We have reasoned this far ourselves,' Saladin put in. 'And we have come to the same conclusion; that those who want revenge, which is the majority of men, do not care about words or dignity or eternal war. So what more is there to say?'

'One thing,' said Arn. 'All cities can be conquered, also Jerusalem, which you now shall do. But not all cities can be held as easily as they were taken. So your question must be, what do we do with such a victory? Can we hold on to the holy city?'

'At this time, when the Christians have only four cities left in Palestine, three of which we shall take very soon, no one doubts the answer, unfortunately,' said Saladin. 'So is there anything more to say?'

'Yes, there is,' said Arn. 'You want to hold Jerusalem for more than a year? Then ask whether next year you want to see ten thousand new Frankish knights in the country, or whether you prefer a hundred thousand. If you prefer a hundred thousand Frankish knights next year, then you must do with your victory what the Christians did. Kill every living thing. If you'll settle for only ten thousand Frankish knights next year, take the city, reclaim your holy sites, protect the Church of the Holy Sepulchre, and allow anyone to leave the city who so desires. It's simple arithmetic. A hundred thousand Franks next year or only ten thousand? Which do you prefer?'

The other three men sat in silence for a long time. At last

450

Saladin stood up, went over to Arn, pulled him to his feet, and embraced him. As he was known to do whenever he witnessed anything sensitive, cruel, or beautiful, he wept. Saladin's tears were famous, much scorned and much admired in the world of both Christians and Muslims.

'You have saved me, you have given me the answer, and you have thereby saved many lives in Jerusalem next month, and perhaps have saved the city for us for all eternity,' Saladin sobbed.

His brother and son were moved by his tears, but they were able to control themselves.

A month later Arn found himself in Saladin's army outside the walls of Ashkelon. He was dressed in his old clothes, which had been repaired and mended, as was his entire coat of chain mail; they were all in better condition than when he had lost them. But he was not alone in wearing the mantle of a Templar knight; the Grand Master, Gérard de Ridefort, was also clad in like attire. He and King Guy de Lusignan accompanied the army more as baggage than as riders. They each sat atop their own camel, holding on as best they could. Saladin had found it safer to put them on animals that they could not ride rather than on horses. The Saracens had amused themselves greatly, during five days of moving camp, as they watched the two valuable prisoners trying to ease their riding pains and at the same time look dignified as they rode in the file of camels just behind the cavalry itself.

Saladin had sent a fleet from Alexandria to meet them at Ashkelon, and the ships already lay at anchor, threatening the city, by the time the Saracen army arrived by land. But the fleet looked more menacing than it was, because it was a trading fleet without soldiers and with its holds empty.

When they pitched camp outside the city walls, Saladin allowed Guy de Lusignan to walk up to the locked city gate.

There he called out for the inhabitants to surrender, and then their king would be set free. What was a single city compared with the king himself?

The residents of the city did not share this opinion, as they soon demonstrated. King Guy's words had no effect but to incite the citizens to throw rotten fruit and rubbish at him from up in the tower by the city gate. They scorned him as brutally as any king had ever been scorned by his subjects.

Saladin was amused by the spectacle and refused to be disheartened by its result. He left the major part of the army in place to start work on taking Ashkelon by force, and he then continued south toward Gaza.

On the walls of Gaza stood a few Templar knights in white mantles, and a good number of sergeants. They did not let themselves be frightened by the insignificant army that now pitched camp outside their walls, nor did they have any reason to feel fear. The enemy had not brought up any catapults or other siege engines to knock down walls.

Nor were they affected by the fact that their Grand Master had just been led up to the city gate. They expected to be threatened, and if they did not surrender, they assumed their Grand Master would be executed before their eyes.

But they would not be budged by such a threat. The Rule was crystal clear in such circumstances. A Templar knight could not be ransomed for gold or other prisoners or in response to threats. The duty of the Grand Master was thus to die like a Templar knight without complaint and without showing fear. Besides, few of them would find it very lamentable to see Gérard de Ridefort's head roll in the sand. Whoever they elected as the next Grand Master was bound to be better than the fool that had caused their great defeat.

But to their dismay and utter shame, something else now occurred. Gérard de Ridefort stepped forward and gave an order as Grand Master that the city was to be evacuated immediately. Every man would be allowed to take his own weapons and a horse with him, but everything else, even the well-filled treasure chests, must be left behind.

The Rule left no room to refuse to obey the Grand Master.

An hour later the evacuation of Gaza was completed. Arn sat on his horse and watched the march out of the city, and he wept with shame before Gérard de Ridefort's treason.

When the last horses in the column of Templar knights had exited the city gates, Gérard was given his own Frankish horse and was bidden farewell and good luck by Saladin with cheerful but ironic words. Gérard said not a word; he turned his horse and rode off toward his Templar knights. Slowly and with heads bowed as if in a funeral procession, they set off to the north along the shore. Without speaking to any of them he moved to the head of the column.

Satisfied, Saladin declared that he had now won two victories. First, thanks to a man with no spine, he had captured Gaza and its well-filled coffers without having to shoot a single arrow. Second, he had made Gérard de Ridefort once again take command of the remnants of the Knights Templar army. A man like Gérard served Saladin better than he served his own forces.

Saladin's men had immediately stormed into the conquered city, but some of them came back, looking agitated and bringing to Saladin two horses which they claimed were Anaza. Such horses were not owned by Saladin or even the Caliph of Baghdad.

Saladin said that he was happier for this gift than for all the gold that was found in the Templars' coffers inside the fortress. When he asked those around him whether these horses found with the Templar knights could indeed be Anaza, Arn told him it was so. The horses had once belonged to him, given to him by Ibrahim ibn Anaza at the same time as he received the holy sword.

Saladin did not hesitate to give them back to Arn at once.

Three days later Ashkelon fell. Saladin spared the city's inhabitants even though they had not voluntarily surrendered the city. He let them all go aboard the waiting fleet that would take them to Alexandria. Since Alexandria had extensive trade across the sea with both Pisa and Genoa, it was only a matter of time before all these Franks from Ashkelon would be back where they belonged.

Now only Tyrus and Jerusalem were left.

On Friday the seventh day of the month of Rajab, the very day when the Prophet, peace be unto him, had climbed to the seventh Heaven from the Rock of Abraham after his miraculous journey from Mecca that night, Saladin began his entry into Jerusalem. According to the Christians' reckoning of time, it was Friday the second of October in the year of Grace 1187.

The city had been impossible to defend. The only knight in the city of any importance outside the almost eradicated orders of knights was Balian d'Ibelin. Besides himself he had counted only two knights among the defenders and had therefore knighted every man over the age of sixteen. But mounting a defence would have been meaningless; it would only have prolonged the torment. More than ten thousand refugees from the immediate surroundings had streamed in behind the city gates the week before Saladin arrived. This meant that the city's supplies of both water and food would not hold out in the end.

The city was not plundered. Not a single inhabitant was murdered.

Ten thousand of the city's citizens were able to pay for their freedom: ten dinars for men, five for women, and one for a child. Those who paid for their freedom were also allowed to carry away their belongings. But twenty thousand inhabitants of Jerusalem were left in the city because they were unable to pay. Nor could they borrow from the patriarch Heraclius or from the two spiritual orders of knights, who like Heraclius had chosen to take with them their treasures in heavy loads instead of saving Christian brothers and sisters from the slavery that threatened those who could not afford freedom.

Many of Saladin's emirs wept in despair when they saw the patriarch Heraclius happy to pay his ten dinars and then leave with a cargo of gold that would have been enough to pay for the safe conduct of most of the remaining twenty thousand Christians.

Saladin's men found their own leader's generosity as naïve as they found Heraclius's greed detestable.

All the Christians who could pay for their freedom then left for Tyrus, escorted by Saladin's soldiers so that they wouldn't be plundered by robbers and Bedouins on the way. When they were gone Saladin remitted the debt for the remaining twenty thousand people who would have been forced to go into slavery because they couldn't pay the ransom or had received no mercy from the patriarch or the knights.

When the Christians were gone, Muslims and Jews began to move in at once. The holy sites that the Christians called the Temple of the Lord and the Temple of Solomon were cleansed with rose water for several days; the cross on top of the *cupola* was removed and dragged in triumph through the streets, now rinsed clean and free of blood; and the crescent moon was raised for the first time in eighty-eight years over Al Aksa and the Dome of the Rock.

The Church of the Holy Sepulchre was closed for three days and closely guarded while they argued what should be done with it. Almost all of Saladin's emirs thought that the church should be razed to the ground. Saladin rebuked them by saying that the church was only a building; the grave crypt in the rock beneath the building was the actual holy site. It would be an empty gesture to tear down the church itself.

After three days he won them over in this matter as well. The Church of the Holy Sepulchre was reopened and entrusted to Syrian and Byzantine priests. It was guarded by the forbidding Mamelukes against any attempt at desecration.

A week later Saladin was able to hold prayers in the newly cleansed and most remote prayer site, the third most important holy site in Islam, Al Aksa. As usual, he wept. No one was surprised at this. He had finally fulfilled the promise he had made to God, to liberate the holy city of Al Quds.

From the point of view of a business transaction, Saladin's conquest of Jerusalem was one of the worst undertaken during the entire long war in Palestine. And for that he had to endure both laughter and scorn by his contemporaries.

But in terms of posterity he had done something extraordinary. His name became immortal, and forever after he was the only Saracen on whom the Frankish lands looked with genuine respect.

Arn had not been present during Saladin's conquest of Jerusalem. Saladin had spared him from those sights, although he did take the city with the gentle measures that Arn had recommended.

Arn now wanted to leave for home, but Saladin pressed him to stay a while longer. It was a peculiar situation; at the same time that Saladin assured Arn that he was free to go whenever he chose, he spared no efforts to persuade him to stay and help.

As everyone could predict, a new crusade was imminent. The German Emperor Friedrich Barbarossa was on his way through Asia Minor with a mighty army. The king of France,

Philippe Auguste, and the king of England, Richard the Lionheart, were sailing across the Mediterranean.

Saladin's opinion was that the coming war would be decided more by negotiations than on the battlefield, because his experience told him that so many new Franks arriving at once would have a hard time fighting. Arn had to agree with that assessment. It was also difficult for him to contradict Saladin in his belief that no one was better as a negotiator than Arn, who spoke God's language fluently and Frankish like a native. He also had Saladin's trust, and he ought to have the same trust among the Franks because he had served for twenty years as a Templar knight in the Holy Land.

This was also hard to contradict. Arn wanted to go home. He was so filled with longing that it made his recent wounds ache, although they had healed well. But he could not deny that he owed a debt to Saladin that would be hard to repay, because on more than one occasion he had spared Arn's life. Without Saladin's mercy he would never come home at all. But he was suffering from having to participate in a war that no longer concerned him.

Yet God showed mercy on the Muslims in more than one instance. The German Emperor Barbarossa drowned in a river, before he even reached the Holy Land. His body was conveyed further in a cask of vinegar, but he rotted anyway and was buried in Antiochia. The German crusade seemed to die with him.

And it happened just as Arn had predicted: only ten thousand Christian Franks appeared after Jerusalem's fall, not a hundred thousand.

Saladin had released King Guy de Lusignan without even demanding a ransom. Faced with the new crusade from the lands of the Franks, Saladin knew that he needed a man like King Guy released among his own people; the king could be of much greater use there than as a prisoner. And Saladin was right. King Guy's return led instantly to endless squabbling about the succession to the throne and treason among the Christians.

But Saladin did make one mistake that he would long regret. King Guy led a Christian army from Tyrus south along the coast in an attempt to retake Acre, which had been the Christians' most important city after Jerusalem. Saladin chose not to take this threat seriously. When King Guy began to lay siege to Acre, Saladin of course sent off an army which would in turn attack the Christians, who were now trapped between the defenders of the city and Saladin's army. Saladin thought that time, camp illnesses, and the lack of provisions would easily defeat the less-than-terrifying King Guy. Had Saladin been prepared to sacrifice many lives, he could have won the war swiftly, but he thought it unnecessary to pay that price.

Such a long delay permitted first the Frankish King Philippe Auguste and soon thereafter the English King Richard the Lionheart to come to the aid of the Christian besiegers outside Acre. And with that Saladin had brought upon himself an unreasonably hard war, just what he had been trying to avoid.

Arn was summoned to Saladin's service, of course, since there would soon be various matters to negotiate. Saladin eventually put together a force of what he thought was a sufficient number of the men he had sent home to a well-deserved rest after a long and victorious war. Then he attacked recklessly, counting on a quick victory.

He had reckoned wrongly in more ways than one. Certainly the newly arrived Frankish and English crusaders were just as unused to the sun and heat as Saladin had been counting on, and it was now the middle of summer. But the Englishmen were used to fighting attacking cavalry. In fact, that was what they did best.

When the first Saracen cavalry stormed across the field toward the Frankish besiegers outside Acre, the sky grew dark in front of the attackers before they even understood why. A few seconds later they found themselves riding into thousands of arrows that seemed to be falling like hail from the sky. And the few riders who avoided being hit, those who were leading the charge and hadn't noticed that no one was following them, rode straight into a shower of crossbow bolts at close range.

It was all over in less time than it takes a horse to gallop the distance of four normal arrow-shots. The field before Acre was a sea of wounded and dying men, as well as horses that lay kicking on the ground or ran back and forth in panic, trampling the wounded, some of whom staggered around in confusion or scared out of their wits.

Then Richard the Lionheart himself attacked at the head of his knights. It was his swiftest victory ever.

Looking on with a mixture of horror and the professional interest of a warrior, Arn had seen what longbows and cross-bows could do. That lesson would never fade from his mind.

And so it was time to negotiate. The first step was to agree to a cease-fire that would allow them to collect all their dead from the battlefield, to the benefit of both sides in the summer heat. Arn was asked to take charge of this himself, since he was dressed as a Templar knight and so could ride straight toward the Englishmen without the risk of being shot.

English soldiers flush with victory, and speaking a language he did not understand, took Arn without delay to King Richard himself. To Arn's relief he turned out to be a Frank rather than an Englishman, and spoke Frankish with a Norman accent.

King Richard the Lionheart was tall with reddish-blond hair and wide shoulders; he actually looked like a king, whereas King Guy did not. From the size of the battle-axe hanging on the right side of his saddle, it was easy to see that he must also be very strong.

Their first talk was brief, since it dealt only with the simple matter of cleaning up the battlefield. Richard the Lionheart wanted to meet with Saladin in person, and he asked Arn to convey his request.

The next day, Arn returned with a message from Saladin that any meeting between the kings was out of the question until it was time for peace, but Saladin's son al Afdal would come to parley. Upon hearing this Richard flew into a rage against both Saladin and his negotiator, and he showered Arn with scornful accusations of treason against the Christians.

Arn replied that he was unfortunately Saladin's prisoner. He had given his word of honour to carry out this mission to act as a go-between for King Richard and Saladin.

Then King Richard calmed down, muttering crossly something about what he thought of giving one's word of honour to an unbeliever.

When Arn returned with the message, Saladin laughed as he hadn't done in a long time. He said that a man's 'word of honour' was only as good as the honour the man himself possessed; it was as simple as that. When Saladin released King Guy without a ransom he had made him promise to leave the Holy Land and never raise a weapon against one of the faithful again. King Guy naturally had sworn on his Bible and his honour and before God and various saints that he would comply. And just as naturally, precisely as Saladin had reckoned with and hoped, he immediately betrayed his oath and was soon proving useful to the Saracens once again as he divided the Christians.

But Saladin's siege of the Christians outside Acre was no longer going very well, since the English fleet was able to blockade Acre from receiving any provisions by sea. The starvation that Saladin had predicted would be to his advantage soon began to strike his own people inside Acre harder than

460

the Christian besiegers outside the city walls. And it was obviously not a good idea to launch new attacks with cavalry across open fields against the English longbowmen.

Saladin lost the race against time. To his despair the garrison in Acre surrendered and turned over the city to King Richard.

Arn and al Afdal now had the heavy duty of riding into the conquered city to acquaint themselves with the conditions which the citizens of Acre had agreed to in Saladin's name in order to surrender without continued strife.

After this it was very difficult to ride back to Saladin, because what his people inside Acre had agreed to were very harsh conditions indeed. Besides the city and all that was in it, King Richard demanded a hundred thousand besants in gold, the release of a thousand Christian prisoners and a hundred specific knights in captivity, as well as the return of the True Cross.

Not unexpectedly, Saladin shed tears when he heard these terms. It was a high price to pay for the two thousand seven hundred souls who were now at the mercy of King Richard. But Saladin's people had agreed to these conditions to save their own lives, and honour demanded that Saladin concur.

Once again Arn and al Afdal rode back to the city known to al Afdal as Akko and to Arn as Saint-Jean d'Acre, which the Romans had called Akkon. Now the negotiations would become slower and more complicated, since they dealt with many practical matters regarding times and places and how payments should be divided up, and how many of the conditions had to be satisfied before the prisoners could be released.

It would take time to sort out such matters. But King Richard let the negotiators from the other side wait even longer, as he celebrated his victory, and allowed his army to engage in games on horseback outside the walls of Acre.

When King Richard finally deigned to speak to Saladin's

two negotiators, he did so with great contempt, saying that anyone who interrupted a tournament was hardly showing courtly manners unless he intended to participate. And then he turned to al Afdal and asked whether he was a coward or did he dare ride with a lance against any of the English knights. Arn translated and al Afdal replied on Arn's advice that he would rather ride with a bow in his hand against any two of King Richard's knights at the same time – a reply that King Richard pretended not to hear or understand when Arn translated it.

'What about you, captured Templar knight, are you also a coward?' asked King Richard derisively.

'No, Sire, I have served as a Templar knight for twenty years,' said Arn.

'If I offer your new master to pay me fifty thousand besants first and the prisoners we spoke of, and then release my Saracens before we receive the remaining fifty thousand besants and the True Cross, will you then ride against my best knight?'

'Yes, Sire, but I wouldn't want to hurt him,' replied Arn.

'You shall regret those words, renegade, for now I give you Sir Wilfred,' snorted the king.

'I need a shield, lance, and helmet, Sire,' said Arn.

'You may borrow those from your Templar knights here in the city, or perhaps they are your former friends. I will see to that,' said the king.

Arn explained a bit listlessly to al Afdal what sort of contest the childish English king had devised. Al Afdal objected at once that it was against the rules to use any weapons when dealing with negotiators. Arn sighed that rules were probably not what the English king cherished most, as long as they did not please him.

Arn had no trouble borrowing what he needed from obliging brothers in the Templar quarters. Soon thereafter he rode out onto the field before the city walls, holding his helmet in the same hand as he carried the Templar shield, to salute his opponent. He was a bit hesitant when he saw how young and innocent this Wilfred looked, hardly older than his early twenties, and his face completely unscarred from battle.

They rode up to each other and paced two circuits around before they stopped face to face. Arn waited because he was unfamiliar with the rules for these games. The young Englishman then addressed him in a language he didn't understand, and he asked his opponent to please speak his king's language.

'I am Sir Wilfred, a knight who has worn my spurs on the battlefield, and I greet my opponent with honour,' said the young Englishman cockily in a Frankish that sounded most clumsy.

'I am Arn de Gothia, and I have worn my spurs on the battlefield for twenty years, and I greet you also, young man. What do we do now?' said Arn, amused.

'Now we ride at each other until one of us lies on the ground defenceless or dead or yields. May the best man win!' said Sir Wilfred.

'Well, I don't want to hurt you, young man. Is it enough if I knock you out of the saddle a few times?' asked Arn.

'You won't win anything by offensive speech, Sir Arn; that will merely cost you even greater suffering,' replied Sir Wilfred with a sneer that seemed to Arn well practiced.

'Bear one thing in mind, young man,' said Arn. 'You are riding against a Templar knight for the first time, and we never lose against tenderfeet in such games.'

More was not said, for Sir Wilfred turned his horse and galloped back across the field, where he wheeled about again, lifted his helmet, and jammed it onto his head. He was using a helmet of the new type that covered his whole face and made it hard to see anything except what was straight ahead.

Arn also rode back to get ready, but more slowly.

They stood facing each other for a while without anything happening. Since his opponent seemed to have turned his gaze toward King Richard's pavilion, Arn also glanced in that direction. When silence had fallen over the crowd, King Richard stood up and stepped forward with a big red scarf that he held in his outstretched hand. Suddenly he dropped the scarf and at once the young knight set off to attack from across the field.

Arn was riding Ibn Anaza, which gave him an advantage so great that his opponent, who came thundering on a heavy Frankish stallion, would never be able to imagine it. That alone would make the battle turn in his favour, but the hard thing for Arn would be not to inflict more than bruises on his opponent.

On his way across the field, Arn at first rode at the same moderate pace as his approaching opponent, and he saw what was clearly the intention: to strike the other man's head or shield, either to kill him or knock him from his saddle. It appeared to be a very dangerous game, and Arn did not want to strike with the tip of his lance at full speed.

Shortly before they met, Arn increased his speed so that Ibn Anaza was galloping hard, and then he leaned as he swung to the left just before impact. This brought him up on the wrong side of his opponent and enabled him to sweep the knight from his saddle with the broadside of his lance.

With some uneasiness he turned around and trotted over to the young man, who lay swearing and kicking in the sand.

'I hope I didn't injure you too badly, because I didn't mean to,' said Arn kindly. 'Are we done now?'

'No, I do not yield,' said the tenderfoot, grabbing angrily for the reins of his horse and getting up. 'I have the right to three attacks!'

464

Somewhat disappointed, Arn then rode back to the place where he had started before, thinking that the same simple trick would probably not work a second time.

He switched hands so that he was now holding the lance in his left hand with the shield slipped over his upper arm so that it would not be seen before they were very close to each other. By then it would be too late.

Again the king dropped his red scarf, and once more the young Englishman attacked as fast as he could make his heavy stallion run. There was obviously nothing wrong with his courage.

This time Arn did not switch sides in the attack. But just before impact he raised his left arm so that the shield came down at an angle across his opponent's lance, as he gripped the blunt end of his lance hard with his right hand. The tip of Sir Wilfred's lance glanced off Arn's oblique shield. In the next instant the Englishman was struck in the middle of his chest as if by an oar, and this time it connected with twice the force as before. The result was the same, except that Sir Wilfred now flew farther through the air before he slammed into the ground.

Yet he again refused to yield.

The third time Arn flung away his shield and held his lance backwards like a club and rode at his opponent with the club lowered until the very last moment. Then with both hands he raised it so that the Englishman's lance flew up and past him while his own gigantic cudgel slid as if on a track along the other's lance and hit him solidly in the face. The helmet saved him from being killed, but naturally he flew off his horse just as he had done twice before.

When Arn assured himself that his opponent was not badly hurt, he took off his round, open helmet, rode up toward King Richard, and gave an exaggerated bow.

'Sire, your young Wilfred deserves great respect for his

courage. Never before has such a young man ridden without fear against a Templar knight.'

'Your tricks are amusing, but incorrect according to our rules,' the king replied crossly.

'My rules are from the battlefield and not from the jousting field, Sire. Besides, I told you that I didn't want to injure your knight. His bravery and nerve will surely be of great joy to you, Sire.'

This childish game had two consequences for Arn. The first and for the moment most important was that King Richard adjusted the conditions a bit for Saladin's payment.

The other result was that a young knight by the name of Sir Wilfred of Ivanhoe, who now took part in his first large-scale war, for the rest of his life would have an easy time with all opponents on both the jousting field and battlefield, except for Templar knights. He would often have nightmares about them.

When Arn went back to the Templar quarters to return the weapons he had borrowed, he was invited to dine with the new Master of Saint-Jean d'Acre, whom he had known for years, ever since they had been at the fortress of La Fève together. His brother had a good deal to complain about when it came to the English king, especially the fact that this man could not get along with his peers. He had thrown the Frankish king Philippe Auguste out of the Templar quarters. After the royal palace – which was where King Richard had moved in, of course – the Templar residence was the next most elegant in Saint-Jean d'Acre. The two sovereigns had begun to squabble so badly about this trifle that the Frankish king had now decided to take all his men and head home. King Richard had also insulted the Austrian grand duke, by taking down the Austrian standard, which hung between the English and Frankish ones up on the walls. He then broke it in pieces and cast it into the moat. Violent brawls had erupted between the English and the Austrians, and now the Austrians were going to leave too. Through these childish actions the Christians had lost half the strength of their forces, but King Richard seemed to be convinced that only he and his own men were needed to retake Jerusalem, together with the Knights Templar. It was an attitude that was as dangerous as it was rash, but this was understood better by those, like Arn and his old friend, who had been at war with Saladin much longer. The mere prospect of having to move all these archers on foot in the burning sun on the road to Jerusalem would cause great suffering when the attacks from Saladin's Syrian mounted archers commenced.

But one thing was even worse. King Richard was not only a moody man who kept inciting trouble for no reason. He was a man whose word could not be trusted.

Saladin honoured the agreement as negotiated. After ten days he would deliver fifty thousand besants in gold and a thousand freed Christian prisoners. However, it would take longer to locate the one hundred named knights who were imprisoned, since they could be almost anywhere in the dungeons of Syrian or Egyptian fortresses.

Because none of the hundred knights had been delivered, it was King Richard's view that Saladin had broken the agreement.

So he ordered crossbowmen and longbowmen to surround a hill outside Acre named Ayyadieh. Then he drove the two thousand seven hundred captives out from the city – the men in chains, the women and children beside their husbands and fathers.

The Muslims found it hard to believe their eyes when they saw what happened next, and once they did believe it they could hardly see through their tears. All two thousand seven hundred captives that were to be released that day according to the agreement were beheaded, impaled on spears, or clubbed to death with axes.

Soon Saracen horsemen began attacking from every direction, moving in wild disarray, howling and out of their wits. They were met by a hail of arrows, and none of them survived the advance. The slaughter went on for many hours before the last small children were discovered, and they too were killed.

Finally only English corpse-robbers were left up by the dead on the hill called Ayyadieh. They went from body to body cutting open the stomachs to search for any gold coins that had been swallowed.

By that time Saladin had long since left the site, where he had witnessed the start of the massacre.

He sat down by himself a short distance from his tent. No one in his retinue dared disturb him, but Arn hesitantly approached.

'This is a difficult hour, Yussuf, I know that, but in this hard hour I ask for my freedom,' Arn said in a low voice, sitting down next to Saladin. He did not answer for a long time.

'Why do you want to leave me just now at this evil hour, on this day of sorrow that will live forever?' Saladin asked at last, trying to stop his tears.

'Because today you have defeated Richard the Lionheart, even though it was at a high price.'

'Defeated!' snorted Saladin. 'I lost fifty thousand besants in gold only to see those I believed I had ransomed slaughtered before my eyes. That is truly my strangest victory.'

'It is indeed a heavy loss,' said Arn. 'But the victory is that you will not lose Jerusalem to this villain. He will not go down in history as anything but the butcher of Ayyadieh and the one who abandoned the True Cross; our children and their children will remember him as a traitor without honour. He has damaged his own cause more than yours.

The Frankish king had already left for home after a childish quarrel about who should live in what lodgings inside Acre. The Austrian grand duke left him for a similar reason, and the German emperor is rotting in his grave in Antiochia. You no longer have a hundred thousand enemies, but fewer than ten thousand under that mad King Richard. And he will soon have to head for home too, I heard, or his brother will seize his land. In this way you have won, Yussuf.'

'But why leave me at this difficult hour when the grief is much greater than the hope of successful revenge, Arn, my friend?'

'Because now I can no longer negotiate for you. Negotiations with that mad murderer are over. And because I want to go home to my loved ones, to my country, my language, and my people.'

'What will you do when you get there, to your country and your people?'

'The war is over for me, that much I know for certain. I hope to be able to fulfil a vow I swore long ago, a vow of love. But what I would now like to know is what was the meaning of it all? What was I doing here? What was God's intention? I fought for twenty years and I was deservedly on the losing side, because God was punishing us for our sins.'

'You're thinking of Heraclius, Agnes de Courtenay, Guy de Lusignan, and such people?' Saladin whispered with a hint of an ironic smile in the midst of his grief.

'Yes, precisely,' replied Arn. 'For such people I fought, but what God intended by it I will never understand.'

'I do,' said Saladin, 'and I will explain it to you now. But first, other matters. You are now free. You took only fifty thousand besants for my brother when he was your prisoner, even though you knew that you could have extorted twice that from me. I believe that it is God's intent that I happen to have exactly that sum left from what I was going to pay to that butcher Richard. The money is now yours, and it is poor compensation for the sword you gave me. By the way, there is a sword waiting for you in Damascus which will probably suit you in more ways than one. I beg you now to leave me to my sorrow. Ride with God's peace, my friend Al Ghouti, whom I will never forget.'

'Yes, but the meaning of it all? You said that you knew God's meaning,' Arn protested, not yet willing to leave. That question preoccupied his thoughts more than the fact that Saladin had showered a fortune upon him.

'God's meaning?' said Saladin. 'As a Muslim I can tell you that it was God's intent that you, a Templar knight, should give me the sacred Sword of Islam that would make me victorious. But as a Christian you might explain it differently. You told me why we shouldn't do with the people of Jerusalem what Richard has just done to the people of Acre. It was advice that I took to heart. And thus it was so, as you advised me. Your words saved fifty thousand Christian lives. That was God's meaning with your mission in Palestine, for He sees all and He hears all, and He knew what He was doing when He brought you and me together.'

Arn got up and stood there for a moment hesitant and silent. Then Saladin stood up as well. They embraced each other one last time, and Arn turned and left without another word.

His long journey home had begun, back to the land where he intended never to raise a weapon again.